THE POTTERIES GIRLS ON THE HOME FRONT

Needing to find a job, Betty Dean is sent into service at Stowford House. The work is gruelling, and her dreams of making something of herself seem further out of reach.

When Betty is forced to leave after a scandalous incident, she feels that her life is over — until a new job on the trams throws her a lifeline. Meeting fellow tram girls Connie and Jean brings the joy of friendship, even if Betty struggles with having to keep secrets from her new pals.

When soldier Duncan Kennedy enters Betty's life, it seems that she may finally find the love she's always wanted. But opening herself up to someone new isn't easy, and when he leaves for the front, she finds herself alone once again.

As the Great War rumbles on, Betty's life in the Potteries is full of its battles . . .

SPECIAL MESSAGE TO READERS

THE ULVERSCROFT FOUNDATION
(registered UK charity number 264873)
was established in 1972 to provide funds for research, diagnosis and treatment of eye diseases. Examples of major projects funded by the Ulverscroft Foundation are:

- The Children's Eye Unit at Moorfields Eye Hospital, London
- The Ulverscroft Children's Eye Unit at Great Ormond Street Hospital for Sick Children
- Funding research into eye diseases and treatment at the Department of Ophthalmology, University of Leicester
- The Ulverscroft Vision Research Group, Institute of Child Health
- Twin operating theatres at the Western Ophthalmic Hospital, London
- The Chair of Ophthalmology at the Royal Australian College of Ophthalmologists

You can help further the work of the Foundation by making a donation or leaving a legacy. Every contribution is gratefully received. If you would like to help support the Foundation or require further information, please contact:

THE ULVERSCROFT FOUNDATION
The Green, Bradgate Road, Anstey
Leicester LE7 7FU, England
Tel: (0116) 236 4325

website: www.ulverscroft-foundation.org.uk

LYNN JOHNSON

THE POTTERIES GIRLS ON THE HOME FRONT

Complete and Unabridged

MAGNA
Leicester

First published in Great Britain in 2022

First Ulverscroft Edition
published 2023

A catalogue record for this book is available from the British Library.

ISBN 978–0–7505–5006–2

Published by
Ulverscroft Limited
Anstey, Leicestershire

Printed and bound in Great Britain by
TJ Books Ltd., Padstow, Cornwall

This book is printed on acid-free paper

To my family for their enthusiasm and to Michael for keeping me on the straight and narrow.

With all my love.

Part One

1

March 1911

As far back as she could remember, Betty Dean could dry plates with a tea towel and not break them. Being the oldest girl in the family, she would be her mother's helper until she had a home of her own. She had been moulded into an ordinary Potteries girl, to expect nothing and not be disappointed. Coming up to thirteen, she was experienced at every job in the house, from housekeeping and cooking to taking care of her family. She was neither adult nor child but was fit for work.

Today had begun like most days. Father and her elder brother, Jeffrey, had already left for the pit. Betty had risen early and cut up bread for the rest of the family and spread it with dripping left over from last night's tea.

She shouted up the stairs. 'Come on, you lot, else you'll go ter school with nowt in yer bellies.'

Their little band consisted of her younger brother, Michael, and younger sisters, Mary-Ellen, and Lily. This left the youngest, Tommy, at home with Mother. They walked to the school at the top of the street and ate their pieces on the way. Sometimes, Michael would ask for more because he had bellyache by dinnertime if he didn't and the other lads laughed at his rumblings, which could be heard all round the schoolroom.

'Shut up yer moaning, Michael,' Mary-Ellen said. 'Yer not the only one what could do with a bite more.'

Lily, the youngest to go to school, said nothing. She held on to Betty's hand tightly, looking up occasionally for reassurance. Betty would smile and squeeze her hand. As normal, they walked around to Dresden Street to meet Betty's best friend, Martha and her little sister Issy. They continued on to school.

The clothes each of them wore were often too big or too small for they were all hand-me-downs. Often they fitted only for a few months, after which, they were too small. As the eldest girl, Betty had second-hand stuff from the pawn shop or the charity basket at the chapel.

The school, split into three classes, had a Dean in each of them. Reading, writing and arithmetic, the three 'Rs' were the main subjects for each class and the ones Betty was most intent her family should attend. The rest, geography, history, drawing, singing, domestic science and needlework for the girls, and woodwork and science for the boys, could be done if there was sufficient time.

Her favourite subject, apart from reading, was drawing. She had, what Mr Wells called, an aptitude for it. She liked to draw people going about their business. And buildings, she liked to draw them too. Things she could see, touch, or feel. She might like to draw flowers and countryside, if she saw enough of them, but she didn't. Yes, overall, she liked school. She could get away from her boring home life, although she had not yet been brave enough to say so to Mother.

* * *

When the bell went for the end of school, Betty packed away her desk, thinking of the book they had been reading during the last lesson, *King Solomon's Mines*. Mr Wells — her teacher for the past two years, and a person Betty admired greatly — always read from boys' books, stories of adventure and bravery, never anything for girls. She enjoyed adventures, but it would be nice to have a change too.

'Betty Dean, a word with you before you go, please?'

'Yes, Mr Wells.' She turned to Michael. 'Get Mary-Ellen and Lily, and wait outside for me, will yer?'

Michael gave Mr Wells an odd look and nodded to Betty, scuffing his feet as he left.

'And pick yer feet up.'

Martha followed her to Mr Wells' desk. 'I'll get Issy and we will be outside an' all.

Betty nodded and stood in front of Mr Wells.

'You're coming up to thirteen soon, aren't you?'

'Yes, Mr Wells.'

'You are aware you can leave school after Easter?'

'Yes, Mr Wells.'

'Have you had any thoughts on your future?'

'Same as the rest of us girls. A job in the potbank at the end of the road, most probably. Me mother'll sort it out for me.'

'Might you consider remaining at school?'

'Oh, no, Mr Wells. We conner afford nowt like that. Like I said, I'll be looking for what most kids round here look for. A job what pays summat.'

'Of course, and I understand staying at school is a . . . difficult subject to raise in many households in this area, but you're an intelligent girl Betty, one of the brighter ones. Don't dismiss the thought out of hand. Think about it. Education is the path to walk if you want to improve your lot in today's world.'

'Not for the likes of us, Mr Wells.'

'Someone must be the first to break out, Betty. Why can't that person be you?'

'Mother's counting on me earning summat as'll put food on the table and help pay the rent.'

'Your Jeffrey's earnings must help?'

Betty nodded slowly. 'I expect so, but we've gorra lot of mouths ter feed.'

'Promise me you'll think about it Betty. *You* are the only person who can change your life for the better. You owe it to yourself to try.'

'Yes, Mr Wells.'

* * *

'What did he want?' said Martha as Betty joined her outside.

Betty recounted his words. She knew staying on at school would never happen, but she felt surprised and pleased.

'He's never said nowt like that ter me.'

'You're not leaving till the summer. He'll probably say summat then.'

'You were always his favourite,' Martha sniffed.

Betty linked her arm. 'Dunner be like that. There's no chance of me staying on any road.'

Martha grinned. 'I'm joking.'

The girls chatted all the way home, which wasn't far. Betty didn't say much. There was nothing she could say that would persuade Mother to allow her to stay on and she would've been narked to hear Mr Wells suggest such a thing. Betty turned. Michael was strolling along behind them and had been listening. Just like him. Always on the lookout for trouble. She poked her tongue out at him.

The County Borough of Stoke-on-Trent, known as The Potteries, was made up of six towns, although it was difficult to know when one ended and the next began. Mr Wells had said in class it was the only place he knew of that had taken on the name of its main industry. Terraces of houses had grown around the potbanks and bottle ovens, and made dirty by the never-ending smuts of soot. Two-up, two-down houses had front doors opening on to the streets and back doors leading to tiny backyards, alleyways, and outside privies. Nearly all the houses were rented and if families didn't pay their rent, they ended up in the workhouse. On Friday nights doors were not opened to callers for fear it was the rent man, or the tallyman come to collect what he was owed.

* * *

They said their goodbyes to Martha and Issy and continued home where they were greeted by the smell of fresh bread and an excited Tommy.

'Mother, Mr Wells asked our Betty ter stay behind at school today. Said as he wanted ter talk about summat. I think it was about her staying on at school.'

Betty glared at Michael, always the tell-tale. 'It was nowt, Mother.'

Too late, Mother's interest was raised.

'Betty duck, what's our Michael going on about?'

'Mr Wells said as how I was doing well at school . . . and would I be thinking about staying on a bit longer.' She lowered her voice for the second part of her reply.

Mother snorted. 'Does he think we're made of money?'

'It's all right. I told him as I'd be getting work on a potbank just like anybody else round here.'

'Good job an' all. Dunner want him putting bright ideas into yer head, do we?'

Michael grinned and wandered off, whistling. Betty licked out her tongue towards his disappearing back.

Once he was out of earshot, Mother said: 'I want ter talk to yer about school, any road.'

Betty sat at the table, resting her head on her elbows. 'Mr Wells thinks I'm doing well. I felt so proud. He said as I need to think about meself and what I want ter do in the future.'

'That's what somebody says what's got no kids of his own. It's true, I'll give him that, Betty, but dunner go getting fancy ideas. I want yer to have a good life but all you'll need is a job ter tide yer over till yer get wed to a man with a bit of cash in his pocket to look after yer, not scratching around from one day ter the next like what we have ter do. I want yer to meet decent people, but we conner afford for yer to get above yerself. It wouldn't be fair to the other kids.'

Betty sighed. 'I know what I've got ter do, Mother. I'll not go getting above meself.'

'Yer growing up so fast. Developing into a regular little lady, aren't yer?'

Betty felt her face colour. It was true. She was . . . developing into a woman. She hadn't expected it to happen so soon. Her body was changing. With seven in the family, nowhere in the house was private. She had to hide herself when she got undressed for fear someone would pull her leg. It was all too new for her to cope with.

'I've bin thinking of putting yer into service. Where yer might meet people with a bit of brass. Yer wouldn't need no extra lessons then.'

'Mother!'

'Yer could catch yerself a man and wouldn't have ter work again.'

Working in service hadn't entered her mind. She didn't know what to think. No one she knew was in service. She would miss school and learning. Would she have to move away? She didn't know anybody around here that could afford a servant. She would like to make something of herself. Mr Wells said she could and teachers know everything.

'Think about it,' Mother hissed at her. 'I can see yer going the same way as me if yer not careful. Loads of kids and a husband what conner earn enough to look after them. Look at Martha's mother, always has excuses why she's gorra bruise or a black-eye. At least yer father dunner use his fists, and his heart's in the right place. But it doesn't pay the bills.

'I don't want ter go in service nowhere, Mother. I'd be all on me own.'

'We dunner have enough room for all of yer now you're all growing up. It's not decent. No, the sooner we can get yer fixed up with a job where yer can live in, the better as far as I'm concerned.'

2

April 1911

'Mary-Ellen? Take the kids to school today. Betty and me have things to talk about.'

'But Mother —'

'Never mind, '*but mother*'. Do as you're told.'

Once the kids had gone, Mother sat Betty down on the three-legged stool in the corner of the kitchen, so she couldn't escape. A breath caught at the back of her throat. She glanced at the clock on the shelf next to the range.

Betty sat on her hands, her fingers holding fast to the wooden seat. If she had been named Elizabeth all those years ago, she might have protested, or said something intelligent in reply to live up to her grand name, but she was only Betty and could think of nothing to say.

'Now listen here, my girl. We've got ter look at yer future. Have a look at this.'

Mother had already spoken to her about getting a job in service. Betty wondered what sort of place she had in mind. It would be different to what she'd been used to.

Mother handed over the local newspaper, *The Staffordshire Sentinel*. It was open on the vacancies page. The advertisement was brief.

Girl school leaver
Reputable, to live in.
Clean and honest for general housework.
Reference required
Box number 2916

She also passed over a letter with fancy writing, from a place called Stowford House. It sounded grand.

'They'll feed yer and give yer a bed. You'll be a skivvy at first but think of the favour you'll be doing for yer brothers and sisters. You conner begrudge them that.'

What about me, Betty wanted to shout, but Mother would do what was needed and even Father would have no say once she'd made up her mind. He would, more than likely, take himself down the pub like he always did when things got tough.

'It'd be a good start. Then, when yer get a bit older, you'll have blokes flocking after yer when they know you've had a good grounding in housework and the like. Get the right bloke and you'll not have to work. All yer want is a job to tide yer over. Yer dunner want to be working as hard as I had ter when you lot come along, all day in the house and half the night charring in offices in Hanley.'

'Where is this place?'

'Near Macclesfield, in Cheshire. Nice part of the country, by all accounts.'

'Never heard of it. Is it miles away?'

'And when has geography been summat as you know much about, our Betty? They want ter see yer tomorrow so come upstairs with me and we'll find yer summat what's decent ter wear so as yer look grown up and reliable. Yer that short yer dunner look old enough ter be out on yer own never mind looking for a job.'

Mother tutted as if it was Betty's fault her legs hadn't grown longer when she tried on both of mother's newest frocks. Betty was only five foot two inches tall, or thereabouts. Mother was taller by three or four inches and much skinnier. In fact, everybody was taller except Lily, and she'd catch her up before the year was out. Tommy didn't count, what with him being a boy.

Mother dressed Betty in her own best coat — tidy but far too long, and tight around the middle. Michael called Betty fat when he wanted to annoy her. She preferred 'rounded'. Mother had only one hat and it wouldn't sit right on Betty's dark, unruly curls. Quick as a flash, Mother ran round to Aunty Ella's and borrowed a hat so that Betty could look presentable. It wasn't one Betty would've chosen and, for the first time, she wondered if having aunties living close by was a good idea.

'You look smart enough for tomorrow.'

'Tomorrow! It's too soon.'

'You'll do as yer told and there's an end to it.'

Once Mother was satisfied, Betty escaped and ran lightly downstairs. She thrust herself into her only coat, grown tighter across her chest in the past few months, and disappeared outside. As the kids were at school, she went for a walk. It could be the last time she would go out into the world as a girl. In future she would be a worker.

She gazed at the rows of terraced houses, some had fires lit as it was only the beginning of April. Wisps of smoke joined with the dark grey fumes belching from the bottle ovens frequenting all the towns that made up The Potteries. She couldn't believe she could be leaving it all behind so soon. Shouldn't she be glad to get away? To make something of herself.

* * *

Betty had to talk to Martha about her feelings. It was difficult to imagine a world where she couldn't just pop round the corner. Who would she have to talk to about the good times and the bad in this new place?

Once tea was over and she had finished helping Mother, she sped to Martha's house. It was Martha who answered the door.

'Hello Betty, I didn't expect ter see yer. I thought as you were poorly with yer not being at school. Come in.'

Once inside, the words tumbled from Betty's lips.

'In service? I thought you'd end up at the potbank, same as me.'

'There's no room at home. I need work with a room so's I have somewhere to live.'

'You mean a toff's house?'

Betty shrugged. 'Dunno, it was advertised in the paper. I've got to go tomorrow.'

Just then, Mrs Owen came into the room and, although it was poorly lit, Betty could see a bruise on her cheekbone, just below her right eye.

'Evening, Mrs Owen.'

Betty said nothing about the bruise. It was best not to. It was well-known in the street that Mrs Owen often walked into cupboard doors.

Mrs Owen lifted her hand and covered the bruise, clearly embarrassed.

'Oh, hello, Betty. Didn't know you was here.'

'I'm off for a job in the morning. It's in service.' Betty

turned back to Martha. 'Mother's coming with me.'

A raised man's voice called from the kitchen. 'Come on woman. I haven't got all day.'

They jumped at the deep voice of Martha's father and Betty made her excuses to leave with the promise she would tell Martha all about her interview as soon as she could.

* * *

Betty and her mother travelled on the train, third class from Hanley to Stoke and then from Stoke to Macclesfield, the last leg taking nearly an hour. It was both exciting and strange, moving without putting any effort into it, listening to the constant rhythm of the train on the tracks. Two boys hung out of an open window further up the carriage and the smell of smoke from the puffing engine forced its way into her nose and mouth, making her cough. At least the whole experience made her forget where the journey would end. How would it feel with the wind gushing over *her* face? Now she was a grown-up, going for a job, and must act in a ladylike manner, not turn up with a black-smoked face and uncontrollable hair.

They walked steadily from Stowford Holt station towards the village green and then turned into the lane towards Stowford House, as instructed in the letter. Allow about an hour for the two-mile walk, it said. They tramped along the gravelly road avoiding the overnight puddles, pats of dung left by farm animals, and mud. Betty had never seen so many green fields — it was so pretty. She'd never seen a place without bottle ovens filling the sky with belching smoke so a person could barely breathe.

They turned left at the village sign, heading away from the comfortable group of houses on their right. Stowford House stood alone at the end of a long private road, surrounded by lawns bordered by hedges and stone walls. Picturesque was the word she was looking for. But when they arrived at the gated entrance of the huge house, flanked on one side with a tower and a huge glass house on the other, Betty made a sharp move to turn back. This was far grander than she could ever have imagined, and Mother too, judging by the way her mouth had fallen open as the house came into view.

'I conner go in there, Mother. Let's go home. Please?'

For once, her mother was lost for words as they stood together, taking in the enormous house with at least three floors. Judging by the number of windows, there would be lots of rooms to clean. Betty's mouth was dry.

'Come on, Mother, let's go before anybody sees us.'

Mother grabbed her arm, but Betty pulled away, pouting. This was far worse than anything she could have imagined. She felt out of place just looking at it. Could she, Betty Dean, live among the toffs who owned this . . . this castle! What would Martha say?

'Now look, our Betty. It'll be a good starting point. If yer can get a reference from a big house like this, you'll be able to come back to Hanley and walk into a lot of fine homes. Or d'yer want to end up on a potbank?'

Mother had the notion working in a posh house and learning housekeeping and the like might help her get a better class of husband. A girl with no husband was a spinster, to be pitied. 'Any husband's better than none, Betty,' she said nearly every week. And Betty believed her cos every girl believes what her mother says in these parts. Father always had a smile on his face and liked to play with the kids. He didn't have much money and liked going to the pub, but then so did all the men in the street. She had to admit Mother worked hard, and Father wasn't a great deal of use in the house.

'Remember to be respectful to the mistress.'

Mother looked her up and down, pulled the shoulders of Betty's coat back so as it didn't look too big and patted it to be rid of anything that shouldn't be there. She had tried to give Betty a fox fur to wear but she wouldn't hear of it.

'Mother! If I go wearing that, they'll think we're made of money.'

She'd said the right thing. Mother was precious about her fox fur.

Mother pushed her towards the gate. 'Go on. Best not be late.'

'Aren't yer coming with me? I conner go in there by meself.'

Mother folded her arms. 'Yer old enough to stand on yer own two feet. I'll be waiting.'

Betty stared at the house one last time. Mother pushed her forward so suddenly Betty almost tripped. Then Mother nodded towards the house.

Betty threw a wobbly grin and walked up the drive. All was quiet, just the sound of her breathing and her heels hitting the stones. What would it be like living in somebody else's home? Living with other people's belongings and nothing much of her own?

She wouldn't dare touch anything for fear of dropping it.

* * *

She arrived at the front door and glanced around her. Seeing no one about, she climbed the three stone steps and rang the brass bell hanging beside the door, surprised at its loudness. She returned to the bottom step and waited, clutching her bag for want of something to do with her hands. She turned and glanced to where her mother was waiting, one person standing still as a statue, her face too far away to read. Betty gulped in air.

The door opened to reveal a tall and confident elderly lady in a black dress, straight backed, with her head held high.

'Me name's Betty Dean, Miss . . . er, Mrs . . . and I've come about the job what's going,' she squeaked. 'General housework it said in The Sentinel. I was told to come today.'

Standing on the top step, the woman towered above Betty. 'It's me you're here to see. Get yourself round to the back door, Miss Dean. Servants do not use this one.'

She pointed towards a tall gate built into the wall on Betty's left.

'Through the gate, round the back and down the stairs. I'll meet you there. Quickly now.'

The door closed silently, leaving Betty alone on the step. She walked round to the back door, trying to gawp through the windows as she passed, but she couldn't see much. Why wasn't she let in through the front door? It was easier than trudging round the back.

The woman was waiting for her. Betty had thought she might have been the mistress of the house by the way she talked. Betty didn't know anyone who talked like she did. Posh talk. But she would hold her tongue until she knew more.

'Come on in and let me have a look at you.'

The woman frowned as she walked in a circle around Betty, weighing her up. 'You look a trifle young, Betty. Have you done *any* work before?'

'Only helping me mother. She says as I'm good and fast. I help with me brothers and sisters. I promise as I'll do a good job for yer.'

'Turn around.'

Betty did as she asked.

'Show me your hands.'

Betty held them out. The woman turned them back and forth and nodded, satisfied, no doubt, they were clean and not ingrained with dirt. It was the last thing Mother told her to do before they left home.

'Mmm, I suppose you'll do. I'm Mrs Stone, the housekeeper, and you'll do as I say.'

'Yes, Mrs Stone.' She bobbed her head quickly.

'You will start the Monday after Easter Monday, the 24th April.'

'So soon?' she heard herself say.

'Are you wanting a job or not, girl?'

Mrs Stone folded her arms and thrust them under her breasts while tapping her foot. She was not one to be trifled with.

Betty nodded quickly. 'Oh, I want the job, Mrs Stone. You won't regret taking me on. I was only thinking about getting meself fixed up with the right clothes an' all.'

Mrs Stone waved the words away. 'I'll give you your uniform before you go. You can alter it to fit. You'll pay for it out of your wages, of course. You will need a reference, so speak to your headmaster. They usually oblige unless there have been any . . . issues at school?'

'Oh, no, Mrs Stone.'

'I'm glad to hear it.'

'Mr Wells said as I should think about staying on.'

'Why didn't you?'

'Had to earn some money for the family.'

Mrs Stone told her a little about the house, which even had bathrooms and more than one inside privy and there was one at the back of the house near the coal hole, for the servants. All the rooms had different names, a parlour, a sitting room, a dining room, a library, an office, and the big glass house she had seen from the road.

Betty was told to wait while Mrs Stone took lengths of printed material from a cupboard in a small storeroom.

'Plenty there for three dresses if you're careful with the cutting out.'

Betty was also given several white aprons with bibs at the front and straps at the back, a plain black dress with a white lace apron for afternoons and evenings, in the unlikely event she was required to attend the family. They might need altering given Betty's small size. She had to provide her own shoes, which must be black and always polished. It was a good thing her only pair of shoes were black. Otherwise, she would likely as not spend her first week's wages on buying stuff to work in and what would be the benefit of that?

Mrs Stone said she would have half a day off a week, and one Sunday every month to which Betty nodded, not knowing whether the terms were good or bad.

'Mind you don't dawdle on your way here, Betty. Start as you mean to go on, is my motto.'

'Yes, Mrs Stone. Thank you, Mrs Stone.'

Betty nodded to her one final time before heading off towards the gates carrying the pile of clothes that would make up her uniform.

It was exciting to think she would be a working woman after Easter. Away from school, she could begin to grow, like babies grew into kids when they started schooling. She might even grow to become a housekeeper like Mrs Stone. After all, she was almost doing that already.

She glowed as she walked back to her mother, who was pacing up and down by the gate. She imagined this walk being part of her regular day and took in a deep breath of fresh air. It was so good not to smell coal fires and smoking chimneys. If she could put up with the toffs, she could make a good life here.

As she reached the gate, Betty could see the anxiety written on Mother's face.

'Yer've been gone ages. I thought as they'd kept yer there — or done away with yer altogether.'

Betty lifted her arms to show the pile of clothes she was carrying close to her chest. 'I start on 24th April. Mrs Stone is me boss. She's all right.'

'And what's all that?'

'Me uniforms. Got to make three dresses for the daytime, alter aprons and a black dress for upstairs use. All by the day I start.'

Betty stood straight, chin up. She was going places, and this was the beginning.

* * *

When Mother told the rest of the family at teatime Betty would be leaving two weeks on Monday, they looked shocked.

Lily burst into tears. 'Does that mean we won't never see yer again, Betty?' Her watery eyes were smudged with tears and her bottom lip trembled.

Betty couldn't expect her to understand. She was only six, after all.

Betty held out her hand to the tearful child. 'I'll come back every month and it'll be like I've never been away. You'll see.'

Mary-Ellen stared. 'Who's going do your jobs about the house if you're not here? It won't be me, will it?'

'I hope as yer dunner expect me or Jeffrey to do women's work,' said ten-year-old Michael, his back straight as if to make himself as tall as he felt he needed to be. 'Our Jeffrey's working and I'll have a job soon enough.' He stuck his chin in the air as if daring anyone to contradict him.

Betty hid her amusement and put on a stern face. 'I'm leaving home to bring in a bit of money and all you lot can think about is who's going to do the housework? D'yer think as I am just a skivvy for you lot?' She stamped her foot on the stone floor of the kitchen, her dark bouncing curls adding their own annoyance. 'Besides it'll be one less mouth for yer to feed and you two girls'll have more room in bed. I'm doing yer all a favour,' she said, hands on hips and a threatening glare.

'Our Betty's right,' Jeffrey murmured, doing his best to hide a grin. 'We'll all have ter muck in. She's done us proud helping Mother with the washing and ironing and keeping this house clean after school, and if she's going ter work for somebody else and get paid for it, we conner stand in her way.'

'Mary-Ellen'll do the washing and ironing. It's

about time you learned summat useful,' said Mother staring at her new helper.

Mary-Ellen sat, lips pinched, arms folded, sulking.

'I'm glad I'm going.' Betty jumped to her feet. 'You'll all have to do some things for yerselves and about time too. I'll come back to see yer on me day off each month, like I said.' She glared at Mary-Ellen. 'But I'll not be coming back to do the washing, ironing, cooking or anything else, I'll tell yer that for nowt.'

There was silence round the table. The faces looking up at her brought home the enormity of what was happening. Betty had to take a stand right from the outset.

Her annoyance soon fizzled out. It was beginning to hit her, from this point onwards, she wouldn't know what her brothers and sisters were up to, whether someone was ill, happy, or sad. All she would have would be letters, if they could be bothered to send them. They would live in different worlds, with different things to talk about, and she would be a train ride away. She would come to know less and less about her own family, be the odd one out, living alone. She had wanted space to be herself in their crowded home, but it came with a heavy cost. When she put it like that, it sounded lonelier than she had imagined.

It would be up to her to make sure she didn't lose touch. She would insist everyone, even Tommy, with a bit of help, write her a letter each month. That way she could begin to bear it, she hoped.

Jeffrey dragged his feet from under the table and stood up. He gave her a bear hug.

'You'll be alrate, our Betty. Dunner werrit. Remember what Mr Wells said? All you've got ter do is set yer mind to it.'

* * *

That night, she lay in bed, curled up with Mary-Ellen and Lily, eyes wide open, unable to sleep.

'Betty?' The hiss of a voice came from the doorway. A young voice. Tommy.

Betty sat up, careful not to bump against Mary-Ellen. 'Are you all right, Tommy?'

He let himself into the room. 'I conner sleep knowing as you'll be gone soon. Conner get it out of me mind.'

'I won't be far away. And I'll come back regular. I promise.'

'Why d'yer have ter go?'

'We need the money and now we're all growing up, there's no room for all of us here.'

'I'm going ter miss yer.'

Betty put her arms around him. 'And I'll miss you so much. You know I will.'

'Can I stay in here? Just for tonight.'

'There's no room, Tommy,' muttered Lily.

'Course there is, just for tonight,' said Betty, on the verge of tears.

'Yes, but you'll have ter get up early.'

'Dunner care.'

As he huddled against her, Betty put her arms around her brother and sisters. Would this be the way of it all from now on? Always saying goodbye. She had to be strong. To think for herself. To be herself.

3

April 1911

Betty arrived at Martha's at half past eleven on the Sunday.

'I was that upset, Martha, I didn't know what to say. I had to come round and see yer and get out of their way, especially Mary-Ellen's. One minute she's showing she'll be in charge and the next she's moaning about having all the work to do.'

'They've been used to you being around and now Mary-Ellen's going to do your jobs, so she blames yer for leaving.'

'But I've got ter go cos they need the space. I'm not the one what wants to go.'

'She'll come round, Betty duck.'

'I hope so. It's going ter be bad enough living with total strangers without her going on at me when I come home.' Betty lowered her voice. 'How's yer mother?'

Martha put a finger to her mouth and glanced towards the kitchen. 'We dunner talk about it,' she whispered. 'She looks better today. It usually happens when Father's been down the pub on a Friday. She tries to keep out of his way until he's slept it off. I tell you, I wish I could go but I dunner think I could leave Mother.'

'She's got the twins to look after her,' said Betty. A tingle in her cheeks told her she was flushing as she thought of Daniel and his brother, Peter, handsome lads of seventeen years.

'But I'll still want to know she's safe.'

Betty shook her head. 'Will you be all right when I've gone? With nobody to talk to?'

'I'll have ter be. You're a good friend, Betty. I hope it all works out. I'm finishing school in June and Mother's taking me ter put me name down for the potbank. So we'll both be working in a few months' time.'

'What will yer do?'

'Whatever they give me, I suppose. I hope it's in the clean end. They say the girls in the clay end are a rowdy lot.'

It was soon time to leave. Betty hugged Martha tightly and dropped a kiss on her cheek. She shot out of the house blinking the tears away, to spend her last afternoon with her family.

* * *

Betty had packed. She felt as if she was leaving for ever, losing her place in the family never to get it back again.

This was what being grown-up felt like.

She had spoken to each family member over the weekend but had saved her chat with Jeffrey until last because his advice was the most important to her.

'You'll look after everybody for me won't yer Jeffrey? And write to me?'

Jeffrey took her hand and patted it gently. 'Yer dunner even need to ask, duckie. Course I will. You may be me little sister, but you're nearly a young woman. You've got to go out and make your way in the world, otherwise yer'll just be downtrodden like the rest of the women hereabouts.'

'I wouldn't call becoming a maid of all work making summat of meself.'

'Yer going to a posh place, Mother says. You'll meet all sorts. Dunner settle for the first man what asks yer. It's a hard world, Betty. Getting a decent bloke ter take care of yer's important.'

'That's what Mother says.'

'And she should know. She runs this house and what she says goes. You know that.'

'I want ter have a good time, Jeffrey. Not to be at someone's beck and call.'

'I know, duck. But one step at a time, hey?' He patted her shoulder. 'You'll be alrate. If anybody can get what her wants, it's you. You can be mighty strong when you have to be. Probably stronger than the lot of us.'

He walked away. Betty was sure his eyes were overly bright. She shook her head. Next time she had to talk to someone about her troubles, Jeffrey wouldn't be on hand to dole out his words of wisdom. The knowledge brought tears to her eyes.

* * *

They all gathered to see her off. She'd hoped to sneak out without being noticed because she thought it might just be too much — for herself as much as for the rest of the family. She was weepy enough alone with Mother, but when everyone appeared, she was thankful to see them, trying to hold back her tears. It mattered to her they had done so; that it wasn't just another ordinary day.

She ate her oatcake rolled up with cheese, and

washed it down with a cup of tea. Tommy couldn't take his eyes off her as tears welled. Lily was upset because Tommy was upset. Betty smiled at him, talked to him. Last night she had asked Mary-Ellen to make sure Tommy and Lily made progress with their reading, and Jeffrey to be extra attentive. Over the years, Mother had been so busy it had fallen to Betty to look after the little ones, and she would miss them terribly. They were her own family within the family.

'Sorry I've been a pig,' Mary-Ellen whispered. 'I'll miss yer.'

Betty couldn't let them see her heart breaking into pieces. She jumped up from the table and rushed to put on her coat, not wanting to cry in front of them now she was a grown-up and on her way to her first job. She hugged everyone in turn. When she got to Father, he slipped a shilling into her hand — to buy stamps, he whispered. The last person she hugged was Mother. The arms encircling her tightened momentarily. Then they were gone, leaving Betty to only imagine they were there.

'Best get on with it, Betty, love.' Mother sniffed. 'Dunner want to be late on yer first day. You'll be back in a month. It's not the end of the world now, is it?'

It sounded to Betty as if her mother was feeling sorry for sending her away.

Jeffrey opened the front door and stood beside it. Giving him a kiss on his cheek, she whispered. 'You will tell me if there's anything wrong, won't yer? Promise me? I couldn't bear not knowing.'

'Course I will.'

She nodded back, satisfied, and picked up her bag containing the newly made uniforms. There wasn't much else in it: two books; spare drawers and other under garments; her best frock for church; and her new Sunday hat. She stepped into the street. Without looking back, she picked up her pace until she was running, and the cool air burned the tears on her face, her shoes thumped the paving stones at the same pace as her heart. She shook herself.

Come on Betty, pull yourself together. You're nearly thirteen and bright as a button, according to Mr Wells, and he should know. For goodness' sake, act like a grown up!

* * *

As directed on her last visit, Betty knocked on the back door of Stowford House and waited.

A girl a few years older than Betty opened the door. Her blond hair — curly to the point of frizzy — matched the freckles on her face. Her blue eyes looked puzzled. Then a broad grin appeared.

'Hello, you must be the new girl. Come in, come in.'

Betty grinned back feeling instantly at home with the older girl's welcome. She stepped through the open doorway into a small hall area where coats hung on pegs. They went through the opposite door into a long corridor, and into the kitchen. There, four people were working busily.

'I'm Kitty, a housemaid. What's your name?' the blond-haired girl said over her shoulder as she led the way through the kitchen.'

'Betty Dean.' She looked around her, eyes wide. 'My home would fit into the kitchen and scullery with room to spare.'

Kitty giggled. 'I know what you mean. You'll wish it wasn't so big after you done cleaning it.'

'Now then you two.' Mrs Stone looked around from the corner where she was writing something on a board. 'I'm glad to see you, Betty. Kitty, take her up to your room so she can change into her uniform and unpack. Then come back here immediately.'

'Yes, Mrs Stone.'

As the two girls turned towards the door, Mrs Stone's voice raised again. 'And be sharp about it.'

'Yes, Mrs Stone,' Kitty nodded and quickened her pace.

Betty glanced towards the large square sink under the window before following Kitty through the doorway. There wasn't an inch of space to be seen under the crockery, pans, cutlery, and other paraphernalia. She followed Kitty into the long hallway. 'I suppose there's always lots of washing up ter be done?' Betty whispered.

'That lot?' Kitty looked surprised. 'It's only servants' stuff. We've already put the posh things away, so they don't get damaged. Don't worry, you'll get used to it. Dogsbody to everybody is what you are.'

The servants' rooms were in the attic. Kitty led her into a room holding two beds, one bare of coverings, the other unmade after a night's sleep. Red-faced, Kitty moved swiftly to tidy her sheets and blanket.

'Sorry about the mess, I was in a rush this morning. Don't let on to Mrs Stone. She's a stickler about tidiness, as you'll find out soon enough.'

'Course I won't. I'm just as bad.' Betty wasn't really, but it sounded friendly to pretend to be.

Kitty smiled. 'Our secret then.'

The bedroom was stark and laid with linoleum for ease of cleaning. A couple of pieces of carpet were laid beside each bed so the servants' feet didn't touch the cold floor, although Betty supposed they would be unlikely to spend much time in there, so what did it matter?

She discovered Kitty was only four years older than her, so she had at least one young friend to advise her. Kitty told her to put on the print dress for what was left of the morning. Betty turned her back to undress and slid the print dress over her head. She was used to undressing in front of her mother and sisters, but this new friend was a stranger.

Kitty grinned at Betty's lack of composure. In Betty's rush to dress, she had put it on back to front. She gave up and collapsed onto the bed shaking with laughter. Kitty shook her head.

'Come here, let me help or it might be time for dinner before we've even had lunch.'

'D'yer have dinner at teatime then?'

'Yes, don't you?'

'No. Dinner's at dinnertime,' Betty shrugged. 'Conner think of it no other way.'

'Well, you'd better start thinking about it otherwise you'll get confused. As far as this house is concerned, it's breakfast, lunch, afternoon tea, and dinner . . . in that order.'

'How many servants are there? I've only met you and Mrs Stone so far.'

'Mrs Stone's the housekeeper and what she says goes. We have no butler as the master thinks it's not necessary. Cook comes next, that's Mrs Hope, but she's always called Cook. She likes it that way. The upper housemaid is Ruth Stevenson. She considers herself to be superior to the likes of us. She deals with Mrs Delhaven personally. Sally Withers and me are the housemaids. Sally's older than me and not too bright, but is a hard worker.'

Betty's face must have looked blank because Kitty suddenly asked: 'Are you still with me?'

'I think so. I didn't realise there was so many.'

'You'll get used to it,' she smiled.

'What about out there?' Betty pointed through the window.

'Well, Levi Hope's the head gardener and general help. He's Cook's husband and better than his wife to work with: down to earth, but a gentleman. Jim Bailey's the master's valet and chauffeur — but you'll only see him when the master's at home. Young John Makepeace is Mr Hope's assistant, and he is helped by Billy Nixon from Hollybush Farm. He loves gardening and helps out when he can, which isn't often these days.' Kitty's eyes lit up at the mention of his name, tinged with what could've been disappointment.

* * *

Mrs Stone looked at them suspiciously as the pair walked into the kitchen, smiling.

'I hope you're ready for work, Betty? Don't let Kitty lead you astray before you've even begun.'

'Mrs Stone! I haven't been leading her astray. I wouldn't . . . well, not on her first day,' she giggled.

'The family is out, Kitty, so you may show Betty round the house to avoid her getting lost if she is sent anywhere. And no dallying. You can do the pots when you get back, so be quick about it.'

'Yes, Mrs Stone. Come on Betty.'

Kitty left the kitchen so quickly Betty had to run to catch her.

'And no chasing about. Remember, you are young women and not children.'

Kitty screwed up her face but righted it again when she saw Betty's grin.

'Mrs Stone's all right most of the time, but now and again she goes off on one. Just keep your head down when it happens. Come on and I'll show you where to find everything.'

Out of the kitchen, they turned right along a stone-flagged corridor and through a door. The servants' area included the butler's pantry used by Mrs Stone, servants' hall, and storerooms, for all manner of so-called essential equipment, to keep a large house going. And where Betty would, no doubt, spend most of her working hours.

Another door led from the kitchen through to the main house up a flight of stone stairs, through a door to the family part of the house with polished wooden floors and rugs. Double doors opened on to a dining room and a table seating ten chairs. She stared around the huge room looking at the heavy furniture to be polished, and the large fireplace to be set and cleaned out every day. Two more sets of double doors gave entry to the garden and to an even larger drawing room, which led to a glass house — an orangery she was told, although she couldn't see any oranges anywhere. Flowers and bushes and all sorts, but no oranges. She didn't suppose she would find any drawings in the drawing room neither.

More rooms followed until her head was spinning trying to get them lodged into her mind: a reception room, a library, a sitting room, and a billiard room. She would never get used to all these names. A wide staircase with a polished banister led up to the bedrooms, eight in all. Some had a dressing room and bathroom, with its own privy. Mr Delhaven had insisted on it when the house was modernised, so Kitty said. It made more work for the servants. An important room for Betty would be the store where all the linen for the house was to be found.

The back staircase had no carpet, just stone steps — which looked as if they might have been added as an afterthought — led to the top floor, and the servants' rooms.

'Us women stay up here. Mr and Mrs Hope have two rooms over the coach house with a small sitting room. Young John Makepeace has a room over there as well. Jim Bailey has a room in the servants' quarters so he's available for the Master if he should be needed.'

'Why is he called Young John Makepeace?'

'His grandfather worked here at one time and he was name John, too.'

They returned to the servants' hall.

Mrs Stone glanced at them and sniffed. 'Go about your business, Kitty. You, Betty, can come with me.'

She took her into the scullery where the crockery from breakfast and the preparation of lunch was waiting for her attention. 'Usually, you will get this done before you go gadding off anywhere.'

Mrs Stone made it sound as if she and Kitty had been skiving, which Betty didn't think was fair at all, but she kept a straight face.

'Betty, I'll set out your duties so do take heed. You start work at six o'clock cleaning the grates, light the fires, clean the fender and fire irons, scrub the front steps, and clean the brass on the front door. You can then have your breakfast with the rest of us. We like to eat together so don't be late as you will not be popular with your colleagues.'

'Yes, Mrs Stone.' Betty's eyes had grown wide. With all those jobs to be completed, how could she not make others late?

Mrs Stone hadn't finished.

'After breakfast, you will help Cook prepare lunches and make ready for dinner. Dinner is five courses and there are regularly visitors to cook for.' She looked down her nose at Betty. 'You will receive instruction on the correct settings at table.'

Betty didn't see how there could be more than one way to set a table.

'The kitchen floor needs a good scrub after food is prepared, and then both sets of stairs. Once the family have finished dinner in the evening, we're all set to prepare the kitchen for the morning. Your main task will be washing the dishes. The servants' meals are breakfast, a light lunch after the family has partaken and then our evening meal is usually about six o'clock, although this varies from time to time.'

By the time Mrs Stone had finished her list of duties, Betty felt quite dizzy. It seemed she would never emerge from the servants' hall. If she was lucky, she might see a couple of hours of daylight during the summer months. She would never get to walk in those lovely gardens and feel the fresh wind on her face.

'Will there be any time for me to go into the gardens, Mrs Stone?'

Mrs Stone's mouth fell open. She laughed; the first Betty had heard from her.

'You won't be doing your jobs properly if you've the time or the energy to wander round the gardens, my girl.'

* * *

Betty was quiet at their evening meal and let the conversation go on around her. The table was laid with several knives, forks, and spoons as if they were about to have a celebration, and she didn't know where to start. She waited to see what Kitty did and was disappointed when a bowl of soup was placed in front of her. Kitty picked up the spoon on her right, so Betty followed. The soup was thick with vegetables and tasted so good.

She was waiting to be excused from the table when a plate of meat, potatoes and vegetables arrived. By the time she had finished, Betty's belly was fuller than she had ever known.

'Anyone want dessert?' asked Cook.

Betty couldn't eat another mouthful — but neither could she refuse.

'Come on lass. Have you nothing to say?'

That was Levi Hope. What had she got to say that was worth talking about? Everything was new, and she had to concentrate. It was the first time she had ever sat down to a meal she hadn't helped prepare, and with adults she didn't know.

Mr Hope spoke again, holding his fork full of food close to his lips. 'How do you feel about your first day? Nice place to work, isn't it?'

Betty could only nod. So much had changed and she felt insignificant. She supposed she would get used to it, given time, but right now, she could only hold her tongue. What she wanted was to crawl under the table where she could be out of sight of everyone.

The conversation moved on to other things and everyone seemed to forget about her. The men talked together over a cigarette after they had taken their fill. Mrs Stone talked to Ruth about a forthcoming dinner the Delhavens were hosting. Kitty made sure food and drinks continued to arrive at the table. Betty's mind was far away, wondering how little Tommy was doing without her.

* * *

On Friday, Kitty showed Betty around the village when the two were required to collect an addition to the greengrocer order. They grabbed their coats and slipped outside to walk down the long drive to the gates, their feet crunching the stones. On the left, Levi Hope was working in the formal garden that was overlooked by the sitting rooms of the house. He lifted a hand to wave and the girls waved back.

Once on the main road, Kitty turned left walking alongside the stone walls bordering Stowford House.

'You know if you turn right at The Green, it will take you down to Stowford Holt where the train stops. That's where you walked from when you came. We'll head towards The Green and turn left into the village.'

The road split each side of the village green where the old iron signpost read, *Stowford Village*. They passed the church on the right and took the left turn to the centre of the village with its three shops, a greengrocer, general merchant, and a butcher. Kitty waltzed into the greengrocers and introduced Betty to Mr Burton, the owner — or the proprietor, as the sign above the shop window said he was.

'Morning Miss Kitty. How's life?'

'So, so, Mr Burton. You know how it is,' Kitty grinned. 'This is Betty. She's just started at the House in my old job.'

'How long have you been there, Miss Betty?'

Betty coloured at his words. She had never been referred to as 'Miss' by anybody before and she suddenly felt quite grown up.

'Coming up to a week now, Mr Burton.'

'Kitty's a good lass. She'll see yer right.'

Kitty's face turned pink. 'Mr Burton, you are a one.'

'Any time as yer need anything, Miss Betty, just pop in. Always like to help where I can.'

'We've come for the order, Mr Burton.'

'Right you are, Kitty.' He disappeared into the back of the shop and returned with a large bag. 'It's not heavy,' he said, placing it into Betty's outstretched arms. 'Good job as it's not a sack of potatoes.'

Betty squirmed under the weight of it.

'Goodbye, Mr Burton,' Kitty winked.

With that, the girls broke into laughter and left the shop to the sound of Mr Burton's chuckles.

'Not much to look at is there?' Kitty said, already bored.

'It's a lovely place,' said Betty, twirling around, trying to take everything in. It was truly beautiful. Houses with gardens, and flowers already in bloom. Trees showering pale pink blossom lined the road. The opposite side was bordered by the stone walls surrounding Stowford House. She was only just beginning to realise how big the estate was. How different from The Potteries, where the sky sat on top of the houses and the horizon was at the bottom of the street.

'Do you see where the Stowford House wall ends? That's the start of the two farms that belong to the house. My young man, Billy Nixon, and his family live in one, Hollybush Farm. Those little houses were the old labourers' cottages. They are tiny, but so pretty. Wouldn't mind one of them, but I don't suppose I'll ever afford to rent anything unless I get myself a rich husband.'

Betty grinned and adjusted the bag in her arms, which was beginning to feel heavier.

'What do you think of your first week, Betty?'

She thought for a moment. 'I miss me family,' she said eventually. 'I've never bin away from them before. Takes a bit of getting used to.'

'I know what you mean,' said Kitty nodding. 'My family live in Macclesfield, so I can usually get back home on my half-days as well as my day off, if I've a mind to.'

'What are the Delhavens like?'

'Mr Delhaven owns three or four silk mills in Macclesfield. They make silk cloth to send all over the country. He's keen on his business and doesn't spend much time at home these days. He is a nice man and fair. He spends a lot of time in the library. Mrs Delhaven likes to socialise and hold parties, or what she calls 'soirees'.

'What's a s . . . swaray?'

'A posh name for a party as far as I can tell. All as I know is it means lots of work for us.'

They laughed.

'There are two boys, not really boys any more, but Mrs Stone always refers to them in this way. Mr Claude's twenty-two, and clever. He's at university in Germany doing something with chemicals. He is much like his father and they seem to get on well. Mr Harry's nearly nineteen and a different kettle of fish altogether. He is at Oxford University studying greats, or so we've been told.'

'Fireplaces?'

Kitty burst into fits of laughter. 'No. It's what posh people call old books and stuff.'

'Oh, I see.' She didn't really, but she didn't want to show her ignorance.

'A law unto himself, Mr Harry is, and does what he wants most of the time. He likes art and books. He's Mrs Stone's favourite. He can't do no wrong in her eyes.'

A single motor car passed them on the way back to Stowford House, and they managed to avoid it in the narrow lane. Betty's mind turned to Jeffrey. He was sensible, like Mr Claude, perhaps with less brains but a big heart. Maybe it came with being the oldest. The feeling of responsibility. The odd times Jeffrey brought home some of his mates, she would watch them through the kitchen window when they were sat in the backyard. Sometimes she could even hear their jokes if the window was open. She liked best the ones that were good fun. She loved Jeffrey to bits, but if the truth be told, he was on the quiet side.

'Anyway, we'd best get a move on, else we'll both be sacked.'

4

May 1911

The first month passed quickly and Betty secured her place within the household following a good reference from Mr Wells, which was read to her by Mrs Stone: *Betty Dean is a bright scholar and always did as she was told in class. I am satisfied she could have done no better and recommend her for future employment.*

When she first started, she believed her family would never be out of her thoughts. It was probably true during the first two or three days, but after that the time went so fast, she could scarce believe she would be on her way home today.

She'd received letters from Jeffrey and Tommy and was glad. Tommy's letter carried the sound of Jeffrey's voice and she chuckled as she imagined the two of them sitting side by side, deep in thought.

It was when she went with Kitty to clear the table upstairs that she nearly burst into tears. She was thinking about Michael and his hungry belly as she saw the half-finished food waiting to be collected from the dining room. There was no danger of the Delhaven household going hungry. One of the five courses regularly served at dinner would have fed Betty's entire family. Some of the plates returning to the kitchen from the dining room were barely touched. These people took so much for granted and had never felt the pain of a churning belly when a body craved for food — when someone had to go to bed and try to sleep away the hunger.

She blinked away the tears that had appeared from nowhere. No point in getting upset over something she could do nothing about. This was how posh people lived. Mother had warned her she would have to toughen up.

At the end of the day, Betty was worn out, not so much from the work, because she was used to that. It was from the panic that she wasn't doing things right. That she wouldn't fit in. That people might laugh at her mistakes.

So far, she hadn't met any of the Delhaven family, but already there was a strong feeling of 'us and them' between servants and family. There was even a hierarchy between the servants. She had expected to start on the lowest rung of the ladder but, here in Cheshire, they didn't even talk the same as she did; *everyone* sounded much posher.

Kitty felt like a friend already, though. With a bit of luck, maybe it wouldn't be long before Betty could climb up to the next rung, too.

The difference between Stowford House and home was she could have a break at home and the jobs still got done. Here, she only had to stand still and someone would be on at her. A kitchen maid was a slave to everyone in the household. Betty didn't like it, but there was nothing she could do about it.

* * *

'Don't forget you need to be back by ten o'clock. That's when the doors are locked. If you're late, you'll be sleeping with the horses. No excuses,' said Mrs

Stone, not looking up from her mending.

Betty felt quite grown up sitting by herself on the train speeding towards The Potteries. She hadn't been allowed to go out of Hanley a month ago and now she had a job, she could go anywhere.

Everyone was there to welcome her, and Betty was glad. Mary-Ellen had helped Mother to cook the dinner, probably because she wanted to show Betty how quickly her shoes had been filled. Betty had laughed. The change in her sister took her by surprise.

As they sat round the table and Mother doled out small portions of weak lobby — a soup made from gristly meat and left-over vegetables — she glanced across at Betty.

'Bet you'll turn yer nose up after what you've bin eating,' she muttered.

A surprised Betty stared back, trying to decide whether Mother was joking. 'Course not. You've bin feeding me all me life. Why should I want any different?' She looked closely at Mother's face and was shocked to see her uncertainty. Surely, she didn't think Betty would look down on any meal she had made. 'I'm always ready for a bowl of lobby, Mother, you know that,' she grinned.

Mother's face relaxed. Betty had said the right thing; although the episode taught her to take nothing for granted as far as personal feelings went.

She spent some time with Jeffrey, hoping to catch up on anything she'd missed, but he had little to say.

'It's only been a month, Betty. Nowt much happens in a month round here. You know that.'

'I don't care. I want to know or else I shan't feel part of the family no more. How have Tommy and Lily been getting on? They looked so lost the day I left.'

'Our Tommy's been subdued. He's missing yer just like you knew he would. I tried to play with him, find things for him to do, but he had nightmares the first few days. I tried to comfort him, but he wanted you.'

She couldn't stop the tears forming when her mind filled with flashes of an upset and confused little boy.

'He'll understand soon, Betty. Dunner go fretting about it. He's started to follow me, now. Mary-Ellen and Lily are too old for him, and ignore him most of the time.'

Betty smiled and threw her arms around him.

'Hey, what's that for?' Jeffrey shook himself.

'For being you. My lovely big brother. Tommy thinks you're the best brother in the world'

'Dunner be daft.'

'I'm not. I won't worry now as I know you and Tommy are such good mates.'

'I ain't going ter babysit him forever, duck.'

'If he grows up like you, our Jeffrey, then you'll have done a good job, that's all I can say.'

'What about you? How are yer really getting on in posh house? Are they treating yer good?'

'As well as anywhere, I should think. We each do our work. I share a room with Kitty. She's a bit older than me. She was the kitchen maid before me. I suppose I might've been lonely if it wasn't for her, surrounded by so many old people.'

Jeffrey grinned again. 'Dunner go calling them old to their faces and get yersen in trouble.'

'Mrs Stone keeps us well away from the family. Only the upstairs maids get to see them regularly. I could meet them in the street and they wouldn't recognise me.'

Jeffrey nodded, although he'd never been near toffs

himself as far as Betty knew.

'Best keep it like that an' all. Dunner want yer getting all high and mighty with us, else we'll have ter take yer down a peg or two.'

'You've nowt ter worry about, our Jeffrey. I could be a piece of furniture for all they care,' Betty grinned and thumped his arm. He pretended to be hurt but he was laughing. 'I'm not goner change cos I'm working with a load of toffs. I'll learn to hold me own.'

It surprised her that the thought might have entered his head. All she wanted was a job to earn some money to help the family. And Mother had chosen it, not her.

She changed the subject. 'Do take care when yer down the pit, Jeffrey. I dunner want you having no accidents. We rely on yer too much.'

'Am always careful, Betty duck.'

Betty helped Mary-Ellen set the table for tea. The table looked so small and empty, compared with what she was used to now. The Delhavens probably threw away more food in a day than her family could eat in a week. She could understand how her mother felt. They could never imagine living in a house where you couldn't see the tablecloth for the food laid in front of them.

When *she* got married, she would care for her family. They would want for nothing. She would make sure of it. One day she would get a better job. A job what paid more money for working fewer hours. She'd heard of jobs like that.

She spent some time with Martha telling her as much as she could without it sounding as if she was boasting. It appeared as if nothing had changed in Martha's life.

Betty accompanied Mother to chapel soon after

tea. She was surprised how normal everything was. Neighbours called out their greetings and passed the time of day, asking her whether she had settled in to her new job. When she had accompanied the Delhavens to the church in Stowford, no one spoke to them and they, in turn, did not acknowledge anyone, just stared at the path in front of them. She concluded it mattered to none of them. She felt glum at that. In Hanley, there was always somebody to pass the time of day with.

More than ever, her visit home made her realise she would have to look after her own future from now on. She was walking in two worlds. She would be the most important person in *her* life, and it was up to *her* to make something of it.

* * *

All too soon her visit was over, and Betty was on her way to the station again. The day had gone by in a whirl. No sooner was she there than she was getting ready to come away. It would be a whole month before she would see them again.

By the time the train headed towards Macclesfield, it had emptied somewhat. She kept a keen look out for Stowford Holt, not wanting to pass straight through and have to retrace her steps. Her eyes threatened to close and she willed them open.

'Stowford Holt! Next stop, Stowford Holt.'

The sound of the conductor startled her, and she jumped out of her seat. She collected her belongings, her bag, and a small box of her mother's homemade biscuits. Betty had tutted at her when the box was placed into her hands. They were to remind Betty of home, Mother had said, but Betty believed Mother still felt she had something to prove to her.

It was half-past eight when she descended from the train. It was a pleasant spring evening, and she could smell the flowers in the hanging baskets as she climbed the steps out of the station. It was a total surprise to find Jim Bailey, the chauffeur, leaning against the car, smoking. Was he waiting for Mr Delhaven? Had he been away too?

When he saw her, he smiled and stood up.

'Evening, Betty. I've come to pick you up.'

Betty stared at the car, shining as ever. 'That's for me?' She looked at him.

'Well, am not here to pick up any other young ladies, as far as I know,' he grinned. 'I'd got nothing else to do, so Mrs Stone thought as I might as well pick you up so's you wouldn't be late.'

She had been looking forward to the walk but that was before she had seen the car. Jim opened the car door for her like she was a proper lady. With a face burning, Betty stepped inside and relaxed. She had felt the train was fast, but the car was even faster. The trees lining the road flashed by so fast, they made her feel giddy.

Back at Stowford House, Betty remembered to thank Jim for picking her up and walked round to the gate and the servants' entrance.

Mrs Stone smiled as Betty walked into the kitchen. 'Well, if it isn't Betty, come back to us.'

'Thank you for sending Mr Bailey to pick me up,' said Betty, returning the smile.

The evening clear-up had not been completed and Betty felt obliged to lend a hand.

Once it was over, Betty asked Mrs Stone if she may

take a bath to rid herself of the dirt and dust of her journey. It was a novelty to stretch out in a deep bath instead of a tub in front of the fire, trying to cover her modesty lest anyone should come in unexpectedly.

As she lay in the bath, watching the steam rise, she sighed deeply. If she kept her two lives, home and service, separate in her mind, she could enjoy both. They were as different as chalk and cheese.

5

August 1911

Working in service wouldn't be so bad, thought Betty, if it wasn't for the bosses. Clean and comfortable, enough to eat, and learning loads of things that would help her when she did get wed — she was beginning to see why Mother had wanted it to be this way.

The family had all sent letters telling her how they were getting on, except Father, who didn't do that sort of thing. Mother was more than capable of speaking for him. She always had in the past so why change now, he had said when Betty asked.

Towards the end of August, Betty received a letter from Martha. More good news.

21st August 1911

Dear Betty

I am ever so glad to write and tell you my news. I've got a job with Jackson's Pottery. It's not as posh as yours, but it's what I've been expecting since you left school at Easter. They came round our school in June, before we left, and looked at our books, I don't know why. Perhaps they were looking to see how neat we were. There was only three of us. I was that proud, I can tell you.

Any road, I was told to go round to see them at the beginning of July. They took us round the decorating end and showed us some of the jobs what we'd be doing and said they would be sending out letters once they had been to the other local schools.

The good news is I start on Monday in the decorating shop. I will be an assistant to somebody what knows what they're doing and once I get good at it, I'll be on piecework. The more I do, the more money I'll get.

Fancy, us both working. I feel quite grown up, don't you Betty?

By the way, Mr Wells never asked me if I was staying on at school. I suppose he'd given up asking by the time I left. It doesn't bother me.

I'll see you next time you come home if you're not too high and mighty. Only joking about your posh job.

Best wishes
Martha

Betty smiled. It was followed by a frown. Although Martha sounded happy enough, Betty thought she noticed a touch of envy, talking about her 'posh' job and not getting 'high and mighty'. She decided to ignore Martha's words — for now. She'd known Martha for ages. She'll come round eventually. Maybe there was good points about living away from home, she chuckled to nobody.

6

December 1911

It was impossible to travel home for Christmas. How could servants be spared when the family needed them? All the staff worked long hours to get the house ready for the festive season. Mr Hope took care of the Christmas tree — a huge fir tree — and transported it to the dining room when the time was right, ready for it to be decorated by Mrs Stone with baubles and tiny pottery toys that came out every year. Kitty took responsibility for gathering holly and other greenery from the garden, and Betty helped Cook with the Christmas food preparation — and what a lot of food they prepared.

They had started preparations on 'Stir-up Sunday' back in November, the traditional day for making Christmas puddings. The cake had also been made and 'fed' with brandy regularly.

Cook handed Betty a piece of paper on which the menu for Christmas dinner was written in a beautiful script. Even Mrs Hope's shopping lists looked a work of art. Betty couldn't believe so few people could possibly eat so much.

Oysters in half shell with horseradish,
Oxtail Soup,
Roast Young Pig,

Roast Turkey, Oyster Stuffing,
mashed potatoes, stewed celery, spinach with egg,
cranberry jelly,
Nut and apple salad,
English plum pudding, wine sauce, calves' foot jelly in glasses, whipped cream
meringue, fruitcake, macaroons, almonds, and raisins,
Toasted biscuit, cheese, olives, sweet pickle,
candied fruit,
Black coffee.

'Well, my girl, what do you think of it?'

Betty looked in amazement at Cook. 'I haven't heard of half these things on here.'

'By the time you've worked with me for a few years you'll be preparing a meal just like this. I have agreed with Mrs Stone to train you as a cook, if you have a liking or aptitude for it. I need someone reliable to help me'

She held up the menu. 'You mean I will be able to cook like this?'

'It'll take time, but with perseverance I'm sure you'll manage. So, pay attention to what I do.'

Betty hadn't thought of cooking, but it would be better than being a maid, wouldn't it?

* * *

The Delhavens always held a large family Christmas dinner, with several relatives travelling from Manchester and Macclesfield. They stopped overnight, which meant the servants worked almost continually, with only a few hours' sleep over the festive period.

Betty didn't expect Christmas Day to be a normal working day, although it stood to reason it would be even busier than normal with all their guests. Betty rose early to make fires and fill coal scuttles. She spent the rest of the day in the kitchen helping Cook to ensure the meal, for fourteen people, was ready to serve shortly after their return from church. Once the food had been prepared much of the hard work was done for the day, though all of the servants were required to help to clear the dining room. In the meantime, Cook prepared an extensive cold table for the evening. Once done, the servants were able to take their Christmas meal, always listening for the ring of the bell summoning a servant upstairs.

Each member of staff put one present under the tree, and lots were drawn. Nothing expensive, there was not enough money for that, especially as most of them had their own families to buy for. But Betty was told it was the thought that counted. It was exciting to know there was a present under the tree for her. She'd only had presents from her own family. Whatever her present was, she would be happy.

Although the staff worked hard, there was a sense of camaraderie within the kitchen even Mrs Stone was prepared to put up with. Levi played the fiddle and Young John the mouth organ, and they sang popular melodies, traditional seasonal songs and Christmas carols.

The servants' hall clock struck ten and Mrs Stone immediately clapped her hands for quiet. She thanked everybody for their day's work.

'Christmas is now over, let us start to prepare the house for the night.'

There was the work of tidying away what seemed to be every plate, pan, and glass the Delhavens owned; beds had to be warmed and fires banked.

* * *

On Boxing Day, all the servants were required to line up in the hall, from Mrs Stone and Jim Bailey at one end to Betty at the other. Before they got into line, Mrs Stone inspected each person to ensure their hands and faces were clean and tidy, with no hair showing. Betty hid a grin at grown-ups being treated like children at school, and didn't complain.

Mrs Stone marched them into the dining room to meet the family, whose chairs had been arranged in a semi-circle waiting for the show to start. All the family were present and, at last, Betty got to see the Delhaven boys. They were both handsome in their own way and Betty blushed as she stood in front of them to receive her present from the family. Presents were practical: dress lengths to make up a uniform to replace a worn-out one; woollen stockings if Mrs Stone had noticed holes or untidy darning. Betty had to admit it was better than using her well-earned wages to pay for them. Nobody thought servants could possibly want anything 'nice' or 'pretty' or even 'fanciful.' Whatever they received, the items were necessary and something they didn't have to use their own hard-earned money to buy.

One night there was a huge party and several young ladies had been invited, no doubt to show off Mr Claude and Mr Harry before they left to resume their studies. Betty was sure it was their mother's way of controlling who might possibly become a future Mrs Delhaven.

Betty and Kitty made excuses to wander through so they could see the toffs enjoying themselves and study the outfits worn by the ladies, knowing they would never afford such luxury, but ogling, nevertheless.

7

January 1912

It was 7th January before Betty was able to celebrate Christmas with her family. By then, it felt as if Christmas was over.

When she arrived home, it was to a house subdued. If there had been any jollity, then the family had worn itself out and there was none left to share with Betty. Jeffrey tried his best for which she was thankful.

Of course, they made a big fuss of her when she turned up, and they took it in turns to give her a Christmas-cum-New-Year kiss, and Betty was thrilled. She had made each of them a small present: a bookmark for Mary-Ellen; knitted hats for Lily and Tommy; scarves for Father, Jeffrey and Michael; and embroidered handkerchiefs for Mother and Martha, thanks to Cook. She didn't know how she fitted it all in, but she did and how pleased she was at their reception.

Betty was careful not to show any feelings when she sat down to eat. Each place at the table was laid with one plate, a knife, fork and spoon, and a cup. It looked so bare compared with the settings at Stowford House. Unlike Stowford House, all the plates were returned to the kitchen empty of food. If Cook had written out a menu, then this is how it might have looked.

Pork Hock with turnip, onions, and potatoes,
Bread and dripping,
Homemade mince pie (one each),
A mug of tea.

Games followed, and even Father and Jeffrey joined in, although they both had early starts at the pit the next morning. They had all tried to make this first Christmas a bit special for her, for which Betty was thankful.

Later in the afternoon, Betty popped over to see Martha to give her the present she had made. In return, Martha gave her a cup and saucer — made by Jackson's Pottery, it said on the bottom.

'I'll be making these all on me own when I go back,' Martha said. 'Fettling handles, and the like. Might even get to decorating them soon.'

They threw their arms round each other and Betty concluded Martha was happy enough now she was a worker like Betty.

She ran back home to enjoy the rest of the festivities with her family. The behaviour of the young Deans had returned to normal, with shouting and arguments, but Betty didn't care. She would just as soon have her simple family Christmas any day.

Part Two

8

April 1914

Betty was running out of stationery and needed to collect paper, stamps, and envelopes from the general store otherwise there would be no more letters written that day and she had promised one to Martha. She agreed to get cigarettes for Levi and stockings for Ruth. The general store was small and there wasn't much choice, so the trip was reasonably quick.

She had just come out of the store, hands full and humming, when she bumped into someone coming in the opposite direction.

'Oh!'

'Someone's in a wee rush this morning! And who might you be?' He doffed his cap to her, and she couldn't help but smile.

He looked about eighteen or nineteen. He had a deep, man's voice. He spoke differently to anyone Betty knew. A kind of lilt. She quite liked it. He was tall, with red hair and blue eyes, and signs of a beard in the making.

Betty smiled. 'Good morning to you too.'

'You're not from these parts?'

'Neither are you by the sounds of it,' Betty retorted.

'I shall go first then. My name is Alastair Macdonald, and I'm a cousin of Billy Nixon. D'yer know him?'

'Billy? Is he walking out with Kitty Merrick?'

He nodded, grinning all the time so Betty had no

choice but to follow suit.

'I'm Betty Dean. I work at Stowford House.'

'Och, I might've guessed.'

'What d'yer mean?'

'You're wearing the same dress as Kitty wears.'

He was nice, Betty concluded.

'Mind if I walk up the street wi' you?'

His height made her feel small beside him. And she liked that. She nodded and they walked, keeping pace, back towards Stowford House.

She smiled as she said goodbye and hoped she would see him again . . . soon.

* * *

It was Kitty's day off. A bleary-eyed Betty watched her as she gathered a few things to take with her. It fell to Betty to do some of her jobs as well as her own. For the first time, Mrs Stone sent Betty upstairs to work instead of the kitchen. She felt a sense of achievement, much better than being confined to the servants' hall.

She spent the morning at her usual tasks of filling and carrying coal scuttles, removing coal dust and candle wax, sweeping floors, and beating carpets, and cleaning. When she returned to the kitchen, she was exhausted. Her legs ached, her head ached, and even her toes ached. She was glad to have a sit down at lunchtime and even more so when Mrs Stone instructed her to clean the silver in the dining room. Although it was boring, she could sit at the large dining table and let her mind wander aimlessly. She had spread out a protector to prevent damage to the table and had laid out everything before her. Surprisingly, she had no interruptions and even began to sing softly to herself.

Betty had been at Stowford House exactly three years. She had grown up a lot and was more confident. The routines of the house rarely changed, and Betty was now well-versed in most jobs. Better still, Cook had been true to her promise made during her first Christmas and had taught Betty a lot about cooking, and how to arrange the food to look appetising on the plate, something she had never really thought of before. She was even allowed to prepare many of the courses for the Delhavens' meals.

She was nearly sixteen and still the skivvy, but she had learned so much. She rarely met the family, but that didn't matter. She got on well with the rest of the servants, and they were the people she had to live with. She knew, as she had always known, that a life in service was not for her — she might still be a skivvy when she was twenty at the rate things were going. She wanted something more, a challenge, and one day she would find what she was looking for.

She had returned home to The Potteries during most of her monthly days off. Because she wasn't there all the time, she could see the changes in her family. Lily was now Mother's help. Mary-Ellen had been working for a year as a jiggerer's assistant on Jackson's Pottery down the road and looked quite grown-up. Michael had just left school and had a job with a fruit-and-vegetable merchants in Hanley. This would no doubt tide him over until he could work at the pit. Little Tommy was a leggy seven-year-old and his face had grown more serious. Even Martha looked more like a woman than the child she had been when Betty left. They exchanged news: Betty about the grand evening dresses at Stowford, and Martha about the local dances and the lads who went there. Betty was keen to show Martha she hadn't changed, and had swaggered round the room pretending to be high and mighty but giggling, the two of them against the whole world.

When the family talked around the dinner table, it was about people Betty hadn't heard of, of deaths along the street, and of a girl from school who had got married when she got into trouble and who now seemed much older than her years. Gradually, she began to make excuses for not going home. The letters she had looked forward to receiving became fewer and sometimes read more like a diary of day-to-day events. Nothing to do with how they felt and whether they missed her. She had moaned to them at first, but quickly realised she couldn't force them. It had happened slowly, but what she had dreaded from the beginning, losing touch, had happened almost without her notice. Things had changed for her too, people she couldn't talk about because nobody round the table knew them. There were all the people who lived at Stowford House and in the village. It was as if Hanley was a million miles away from Macclesfield.

And now, there was Alastair Macdonald. He looked strong, manly and he had passed the time of day with her. Maybe there would be an opportunity —

— The clock chimes returned her mind swiftly to the job in hand. It was time for the servant's evening meal. She should be helping Cook to get it ready.

Betty returned to the kitchen.

'Have you finished polishing the cutlery?' asked Mrs Stone.

'Yes, all cleaned and put away, and I have put the polish into the store cupboard, the rags into the wash along with my white gloves.'

'At least you remembered to wear gloves this time. We'll make an upstairs maid out of you one day.'

Betty helped Cook to prepare their evening meal and when she sat down, she gave a large sigh and yawned.

Cook glanced round the room. 'Kitty not back yet?'

Ruth entered the room on the tail end of the conversation. 'I haven't seen her. Has anyone else?'

All the staff were in the servants' hall now and all of them shook their heads.

When nine o'clock came with still no sign of Kitty, Betty began to worry. Kitty usually returned from visiting her family by half past six. She had late nights, but not after visiting family. And now it was almost dark, and she'd be walking from Stowford Holt on her own.

Time ticked by.

Where on earth was she?

* * *

Ten o'clock.

Mrs Stone came into the servants' dining room, where the staff had gathered. 'Where is Kitty?'

She was met with blank looks.

'Well, she'll sleep in the coach house, tonight.'

'That's me going to bed then,' said Young John Makepeace, with a glint in his eye and a wink at Betty.

Mrs Stone glared at him and walked out without a word, indicating to Betty to follow her.

'Do you know what's going on?'

'No, Mrs Stone. She never said nothing before she went. It's dark and there's no more trains tonight.'

'Finish off the rest of your jobs and get to bed. You might be doing some of Kitty's work tomorrow.'

Betty was thoughtful when she went to bed. She undressed, drew back her bed coverings and plumped up the pillow. She opened the drawer to the bedside cabinet to take out her book to read for half an hour, although she had no idea how she would manage to concentrate.

That's when she saw the note, written in Kitty's hand.

She picked it up, turning it over, and read the words *To Betty, in confidence*. With her heart thumping against her chest, Betty opened the note and slowly sank onto the bed, her hand at her neck as she pulled at her collar and tried to breathe.

Dear Betty,

If you are reading this note, then you are probably in our room wondering where the heck I am. Everything has happened so quickly. I wanted to tell you, but I was sworn to secrecy.

Believe it or not, by the time you read this I will be married to Billy Nixon. I will not be coming back to work at Stowford House and will be living at Hollybush Farm instead. Both families are happy with the arrangements. I do hope you are happy for me, Betty. I know I am doing the right thing.

Do you think you could pack up the rest of my belongings and bring them to the Farm? I would love to see you. Please do not tell anyone about this note. I will tell you more when I see you, but you don't have to worry, Betty, because I am fine. In the meantime, take care of yourself. You might even get promoted to my job because you are a good girl, Betty. So do your best and who knows what might happen.

Yours

Kitty Nixon

PS Mrs Stone knows. I have left her a note too.

Kitty married!

The words jumped off the page in front of her eyes. Kitty wasn't ill: she'd gone and married Billy without telling anyone. And thank goodness Kitty left a letter for Mrs Stone too. She wouldn't have liked to be the one to break the news to her.

It felt odd to sleep on her own without the gentle breathing of someone else. She had never slept alone in her life, and it kept her awake. It was while she was lying in bed trying to force herself to sleep there was a knock at the door. 'Betty, it's Mrs Stone. Can I come in?'

'Yes, of course.'

Mrs Stone opened the door. She was in her dressing gown, her hair loose hung round her shoulders making her appear younger than her fifty years.

'I've received this note from Kitty. She won't be back tonight. Apparently, the girl has gone and got herself married.'

'Yes, I've had a letter as well.'

'She's married Billy Nixon today at Macclesfield Registry Office. There was a space in the diary, and they took it otherwise they would have had a long wait.'

'That's good news, isn't it?'

'Not for us. Kitty is . . . was employed as a live-in housemaid. I daresay Mr Nixon will have something to say if she begins her married life here and not at home,' said Mrs Stone in a dry voice.

Betty didn't know whether she was joking or serious. It wasn't like her to joke about something important.

'So, Betty, I want you to gather all of Kitty's personal belongings together and take them to Hollybush Farm before breakfast.' She sighed. 'I will tell everybody the news while you are out. If you see anyone you are to say nothing about the matter. Is that clear, Betty?'

Betty nodded.

'You can collect the groceries for Cook on your way back and that will be where I shall say I've sent you. Good night, Betty.'

* * *

It was about three-quarters of a mile to Hollybush Farm, and it gave her plenty of time to think about Kitty and her wedding. She had begun to have her suspicions there was more to it. She had thought they were friends and could tell each other anything. But supposing Kitty was . . . suppose she was . . . expecting? Even to think such a thought made her cheeks burn. She and Billy had . . . done things no young woman should ever do outside of marriage. Kitty wasn't like that.

She opened the large gate to the farm and walked steadily towards the front door. Kitty must've been keeping a look-out for her because the door opened before Betty reached it.

'Oh, Betty. Thank goodness it's you.'

'Hello, Kitty,' she smiled, suddenly nervous.

Kitty's face was flushed too. 'You'd better come in.'

Betty passed through the door in front of Kitty, walked along a short hall and into a kitchen, which was mostly filled by a large table.

'Pop my stuff in the corner, Betty and I'll put the kettle on.'

'I used my case, so I'll need to take it back with me.' Betty put the case in the corner and turned towards the table wondering what to say. Usually, the pair had no trouble in talking. Betty's eyes wandered down to Kitty's belly and, without asking, she knew why Kitty's marriage had been arranged so quickly and wondered how she hadn't noticed before.

Kitty had seen the look and pulled her cardigan tightly around her waist.

Betty smiled. 'I did wonder, Kitty. What with it all being so quick.'

'It wasn't supposed to happen. We'd had a good night out and Billy . . . well, he . . . sort of got carried away. And I . . . well, I did too. We couldn't help it. But we were thinking of getting married before this happened.' She pointed at her waist and stared at Betty as if daring her to contradict. 'We love each other, Betty.'

'And you don't regret it now yer expecting?'

Kitty shook her head. 'It would've been better happening the other way round and we could've had some time together before a baby came, but . . . I've got everything I ever wanted, Betty. I knew I'd have to leave Stowford House. I can't do my job if I can't live in.'

'What'll you do when the baby's born?'

'Don't know. Help on the farm for one thing. If I do anything outside the farm, it'll mean somebody having to take care of the baby and it won't be cheap. I do believe I'm lucky it was Billy. He's a good man and he'll take care of us.'

Betty's face became serious and she stood up. 'I'll

be making tracks. Mrs Stone warned me not to take all day,' she grinned.

The two girls gave each other hugs and Kitty showed Betty to the door.

'Come back and see me now and again, Betty. I'll miss you.'

Betty nodded. 'I will, I promise.'

On the walk back, her thoughts were with Kitty. She seemed happy enough and, in a few short months, she would have the makings of a family. At least she knew where her life was going. But it didn't make it right. What would Martha have thought about her visiting a girl who had got herself into trouble? Did Alastair know?

Betty stopped walking. Here was her first opportunity to get on in her life. Why should Mrs Stone employ another housemaid when Betty was perfectly capable of doing the job? Why not get a new skivvy instead?

Betty returned to the House and immediately went to the servants' hall in search of Mrs Stone. She was sitting at the small oak desk in the butler's pantry, working. Betty knocked and walked in.

'So, you're back. Did you see Kitty?'

She nodded.

'And did she mention the other . . . delicate matter?'

'You knew she was expecting?'

'I guessed. So now you know why she will not be returning to this establishment. You should learn from that, Betty Dean. You'd best start work, the mornings nearly gone.'

* * *

After breakfast on Sunday, Mrs Stone called Betty into her room.

'Yer look a bit peaky, Mrs Stone, if yer don't mind me saying?'

Mrs Stone gave her a quick glance and then shook her head as if she meant to say something.

'Would it be wrong for me to get yer a cup of tea?' Betty persisted. 'No, Betty. I am quite well. I just needed a rest. Nothing more. I must set about filling the job as soon as possible. I —'

'That's why I —'

'For goodness' sake, Betty, let me finish. You're a one, aren't you? Always something to say. Let me get my words out first . . . if you have no objection?' She smiled thinly.

'No, Mrs Stone. I'm sorry.'

'Now we have sorted out the . . . delicate matter relating to Kitty, I need to find a replacement for her —'

'Th —' Mrs Stone's eyes warned Betty about saying anything more.

'Of course, I need to find someone quickly.'

Betty squirmed in her seat desperate to interrupt but not wanting to annoy Mrs Stone any further.

'I have decided to promote you.'

'That's what I was just going to say.'

'I'm glad we agree,' said Mrs Stone dryly. 'You've worked hard in this establishment, and I've been satisfied with your work. You're a capable girl, and you deserve it. You will mainly work upstairs under Ruth Stevenson, but I need you to continue your duties below stairs until a new kitchen maid can be found. Have a look at Kitty's uniform dresses. You are not too different in size, although the hems will need taking up.'

Mrs Stone stood up, signalling the end of the conversation. 'You will commence your new duties on Monday, so make sure you have your uniforms sorted by then.'

Betty nodded to Mrs Stone and scraped her chair back. 'Thank you, Mrs Stone. I'll do me best for yer.'

Finally, Mrs Stone smiled. 'I'm sure you will, Betty.'

She let herself out of the butler's pantry and walked into the kitchen. It was empty. She couldn't speak to anyone, not at this moment, so she was thankful. She was buzzing inside. She hurried upstairs to her bedroom and shut the door quietly not wanting anyone to know she was in there until she had regained control. She was grinning from ear to ear.

Mrs Stone told everyone at lunchtime about Betty and they all congratulated her.

Kitty was talked about in dark corners within the house. Nobody dared disregard Mrs Stone's orders not to gossip. But they had guessed for themselves. Her ban might even have confirmed their suspicions.

That night, Betty spent her spare time altering the dresses while thinking of Kitty, in bed with her new husband. Kitty, who had always appeared so upstanding in her character.

Sorry as she was for her friend's employment to end as it did, she couldn't help but be happy at her newfound promotion. How pleased Mother would be when Betty wrote and told her. She wrote to Martha telling her the good news but decided to say nothing about Kitty. Better wait until she was home. Martha was a bit prudish about girls who got into trouble.

She hugged her knees. She was no longer a skivvy; Betty Dean was going up in the world.

* * *

On Ruth's day off, Betty had to assist Mrs Delhaven. On her first day she was so worried about doing something wrong that she spilled the tea she was serving into the silver tray, causing the saucers to be swimming in it. Red-faced, with cheeks so tight she could barely open her mouth, Betty apologised. She was about to remove it when Mrs Delhaven's arm knocked the tray and tea spilled over Betty's apron too.

'So . . . so . . . sorry, Madam, I'll bring some more.'

'And do get changed, Betty. You look as if you've just got out of the bath.'

Betty fled from the room carrying the tray, swimming in tea. Tears splashed into the brown liquid threatening to cover the carpets to add insult to injury. When she entered the servants' corridor, she laid the tray down carefully on the floor and wiped her face on her handkerchief, not wanting to show her distress to anyone.

Mrs Stone was humming to herself in the butler's pantry when Betty got there.

'That you, Betty? Everything all right upstairs?'

'Yes, Mrs Stone. The mistress has asked for another pot of tea. I'm about to take it up.'

Mrs Stone walked into the kitchen with a handful of side plates and her mouth fell open at the sight of Betty.

'Betty! Look at your dress. You can't go back upstairs looking like that. Here, put this apron on. The bib will cover most of the stain — and be more careful.'

Betty quickly doused her face with water and wiped it with a towel. She would have to do. She picked up a clean tray, with clean cups and saucers, and a new pot of tea, and made her way slowly to the sitting room.

'Ah, Betty. Put the tray down carefully this time.'

Betty felt a hot wave wash over her. 'Yes, Madam.' She did as she was bid. 'Will that be all, Madam?'

'Yes Betty. You may go. It is your first day on your own serving the family. We shall say no more about it.'

'Thank you, Madam. That's . . . that's . . . good of yer.'

"You', Betty, not 'yer'. If you want to continue working upstairs, you would do well to remember to speak properly.'

Betty nodded for fear of prolonging the conversation and departed, thankful to return to her lowly life below stairs. Upstairs or downstairs — there must be more to life than this. Perhaps Kitty has got it right after all.

Betty told Ruth when she returned. Ruth's immediate gasp of shock was quickly replaced by a peal of laughter — not quite the reaction Betty was hoping for.

'You're a funny one, Betty. It sounds like Madam wasn't too upset. It's unfortunate it happened on your first day, but you must be careful in the future. You don't want to make a habit of it. You'll have her thinking I'm not teaching you properly.'

Ruth was an upright woman in her late twenties and wasn't prone to laughing when things went wrong. Betty thought she should laugh more often. It suited her.

9

May 1914

Alastair Macdonald was waiting for Betty outside the church on Sunday. She smiled, surprised when he fell into step with her for everyone to see.

'Hello Alastair. How are you?'

'Am grand, as they say.'

Betty didn't quite know what to say next. 'The spring flowers are doing nicely.' She thought it sounded rather lame.

He nodded. 'Wouldna disagree with yer, lass.'

Their talking dried up.

Did he have a reason for joining her, or was he passing the time of day?

'I . . . I, er . . . wanted to ask you, Betty? Would you meet me later, for a walk, maybe?' He stared into the distance, awaiting her reply.

'I'd like that.'

He turned and grinned. 'I'll meet you at the gates then, at two o'clock?'

Unable to speak, she nodded and managed a quick smile. After he had gone, she was unable to believe what had just happened. A lad had asked her out. Her, Betty Dean, walking out with a bloke like Alastair Macdonald. Imagine what Mother would say!

The afternoon couldn't come quickly enough.

Her choices of outfit had grown in the years since she had first arrived, all were homemade. She chose a becoming pale blue because her best hat — she had two now — matched it. Over the top she wore her coat

She walked down the drive, waving to Levi Hope as she went. No doubt he could see Alastair waiting for her. She was glad. She held her head up high. She was walking out with a lad, and she had a witness to prove it!

'Afternoon, Betty.'

'Hello, Alastair,' she said, shyly.

'Where shall we go?'

'Don't mind.'

With unspoken agreement, they walked towards the station at Stowford Holt. The silence at first was a little uncomfortable.

'Where d'yer come from. You sound so different.'

'Scotland. It's called Pitlochry. A place you've probably never heard of, not many have. It's beautiful, surrounded by hills and trees. I used to work on the Blair Tummel Estate where me folks work. Belongs to the Duke of Caithness. A while back, I was sent down here to work at Macclesfield Hall, which also belongs to the Duke.'

'Sounds posh.'

'It is, but I work in the grounds. I'm an assistant gamekeeper.'

'What's one of them?'

'I look after the game birds, such as pheasants and grouse, and shoot the vermin that go after them . . . rats . . . or poachers.'

'You mean you . . .' she couldn't say it.

'Yes, I kill them. Usually with a gun. I'm joking about the poachers, Betty, I'm not allowed to shoot them!'

She laughed. 'That's a relief.'

'I spend all my life looking after these bonnie birds so the toffs can come and shoot the lot of them in August. Crazy, but it pays well, and I get to practise my shooting.'

'Oh, my!'

* * *

Happily for Betty, the new kitchen maid, or skivvy, joined them at the end of May.

She was brought into the kitchen by Mrs Stone and introduced to everyone.

'This is Christine Williams, and she comes from Crewe. She is fourteen years old and left school at Easter. She'll be nervous, so make sure to give her a warm welcome. Betty, you will show Christine the ropes, just in the same way you were shown.'

'Yes, Mrs Stone.'

Betty thought Christine was a lucky girl to have been allowed to stop on at school, but then consoled herself when she realised the new girl had ended up in the same position as she had. Betty remembered how Kitty had helped her in her first few days and resolved to do the same for Christine.

'I have decided to move the spare bed out of your room, Betty, and make use of the end room. It will need a good clean and airing. It can be your first task with Christine,' added Mrs Stone. 'You'll be glad to know you will not have to share any more.'

10

August 1914

At the beginning of August, there came dreadful news. The likelihood of a war in Europe was increasing by the day. *The Staffordshire Sentinel* said Austria-Hungary had declared war on a place called Serbia. All the servants were talking about it over their evening meal. It was far enough away for it not to concern us, they said. But, even so, it might be difficult to contain because Russia was threatening to mobilise its troops too. There was a map. All the countries looked close together but were miles away from England. Surely the Germans wouldn't cross the sea to fight.

During their mid-morning cup of tea, Betty wrote to Jeffrey asking him to promise he wouldn't go to war unless he was forced to. There was no point in doing anything daft when he had the family to support. He couldn't expect Father to do it all by himself.

She asked Mrs Stone if there was anything she could collect from the village when she went to post her letter.

'I was going to tell you to pop down there for me. Will you call at the butchers on your way back? He's got some meat put to one side for me.'

'Course I will. Can I go now? I've written to Jeffrey, and I want it to catch the post.'

'About the war coming any day?'

Betty nodded. 'I want to stop him from getting

involved.'

Mrs Stone laughed. 'And you think you can stop him, do you? If I know anything about men, he'll do as he wants to and no messing.'

'He'll listen to me. Always has, always will.'

Mrs Stone raised her eyebrows. 'You're a pretty stubborn madam, I'll give you that, Betty.'

She thrust her arms into her coat and grabbed her hat, before shooting out of the house.

The first thing she did was post her precious letter. Once it was done, she felt more relaxed and tried to whistle as she strolled along to the butchers.

'Hello, Betty. How are you?'

She turned to find Kitty smiling. It looked as if she'd just come out of the greengrocers. Her bag was full.

'Hello, Kitty. How are you and the little one?'

'Little one is fine. It knows how to kick.'

'Perhaps it's a boy?'

Kitty's hand went to her belly as if trying to protect her unborn child. Embarrassed, Betty turned away. What if Billy Nixon went off to fight and Kitty was left to cope on her own? At least she would be a married woman and not a fallen one. How would *she* feel if she was in her friend's shoes?

Kitty's eyes filled. 'The thought of my Billy fighting makes me feel sick. Who's going to work the farm if the men are fighting? Who'll look after me and the baby?'

'It might blow over, yer never know.' She put her hand on the mum-to-be's shoulder and gave it a rub as if she was helping a child to feel better.

She didn't really believe her comment and she could see Kitty didn't either. 'Levi Hope has taken to reading the news to us, so we all get chance to find out what's happening at the same time.'

'Trying to take over, is he? Sounds just like him.'

'I think it's his way of trying to stop himself worrying too much. Some people must talk, otherwise they'd go mad with worry. Others bottle it up. Who knows which is best, Kitty? Let's hope nothing comes of it and it's just a storm in a teacup.'

'A bloody big teacup if you ask me!'

* * *

It wasn't a storm in a teacup.

Four days later the country woke to find itself at war with Germany. Fewer than twenty-four hours later the mobilisation of the territorials and army reservists had begun. The newspaper reported they were making ready to leave at a moment's notice for their units. Registration papers were delivered by messengers on foot or bicycle. The post offices were open day and night to register reservists and give them the three shillings to which they were entitled.

The talk around the breakfast table was all about war.

Levi Hope read out the headlines in the morning newspapers. It said the news had come so quickly even tramcars had been recalled enabling reservists on duty to respond to the call to arms. Some men left immediately. The feelings of those men must've been unimaginable. What their families thought as they said their goodbyes, Betty couldn't contemplate. The nine forty-one morning train from Manchester to London was reported as carrying well-nigh a thousand men, loyal and ready. To add to the complications, the trains had been taken over by the government to make sure troops could be moved to where they were needed. Goodness knows how people would get back from their Potters holidays in Blackpool or Rhyl.

Mr Delhaven had risen early and had taken *The Financial Times* to his study to read, so Mrs Stone said. Ruth said he never took his eyes off it when she went in to take him a pot of tea. It wasn't like him, for he always passed the time of day with her.

Betty was desperate to get home to see Jeffrey. Now war was unavoidable, he might break his promise about not joining up. It was one thing to agree not to do something that might not happen, but it was entirely different when the thing you dreaded most became real. She had to know, and letters would take too long. She spoke to Mrs Stone and promised she would be back before nightfall. Surprisingly, Mrs Stone was quite sympathetic and said they would manage without her for a day, but it would be a one-off and she was not to expect further consideration for time off, for whatever purpose. Betty could've hugged her but managed to stop herself before both regretted it.

Much to her disappointment, she arrived at the station only to find there were no trains today. The newspapers were right.

* * *

The following morning, Betty finally received a reply from Jeffrey. He knew she wouldn't rest until she had received word from him. She picked it up and kissed the envelope, then ran to the nearest privy to read it in peace.

3rd August 1914

My Dear Betty,

I received your letter today. I can tell by its tone you must have been out of your mind with worry given you are so far away. I have no intention of taking the Colours. My job at the pit is required and I do not have to leave it unless I decide I must, so you can put it out of your mind, right now. I am bound to do as you ask. Father is too old and can't fight and thank God, our Michael is too young.

I believe it will feel rather strange to be one of the few young men walking around the town but no doubt I shall get used to it in time.

What a disappointment for you to not make it home, Betty. I'm sure everybody would have been glad to see you.

Rest assured, dear Betty, I shall be caring for everyone at home, as before. Nothing has changed since you were last here.

Take care of yourself and come home when you get the opportunity.

Your loving brother
Jeffrey xx

Tears were quick to blur her eyes. His letter was light and told her what she wanted to hear. Thank goodness he would not think of leaving them. It came to her suddenly he might have had other thoughts if she had been at home to take his place.

She smiled and kissed his letter again before returning it to its envelope and slipping it her pocket to read again later.

* * *

The summer of 1914 had been perfect as far as Betty was concerned. The weather was splendid and the attention given to her by Alastair made her feel special. But all this came to an end when the war started.

Betty agreed to meet Alastair in the village on her half day off. They had plenty to talk about as they walked for miles around the lanes. Alastair had been told by the head gamekeeper not to worry about going to war, as his lordship would ensure he stayed to look after the birds. But he would not be able to see Betty for about a month as it was the start of the grouse shooting season on 12th August. He explained it was called the Glorious Twelfth, but he didn't think it would be 'glorious' for the birds.

When they got back to the village, the pub was open, and people were sitting in the garden at the back. Betty didn't normally go into the pub, so Alastair went in for the drinks. As he turned the corner, two youths bumped into him, and their drinks hit the ground.

'Watch out!' he shouted.

'Sorry, Jock. I didn't see yer,' one of the youths said.

'I'll make you sorry,' Alastair grabbed the youth by the collar and looked as if he was going to punch him.

'Oh no you won't.'

No one had seen the constable approaching.

'Not you again. Be a good lad and let go of the boy. I'm sure he didn't do it on purpose,' he said to Alastair, who looked down at his soaking trousers, and then let go of the youth's collar.

'Sorry, officer,' said Alastair. The two youths also apologised and offered to pay for more drinks, but Alastair declined.

'Be on your way, Mr Macdonald.'

The officer waved them on to Betty's embarrassment. 'I thought you were going to hit the lad,' she said

'Ach, no. I was just giving him a fright. I'm sorry Betty, I didn't mean to scare you. I was upset at the mess he'd made on my only suit.'

'Why did the officer know your name?'

'It's a small place. He knows everybody's name'

That evening Betty thought about what had happened and didn't know what to make of it.

* * *

The war had been going for just two weeks, but its effect on Stowford House had already been felt. Mr Harry Delhaven was already in the army at the outbreak of war, and was involved from the outset.

Among the servants, Levi Hope was too old, Young John Makepeace thought about volunteering, but was persuaded by Mr Delhaven to remain to look after the grounds. Mr Bailey volunteered. and Sally Withers left for a factory job making insulators for telegraph poles.

Levi and Phyllis had only one son, a sailor in the Royal Navy. He was a petty officer on HMS Iron Duke and was at Scapa Flow. Mrs Stone did not have anyone she was willing to talk about.

Christine Williams seemed the most affected as both her brothers had volunteered.

* * *

As her time drew closer, Kitty grew more anxious. At first, she talked about the baby and whether it was going to be all right, and then her anxieties moved to herself and how the baby was going to be born. She made Betty nervous in a way she had never felt when her mother had gone into labour.

A few days later, Billy called at Stowford House to say Kitty had given birth to a boy overnight. Master Davy Nixon had arrived.

It was nice of Billy to call.

11

December 1914

Betty arranged to meet Alastair at the gates to Stowford House on her afternoon off. She watched him as she walked. He was pacing up and down as if wrestling with a problem. She frowned. Whatever was on his mind was taking all his attention, for he didn't notice her walking towards him until she had almost reached him.

'Hello, Alastair.'

He jumped at her words and nodded at her before falling into step with her.

She glanced at him. 'Are you all right?'

'Course I am. Why wouldn't I be?' He seemed defensive.

'You didn't see me until I was almost on top of yer.'

They were walking towards the village. He said nothing. Then, moments later, he seemed back to his normal self.

'Are you going home for Christmas?'

'Well, I go back on the 27th. I suppose it's near Christmas.'

'Mmm.'

She knew him well enough now to know when something was playing on his mind. She stopped walking. 'Come on. Out with it. What's up with yer?'

He grinned. 'I've volunteered. For the army.'

Betty froze. 'You've enlisted? Without so much as a

word to me?'

Alastair shrugged. 'Thought you'd be pleased to be walking out with a soldier. Lots of other lasses do.'

'I'm not other lasses.' She shook her head. 'I conner believe you'd do that to me. Please say you're joking?'

He took her hand. 'I'm not.' His eyes caught hers. 'Look, Betty, I'm handy with a gun and I think that's where I belong. Surely you would agree?'

She licked her lip and tried to draw her hand away, but he held it fast. 'If I try hard enough, I think I can understand you joining up. But doing it without saying a word, I don't understand.'

'Ok, I should've told you, lass. But I'm telling you now, aren't I?'

'Yes, when you've done it. Tell me, would you have still enlisted if I had asked you not to?'

Alastair stared at her without a word.

'You never gave me a thought, did you?' How could he have been so insensitive? 'You should've said summat.'

Only the clicking of their shoes on the pavement broke the silence as they walked. It was, therefore, a surprise when they passed through one of the gates to Hollybush Farm.

'I thought we could talk here. No one around to interrupt us.' He waved his arm towards the top field.

'When do you leave?' She held her breath.

'Tomorrow.'

'So soon?'

'It's for training before I get posted. I'll come back before I . . . go anywhere. To be fair, I didn't expect it would happen so quickly.'

She closed her eyes. Without warning, his lips descended on hers. She tried to push him away, but his arms tightened around her. She struggled, but the feel of his lips on hers sent strange feelings through her body. They had kissed before. Of course they had. But not like this. Not with so much urgency. Gradually she stopped fighting him and kissed him back, their lips becoming more persistent.

When he gradually pulled away, she almost fell.

'Oh, Alastair. I don't think I can bear you going away.'

'Think about it, the next time you see me, you'll be kissing a man in uniform. It'll be special.'

'You don't need a uniform to be special to me.'

He stared at her and then grabbed her arm. 'Come with me, Betty. I know a place.' He pulled her behind him.

'Where are we going?'

He ignored her and carried on striding through the damp grass. He stopped close to the last barn, full of hay bales for winter feeding of the animals. Once inside, he let go of her hand and headed towards a window that barely let in the light. The fresh, sweet smell of the hay was enticing, as was the expectation of more kisses to come.

He climbed two or three bales and held out his hand to help her climb up to join him.

'Up there . . . I can't.'

'Come on, Betty. You can.'

His voice pleaded with her, and her heart couldn't refuse. She took his hand and he pulled her up towards him. Once she was in his arms again, he kissed her urgently, She couldn't help but respond.

'Oh, Alastair.'

He groaned and pushed her down, his eyes burning into hers. He lowered himself beside her, his hand moving down her body until she could feel it touching the top of her leg. She struggled but there wasn't much heart in it. She wanted him. A stirring deep inside needed him to carry on. Hot air touched her ears as he murmured her name over and over. He opened her coat, and his hand grazed her breast. She wasn't prepared for her body's response. She pulled him close entwining their bodies. His hand moved from the top of her leg until she cried out in shock and longing. She had never meant to go this far. He pushed against her, again and again.

Suddenly, it was over.

He rolled away from her, spent.

Her breaths were coming quickly, her chest heaving. He turned his head to watch her, waiting for her to say something. She couldn't look at him. Through the open doors of the barn she could see clouds passing. The sky was still light, but she felt she had been here, in this barn, for ages. A thrill washed over her. She had done it. Her first time. And tomorrow she would lose him.

'You're mine now, Betty lass, and wherever I am, I'll be thinking about you, I can promise you. I love you, Betty Dean.'

How could she bear to lose him, even for an instant, so soon after the experience of this day?

When she walked back into Stowford House, she felt all eyes were upon her, that she had somehow become a woman. Her cheeks burned when anyone looked at her as if they could, through reading her face, know exactly what she had done.

In bed that night, it surprised her she hadn't given a thought to the consequences of her actions.

It was a week later, and with some relief that, for the

first time in her life, she was glad to have the stomach ache usually accompanying her monthlies.

* * *

Another letter arrived from Jeffrey. She slipped it into the pocket of her dress beneath her apron and sat waiting to be dismissed. She jumped up as soon as the words 'you may go' left Mrs Stone's lips. She had her instructions for the rest of the day and felt she deserved a few moments by herself to read her letter.

She bounded upstairs and into her room, closing the door quickly behind her. Leaning back against it she breathed deeply to recover her breath, then she moved forward and sat on the edge of her bed. Slowly, she peeled back the envelope and began to read.

21st December, 1914

Dear Betty,

Please don't be angry, dearest Betty. I have enlisted in the army and, as I say those words, I can hear you shouting 'why' in my lughole. Betty, in my mind, I do need to go. I can't let all those blokes go to fight for what is right and me stay behind. I know the next words to leave your mouth after reading this letter will be 'For Heaven's sake you're needed here. The pit needs you and your family needs you.'

Well, you'd be right. I feel slightly mad for doing it, but my conscience is clear, Betty duck. I would feel guilty for the rest of my life if I didn't go, and I don't know whether I could cope with that. Besides, the war might well be over before I am required overseas.

I know you will take care of things at home even though you are far away. Mary-Ellen is growing up and has taken over your place well. I had to write and tell you before you come home for Christmas, for I would never have the courage to tell you face to face. I must report for training on 29th December so I will see you at Christmas. Please try to get home before I leave.

Writing this letter has almost broken me. In sparing your heart, I have damaged my own. I am so looking forward to seeing you before I go. You and all the family will be in my mind constantly.

Take care, little sister. Be brave. Get out of life whatever is most important to you and remember, you are loved, always.

Jeffrey xx

No. No, no! She dashed away her tears with a fist. She felt sick and her head was spinning. Why did he have to go and enlist? As a miner he was important to *this* country.

He. Didn't. Have. To. Go! Each word was accompanied with a fisted hand hitting her pillow.

If she'd been at home, she might've talked sense into him. How like him to leave off telling her until it was too late to do anything about it. But he was afraid she might talk him out of it. Her heart was racing and she tried to calm herself. She was no good to anybody in this state.

He had done exactly as Alastair had done. Did nobody care about *her* feelings? It was as if she didn't count.

She returned to the kitchen, but she couldn't get him out of her mind. He was doing what he thought was right . . . what he could live with.

Stupid, stupid man. She banged the table with her fist.

'Whatever's the matter, Betty?'

She showed Mrs Stone the letter.

'I thought something wasn't right with you, Betty. It's only to be expected, child. But still a shock when it comes.'

'But he didn't have to, Mrs Stone. He's a miner. He doesn't have to go.'

'I'm afraid it's not only the government that can tell a man what's right. It's what he feels in here.' She thumped her hand against her chest. 'And if this tells you to do something, then you ignore it at your peril, for you have to live with the consequences.'

* * *

Betty thought about Mrs Stone's words as she was getting ready to leave Stowford for her Christmas on the 27th. All the staff had been given an additional day, to reflect that family visits were important in times of war. When she met Jeffrey, should she show anger or disappointment? Tears of sadness or appreciation of his actions? She couldn't decide.

She wrapped herself up and wore her new gloves for the first time. Even so, the snowy, icy walk to the station was tough going. Her cheeks felt chapped in the strong wind and, periodically, she would walk backwards to give her numb face a chance to recover. It was a relief to step aboard the railway carriage and relax.

Luckily the snow had turned to rain by the time she arrived at Stoke station so the walk home to Hanley helped clear her head. She arrived home to find everyone there, including dearest Jeffrey. At the sight of him, she dropped her bag and leapt into his arms.

He hugged her tightly. She felt warm, protected, loved. He was breathing heavily. She pushed him away gently and looked into his eyes sensing he was waiting for her response to his news.

'Come on, yer daft wench. Let's be having yer inside afore yer catch yer death,' he said.

His troubled eyes rested on her when he didn't think she was looking.

'It's right good ter see you an' all, Jeffrey.' She forced a grin, and lapsed into local words naturally now she was back home, not wanting to stand out as being different. The more at ease her brother felt, the more she would get out of him, and she had to make the most of it while she had him in her sights.

All the family were there, laughing and making light of what was to come, but Betty wasn't fooled. Underneath all their bravado, Jeffrey's news lay heavy. Faces looked from her to Jeffrey and back again, waiting for him to be the one to raise the subject. It was as if something or someone was in the room with them. She couldn't trust herself to speak of it.

Later, when they had the opportunity to be alone, she took a walk with him, pondering on how to raise the matter to best effect. Her breath came shallowly.

It was Jeffrey who broke the silence.

'Come on, Betty, out with it. Yer didn't come all this way to walk with me and say nowt.'

'Oh, Jeffrey. Why did yer go and do it? Join up when yer promised me yer wouldn't.'

He had a sheepish look about him. 'It was what I had ter do.'

'But yer didn't. That's the point.'

'You dunner understand. So many people have taken the Colours. But many more are needed. You've seen the notices in the newspaper, '*YOUR KING AND COUNTRY NEED YOU.*''

'But we need yer at home. The pit needs yer, else everybody's going ter be damn cold if all the miners go off, won't they?' She tried to laugh at her joke.

'I'm a fit, working bloke, Betty, not married with a family. I conner be working over here when men are dying in foreign parts, especially family men. Looks as if I'm avoiding going, a coward. A sergeant from the Royal Engineers spoke to us all before we went on shift a few weeks ago. He told us how important our mining skills would be. On top of that, I'm getting sick of dirty looks from posh women with big hats. They never stop ter think or ask why I'm not in uniform. They just glower and tut. The only time I can forget is when I'm asleep and Heaven knows even it has been interrupted now, what with the dreaming.'

'But you've got people relying on yer.'

'Betty, I have ter do this, otherwise I'll go mad. I dunner see as it could be any worse than staying here and being sick at the thought of staying behind.'

'Oh, Jeffrey.' Her eyes were stinging, and she felt drained. She could fight him no longer. 'I'll think about you every night and pray for yer an' all. Promise me you'll take care of yerself?'

'I'll come home when it's all over and celebrate a job well done.'

He lifted a dark curl of hair off her face where it had fallen. She blinked and caught his hand with her own. 'I'll hold yer to that, Jeffrey Dean. And woe betide yer if yer don't.'

They both laughed. She leaned forward and he gave her another hug.

And that was that.

They made the most of their late Christmas, everybody hoping against hope the war would end quickly. They played games, drank a little too much and sang bawdy songs to take their minds off what was to come. Betty had a feeling Mother had spent far too much money on food as if to feed Jeffrey up before he went. Betty gave her as much as she could out of her wages so as the rest of them didn't go hungry in the weeks after the festivities.

* * *

It was a thoughtful Betty who returned to Cheshire. The hug Jeffrey gave her as they parted was strong, as if it was going to be the last she would receive from him, and she hugged him even more. She really didn't see how she could carry on working when he was likely to be heading towards danger the further he got away from her.

She had walked to Stoke station in the rain. The grey sky was already darkening for another long winter night. Rain had soaked through her coat and her hat had drooped about her face. She was glad to be at the end of her journey and to see Levi waiting for her at Stowford Holt with the pony and trap, and she thanked him.

She opened the door to the servants' entrance, took off her hat and shook away as much of the rain as she could. Only then did she step inside. The hall was dark and uninviting. Another sigh escaped from her disappointed lips. If she had been at home, she would've had people around her who cared about Jeffrey, people who could talk about the old days and not think about the future.

They were all standing there, some working, others just chatting.

'Hello everybody,' she said in as bright voice as she could manage.

'Hello, Betty,' said Cook giving her an anxious look. 'It's good to have you back, child.'

As she nodded back, Cook whispered: 'Did you manage to see your brother?'

'Yes. He is leaving tomorrow for training. I think he's all right.'

It was nice of Cook to ask.

'You'd best get changed and get yourself back to work before Mrs Stone returns from the village. She thought you'd be back by now, Betty,' said Ruth Stevenson.

12

January 1915

Time passed by so slowly, Betty found herself asking for jobs to do to stop her mind from thinking about the two boys who had been in her life and who were now absent. How strange she should miss Jeffrey when she had seen him so rarely since working at Stowford. Now, she couldn't get him out of her mind. In the future, the war would determine if and when she would see him again.

It was the end of January and Alastair was expected in the early afternoon When she drew breath, the air left her body noisily and caused Ruth to ask her if she was all right.

At half-past one, she threw on her coat and escaped. She ran towards the gates to where Alastair was waiting. He was smoking, but stubbed it out as soon as he saw her.

'Ah, Betty lass. It's good to see you. Have you missed me?' He broke into a grin and opened his arms.

She flew into them oblivious of the possibility of watchful eyes. 'I couldn't wait. I've been counting the hours.'

He swung her off her feet and she laughed with the joy of it all.

'Come on, let's make the most of me being here We'll go to the barn.'

Her body responded before she was able to say a

word. 'Do you think we should?' She asked the question, but she already knew the answer. She wanted his kisses, and they could hardly do that in the street.

As they walked towards Hollybush Farm, he talked about his basic training and the endless marching, about the men he shared with and the officers who were training them. She was disappointed he didn't ask about her life, but supposed he would, eventually.

They arrived at the barn and ducked inside. The hay they had lain in was still there, as if waiting for their return. They looked at one another. His eyes were bright, burning, and she couldn't look away. She didn't want to. She wanted him to want her. He undid the buttons on her coat slowly and slid his hand inside. She caught her breath and leaned towards him, wanting him to kiss her. He didn't. He threw her coat on the hay and took her in his arms. At last, she was where she wanted to be.

He lay on top of her, his body hard against her.

'I've been thinking about this, Betty. Every day I felt good because I knew you were waiting for me.'

He caressed her face and moved against her. She was overcome with need for him until she could think of nothing else.

Then it was over, and he rolled away. Only then did she feel the cool air of the January day brushing against her.

'I canna tell you how much it means to me to know you're here, waiting for me, Betty.' He took out a packet of Woodbines and offered her one.

'I don't,' she said.

He was still watching her as she slipped into her coat. She didn't mind. She wanted him to see her. If they stayed here, talking, they might even do it again.

Maybe she could do something, to show how much she wanted it? But she didn't know if girls did that sort of thing.

13

February 1915

On the Saturday of Alastair's leave, he told Betty he had promised to visit his parents in Pitlochry. The train would take him most of the way and he would be back to spend some time with her before leaving for his sharp-shooter training.

On the Wednesday afternoon he was due back, Betty had done her jobs and was standing outside near the back door and could hear voices in the workshop adjoining the coach house. She had been counting down the days to Alastair's return and it had almost arrived.

She wandered over to the workshop to find Young John Makepeace in there.

'You talking to yerself, John?' She grinned as he looked up to see her, arms folded with her head on one side.

'Course not, although it's likely to be the only time I get any decent conversation, I might add.'

'Well, who —'

'You're taking a chance coming over here, Betty. Women don't grace these parts very often.'

It was Levi Hope, wearing a leather apron and carrying the tools to a bench at the back of the workshop.

'Hello, Levi. Thought I'd come and see what you boys are up to.' She felt happy and giggles mounted up inside her.

Her happiness at Alastair's impending return bubbled over. She wanted to share it. She walked into the workshop, swaying her hips, and in the mood for banter.

John laid down the set of reins he'd been working on. 'We're busy, but not too busy to talk to the likes of you.'

'I've got more than enough to do, even if you haven't, lad,' murmured Levi banging a piece of metal with a hammer of some sort.

John stood, hands on hips and swaggered towards her. 'So, what do you really want, Betty.'

She laughed. 'What are you offering?'

'Go on, John — why don't you tell us all what *you* want.'

Betty swung round. It was Alastair, in his uniform, standing in the open doorway. She gave him a huge smile and ran towards him. His face looked like thunder; his eyes overly bright. She faltered. She had never seen him looking like that.

'We were just chatting, Al —'

'Just chatting? It didn't look like just chatting to me.'

John stood his ground. 'Come on Alastair, we were just having a bit of fun.'

'Fun! That's what you call messing around with my girl.'

She glared at Alastair. 'We weren't doing nothing wrong. I was waiting for you. I just came out for a chat.'

'I know what my eyes saw.'

His face looked overheated. His hands clenched and unclenched by his side as if he was fighting with them. Betty put a hand on his arm to lead him away, his muscles hard and strong, but he shook it off, still glaring at John. Suddenly he lashed out and landed a fist on John's cheekbone. He tumbled backwards until his legs gave way and he was flat on his back.

'Stop it!' She screamed and tried to pull Alastair away.

He grabbed hold of Betty's upper arms tightly and pushed her away. She tripped and fell. She got up and tried again. His eyes glazed as if he didn't recognise her and went to kick John in the ribs.

Levi came running from the back of the workshop. 'What the hell's going on?'

Alastair looked surprised to see him as he stood over John Makepeace. 'I didn't know you was here,' he said finally, stepping away from John's prone body.

Betty rushed over to John and knelt beside him. 'Are you all right?'

He lifted a hand to his cheek. There was a red slit and some blood oozed out of his mouth. 'I will be when I've flattened that idiot.'

'That's my girl you're chatting up. Don't you think I know what you're doing?' hissed Alastair. 'Come with me, Betty.'

She stood transfixed. Never, in the six months she had been seeing him, had she witnessed such behaviour. It was as if the violence had taken him over and he didn't know when to stop. Never, for one minute, did it enter her head he would hurt her. She rubbed her arms and could still feel his fingers holding her, pressing into her skin.

Betty helped John to his feet. 'I think you'd best go, Alastair,' she said not taking her eyes off John.

'But what about —'

'Do what the lady asks,' said Levi, still with the

hammer in his hand. 'If you go now, we'll speak no more about it.'

Alastair stared at the group and shook his head.

'I need to talk to you, Betty. Please.'

'I'll let you know,' she said.

She begged Levi and John to say nothing of Alastair's behaviour. John promised to say one of the horses had kicked him and he would take care not to get near his back legs in future.

'You do know he's got a reputation. Has difficulty controlling his temper at the best of times. We'll have to speak to the Master,' said Levi, his face full of concern.

She couldn't let Levi or John do that. Maybe Alastair had some reason for his outburst. 'Please don't, he's always been fine with me.'

'I'm warning you, Betty, and you should take heed,' said Levi with a troubled look. 'I didn't know as you and him . . .'

'Like I said, he's never touched me before.' She might have been blushing as she finished speaking, and her voice sounded unsure even to herself.

An hour later, Alastair was back. 'Come with me, Betty. I'm going on Saturday. I need to talk to you. To explain.'

'I can't.' She needed time to think, and she needed answers. 'I'll see you at two o'clock on Friday at the entrance gates.'

She closed the door.

* * *

She slept badly. Throughout the following day, she couldn't get Alastair's anger out of her mind. The violence he had shown to John Makepeace and his anger against her — for what? Had he been jealous at catching her enjoying herself with somebody who wasn't him? If Levi hadn't been present, she didn't know what he would've done and whether she could've stopped him.

Martha's mother came to mind. Her occasional black eyes, and the bruises she tried to hide. Was that how *he* had started? Martha said he was always sorry for his actions and promised never to do it again — until next time. Even her mother had stopped trying to make excuses for him.

She realised Alastair was going to be the same. It was John's fault for having a laugh; it was Betty's fault for being there. It would always be someone else's fault.

No matter what she thought of Alastair, she would not put herself through all this. By Saturday evening she had made up her mind. She would tell him it was over between them.

* * *

'Thank you for walking with me,' Betty said, as Levi and John accompanied her down the driveway to meet Alastair.

She was going to tell Alastair it was over between them and was nervous of his reaction, and they had agreed to go with her instantly.

'We'll cut some branches off the large oak, John. The one broken in the wind at the turn of the year.'

John grinned. 'You don't have to worry, Betty. We'll see you right.'

She couldn't help feeling relieved to know they

would be near to the entrance — just in case.

Alastair was waiting at the gate. He smiled at her. Levi and John began working on the tree.

'I don't know what came over me, Betty. I won't do it again. I think it was the thought of me going away and leaving you with the likes of him,' Alastair nodded towards John.

She stared at him. Surely he didn't have it in his mind she would fall for the first person she met while he was away.

'I don't know what you think I am, Alastair. I wouldn't do summat like that behind your back.'

'You don't know that.'

She placed her hands on her hips. 'So, *you* say you won't do it again and I must believe you, but when I ask to do the same, you say *I* don't know my own mind?' her voice grew louder.

'I'm trying to tell you how it was for me.' His teeth were clenched. He grabbed hold of her and pulled her towards the copse opposite the gates, and out of sight of Levi and John. She gulped. No one would be able to see them. She struggled but his hands held fast.

'Alastair, let me go or else I'll scream.'

He was dragging her. 'No, you won't, or I shall tell them what you've been up to. What will they think of you then?'

He stopped so suddenly she cannoned into him.

'Betty, lass. I'm sorry for things getting out of hand yesterday. I'd rushed over to see you when I got back and when I heard you laughing with him in the workshop, I thought you and him were —'

'Were what?'

'You know . . . having fun.'

'We were, Alastair. We'd been working hard and we

were chatting.'

'You sounded as if you were . . . getting close.' He looked down at his cap.

'What? With Levi working in there?'

'I didn't know?'

Betty shook her head. 'So you just went for John. Why? To teach him a lesson?'

'We're good together, Betty. We were meant for each other.'

'I thought we were, too. Now I'm not so sure.'

'I did it because I love you, Betty.' He grabbed her arms and shook her. 'Can't you see what you mean to me?'

Her eyes opened wide. Until yesterday, she had thought she loved him too, and couldn't bear the thought of him going away. But things had changed.

His face became redder. His fists clenched and unclenched.

'I'm sorry. You can see how much you mean to me. We belong together.' He lifted his hand and stroked her head, gently, the brutishness all gone. He wasn't the same man. She hesitated.

'You're not listening. You frightened me. It's over Alastair.' She stepped back a pace, but he moved forward and held her jaw, tightly. 'You're hurting me.'

He held her. Trapped. Her breaths came thick and fast.

'I'll tell you when it's over. I know you're upset, so I am going to forget you said that. I'm going to fight for my country, but I'll always come back for you. I promise.' His eyes burned into her.

She shook her head. 'Alastair, listen to me, I never want to see you again.'

She pulled away and hurried towards the gate

in time to see Levi and John walking towards her. If Alastair was going to come after her, he must've changed his mind.

Levi's eyes searched hers. 'You all right, Betty? We were worried about you.'

She turned. Alastair hadn't moved. He had watched her walk away.

'Yes, Levi,' she nodded. 'I'm all right now.'

* * *

Mrs Stone handed out letters to all the staff just after eleven o'clock. Betty watched faces change from anxiety to relief, always a comfort. In Betty's case, recognising her mother's uneven and spidery writing on the envelope, she begged Mrs Stone for ten minutes to herself so she may read it. After a quick nod, she bounded out of the kitchen and up to her bedroom.

Her mother didn't beat about the bush but came straight out with her news. Mr Percy Owen, Martha's father, was 'missing in action' in Flanders. The news was all round Wellington Road, she said. The family had all their curtains closed and nobody answered the door.

Betty's hand shook as she read the letter for the second time. Whatever must Martha be going through? If only she wasn't so far away, Betty could help and support her.

She was longer than she intended and Mrs Stone looked annoyed when she returned. However, one look at Betty's face would have told her the news was not good.

'Sit down, dear. Looks as if you've had a shock.'

Betty took a deep breath and blurted out the contents of the letter before bursting into tears. What she couldn't take in was how she felt about it. Percy Owen had been a bad husband and father, but he was still a member of the family.

In the circumstances, Betty swapped her day off with Ruth so she could go home on Sunday.

* * *

The house was quiet when Betty arrived home mid-morning. There had been no time to let them know she was coming, so they were probably at chapel. There was no point in her sitting alone, waiting for them to return.

She closed the door and hurried up the street to call on Martha, and hoped, given the circumstances, her friend would be at home. As Mother had written, all the curtains were drawn and there were no signs of anyone being at home.

She knocked on the door.

No one answered.

She thought she might catch someone if she went down the back alley and knocked on the back door. She stepped into the darkness of the alley, listening to the echoing of her heels in the narrow passageway. The kitchen curtains were open, and she could see Martha sitting with her arm around her mother.

Martha glanced up and gave a tremulous smile, said something to her mother, and then walked towards the back door to let Betty in. They fell into each other's arms until Martha could step back and blow her nose.

'How are yer?' She deliberately kept her voice low.

Martha shrugged. 'Dunno how I feel right now. Since he's been gone it's been fine. It's such a relief to come home and not have to wonder if he'd given Mother a pasting for summat she had or hadn't done. I know Mother felt so, too. But he's still our dad and I conner believe he might never come back. He was just young enough to be on the reserve list and the thought of being back in the army excited him.'

Betty's heart went out to Martha. Whichever way she looked at this, Martha would feel racked with guilt and relief.

'How's yer mother?'

'Same, but she feels guiltier. She says as she should grieve for him, but the tears won't come. Why should he make us feel like that, Betty?' Martha blinked and shook her head.

'Are you all right for money?'

'With most of us working, we should manage.'

They went into the kitchen so Betty could pass on her condolences to Mrs Owen. Issy was in there too. The three of them talked until dinnertime and the occasional knock on the door went unanswered.

She returned to Wellington Road where everybody was getting ready for Sunday dinner. Seeing Betty's face, Mother realised where she had been. They hugged. But soon, the Dean household returned to normal.

All the trouble Betty had had with Alastair came flooding back as she made her way to Stowford, comforted by the thought she had narrowly escaped placing herself in the same situation that had tormented her friend's family.

14

March 1915

Jeffrey's first letter sent during his training reduced her to tears. He was so far away, and her family too distant to gain any comfort from them. At least the family had each other; she had no one to hug, console, nor comfort her. Wasn't everyone in the same boat? Caring for all the men who had left their homes to go off and fight would take everyone's strength away. There was none left for the people grieving at home. Who knew how long it would be before the end was in sight?

She opened the cupboard beside her bed and reached for the letter she'd received that morning, to read it once more, touching something Jeffrey had touched.

9th March 1915

My Dear Betty,

Hope you are well and still enjoying your job in that big house with all your cronies. We are nearing the end of our basic training and will be selected for service units shortly. The training was hard. I thought I was fit but this training made me realise I wasn't. I don't know how the others have survived. Not sure I'll get leave at the end of my training. I will let you know if I do.

I do hope you manage to get home regularly, Betty. Our mother needs to let go of some of the burden she carries now she doesn't have us to lean on. Father tries his best, but Mother makes all the decisions.

Do you remember the photograph we had taken on the chapel outing just before the war started? The one of all of us, sitting in a studio looking prim and proper? I carry it round with me in my breast pocket. I take it out each night and look at it. I don't let anyone see. I'm not a crybaby. It brings you all close to me.

I shall write to you and Mother as often as I can. Write back to me, won't you? We soldiers live for our letters from home, even now, when we are still in England. When we are at the Front it will be doubly important because it will show there is some normality somewhere in this crazy world.

Think of me.

With much love
Jeffrey xx

He's lonely.

She screwed up her eyes hard and asked God to take care of him and all the soldiers who couldn't be with their families. She stared out of the window, letting her thoughts travel beyond the gardens and the fields surrounding Stowford House to the houses centred on the far side of the village green. How many of the young men who lived in those tiny houses had left a big hole in the hearts of their families and were now in foreign parts? She no longer felt sixteen; she felt old. She dropped a kiss on the letter and returned it to the cupboard. She would write back to him that evening, knowing he would be waiting for it.

But there was one thing she couldn't tell him: she had missed one of her monthlies.

* * *

When all her duties had been completed, Betty climbed the stairs wearily to her room and closed the door before slumping on the bed. Her mind went to the last monthly she remembered. She was due her next. She went cold. Her skin tight. She couldn't be . . . She thought back to Kitty and how some of the servants had sniggered in corners when they heard the news. And Martha, what would she say?

She couldn't be expecting. Had the worry about Jeffrey and the upset with Alastair affected her cycles?

Betty sighed and got up to undress, the cold air making the hairs on her arms stand up. She had pulled her nightgown over her head and climbed into bed before she remembered she needed to write to Jeffrey. She reached into her drawer and pulled out his letter, her writing pad and ink, and began to write what she hoped would be a positive response.

13th March 1915

Dear Jeffrey,

I was so pleased to get your letter today and wanted to write straight back. You sound a little lonely, dear brother. I hope you might feel better when you get to read this letter, although I have little to say now. I am quite well. I still go back to The Potteries on my days-off. Mother seems to be coping well. I think Mary-Ellen is taking her housekeeping work seriously. It's a big help.

I'm surprised you were not considered fit, after all the hard work down the pit. I dread to think how a teacher, or an office clerk would have measured up.

It nice to know you have the chapel outing photograph. I had forgotten about it, but, now I know you have a copy with you, I will do the same. At least we will be looking at the same picture.

Mr Harry is home now. I don't know how long he will be with us. It would be nice if he stayed a couple of days and received guests so things might feel normal again even though there will be extra work for everyone.

Well, my dear Jeffrey, it is quite late, and I must go to bed if I am to get up to do my jobs in the morning. Please take care of yourself.

I will look forward to getting your next letter when you have time to put pen to paper.

Sleep tight,

Your loving sister,
Betty

Satisfied, Betty slipped the letter into an envelope and wrote the address neatly. She laid it on the chest of drawers to remind her to post it the next day, before putting out the light and attempting sleep.

15

April 1915

When Betty missed the first one, she suspected she was in trouble. Sometimes she was late, but she always had her monthlies. Now she had missed two and there could be no shadow of a doubt. It would be born in October. She was not ready to say the proper word — not yet. How could she possibly be ready to welcome the little mite into the world when she wasn't even a grown-up herself? How could she look after it and work to keep a roof over their heads?

With so much on her mind, Betty's regular visit home would be a subdued affair. It was on a Wednesday this month, which meant only her mother would be at home and, if she caught the later train not only would everyone be at work, but Tommy and Lily would be at school.

Betty sat alone on the train as it pulled out from Stowford Halt. It had been her mother's idea to improve her chances in life by working in a grand house, and, as the years passed, Betty came to realise it was a good opportunity. She was supposed to be the clever one and here she was, returning home with her tail between her legs, and a baby in her belly.

Her body rocked back and forth to the steady sound of the train on the rails. She tried to concentrate on what she would say to her family, but she wanted to scream and bury her head somewhere where no one could find her.

The walk from Stoke station was pleasant, skirting the park for a lot of the way. She arrived at Wellington Road and entered by the back door into the scullery. As expected, Mother was alone. Now the family was older, Mother took in mending and sewing, mostly from the posh houses near the park. Today, she was working on a set of heavy curtains.

'Hello, Mother.'

'You're later than usual. I had a terrible job getting our Tommy to go to school. He thought you would be here early like you usually are.'

'I missed the first train and Mrs Stone made me wait until I had a drink and something to eat.'

'Well, you can get Tommy and Lily at dinnertime. They'll enjoy having their big sister walk them home from school.'

Betty helped with some of the sewing and the morning soon went. She had to find a way to tell Mother. Her mouth was dry and Mother had given her the odd funny look and Betty had looked away. Could she just come out with it? Her chest felt tight. She could barely breathe. The words wouldn't come.

Dinnertime arrived and Betty walked up to the top of the street to pick up Tommy and Lily, who were overjoyed to see her. Lily told her all about the morning lessons and that she had got a star for sums. Tommy was just pleased to see her. He held her hand all the way back, looking at her most of the way home, saying nothing.

The two children took their boots off in the scullery. Mother had their pieces of bread ready, and they tucked in heartily. Betty and Mother sat down to have their dinner. Betty had no appetite, but she would try her best to eat.

'I've got us a treat today.' Mother proudly opened the grease proof paper holding two ounces of brawn.

It was too much for Betty. Nausea had her rushing to the privy. She felt awful. How could a girl keep her predicament quiet when she suffers so?

On her return, she got another strange look from Mother. The brawn butties were ready along with a mug of tea, and Betty did her best to eat most of it. Soon it was time for the kids to return to the school and Betty walked them back. Lily met her friend and walked on ahead.

'Have yer missed me, Tommy?' Betty said, wistfully.

'I dunner want yer ter go away no more. It's not the same when you're not here.'

'But I'll always come home again. I've got ter go and earn some money, Tommy. Just like our Mary-Ellen and Michael.'

'Dunner yer like us no more?'

'Whatever gives you that idea? Am telling yer, Tommy, there's no room here for me. But I keep coming back cos I love yer. All of yer.'

Try as she might to forget, the more she talked to Tommy, the more her mind turned to the baby growing inside her. If she didn't tell Mother now, it would be hanging over her until her next visit. She couldn't cope with that.

* * *

Mother was waiting, hands on hips.

She knows.

'I think you've got some explaining to do young lady, but before you say a word, sit yerself down and have a drink of tea.'

Betty sank into a chair by the window. She was glad Mother had guessed. It saved her from having to come right out with it.

Mother poured the tea.

'I expect you don't want much more . . . in your condition.'

'No,' she whispered.

'I want to know everything, Betty. How far gone are yer?'

'Three months, I think. I've missed two monthlies. I'm so sorry.'

Mother shook her head. 'I never thought as I'd see you in trouble.'

'I'm so sorry.'

'Sorry? Is that all you can say?' Mother's voice grew louder. 'You bring shame to this house and you're sorry! Thank the Lord you arrived after everyone had gone.'

Betty hung her head. 'I don't know what to say.'

'Were yer forced? Is that it?'

Would it be the end of it if she said yes? She doubted it. She shook her head. The look on her mother's face had frozen her tongue.

'Whatever will yer father say?' Mother took a handkerchief out of her apron pocket and dabbed her eyes with it.

'I really am sorry.'

'So yer keep saying, but sorry's not going to undo the matter, is it? I think you'd better tell me what happened, our Betty. And I want no lies.'

Betty had prepared herself for this. Late into last night she had resolved to tell the truth.

'There was this lad —'

'What lad? What's his name?'

'In Stowford. I was walking out with him. He was from Scotland and worked on one of the Duke of Caithness's estates. He was nice. I even thought I might ask him to come home with me so's he could meet you and Father. Then, the war started, and he enlisted. One day, near Christmas, we . . . we got carried away and . . .'

'And you let him have his way with yer.'

Betty nodded, unable to look at her.

'Stupid girl! Dunner you know a lad'll say anything to get into yer drawers?'

Betty flinched and her face burned.

'You're supposed to be the intelligent one an' all.' Mother shook her head. 'What's his name?'

'Alastair.'

'Your Father will want to speak to him —'

'No!'

Mother's eyebrows shot up her forehead at the vehemence in her voice. 'You'll do as yer told, my girl.'

'I wouldn't marry him if he was the last man on earth. He has a temper. He's violent and he hit me, and I am *not* going to end up like Martha's mother.'

'You never said.'

'Well, I'm saying now, Mother. It was jealousy.' Betty told her how Alastair had attacked Young John Makepeace.

Mother paled. 'Oh, Betty duck, why didn't you say so before?'

Betty shrugged. 'I still did what I did.'

They sat in silence.

'That's it then. You conner marry him,' Mother sighed. 'You won't be the only girl left expecting when their sweethearts go off to war. We'll fob off anyone as asks. We can say you was engaged, and he was going to marry you next time he got leave, but he got killed. I'll have ter think about it. In the meantime, you'll say nowt to no one, do yer hear me, our Betty? No one, not even yer brothers and sisters. Not until we decide what ter do.'

Mother paced the floor.

'What about Father?'

'We'll deal with him. He'll be angry and embarrassed. You know what he's like when it comes to other people knowing yer business. You'll stay here until I've spoken to him.'

'What about Stowford House? They're expecting me back.'

'One problem at a time, Betty.'

* * *

As soon as Father walked through the door, eyes red-rimmed with coal dust and no doubt looking forward to a good wash, Mother sent everyone out except Betty. The kids protested but did as they were told. Mother spread out an old newspaper on the chair by the table so as Father wouldn't leave it dirty.

'What's going on?'

He looked tired. The lump in Betty's throat nearly stopped her from swallowing. He had never hit any of them, but she couldn't bear letting him down like this. Her eyes filled. It hurt her more than a slap across the face would've done.

They sat round the table. Mother put her hands together and looked from one to the other. Betty thought she was about to tell him her news.

'Tell your Father what you told me, Betty.'

Father frowned. 'Tell me what?'

Betty started. Hadn't Mother said she would tell him? Her heart sank. She was being made to pay after all. The words left her lips quietly as she told him everything she had told her mother, including the fight. He never spoke a word.

When it was over, he sat still, his knuckles white. He lifted first one fist and then the other, slowly banging the table.

'What the hell were yer thinking, Betty?' he said, shaking his head. 'I never had you down as a girl as would get herself into trouble.'

Betty hung her head.

'I've a bloody good mind to go up to Stowford and sort him out for touching one of my girls.' There was no doubt he meant what he said.

'No, Father. It won't do no good. He's at the Front and I'm never going to marry him.'

'Marry him? That's the last thing you'll do, my girl. I was going to go there and give him a bloody good hiding!'

'That's not the way, Charlie. Think about it. We conner let anybody know what's happened — for the sake of our Betty. What will people say when they find out. We need to come up with a story and stick to it. You just said as he's at the Front. We can say he died serving his country.'

'You mean tell a lie?'

'Can you think of summat better to say?'

Father stared. His shoulders fell. He shook his head.

'We can say she was set to get married the next time he came on leave — but he got killed before he could come back.

'That means everybody'll know what I —'

'You should've thought about that at the time, lady.'

Betty almost burst into tears.

'I'm sorry love, but we must be very careful. We must agree a story to tell the family — and stick to it. We only say what we have ter.'

The three of them looked at each other.

'What about Jeffrey?'

'Not even him, Betty. We tell only people we need to tell.'

'You know I shall have to leave Stowford as soon as they know I'm expecting.'

'Yes, you can go back tomorrow and tell them yer have ter finish cos of family troubles. Give them a week's notice and say nowt else to nobody.'

⋆ ⋆ ⋆

All sorts of emotions ran through Betty as she walked into Stowford House. The first person she met there was Ruth.

'*You* are in serious trouble, Betty. Mrs Stone was going up the wall last night when you didn't come back. Wherever have you been?'

'Hello, Ruth.' Betty carried on walking.

'Well! Who does she think she is?'

Betty ignored her and found Mrs Stone in the butler's pantry going through some paperwork. She looked up at Betty, waiting at the door.

'Good of you to turn up today.' Mrs Stone's face lived up to her name, her eyes taking in Betty's outside clothes.

'I'm sorry, Mrs Stone. I need to talk to you.' Betty didn't wait to be invited, she stepped inside and closed the door behind her. Mrs Stone looked startled and sat up straight. 'I am sorry to say there was a problem at home yesterday, which I conner speak of, but I shall have to leave at the end of the week.'

Mrs Stones eyes bulged. 'You always have something surprising to say, Betty. It was the last thing I was expecting. Why, when you are doing so well? Are you ill?'

'Like I said, it's personal and I'm sorry.' Betty stood firmly, her chin up, feeling pleased she was having this conversation on her terms.

'Well!' Mrs Stone sat back in her chair. 'I'm disappointed, Betty, but it sounds as if I can't talk you round. I will accept your notice.'

'Thank you.'

When questioned by the other staff, Betty could not be persuaded to say anything about what had happened. It was a long week and she kept herself to herself for most of it. When Friday came, it was a relief to gather her belongings together and to leave the Stowford part of her life, and all that had happened, behind her.

16

May 1915

It was as if the clock had been turned back. Three to a bed, less room and plenty of arguments, which could only get worse as the weeks passed.

'We can have yer living at home for a week or two, Betty, but we need to find you a job with somewhere to stay.'

'Will anybody take me on like this?' Betty spread her arms and pointed to her stomach.

'Somebody will — if they're desperate. You'll just have to keep trying.'

Betty scanned the newspaper and wandered around corner shops looking at cards in their windows.

It was her mother who discovered a possibility. She arrived home from chapel on Sunday in a state of excitement.

'I was talking to Iris Shenton, Betty. She lives near to Hanley Park and her's looking for somebody urgently to do for her, and she has a room an' all. It's perfect. Just dunner tell her as you're expecting.'

'Yer want me to lie?'

'Yes, if yer know what's good for yer. She has difficulty in moving around, and she's desperate. She says as she'll see yer this afternoon.'

Betty couldn't eat her dinner and set off to see Mrs Shenton, unable to believe her mother wanted her to lie to a member of the congregation. She thought her mother to be an upstanding woman, but Betty was disappointed in her behaviour.

She wouldn't be able to keep her secret for long because she was sure she would be showing quite soon. Already her waist felt thicker and her breasts felt larger.

* * *

As Mother had said, Belgrave Road was opposite to Hanley Park. It reminded Betty of the countryside around Stowford House. From the outside the house looked to be a larger-than-average town house, but not overly so, and well kept. She had dressed smartly — it was one of the things Mrs Stone always insisted upon — and knocked at the door at exactly two o'clock as Mother had instructed.

Almost immediately, the door opened.

'Hello dear, you must be Betty. Come in.'

Mrs Shenton turned to walk slowly along the hall, leaving Betty to follow. It was easy to see she was in pain as she moved. To answer the door so quickly, she must have been sitting in the hall waiting for her.

The house was full of furniture, knick-knacks and strange objects that must have had some hidden meaning to Mrs Shenton: a monkey sitting cross-legged; an elephant as big as a cat; and a huge shell.

'That's a conch, my dear. Put it to your ear and you can hear the sea.'

Betty did as she was bid. There was a rushing sound. She had never seen or heard the sea. She lifted the conch and listened again with her eyes closed, letting her imagination run.

'What a lovely sound.'

Mrs Shenton invited her to take a seat in a sitting room overlooking the street and, beyond, Hanley Park with its tall trees and landscaped gardens.

'You've got a lovely view, Mrs Shenton.'

'Thank you. It was what my husband wanted.' She sighed. 'I am grateful for it. If I was forced to look at houses from my window, I should get very bored indeed. So, please call me Iris and tell me a little about yourself.'

'I . . . er . . .' She had prepared nothing. She hadn't expected to talk about herself so quickly.

'Don't worry, Betty. I am acquainted with your mother through the chapel, but I would like to know a little about you. I'm not probing for anything you are not prepared to talk about. We all have our secrets, I'm sure.'

'I come from a large family, Mrs Shenton. That's why I'm living out. No room at home. I left school at nearly thirteen and went into service, so I have over four years' experience.'

Mrs Shenton nodded. 'You left school early?'

'We couldn't afford it. I worked in a big house, starting as a kitchen maid, and then became an upstairs maid when someone left. While I was the kitchen maid, Cook taught me how to prepare meals for the household. Showed me all the techniques. I especially enjoyed making puddings — sorry desserts — and was even left in charge of the kitchen on her day off. She also taught me how to manage food to get the best out of it. I became an upstairs maid but I still liked to help with the cooking.'

'You sound a very competent young lady.'

She wasn't used to compliments. Heat climbed up to her neck. She managed a smile.

'One point I am strict on, Betty, is no gentlemen callers. It doesn't do for ladies on their own to have gentlemen in their homes.'

'You won't have no trouble with me, Mrs Shenton. I can say for definite.'

'I daresay you can now, but it won't always be the case. You're an attractive young lady.'

Betty felt unsettled at the compliments, knowing what she was hiding.

Mrs Shenton was comfortable rather than well off. She and her former husband, a doctor, had one child, a daughter named Victoria, now married, who lived in the neighbouring town of Newcastle-under-Lyme and visited every Sunday. After her husband died, Mrs Shenton had been taken ill and now suffered with arthritis, which, some days, prevented her from getting out of bed at all.

As Mrs Shenton continued to speak, Betty was getting more and more anxious. The woman obviously needed help and she couldn't leave things as they stood.

'As far as pay is concerned, Betty, it will be —'

'Hold on, Mrs Shenton. I . . . there's summat I need to tell yer before you go any further. I can't let you go on without yer knowing.' She took a deep breath. It was a shame; she was sure she would have worked well with Mrs Shenton, but she couldn't keep her secret any longer. 'I think you should know . . .' Another deep breath. 'I'm expecting.'

'You're . . . ?' Mrs Shenton looked down at Betty's hidden belly.

She nodded miserably. 'I would love to do this job, Mrs Shenton. But I couldn't keep it from you.'

'I see.'

'So, I won't take up no more of yer time. Thank yer for seeing me.' Betty rose to her feet.

'Hold on a moment. What makes you so sure I wouldn't want you to work for me?'

'You couldn't possibly! Not after I tried to —'

'Deceive me?'

Betty's face could not have been redder. 'I'm so sorry.'

'Sit down.'

She did as she was told, although she wanted to run, hide her face, anything rather than sit in front of this woman.

'I would like to hear a little more from you. When are you due?'

'October.'

'So, we have over six months. What about the father?'

Betty swallowed. *Here goes*. She recounted the story she had reluctantly agreed with her parents. A pang of guilt shot through Betty as the lie left her lips.

'I'm so sorry,' she finished.

There was a pause before Mrs Shenton continued. 'Then I think it could work well. I am on my own and in need of help, and you are in need of work and somewhere to stay. I see no reason why it shouldn't be a help to us both.'

'But —'

'You're wondering why I would take you on given you were not entirely truthful?'

'Well, yes.'

'I would take you on because you told me. You must've wanted this position badly and yet your conscience wouldn't allow you to lie. So yes, the job is yours — if you still want it?'

'Oh, yes, please.'

Mrs Shenton's face took on a stern look. 'You might tell your mother I admired your honesty, Betty, and you got the job on merit.'

She frowned. How did she know Mother — ?

'I also admire your loyalty.'

Mrs Shenton had guessed Mother had put her up to it. She was far cannier than Betty's mother had given her credit for.

It was all settled. Mrs Shenton agreed to say nothing to her daughter about the forthcoming birth until it was necessary, and Betty was to commence her duties immediately.

* * *

Betty was thankful as she made her way back to Wellington Road to tell her mother all had gone well. She opened the back door to a house full of noise, Mother shouting at Tommy and Lily who were arguing about something or other.

'Hello everybody, it's me!'

Tommy squealed his excitement.

Mother waved to her. 'Come into the scullery. I need a word.'

Betty did as she was bid.

Mother whispered: 'Everything go well today?'

'I've got the job. I like Mrs Shenton,' Betty whispered back. 'She made me feel welcome. Her daughter visits on Sundays, which means I can have every Sunday off.'

'Well, you keep yer nose clean and yer should be all right for a while. Once you've got your feet under the table, yer can tell her about the baby.'

'I've already told her.'

'Yer told her? I thought as we were keeping it quiet and telling nobody.'

'I couldn't. She was so nice . . . I had to tell her. It made no difference. In fact, she said she would take me on because I had been honest and told her.'

Her mother's face turned pink.

'We'd better tell your Aunty Ella —'

'No, Mother. Nobody at all. And tell Father to say nowt as well.'

Mother turned on her. 'D'yer honestly think yer father'll open his mouth to anybody about this?'

Betty's lower lip trembled. 'Thank you.'

* * *

Betty made sure she arrived at Belgrave Road prompt at ten o'clock, as agreed. It wasn't far to walk. She knocked on the door and was surprised when it was opened by a tall, prim and proper-looking woman with a severe face that had trouble raising a smile.

'Hello. My name's Betty Dean, the new housemaid. Mrs Shenton's expecting me.'

Betty wondered whether to shake her hand, but the woman stepped quickly to one side and waved Betty into the hallway. A little confused, Betty walked in front of her into the sitting room where she had sat with Mrs Shenton the previous day.

'Hello, Betty dear.'

Mrs Shenton beckoned them both to sit and then continued.

'Betty, this is my daughter, Mrs Victoria Hayes. I'm afraid she has come to check you out. She does not like to think I am inviting strangers off the street to live in my home. I did mention I was acquainted with your mother through the chapel, but I expect she needed to see you for herself.'

Betty bit her lip, concerned at being 'checked out'.

Mrs Shenton caught her concern and gave an almost imperceptible shake of the head, which Betty took to mean *say nothing* or *don't worry*.

'Miss Dean . . . Betty, my mother has been unwell for some time and needs a little looking-after in addition to household duties. I have made it my business to meet any person invited into the house so I may satisfy myself as to their good character.'

Betty nodded. It was something a concerned daughter would do.

'My mother and I expect you to be of good character, upstanding and honest in your work. Can you assure me you will meet our expectations?'

'Victoria, dear. I talked to Betty at length yesterday and am satisfied as to her good character.'

Betty sent Mrs Shenton a silent *thank you* as Victoria nodded.

'I will keep an eye on you initially, Betty. I pay Mother a visit every Sunday, so I shall soon know if things are not up to standard.'

Mrs Shenton gave Betty a wink and straightened her face quickly.

'Consequently, you won't be required on Sundays from after breakfast until I return from chapel. You can do as you wish as Victoria will be with me the rest of the time.'

'Thank you, Mrs Shenton.'

Victoria showed Betty upstairs to her comfortable-looking bedroom. Although small, it was bigger than her room at home and she had it all to herself. She noticed the little writing desk by the window with a view over the park. It all looked so grown-up.

'Thank you. I shall look after Mrs Shenton. I have younger brothers and sisters at home, and I have looked after them for a long time now.'

Victoria nodded, still without a smile. 'I'm glad to hear it. But there is a difference between caring for children, and caring for adults who are not as well as they might be and who are determined to look after themselves. Now, I suggest you unpack your things. Then familiarise yourself with the kitchen and get to work.'

⋆ ⋆ ⋆

Betty settled in quickly. She unpacked her belongings, which looked lost in the large wardrobe in her room. She laid her pen and ink on the desk along with her writing paper and was quite satisfied when she had finished.

As she descended the stairs, she passed Mrs Shenton's room — it, too, overlooked the park. The window had two chairs facing outwards. She could imagine Mrs Shenton looking at the view. She was a little surprised to see a modern bathroom and separate privy on both the upper floors. A privy and bath to herself!

She returned to the ground floor and headed to the back of the house. The kitchen was well appointed with a smart-looking range and a nice large table in the centre for food preparation and baking. Next to the kitchen was a scullery with a large sink, mangle, and dolly tub. Outside there was a yard with a coal house and privy.

She completed her first task by preparing a pot of

tea for Mrs Shenton and Mrs Hayes. She couldn't find any biscuits but could easily make some. She would give the kitchen a good clean and then make a cake for tea, if she could find the ingredients.

Betty stood back and put her hands on her hips. A month ago she was in a different world. This was her kitchen to organise, her meals to plan and her house to keep clean and tidy. This was her house to manage.

* * *

Since the beginning of the war, Betty had started to take more than a passing interest in the newspapers. She regularly read the local papers and often popped into the library to research which news articles were hitting the headlines. She and Iris would often spend time in the evening discussing news.

When she called in at Wellington Road, she might pick up The Sentinel, but most of the time she spent with her brothers and sisters. Mother, always up-to-date on births, marriages, and deaths, added the casualty lists, which were growing longer all the time, to her regular daily reading.

Suddenly, a gasp from Mother caught her ear.

'What's up, Mother? What've yer found?' said Betty.

'Look at this.'

Betty moved to stand over her mother who was sat at the table, unable or unwilling, to take her eyes off the paper. Betty croodled down to read the tiny text.

Death in Action

Pte Horace Wells, Norths Staffs Regiment, a well-known schoolteacher from Hanley, has been killed in action. Pte Wells has a brother in training in England.

Tears sprung to Betty's eyes as she remembered her last conversation with Mr Wells. How he had made her feel when he said she was a 'bright girl'. He must have been one of the older men to go to war. Had Martha seen it? And why didn't they know he had a brother?

17

June 1915

It had been a month since Betty had started to work for Mrs Shenton. She was getting a routine going and enjoying organising the household. She always seemed to be busy with cooking, cleaning, washing, ironing, and, most of all, helping Mrs Shenton. Iris, as she kept reminding Betty to call her, had said it was important to keep her independence and show Victoria she was managing. Her daughter had the idea she should live with her in Newcastle-under-Lyme, which Iris was insistent she would not do. Betty thought Iris didn't like the idea of being bossed about, and Victoria was just the sort of person who would boss anybody.

It was Sunday. Betty sang to herself in the kitchen, nursery rhymes mainly, for the baby who she had a notion could hear her songs. She had just taken a sponge cake out of the oven, and would decorate it after Iris's breakfast, and then have the rest of the day to herself. As her condition was showing, she avoided going outside, except to deliver the shopping orders to the Co-operative. It was a nice sunny day and she decided to put on her baggiest coat, despite the heat, and take a walk around the park in the morning. Most of the people she knew tended to take their Sunday exercise in the afternoons. She would then spend the rest of the day in her room and maybe even do more baking later. While she was waiting for the cake to cool, she made a list of items she needed for the coming week.

A knock came on the kitchen door. It was half-past eight, too early for Victoria, who wouldn't use the back door anyway.

She laid her pencil down and opened the door to reveal Tommy, out of breath and with a bright red face as if he'd run all the way from Wellington Road.

Betty stepped back to let him in.

'Whatever's up?'

'Mother told . . . me to come. I've . . . gorra . . . message for yer.' He forced the words out between breaths. He tried again but she put up her hand to stop him.

'Sit yerself down. You'll pass out if yer dunner get yer breath back.' She pushed him towards a stool and when his breathing became more natural, Betty allowed him to speak.

'What's got yer all in a tizzy?'

'Our Jeffrey's come home and Mother wants you home for eleven o'clock at the latest.'

'Jeffrey's home! When did he get here?'

'Last night after tea. I was in bed, and I heard his voice. He came up to see me.'

'Is he alrate?'

'Yes, champion. He's been promoted to sergeant. He's got three stripes! Mother said you've got summat ter tell us an' all.'

Betty's smile disappeared. 'She said that?'

Tommy nodded. He stared at her belly. She picked up a towel to hide it. He probably didn't realise what he'd seen.

'What've yer got ter tell us?'

'Never yer mind, our Tommy. You'll find out soon

enough.'

So, it was to be today, when all the family would be told what she had been trying to hide for so long. What would they think of her? She had been meaning to put pen to paper to tell Jeffrey, but how could she give such news in a letter? In the end, she had said nothing.

* * *

Betty opened the door to Wellington Road with trepidation. Michael was the first person to see her.

'Our Betty's here.'

She forced a grin and wrapped her coat round her tightly as all eyes turned towards her.

'Glad you've noticed.' It was all she could think of to say to him. She was wearing a loose-fitting dress she had made for herself to wear during these later months.

The door to the upstairs opened and in walked Jeffrey.

His face lit up when he saw her. Betty's heart sank. His first action would be to hug her, and he was bound to find the shape of her had changed, even though she was still wearing her coat.

'Hello Jeffrey, it's good to see yer,' she said, and sat quickly before he had a chance to get close. She couldn't bring herself to look at anyone, least of all him, who would soon know exactly what she had been up to. Watching his disappointment in her would be hard. Her whole body began to shake. Short breaths had her almost panting. Would he think her a slut?

'Aren't yer going to take yer coat off? You must be boiling' said Mary-Ellen as she helped Mother to lay the table.

'Leave her be.' Mother threw Betty an anxious look and then spoke out in a loud voice claiming everyone's attention. 'She'll take it off when she's good and ready. Any road, now everybody's here, there's a family matter what needs discussing.'

Father wouldn't look at her. He just got up and put on his cap and walked out. Michael and Mary-Ellen were making faces at each other across the table, and Jeffrey was staring at Mother expectantly.

Tears welled up. Betty knew he'd be angry, but she wanted, no needed, Jeffrey to accept it. For better or worse it was out of her hands. She fixed her eyes on her hands clutching each other on the table showing white knuckles.

'As you know our Betty came home in April. She had to leave her job because . . . because she's expecting.'

Gasps ran around the table, with a loud shriek from Mary-Ellen.

'Expecting what?' asked eight-year-old Tommy.'

His question met with complete silence. Betty's face grew hotter. She couldn't look up. She felt degraded, humiliated, ashamed, and ready to run anywhere to get away from the silence pounding in her ears. She could feel their eyes on her.

At last, she dared to look up.

Lily was bright red. Mary-Ellen and Michael were sniggering to each other.

'And everybody says Betty's the clever one,' snapped Mary-Ellen.

Mother glared. 'Shut-up, Mary-Ellen!'

Worst of all, Jeffrey was looking at her, his eyes half closed, his face unfathomable.

She tried blinking away tears, but more soon followed.

'Betty's going to have a baby,' said Michael, almost in awe.

'But she can't. She isn't married,' piped up Tommy who, in his childishness was the only one of them feeling free enough to say it.

'Who's the father?' said Jeffrey, stony-faced.

'Someone from Stowford.'

'So, you *do* know. That's a start, I suppose.' Jeffrey banged his fist on the table, and everyone jumped.

His sarcastic words came like a slap in Betty's face. Jeffrey, the one she relied on in all matters, bowed his head and shook it as if he couldn't believe his ears. She had let him down, let them all down, badly. But to have him look at her with such disgust was more than she could bear.

The younger Deans looked from one to the other, frightened to say anything at all.

Betty burst into tears.

Mother stood up. 'Our Betty's done wrong, but it has happened and we must make the best of it. All you need to know is that she was going to get wed but the father was killed in Flanders. Remember, it's family business. Nobody else's. So dunner go gossiping. There'll be enough of that from the neighbours.'

She looked at each of them, waiting for their answer, and returned to her seat.

Nobody had moved to comfort Betty.

Finally, Jeffrey got to his feet, sniffed, and stood shaking his head.

'Jeffrey?' Betty didn't recognise her own voice; it was so soft. 'Jeffrey?' This time a little stronger.

'I canna say nowt, Betty. I need time.' He put his

hand in front of him as if to stop her going to him. Then, he followed Father outside.

She cupped her head in her hands. Quietly, her heart broke.

* * *

Sunday dinner was eaten in silence. Betty stirred peas and gravy round the plate, unable to eat a thing. While the younger ones had no trouble at all, Father and Jeffrey returned but ate little and took themselves off again without speaking. In the end, Mother sent everyone out with various jobs to be completed. Mary-Ellen volunteered to wash up, but only to listen in and Mother soon put a stop to it.

Now they were completely alone.

'Thank the Lord that's over with,' Mother said, slipping into a chair.

'I dunner think I'll ever be able to come back here. They all hate me.'

'They'll come round, given time.'

'Jeffrey's so angry with me — I can't let him go back to war without talking to him. What if summat happens to him?'

'You conner go blaming yerself for everything what happens. When he gets back to war, he'll have other things to think about. Give him time.'

'When does he go back?'

'Tomorrow morning.'

'D'yer think I should come back tomorrow? Make him understand?'

'Dunner think as it'll do no good. You're his little sister — he's bound to feel angry.'

They sat in silence for a while.

'Is everything going all right with you.'

'It was until today.'

Mother and Betty looked at each other and then burst out laughing, followed by floods of tears. Betty said she wanted to go back to Belgrave Road and have a nap.

'Please tell Jeffrey I'll write to him soon'

'I will. Now go and wash yer face, Betty duck, cos yer eyes is all puffed up. Yer conner go out on the street looking like that.'

She dragged herself into the scullery and patted her cheeks with lukewarm water from the kettle and dried her face ready to meet the outside world again. Even when she had first left home, she had never felt so alone.

* * *

Betty let herself out of the house and more tears followed. She didn't want to see anybody and kept her head down as she headed along the road. She turned the corner and bumped into someone walking in the opposite direction. It was Martha.

'Hiya, Betty. Haven't see yer for . . . whatever's the matter?

Martha put her arm round Betty, making her cry even more.

'I'll walk with yer. Have yer bin home?'

Betty nodded.

'So, why the tears? Has summat happened?'

'I can't tell yer. It's a secret.'

'Let me walk with yer then. Make sure yer all right.'

Betty sniffed as they walked in silence. She couldn't stop herself. 'Martha — I'm expecting.'

'Yer conner be, yer not married.'
'I mean it, I'm expecting.' Betty opened her coat and Martha's eyes widened when she saw her belly.'
Martha took her arm off Betty's shoulder. 'You're . . . oh, no, not you.'
'Mother's just told the family. It was horrible, Martha. Really bad and our Jeffrey's not speaking to me.'
'Isn't he?' Martha sounded miles away.
'I don't want him going back to war with us not speaking. Supposing summat happens to him?'
Martha bit her lip. 'It'd be your fault.'
Betty thought she hadn't heard properly. 'What d'yer mean?'
'I said as it'd be your fault. What did yer expect? You know what people think about girls who . . . who go with men, never mind them what get pregnant.'
There was emphasis in the way Martha said the last word, the word no one should speak of. It had been on the tip of Betty's lips to tell her of Alastair's hot temper and violent ways. But she didn't.
'I didn't go with *men*, as you put it. We were walking out for a long time. He volunteered for the army and got himself killed.'
Martha's face changed, as if she might've begun to feel sorry for her harsh words.
'But you still did it, Betty — and yer not wed. That makes you nothing better than a —'
'Don't say what's on your lips. You don't know the full story'
'I know — I don't need a picture — you've done summat bad and there is no excuse.'
Betty's lip curled. How dare she say such terrible things. Her eyes bored into Martha's, and it was Martha who turned away first.

'Is that what you think?'
'Dunno.'
'How can yer say that? We're friends.'
'Dunno what me Mother'll say.'
'You can't say nothing, Martha.'

A group of men walked in-between them. Betty waited until they had passed. 'I've promised Mother I'll tell nobody,' she hissed. 'Promise me.'

'She's bound to find out.'

'We'll have ter see, then won't we.'

* * *

Betty walked briskly up to the chapel just as the congregation were leaving. She waited until Iris had finished talking, then walked steadily back to Belgrave Road. When they got into the hall, Betty helped Iris take off her outside coat and they moved into the lounge.

Now the two of them were home, Iris asked if there was anything the matter. The tears were uncontrollable as Betty poured out all that had happened. Every time she spoke these days she started blarting.

'Martha, my friend what lives down the road had been a real . . .' She couldn't say the word she wanted to say in front of Iris. 'She was nasty. She looked down her nose at me as if I was nowt but dirt.'

'Having a baby out of wedlock carries a stigma, Betty. To a lot of people, it's something best not talked about. It will have come as a shock to her. She'll get over it sooner or later and if she doesn't, you will be better off not counting her among your friends.'

'Even our Jeffrey's not speaking to me. Mother's had us all round the table. Father walked out as soon as she began talking and our Jeffrey . . .' More tears welled up.

'You can't expect anything else from those who love you, Betty dear.' Iris's voice was gentle. 'You'll have to give them time. They love you and you love them. As for your Jeffrey, he's your brother, but he's also a man. It's hard sometimes for men to accept their sister has had . . . relations . . . with a man. You will always be his sister, who he has protected since childhood.'

Betty's weeping grew softer. She nodded. Iris was right.

'Do you think I should talk to him tomorrow — before he goes back?'

'You must do as you think fit. He has had a huge shock and he'll need time.'

'That's what Mother said. But I don't think I can cope with him going away like this.'

'Leave your decision until tomorrow. When your head is clearer.'

Iris suggested Betty have a rest, but instead she settled back to her normal Sunday evening work. It helped to take her mind off things. Iris stayed with her and chatted away.

Gradually, Betty began to smile again.

* * *

As it was, Betty had no need to go back home to see Jeffrey. He appeared on Iris's doorstep just before ten o'clock the next morning, all kitted out ready to head back to his unit. He had a sheepish look on his face.

'D'yer think as I may come in and talk ter yer for a few minutes?'

'Jeffrey! Oh, am that pleased ter see yer. I was going to try to talk to yer before you went back.'

'Well, am here now . . . if you'll let me in?'

'Come on then. I'll let Iris know.'

She was back almost immediately. 'Iris says I'm to show you into the sitting room.' She beckoned him to follow.

She stood beside the fire grate. He looked surprisingly nervous. She wanted to run to him but held herself in check. She needed to hear what he had to say.

'I'm on me way back, but I had ter see yer afore I go. I'm that sorry, Betty, duck. It was the shock talking yesterday.'

She nodded.

'You're me little sister — one of them at any rate. I couldn't believe it'd happen to yer. I've always protected yer. And now, cos of this bloody war —'

'Oh Jeffrey. Dunner blame yerself for not being here.' She threw herself into his arms. The bump in her belly touched him. She hadn't meant it to. She had just wanted to hold him and not let him go. 'You're a good brother and I love you.'

He pushed her gently away from him.

'I must ask yer, Betty and I want yer to be honest. Did he force yer?'

His face had an earnest look, and he was holding his breath for her answer.

'No, Jeffrey, he didn't. It was just a moment. I thought a lot of him and we were going to get wed.'

Jeffrey pulled her close, not seeming to mind about her bump. She held him tightly.

'I'll be thinking about yer, duck. When I'm out there. You *will* take care, won't yer?' His hand moved to wipe her wet face, his eyes searching her's.

'You don't know how glad I am you came.'

Soon after, he left. Betty sat on her own, letting the tears fall, but this time, they were tears of relief.

* * *

Betty had decided to call at Wellington Road after tea for a chat. A cloud of depression hung over her and she needed fresh company.

She stuck with her heavy winter coat to hide her condition and kept her eyes looking forward as she drew closer to home. Would she ever feel comfortable in this street when everyone knew who she was and what she had done? She wished she could call on Martha to talk, to explain, but after their big argument, she hadn't dared knock on the door. Neither, it seemed, had Martha approached her. Someone was going to have to make the first move if any progress was going to be made.

Mary-Ellen had just finished washing the dishes and Mother was putting the dry crockery away.

Mary-Ellen glanced her way. 'You look fed up, Betty. What's up with yer?'

'Oh, this and that,' Betty sighed in such a way it brought her out in a fit of giggles.

Mother smiled. 'That's better.'

Boots thumping in the yard heralded the approach of Michael.

'Hey up Betty. Did yer hear about the Owens?'

'What about them?' she asked, wondering what could possibly have happened now.

'They've gone.'

Betty frowned. 'Gone where? What are you on about?'

'They've moved, to Tunstall. They're living with

Mrs Owen's mother in a pub in Tunstall.'
'That'll be The Potter's Wheel where Mrs Owen was brought up,' Mother said.
Betty's heart thumped in her chest. 'Martha would never leave without telling me.'
'That was before . . . you know,' said Mary-Ellen, nodding towards Betty's stomach.
Betty ignored her. 'Did they do a moonlight flit?'
He shook his head violently. 'No, they packed up their furniture on a cart and just left. Issy told me they couldn't afford the rent since her father went missing.'
'How come yer know so much about them?' asked Mary-Ellen.
'Just do.'
Mary-Ellen sneered. 'I supposed your girlfriend told you.'
'Issy's not my girlfriend,' Michael shouted, but his crimson face said otherwise.
Betty wanted to ask more, but she couldn't. She had hoped she and Martha would become friends again soon, but for her to leave without saying a word, was too much. If Martha was still too angry to say goodbye, then she was no friend.
And that was the end of it.

18

September 1915

When comparing the two jobs she'd experienced, Betty would say the job with Iris Shenton was harder work, given she was responsible for the entire household. Being the only servant was sometimes lonely, but she wouldn't have exchanged it for Stowford for anything. Here, she was needed and appreciated, and it meant more to Betty than she could put into words. Iris always thanked her. That was worth a little hardship.

Betty had created her own routine for looking after the house and preparing all of the meals. She hoped Mrs Stone and Cook would have been proud of her achievements.

Iris had just had her sixtieth birthday but looked older to Betty's seventeen-year-old self. Maybe it was the way she walked, or the lines of agony that periodically crossed her face when her arthritis caused her considerable pain.

As the year moved towards autumn and Betty's condition began to show, she went out less and less. They talked about the baby and Iris spoke of the young Victoria, much to Betty's amusement. Of late, she had begun to read to Iris during the evening, once all her duties had been performed. It was comfortable and Iris relaxed, which helped the pain. Sometimes, Iris dozed and, during those times, Betty would stop and tiptoe from the room and busy herself, not too far away, and with one ear listening for her to awake.

As for her child's father . . . she had, deliberately, not given her address to Alastair, and had asked Mrs Stone to tell him nothing if he should ask. They had split up and she had no intention of seeing him again. Instead, she concentrated on her new life.

Iris was a nice old soul. They always had a natter once Betty had prepared everything for Iris to get out of bed, grate cleaned out, kitchen fire kindled, and table laid for breakfast. There wasn't much washing to do, mainly dresses, which Iris insisted on changing every alternate day even though she rarely had visitors. And there were her smalls, which Betty soaked overnight before washing them thoroughly in the sink and putting them through the mangle. Housework mainly included sweeping carpets, dusting the heavy furniture and, once a fortnight, cleaning the windows inside. A man came every other week to clean the outside windows, to be rid of the sooty film coating them. On Fridays, she sat with Iris and made a list of shopping items to get, if available. Iris would leave it to Betty to decide on replacements if the shops no longer had her favourites due to the war.

Betty usually visited her mother during the day, fitting it in with doing errands for Iris. That way, she could avoid everyone and still catch up on all the latest news: who'd gone off to war; who had been sent home; and, sadly, who would never come home again. How strange it was when she had heard one of her old classmates had been killed. That they were old enough to fight was shocking. They were men — killed fighting for their country — but to Betty they were still boys.

* * *

'Iris, have you started to look for someone to replace me yet?'

'No dear, I was rather hoping you would want to stay with me.'

It took a moment or two for the words to sink in. Betty stared at her with a look of astonishment, followed quickly by a broad grin.

'I'd love to. But I don't see how that would work. I would have to be popping home to feed the baby. Mother has said she would look after it so I can work, but I think she expects to feed it watered-down cow's milk as soon as she can so I can get a job in a potbank.'

'No, Betty, I was thinking of something totally different. I'm suggesting you have the baby here and live here, with the baby, while you work for me.'

'You really mean it?'

'Yes, it makes sense. You want somewhere to live and have your baby. I have the room. You will be able to continue your current role and we get on well together. It will be nice to have the sound of a baby in the old house again.'

'I will be able to feed the baby meself, which will be much better. But babies make lots of noise, Iris. I remember that from my little brothers and sisters.'

Iris smiled wryly. 'I may look old, Betty, but I did have had a baby of my own. Victoria may look all prim and proper now, but she had a good pair of lungs on her and made sure we all knew about it.'

'What I mean is, I dunno I can put on you like that.'

'But you haven't asked me for my help. I have made the offer to you, which you may accept or reject. That, my dear, is down to you.'

'What will Mrs Hayes say? Won't she think I'm taking advantage of yer good nature?'

Iris laughed. 'Leave Victoria to me.' She put her hands together on her knee, matter of factly, as if ending the conversation. 'Of course, you can have time to think about —'

'I don't need time, Iris. Thank you so much.' A load had moved off Betty's shoulders. The huge responsibility she had taken on was beginning to feel all too real. She had so much to put in place to make it work. It had to.

* * *

Betty heard a key in the lock and the front door open. She swore to herself. It could only be Victoria. She was usually out of Victoria's way by the time she arrived, but today she had stayed to finish a job she had been meaning to do but hadn't quite got round to it. She scrambled to get into her large apron so as to cover her ever expanding belly — but she was too late.

Betty tried to act naturally but only succeeded in looking flustered. 'Good . . . morning, Mrs Hayes.'

'Good morning, Betty. No need to rush. I'm here early because I need to talk to you on a matter of some importance.'

'Oh!' Betty continued to struggle with the apron and swore under her breath.

'Don't worry about hiding your condition. I've known for some months now. I also know about your understanding with my mother regarding what will happen when your baby arrives.'

Betty washed and quickly dried her hands to give

herself time to think. 'Mrs Shenton's been good to me,' she said over her shoulder.'

'Mother is like that, but some people can take advantage of women like her. She enjoys your company, and everything has gone smoothly since you began working here. So, I told her I would be happy with the arrangement —'

'Thank you for that —'

'Let me finish.'

Embarrassed, Betty looked at the floor.

'I am happy with the arrangement so long as it doesn't wear on Mother. If I find you are putting on her then I will take steps to terminate your employment. Are you clear?'

'Yes, Mrs Hayes.'

'Victoria will do.' She smiled. 'I'm sure we shall get on splendidly, Betty,' she said and out she walked.

* * *

Betty and Iris sat together to have their lunchtime meal, as usual, and the conversation naturally turned to the baby.

'Do you have everything you need, Betty?'

'I think so. We still have the baby clothes and paraphernalia from when Tommy and Lily were born. I can use a drawer out of the chest in my room for a crib. We still call the top drawer in Mother's room the 'baby drawer' as I think we've all been put to bed in it.'

'I think we can do better. In the one of the back bedrooms, I'm sure I stored some of Victoria's things. I suggest you have a look in there to see what you can find.'

‘Oh! Thank you, Iris. I’ll do that.’

‘On another matter, what is going to happen for those few weeks either side of the baby’s birth?’

‘Well, Mother worked in the house until she had us. She stayed in bed a few days and then things returned to normal, just another mouth to feed.’

‘But it might not be the same for you.’

‘She has promised to help out if I’m not able to.’

‘You seem to have it all under control.’

‘We dunner want to let yer down, Iris. You’ve been so good.’ ‘I’m sure we will work it out between us.’

19

October 1915

Betty had made bread and left it to rise, before a spring clean throughout the bedrooms and bathroom. Iris had laughed at Betty's industry. She said it was known as 'nesting', when the mother begins to ready herself for the forthcoming birth.

'Usually, it happens close to the birth,' said Iris, looking doubtful.

'I hope not, cos I'm not ready. I've got ages yet.'

'Let's hope the baby knows. Do you have any names in mind?'

'No. I mightn't make up my mind until the baby's born. Supposing summat goes wrong?'

'There are problems associated with birthing, I'll not deny it. Do look after yourself and eat well. Have you been in touch with the midwife?'

Betty shook her head. 'I've bin meaning to. I don't think Mother wants to be out with me in public.'

'But you must see someone. You might need their help when the time comes.'

'Mother had no problem and she's had six of us. I think as she was planning to deliver it herself, what with her experience.'

'I've already told you it doesn't necessarily follow you will have the same good fortune. Promise me you'll arrange to see someone. I'll come with you if you want me to.'

'No, Mother'll come with me, if I ask.'
'Please do, Betty. It's important.'

* * *

Betty began to sort out the back bedroom as Iris had suggested. It contained lots of things belonging to Iris's husband and hadn't been touched since he passed away. Much of it would be thrown away, Iris said, but first it had to be checked. Betty made piles of clothes, books, medical tools and equipment, items she could only guess the purpose of. The baby was making itself known these days. She took things carefully and rested when she could. Though it was early October it was still warm and, even with all the windows open, she felt hot and sweaty. The sooner it was all over, the better. Then she could relax knowing her work was ready for Mother to take over. She loved to place her hands on her belly as a kind of hug so the baby would feel her close.

Iris's voice sounded from the bottom of the stairs.

'Betty dear, I think it would be wise for you to stop now.'

'I'm fine. Nearly done.'

She had found a lovely wicker Moses basket and the frame of what looked like a cot. She moved a matching pair of leather suitcases towards the pile of clothes hanging over a chair that had seen better days. The cases were both heavy and she tried the locks expecting to find more papers or books. Instead, one of the cases contained baby clothes, and squares of cotton towelling, which she could make use of as nappies.

At that moment, Iris joined her.

'Look what I've found,' Betty smiled.

They examined the suitcase of clothes: baby clothes mainly, some knitted with the tiniest of stitches. At the bottom of the case was the most beautiful dress she had ever set eyes on.

'That's Victoria's christening gown. My mother made it for me. She loved to embroider, and it wasn't something I was good at.' Iris smiled. 'If you are having the baby christened, you may borrow it.'

Betty's eyes opened wide. 'I don't know if I would dare. Supposing it got damaged?'

'I know you well enough to believe you wouldn't let it happen, otherwise I wouldn't offer it to you.'

Next, they came across a metal machine of some sort. It was heavy when she pulled it towards her. She stared at it, dusty and complicated but seemingly in good condition.

'What's this?'

Iris moved towards her. 'Oh, I thought that old thing had been thrown away ages ago.' Her fingers ran over what she called keys, as if they knew where they were going. 'It's a typewriter. My husband typed up documents and his patient notes on it. I sometimes helped him. It takes me back to happier times.' She sighed.

'A typewriter?'

'Yes, you feed paper in here . . .' Iris pointed to a valley at the top of the machine. 'Then, using the keys with the letters and numbers, you can type all sorts of things. They are used in many offices.'

'How wonderful.'

'Try it for yourself. I'll show you how to use it.'

Betty grew excited as she thought about using a machine like posh people in offices used, and could barely contain herself.

Iris fed paper into the machine until it was in exactly the right place. Using two fingers, she pressed down the keys and, as she did, words formed on the paper. It was so simple.

Betty sat in front of the machine and gently pressed down the letter A. Nothing happened. She tried again but still nothing appeared on the paper.

Iris chuckled. 'You will need to press the key with more vigour, Betty, dear. It won't break.'

She tried again — and this time, it worked. She tried another and soon, every key she pressed left its mark on the paper.

'Thank you for letting me have a go, Iris. Why are the keys not in the right order? It will take ages to find them.'

'I don't know. Perhaps the keys most used are towards the centre. Anyway, I don't use it. Take it to your room, and you can practise in your spare time.'

'Do you think I could?'

'Of course. It's an excellent idea.'

* * *

It was the 24th. Betty was in the kitchen planning her day's activities when the pains came. She doubled up, wondering what she had eaten to give her bellyache. When a second came, and then a third, it dawned on her that her baby would wait no longer. A wave of heat washed over her.

'Iris! Iris! Call for the midwife, will yer? The shop at the end of her street will tell her.'

Iris left the door on the latch and sat with her as Betty fought the panic, doing her best to stay calm. She couldn't believe how relieved she was when Mrs

Rawlinson, the midwife, bustled into the room and had everything organised within minutes. Soon after, Mother arrived and agreed to stay with her until the baby was born.

Betty had no control over what was happening. The pain was unbearable. All sorts of emotions passed through her mind, reminding her of Kitty's questions just before Davy was born. How would the baby get out? What if it got stuck? What if there was no milk? How long would her labour last? Would she die? She had laughed at the time, but . . .

'Short, quick pants is best,' the midwife said in a voice loud enough to overcome Betty's screams. 'It'll soon be over.'

How could Betty believe that when she'd been in pain for hours? Lily and Tommy were quick to arrive it seemed, yet here she was, weak with exhaustion, and still it went on. It wasn't fair!

On and on it went until she just wanted it to go away.

Then, with one last push that travelled all the way up her body, it was over.

Drained, Betty fell back on to the pillow, unable to move and closed her eyes. Then the sharp cry of a new-born filled the room.

'It's a little girl, Mother.'

Betty's eyes shot open to see the midwife grinning broadly. 'And she's a right beauty, just like her mummy.'

Mother stood beside the bed, unable to take her eyes off the baby. Betty held out her arms as the midwife wrapped the baby in a blanket and handed her over.

Betty felt tears forming. This tiny scrap would be

dependent upon her for the next umpteen years.

'Thank you, so much, Mrs Rawlinson, I dunno what I'd have done without yer.'

'Yer Mam would've managed. It was straightforward enough.'

'Well, I'll thank yer all the same. What's yer first name, if yer don't mind me asking?'

'Hannah. I don't hear it that often these days. I'm always called Mrs Rawlinson.'

'It'd be a lovely name for my baby.' Betty looked from the tiny baby nestling in her arms to the red-faced beaming midwife and back. 'Hello, Hannah. Meet Hannah Iris Dean.'

Mrs Rawlinson kissed Hannah's hand. 'You should get some rest, like I said. I'll talk to yer mother on what to do next, although she probably knows. I've delivered a few for her in the past.'

Hannah Iris Dean was borne at seven o'clock in the evening.

Mrs Rawlinson disappeared, taking Mother with her, leaving Betty alone with her baby — *her* baby. There was nothing Betty could do now except sleep. She had a baby girl. No matter how many times she repeated those words, she couldn't take them in.

'You are so pretty, Hannah.' Gently, she touched the softness of the baby's chin and her eyes opened and stared up at Betty, who was suddenly overcome with a powerful emotion to do whatever it cost to protect her daughter.

A knock came on the door. It was Iris. 'Mind if I come in? Oh, my word, what a lovely little thing. You must be proud of her, Betty.'

Iris stroked Hannah's head so gently; the baby closed her eyes. She couldn't have looked more contented.

'Do you have a name for her?'

Betty smiled. 'Iris, meet my daughter, Hannah Iris Dean.'

Iris caught her breath as she heard the name. Smiling through her tears she leaned over and dropped a kiss on Betty's forehead.

* * *

'Taking care of her will be your job for the next twenty years,' Betty's mother said later, when she came in to 'do' for Iris. 'Your life will not be your own from now on, I'm telling yer.'

Mother's words only reinforced the enormity of what had happened. The responsibility she'd taken on. Feeding, clothing, upbringing, caring for her in sickness and in health. All would be down to her.

She felt alternately hot and cold. 'Whatever shall I do, Mother. I'm frightened.'

Mother busied herself and was soon ready to leave, everything prepared for Iris and Betty for the rest of the day. She would be back in the afternoon.

'You'll have to get Hannah's birth registered, your father always did mine, soon after the birth. I can do it for you if you like. Have you thought about what you are going to put for the father's name?'

Betty thought for a moment. 'Do I have to? I don't want his name on it. I just want her to be a Dean and nothing else.'

'I'll see what they say when I get there.'

Mother returned in the afternoon as promised and handed over Hannah's birth certificate, with a smile. Betty read the contents. The father's name had been left blank.

'They told me at the office it was the best way.'

Betty looked at the certificate again. There it was, in black and white: Hannah Iris Dean.

Later, when they were on their own, Betty whispered to Hannah: 'This is proof Hannah, you're a Dean and always will be.'

20

December 1915

Betty stayed with her family on Christmas Day. Their first Christmas without Jeffrey wouldn't be a happy one — the sight of his empty chair was unbearable. The rest of the family were used to not having him around, but whenever she entered a room, Betty couldn't help looking for him. Tears would fill her eyes and she would make some excuse: she had been cutting up onions; or the steam of the kettle had made her eyes water; or smoke from the fire had irritated them.

On the other hand, Hannah brought everyone much-needed joy. Not a replacement, but a welcome addition to the family and they all took turns to show their appreciation of her presence.

Once, Betty slipped outside and looked up at the stars, wondering if they were looking down on Jeffrey too. She couldn't see many; the smoke-filled sky kept the stars to itself. There would be many more where he was, she was sure.

In the meantime, she had thought up some party games to keep the younger kids happy and give her mother a rest. Betty could see it in her face. She wanted to do her fair share of caring for the family, but it was a relief to leave and to be back to usual routine once the festivities were over. What with caring for the family and for Hannah, her days were filled. She hadn't realised how much work there was in looking after such a tiny person.

21

January 1916

Betty felt she was beginning a new life, pleased to have her body back to herself. It was the time to take control.

Hannah was the most beautiful baby Betty had ever seen, dark-blue eyes and a hint of red hair. She wanted to show her off to the world . . . but she couldn't even show her to Martha.

Iris was quite taken with Hannah, too, and even sat with her, telling stories while Betty worked. The young mother was surprised how much she was able to do after giving birth, and life at Belgrave Road soon returned to normality. Those long days spent in service at Stowford House stood her in good stead. She had often worked from six o'clock in the morning through till midnight, so the feeding of Hannah and the broken sleep affected her less than she expected. Mother only needed to come in to help Iris in the first few weeks.

She had bouts of anxiety when she was left alone with Hannah, doubting her ability to look after one so young who was totally reliant on her. Night-time was the worst when they were on their own. She wasn't a good enough mother to stop Hannah from crying and it hurt her desperately to think so. She would pace up and down the room, with Hannah in her arms, wishing she was back home where she would at least have someone to talk to, even if it was only Mary-Ellen. And then, once Hannah was asleep, Betty would wake up every hour to check she was still breathing.

Betty was glad she had done as Iris had advised and got Hannah Rawlinson to look after the birth. Even though she was told it was a straightforward birth, she would have panicked when the pains started, she was sure of it. Mother had grown used to saving coppers where she could. The birth of Betty's baby was not the time to think of saving money. Betty was learning to protect herself. From now on, she would be protecting herself and Hannah.

Most of the people Betty knew from Wellington Road and school were aware of her circumstances. It was impossible to keep anything like that quiet. Now she had no reason to hide away, she started going out into the world again when she could, strolling round the town and the park with Hannah in the pram. Betty hardly ever went out on her own — she always tried to take Hannah in the pram. Sometimes, Iris would come for a short walk with them, too. The only place she never took Hannah was to the chapel on a Sunday evening, when she walked Iris back. They might preach forgiveness and understanding inside, but Betty was wise enough to realise it did not spread to unmarried mothers.

Initially, even Mother's neighbours refused to speak to her. Betty lifted her nose to show she didn't care, although she was sorry her mother had to put up with it. Mother swore she didn't mind if people were small-minded. Even though they told everyone Betty was to be married when the father was next on leave — but he never came back. The neighbours were prepared to accept, but not condone, what she had done. She had her family and that was all that mattered. Much as she loved her daughter, Betty felt the guilt would stay with her forever.

22

September 1916

The war in Europe had been going for over two years with no end in sight. Since the beginning of July, the British had been attacking the Germans on the River Somme and the battle was still raging.

At home there were shortages of lots of imported items as the Germans attacked ships bringing supplies to Britain. Britain blockaded German ports to prevent their trade.

There were a lot more women wearing black now, and the telegram boy on his bicycle was feared in every street.

Betty sat on her favourite chair in the kitchen next to the range, nursing Hannah, who was sleeping peacefully. Surely it would be over before Hannah was old enough to understand, wouldn't it?

* * *

Iris had suggested Betty have the typewriter in her own room so she might teach herself, at her own convenience, to use it. If she mastered the heavy keys and remembered where the letters were, she might get a job in an office where she could better earn her keep and pay her way for Hannah's upbringing. It had been slow at first, spelling the words, looking for the right keys and then pressing so hard enough on the round keys to make contact with the paper that her fingers ached. Gradually, she thought less about the spelling and her fingers found the keys of their own accord. For practice, she typed out articles from *The Sentinel* and magazines. That was a while ago now, and even Hannah seemed to settle when she heard the clacketing of the keys.

Iris strolled into the kitchen as Betty was preparing the food for dinner. 'Dear, I have something for you.'

Betty washed and dried her hands.

Iris passed her a sheet of paper. 'What do you think of this?'

The local Workers' Educational Association had put out an advertisement offering a bookkeeping course for anyone looking for an office job. It would take place one evening a week, and so would be suitable for people who worked during the day.

Surprised, Betty glanced at Iris. 'Looking after books?'

'In a manner of speaking,' smiled Iris, 'but not the sort you are thinking of. When people are in business, they are required to keep books about the business, such as how much money the company has, who owes money and who is owed money by the company. It would look fine if you were to do such a course and then apply for a post in an office, would it not?'

Betty opened her eyes wide. 'I can't do nowt like that, Iris.'

'But did you not say your teacher said you were bright?'

She laughed. 'Yes, he did, but I don't think he meant nothing like that.'

'You don't know until you have tried. I thought you wanted to improve yourself?'

'Yes, but —'

'No buts, Betty. You need to plan. To build a future for you and Hannah.'

'Girls like me work in potbanks and the like until they find husbands, get married and start a family.'

'No such thing as 'girls like me', Betty. We do what we can to make progress. This war has taught us that women are capable of a lot more than they think. Open your eyes and look around you, especially now you have Hannah, I would say.'

She stared at Iris. It had taken confidence to walk up the drive to Stowford House, and what about applying for her current job when she knew she was expecting and there was every likelihood of her being turned down?

'You're right. I'll go around there and enrol after tea tonight.'

'Good girl.' Iris took hold of Betty's hand and patted it.

She returned to the preparation of food and, not for the first time, thanked the Lord when he sent her to Iris's door.

* * *

It was with some apprehension she opened the door to the building on the first Monday evening of the course. Several people had already arrived and, much to Betty's relief, there were six women. The work was easier than she had thought and a lot of it was commonsense.

One thing Betty was beginning to realise: it was better to try something before believing it was impossible.

23

October 1916

It was early October and a Sunday, so Betty, now eighteen, was not required. Briefly, she spoke to Victoria, who had arrived as Betty was getting ready to take Hannah to spend a few hours with her grandma and Lily.

After dinner, she left Hannah at Wellington Road and set off briskly towards Hanley and the shops, pretending she could afford to treat herself. It was a good job the shops were closed, otherwise the temptation to buy something for the sheer sake of it might have proved too strong.

She turned to the right and came to Webberley's Bookshop, a recent addition to the town, and stopped. Each window contained a small number of books to tantalise passing shoppers. How nice it would be to lose herself in a book like those in the window. She loved reading and had enjoyed reading out to the class at school. What differences would she have made to her life if she had stayed at school as she had wanted to?

The Card by Arnold Bennett caught her attention. Beside the book there was a note saying he was a local writer. Perhaps it might suit Iris. She would ask her when she started work again tomorrow.

A young woman, also attracted by the shop window, stopped beside her. Betty glanced her way. She looked of a similar age but was taller and slimmer, with the belt of her coat pulled tight. The woman must have felt Betty's eyes on her because she looked across with clear, hazel eyes.

Betty grinned and the girl smiled back.

Betty took the bull by the horns. 'Hello. Some nice-looking books in here.'

'I wish I could afford to buy some. It'd give me summat to do when I'm bored,' said the woman.

Betty nodded. 'I know what yer mean. So much yer can do when you've a bit of money in yer pockets. Me name's Betty by the way. Am in lodgings near the park, in service.'

'You're local then. I thought so cos of the way yer talk. Like one of us.' It wasn't a question; it was rather as if she was mulling it over in her mind. 'I'm Jean Wright and I'm not far from the park. In Ware Street.'

Delighted, Betty clapped her hands. 'That's lovely. D'yer live with your family?'

Jean shook her head. 'I left home cos I couldn't get on with them.

It was Betty's turn to nod. 'I get on all right with mine. There's just too many of us to fit in one small house.'

Jean laughed, a nice warm laugh. 'Oh, I see. So, you had to move out?'

'I was in service in Macclesfield, and I came back to Hanley about eighteen months ago and am in service again. Me family's always lived in Hanley. Today's me day off so I decided to have a walk.'

Betty noticed immediately the girl's nails were bitten to the quick. Maybe she was a nervous soul. 'Do yer fancy a walk?' she said. 'Unless you've got somewhere to be?'

'I'd like that.'

The two of them walked down Percy Street, towards Burton & Dunn's Department Store, past the library in Pall Mall, and back towards the bookshop. Betty hadn't had time to visit the library since she returned and decided to do so the next time she was in Hanley. Perhaps they would have a copy of *The Card*.

Jean said she worked as a flowerer on Newtown Potbank in Etruria. It was a fair walk of a morning she said, but it wasn't that bad. She could catch a tram if she had a mind to, but mostly she didn't. She needed the money, and it did no harm to stretch her legs when she was sitting on her backside all day, she finished with a laugh.

'What's a flowerer?'

'Makes flowers out of clay, petals, and the like. Yer must've seen them in the shops . . . little bowls of flowers? The sort of thing yer mother would like.'

'I do for a woman, you know, shopping, cleaning, cooking, and the like. It's all right, but I never get ter meet nobody. I like her, but it's good ter talk ter somebody me own age, I don't mind telling yer.'

Although Jean looked a rather solemn girl, when she opened up, she was very nice.

'I don't go out much meself,' Jean had said. 'I suppose I should but not knowing nobody, it kind of scares me a bit.'

'Why?'

'I suppose I've become nervous about meeting people.'

'You talked to me and yer didn't know me.'

Jean smiled. 'You're the sort of girl who could talk to anyone and they could talk to you.'

Betty giggled. 'Dunno whether that's a compliment

or not.'

Jean covered her face with her hands. 'Oh, I see what you mean. No . . . no, it's a compliment. I wish I was like you.'

'D'yer know summat?' Betty put her head on one side and stared thoughtfully at the tall, slightly worried girl beside her. 'I'm sure we can be friends. I just know it.'

She was surprised they got on so well. Nevertheless, she decided to keep Hannah a secret — for the time being. After the rejection she had received from Martha, she was not about to risk a new friendship going the same way. She would tell when and if the time was right, and not before.

24

November 1916

Mother was happy to look after Hannah. She said a brisk walk would do Betty some good.

Betty and Jean planned to walk along the Cauldon Canal. It wasn't a picturesque walk. Town and countryside mixed with large barges full of clay and coal, and the like, working their way between the potbanks along its length.

'Have you ever been dancing, Jean?'

'Oh yes. I remember one time, when I was fifteen and taller than the boy who had asked me to dance — I'd never been before — and he dragged me on to the dance floor for a spot of barn dancing.'

Betty laughed and clapped her hands. 'Did yer have a good time?'

Jean bit a nail on her left hand and shook her head. 'I would've enjoyed just watching, but the lad asked me. I said no, but he took no notice. He shouted the first two steps over the noise of the band. I was on the dance floor being pulled round, with me feet going everywhere except where they should be.'

Jean's face was scarlet. It stopped Betty's laughter dead. 'Whatever did you do?'

'I tried to pull away. I trod on his toes — not on purpose. He was pulling me this way and that. Honestly, Betty, the room was spinning. Then he pulled me close. He had bad breath and shouted, 'You bloody bitch, you nearly broke me sodding toe.' So now, I go along sometimes, but I don't dance.'

Betty stared at Jean. It was bad enough being small. How much worse was it for Jean who was so tall? No wonder she walked with her shoulders hunched up.

'That's terrible. You could be having such fun, I guarantee it.'

Jean shook her head. 'I doubt it. I'd look silly.'

'The lad was a stupid fool. Forcing a girl who says no on ter the dance floor ter do a barn dance and then moaning when she treads on his toes? I know who I think the fool was.'

Jean swallowed and then they burst into fits of laughter.

Betty lifted her arm as if to take an oath. 'We, Jean Wright, and Betty Dean, are going ter practice some dancing steps so we can go together. I refuse to let some stupid lad spoil it for yer, cos he'll spoil it for me an' all and I dunner like that one little bit.'

They carried on walking in silence. Already, it felt strange to be parted from Hannah.

Betty sighed. 'I'm bored. I want summat more exciting in my life than cleaning up after everybody. Iris is wonderful, but it's not what I really want to do.'

Jean laughed at Betty's screwed-up nose. 'Life is boring when you have to work all day, but you've got no choice. Pound notes dunner grow on trees, duck.'

'I know, I know. I'm talking about wanting summat out of my life. It's so boring. Aren't yer bored making petals all day?'

'All jobs are boring. What would yer do then . . . if yer looked for summat else?'

Betty shrugged. 'Dunno. What's it like at Newtown potbank?'

'Same as everywhere else, I suppose. There's women's work and men's work. Working the machines is men's work, so if yer can get one of those you'd be all right cos they pay better, although not much. But we're not taking on now. We're not too badly off as there's no pots coming in from Germany. Some potbanks have closed until after the war. Their workers are either in the Colours or looking for other jobs.

'I'm going to start looking in January. I don't want ter leave Mrs Shenton on her own over Christmas.'

'That's good of yer.'

'Are you being sarky?'

'Dunner be so prickly,' Jean said quickly. 'I'm not being sarcastic. Not everybody would even think about Mrs Shenton in your position. They'd just go and have done with it.'

'I do feel a bit mean,' Betty sighed. 'It seems as yer always have ter let somebody down if yer trying to better yerself.'

'That's not true. If you want to go and do summat then you owe to yerself to try.'

* * *

Jean had, Betty felt, deliberately said little about her past. In Betty's eyes, Jean came over as shy, someone used to keeping herself to herself. All Betty knew about her was she lived on her own in Hanley, she was embarrassed about her height and bit her nails when nervous. She vowed to find out a little more on their next meeting. It was nearly Christmas, and she should know something.

Their next get-together was spent in Jean's room.

'I hate this room.'

'You only need a few knick-knacks to make it cosy. Nowt too expensive.'

'I don't really look at it. I prefer the world of my books, to be honest.'

'What about your friends?'

Jean shrugged. 'I don't have any . . . apart from you.'

'You don't?'

Jean shook her head.

'What about family?'

'There was me mother and me little sister. When father died, we went into Stoke Workhouse cos mother couldn't keep us. She had no family and couldn't look after us, cos me sister was just a baby. Me sister got pneumonia and whooping cough — she died. Mother couldn't cope and took ill and that was it — she was gone an' all.' Jean spoke matter-of-factly, staring straight ahead.

Betty sought out her hand and squeezed it, wanting Jean to know she cared.

'I'm all right now, Betty. It was a long time ago. I had a friend and, when we reached sixteen, we set up together, to rent this place. She went off with some fella, and I've been here by meself.'

Betty was quiet, thinking about all Jean had said. Poor girl. Her own life felt rich by comparison.

25

December 1916

Iris had arranged to spend the festive season with Victoria and her family in Newcastle-under-Lyme, and Betty accompanied her on the tram to meet Victoria there. She would return on 27th December so, for Betty, Christmas would actually be at Christmas this year.

She returned to Belgrave Road, where Lily, who had been looking after Hannah, was waiting. Lily was a much more level-headed girl than Mary-Ellen, and more responsible. They chatted for a few minutes. Then Lily left.

Iris had insisted they have a Christmas tree for little Hannah, and Betty hung festive decorations around the house and in the bedroom she shared with Hannah.

Betty was responsible for looking after the house while Iris was away and was determined nothing would happen to betray this trust. She returned to the house each evening, as it was important not to disturb Hannah's routine, but was determined to spend as much time as she could with both her family and daughter.

* * *

Betty and Jean arranged to go to the Christmas Dance at the Victoria Hall on the Saturday before Christmas.

Each time she went out on her own, a twinge of guilt would steal over Betty when she was having a good time. Was it wrong of her to leave Hannah in her mother's care, again? Was she being selfish?

Jean was flushed with excitement when Betty arrived at her lodging house that evening. She admitted she was looking forward to the dance and would happily dance until midnight. Betty would have to think on her feet to explain she must return home at about ten o'clock, as she had Hannah's feed to get back for. Mother had said she could have cow's milk this time, but Betty preferred to keep her daughter on her normal routine.

They arrived at the dance hall early to get a good seat near to the dance floor, where they would be more noticeable to any young men who happened to be looking for a partner.

The music was loud and echoed through the hall. They could barely hear each other speak, as the band played an arrangement of *Roses of Picardy* as a waltz.

There were three tables to choose from. Several women were sitting in chairs around the walls and appeared to be happily chatting to one another. Betty wondered how many were desperate for a bloke to ask them to dance. Some were dancing with each other, and she saw them casting their eyes around the hall searching for signs of men without women, smiling encouragingly if a man should look at them, but wouldn't think of making an approach themselves.

'Dunner think we'll be in luck tonight, Jean.'

Just then a group of young men waltzed in, loud, laughing and joking. It was obvious they had started drinking elsewhere. Soldiers on leave and out to have a good time while they still could.

'What d'yer reckon?' Betty jerked her head in their direction.

'They're a bit loud.'

'Yes, but they're having fun by the looks of it. We should make the most of it, don't you think?'

'We haven't seen you in these parts. Can we tempt you to dance?'

The girls glanced up. Two young men had stopped beside their table. One grinned at Betty and held out his hand to her. He had twinkling eyes, dark hair, and a dark moustache.

'Ladies, I'm Duncan and this is my mate, Arthur.'

The second lad nodded without looking at them. Duncan raised an eyebrow waiting for Betty's response.

She gave him a broad smile and turned to Jean, who was looking a little uncertainly at his friend. Jean was backward about coming forward at the best of times.

'Ta very much. I'm Betty.' She stood up. 'And this is Jean.' She locked her eyes on her friend and pulled her out of her seat.

When they reached the dance floor Betty easily slid into Duncan's arms and he whisked her away, leaving Jean to sort herself out. He was tall and she melted into his arms. She had been taught to dance at school and had sniggered as embarrassed boys jerked their way round the floor. She would hear them counting steps under their breath. As Duncan whirled her around, she had to admit he was a good dancer.

She caught the looks on the faces of some of the girls sitting at the tables. This was what it was all about. Meeting boys and young men because, if she didn't, she was never going to meet the man of her dreams, the man who would take care of her for the rest of her life. Fewer and fewer men were left in The Potteries since conscription began. Unmarried men were among the first to go. How many would live to become husbands?

A tingling sensation ran up and down Betty's back where Duncan's hand was resting. She was so glad she had talked Jean into coming along. Even wearing her new shoes with high heels, she had to crick her neck to look at him. She smiled. Tall, dark, and handsome — she should be so lucky.

She looked over her shoulder to Jean dancing with Arthur. She looked uncomfortable. Standing with her back straight, she was taller than him. In fact, Jean was taller than many of the men and boys Betty knew. She giggled even though she knew she shouldn't.

Duncan must have felt her body shake.

He put his lips against her ear. 'You all right, Betty?'

'Oh, yes. Just watching Jean and Arthur.' The touch of his lips sent sensations though her body, taking away her ability to concentrate.

He looked in the direction Betty pointed. Jean plainly was a few inches taller than Arthur. His eyes were almost looking at her chin. Betty made a mental note to suggest Jean did not put her hair up when they went to a dance. She looked even taller.

His eyes closed. 'Bugger!'

'What's up?'

'Arthur worries about his height. He's mighty self-conscious. Thinks every girl'll laugh at him. Didn't realise how tall yer mate was. I could've swapped. We've been away. Army. Arthur gets a bit . . . anxious these days.'

Betty raised her eyebrows, in pretend annoyance, to make light of his words. 'Do you usually choose a girl by her height then? Or was it a case of any girl'll do?'

'Course not. I chose you, didn't I? Just saying I could've saved Arthur the embarrassment.'

It was nice of him. His voice was low, but deep and she wanted to keep him talking. 'Don't suppose you're allowed to say where you've been?'

Duncan touched his nose knowingly.

Betty laughed. 'How long have you been fighting?'

His face clouded over. 'I've just finished my training in the Royal Field Artillery. I'll be on my way to France after Christmas, the 27th to be precise. So, in reply to your question, I've only made it to Catterick so far!'

When the dance was over the four returned to their table. Jean seemed happy enough to sit and chat with Arthur, so Betty and Duncan spent most of the evening dancing — and it felt wonderful. He was easily the best-looking man there. As she flew round the room in his arms, she felt sorry for those with no partners, but not sorry enough to let him go.

When Duncan and Arthur went off to get some drinks, she flopped onto a chair next to Jean so she could hear when she spoke.

'Are you all right? Why did yer stop dancing?'

Jean shrugged. 'He didn't say much when we were dancing. When the music stopped, he came back ter the table and we've sat chatting. He seems very nice but nervous.

'Duncan says as he's got one or two problems.'

Jean sighed. 'Yer conner see it from the outside, Betty, but there's bound to be men what's hurting on the inside. Being trained to kill. It's not right.'

They were quiet for a moment.

When the men returned, Betty and Duncan sipped their drinks in-between visits to the dance floor. But ten o'clock came all too quickly. She made an excuse she had to be home early to help her mother out. Duncan's arm, which was resting on the back of her chair, slid to Betty's shoulders, causing a hot flush. She didn't want to go, but she had to return to Hannah. Quick as a flash, Duncan's arm moved and he was reaching in his pocket for something. It was a piece of paper. He wrote on it and folded it into quarters.

'Put this safe. It's me address. You might think of writing to me, if yer get the chance?'

She couldn't let him go like that. She had hoped he would suggest walking them home. It was down to her.

'You said you were leaving on Wednesday. Would you like to meet at the boating lake in Hanley Park at two o'clock on Tuesday? We can talk a little more?'

His eyes lit up. 'Yes, I'd like it very much.'

He dropped a kiss on her forehead. It made her jump.

'Sorry, I wasn't being forward or anything.' He flushed.

'No, it's me. I wasn't expecting it.' She kissed him back and smiled. 'See you on Tuesday, Duncan.'

He hesitated, as if he didn't want to go, then he and Arthur walked away through the dancers.

The two girls collected their coats and stepped outside. He was nice, a bit like Jeffrey, looking out for his mate. She compared a lot of men to Jeffrey these days and, if Duncan turned out like him, she would do very well.

They arrived at Jean's boarding house first and stood for a moment in silence.

'Ready to —'

'I'm sorry about —'

The two spoke out at the same time. Betty smiled. 'You go first.'

'I'm sorry I wasn't better company. You must think I'm a miserable cow.'

Betty was surprised. It sounded more like something she would say. 'Did Arthur behave himself, Jean?'

'Oh, yes. It's nothing like that. I just got the impression Duncan had dragged him here and he was going through the motions. So, when he said he'd take me back to our table, I agreed and that was it.'

In bed later, Betty took out the note Duncan had written. *71766 Cpl Duncan Kennedy, 75th Royal Field Artillery Brigade, BEF, France.*

⋆ ⋆ ⋆

Betty walked purposely down to the boating lake in Hanley Park to meet Duncan. Had she been too forward in suggesting a meeting, to a random bloke on the strength of an evening at a dance?

Duncan was already waiting for her and strode towards her, smiling. He was wearing his Royal Field Artillery uniform with its two stripes and insignia. He looked so smart.

'Thanks for coming, Betty. I wanted to see you again . . . to make sure you were real.'

She laughed. 'Same here. I might've dreamed you up.' She knew her eyes were twinkling and his were the same.

'We had a good time at the dance.'

'The time passed so quickly.'

She was unsure what to say next. Having him here, to herself, was different to talking in a crowded, music-filled dance hall. After Alastair, she was determined to choose carefully.

Duncan had already made an impact on her.

'Do yer have any —'

'— Tell me a little about yourself, Betty.'

They laughed.

'I'll go first.' She told him about being in service. How she had moved from a big house to a much nicer one where she got on well with her employer. She talked about her large family and how much she had missed being with them, particularly Jeffrey away in Flanders, and Tommy and Lily who she wished she could spend more time with.

She took a breath. 'I also have a daughter. She's nearly fourteen months old.

'You're married?'

'Her father died in the war. There's just me and Hannah.' She watched his face, but he just nodded. 'What about you?'

'Me? I used to work in the office of the North Staffordshire Railway Company doing paperwork and financial stuff.'

'Then we have summat in common. I taught meself to type and am doing a bookkeeping course. I hope to put it to some use in an office after the war. What about your family?'

'My father is Sean and I have a sister, Susan. Both Mother and the baby died three years after Susan was born.'

'I'm so sorry to hear.'

'Susan's sixteen and works in Burton & Dunn's.'

Betty looked suitably impressed. 'What do you do in the army?'

'After I did my basic training, I was sent to gunnery school, the Royal Field Artillery.' He pointed to the insignia on his shoulder. 'We work behind our lines and trenches, and support the infantry on the battlefield. When our lads advance it'll be my job to aim the gun and calculate the correct angles to hit the target. I operate what's called a medium field gun. It's not huge, so we can move it around quickly when needed.'

'How do you know if you're firing in the correct place?'

'Observers let the gunnery officer know and he issues corrections to us gunners on where to fire.'

She didn't want to waste a moment of the time they had left. She talked and he listened. Then he talked and she listened. They laughed and joked, and she never noticed the ache in her legs until he had waved goodbye to her.

'Betty, I need you to listen to me now.' His face became serious. He slid a piece of paper into her hand. 'I know it's a bit maudlin, but I need to tell you: I gave you my army address so as you could write to me.'

'And I will, I swear.'

'I know you will, but I want you to write to Susan, too. I need you to tell her your address. God forbid, but if anything should happen to me, the army will tell my family.'

'Duncan! Don't speak of it.'

'Shh.' He put his finger on her lips. 'I need to know you will be told if the worst happened. I couldn't bear you not knowing.'

Finding out more about Duncan had both pleased

her and upset her. The talk of guns and of needing to know she had the address of his family had really brought home to her the desperate nature of fighting this war.

* * *

Duncan's train was leaving Stoke at nine o'clock, still two hours to go before she had arranged to see him off. She busied herself, but kept an eye on the clock, not wanting to have a last-minute rush to the station.

Lily arrived at Belgrave Road promptly to look after Hannah, and said she'd decided to take her for a walk around the park, so set about dressing her in warm clothes.

'When do yer want me to bring Hannah back?' asked Lily

'I'll come ter Wellington Road before lunch. Mrs Shenton will be back by then.'

'Yer look nice.'

'Thank you, Lily. If it rains or goes colder then you go home straight away.'

'Yes, Miss Dean.' Lily completed a perfect curtsey. The sisters laughed.

What Lily had said was true, Betty had taken great care of her appearance and had touched up her lips with lipstick, though not too much.

They parted company at the park gates. Soon, she was on her way to the station. She had arranged to meet Duncan outside the front doors, opposite the North Stafford Hotel. The clock inside the station told her she still had half an hour to wait. She walked down to the railway bridge spanning another road across the city and watched cars, bicycles, and delivery carts heading for the town. She walked back to hear the arrival at platform three of the eight-thirty-two to Manchester. The platforms filled with black smoke as the train came to a stop. She watched the passengers flow out of the station and into the street. Some had people waiting for them, others appeared to be on their own.

A cold draught from the open doors of the station swirled round her legs and she could barely feel her feet as she stamped them to get the blood flowing. She smoothed her hair out of her eyes, hoping the sudden wind hadn't played havoc with it.

'Sounds like you're in an awful temper, Betty Dean.'

She swung round. 'You did that on purpose!'

He laughed. 'I like watching you.' His face sobered momentarily. 'I want to keep a picture of you in my mind as long as I can.'

Betty stared at him. It was as if he could read her mind, and yes, she wanted the same. When they arranged to meet in the park yesterday, it was because she wanted to write to him, to keep him company while he was away, and she wanted to know him a little more about him before he went. After their walk together, she realised it was more than that. She didn't want him to disappear out of her life and not know whether he was alive or dead.

Three men dressed in khaki arrived at the door of the station and began to smoke and tell jokes. More joined them. Another train must have come in. She hadn't heard the announcement because she was concentrating on Duncan. He pulled her to one side, so they wouldn't be interrupted. Even so, he had to shout to make his words heard.

'I'm glad you came, Betty.'

She quite liked the echoey noise of it all. The platforms littered with people, either meeting others, or saying their goodbyes, slow and tearful, often a quiet holding of a loved one. It was the first time she'd said goodbye to a man going off to war. It was exciting, but painful.

Suddenly self-conscious at the look in his eyes, she had to hold her arms firmly at her side to stop herself from flinging them around him, worried she'd make an ass of herself.

'Promise again you'll write, Betty.'

She nodded vigorously. 'I will. And you take care of yourself.'

'Don't forget about Susan. Write to her, or better still, go and see her.'

'What'll they think if I turn up on their doorstep?'

'I've told them about you. I need to know they can get in touch with you if anything should happen to me.'

'Don't say that.'

'I have to, Betty. I told you I did. You know only too well what can happen, to any of us? To be truthful, I would ask you to walk out with me, if I wasn't going away. You don't have anyone else, do you?'

'No, I don't. I *will* write. I promise.'

He caught her in his arms and kissed her full on the lips in front of everybody. But she didn't care and kissed him back. Then, his train was announced. And he was gone, leaving her waving madly on the platform.

* * *

Once Duncan had gone, she felt deprived. She had known him for so little time and yet he filled her mind. She hadn't told Jean about the two meetings and wondered if she had seen Arthur since the dance.

Anyway, it was New Year's Eve, and it seemed the best of excuses to put pen to paper.

31st December 1916

Dear Duncan,

Thank you for a lovely time at the dance. It was good to talk to you, and I was even more pleased when we met again in Hanley Park on Boxing Day. As you suggested, I have written to Susan and hope to pay a visit soon. You know I am from a large family, so it is quite different to yours. We have each other to lean on, while your father and Susan have only each other.

I was proud when you asked me to see you off at the station. You looked so smart.

I hope you had a good journey back. You didn't say when you would be going overseas, so I can't imagine what you are doing now. Are you very busy, or have you already set off? When my brother, Jeffrey, went, I couldn't stop thinking about him and what he might be facing. But, somehow, I needed to know. It's almost like hitting yourself to prove you are awake: you know it is going to be painful, but you do it anyway. You will think me stupid now!

It will soon be 1917. Let's hope this war is won and we can return to normal.

I'm sure we shall have lots of news to pass on. Write to me soon.

Best wishes
Betty Dean

26

January 1917

Betty took Hannah out in the pram when she paid some bills and collected new linen from the drapers. During the time she spent on her own, she thought about this idea of bettering her prospects. At fifteen months, Hannah, was too young to be engaged in conversation, but watched her mother from the depths of her pram with a thumb in her mouth.

The bookkeeping course was going well. Betty felt she was as good as anyone else undertaking it. She had also mastered the typewriter; her typing was quicker, with fewer mistakes. She was even typing correspondence for Iris. When the bookkeeping course finished, she was going to learn shorthand.

She hummed as she opened the back door to Iris's and dropped the shopping on the kitchen table, but as she pushed the pram inside and took off her coat there was a faint sound. She walked slowly towards the hall.

'Is that you Iris?'

'Betty? Thank goodness.' Iris's voice sounded weak, not like herself.

'Where are yer?'

'I'm upstairs.'

She raced up the stairs two at a time. At the top she saw a foot sticking out of Iris's bedroom.

'Oh, Iris . . . what have you done?'

'I slipped and fell. I couldn't get up.' She voice sounded weak. 'I've been lying here since just after you went to the shop.'

Betty bent down and felt Iris's arms and then her legs.

'Ouch!'

'Sorry, did I hurt yer?'

'It's my leg. I might have twisted my ankle. I tried to get up, but I couldn't put any weight on it.'

'Does it hurt anywhere else?'

Iris shook her head and closed her eyes.

'Let me help you to your bed if you can stand up.'

Iris gave her a painful nod and that's when Betty realised how shaken the elderly woman was. She would never contemplate lying on her bed during the daylight hours.

Betty telephoned Victoria to explain what had happened, and the daughter ordered her to call out the doctor. 'I shall be over directly.'

She stayed with Iris as much as she could, to check she didn't get any worse. The doctor called after lunch and agreed the ankle was swollen, but not broken, and Iris must rest in bed for two days before contemplating walking on it.

* * *

Victoria arrived just after the doctor had left. She let herself in and rushed up to her mother's room, where she immediately took charge, much to Iris's protestations that she was managing, with Betty's help.

Betty smothered a grin. She could understand why Iris had fought to keep her independence. Victoria could be a little overpowering.

'I'll leave you with Victoria now. I need to do somethings downstairs.'

'Betty, when I came in it sounded as if Hannah has just awoken. She will probably need you. When you are able, will you get Mother and I a pot of tea?'

'Of course,' she smiled.

As she left the room, Victoria's voice grew fainter but Betty heard her words clearly.

'I do wish you'd listen to me. You need more rest at your age. Please be careful. I can't always come rushing over to help you.'

'I didn't ask you to, Victoria. Betty and I were managing perfectly well. And she has plied me with tea since I woke up.'

Betty could hear Victoria speaking as she went about her tasks. Once she'd had a bite to eat and Hannah was fed and changed, Betty set about making the tea for upstairs. There was no doubting Victoria's concern for her mother and she was relieved the woman had rushed over, for Iris's sake.

She reached the top of the stairs and knocked politely on Iris's door as she always did.

'. . . I'll speak to the solicitor, and we can find out more.'

Victoria said nothing more as Betty served the tea. Half an hour later, Victoria entered the kitchen.

'Mother appears to be well enough, Betty. But do call me if she needs me, won't you? I will come back on Saturday afternoon at two o'clock to make sure all is well.

Betty nodded. 'I will.'

* * *

Victoria was as good as her word and arrived promptly. With a quick nod to Betty, she went straight to Iris's room and closed the door. She seemed in a rush, so Betty gave them a little time together before interrupting them to take away her lunch tray.

A couple of hours later the door was still closed. Betty decided she couldn't wait any longer to serve afternoon tea. She knocked on the door and entered.

It was Victoria, as usual, who spoke first. 'Put the tray on the table and sit down. We have an important matter to discuss with you.'

It didn't sound good. She placed the silver tray on the table in front of them. She had an idea the discussion would not be to her benefit.

'Now, you've seen at first-hand how frail my mother has become in recent weeks.'

Iris had had one or two minor mishaps recently, but nothing that would be a cause for concern . . . except this fall, Betty was about to say, but Victoria continued.

'Mother and I have spoken at length and have agreed it would be best if she moved in with me. It is not good for her to be looking after this huge house on her own when she has no need of it. You too must be finding it difficult, with the baby, trying to juggle all this and look after her.'

'It's not too bad, Victoria. Mother takes Hannah during the day whenever I need her to.'

'That's the problem, Betty. You can't give your full attention to my mother and have the responsibility of the child too. You are being stretched too much and it could be damaging to my mother's health when her arthritis is getting worse. Because of that, I have insisted Mother takes steps to move in with me permanently.'

It was bound to happen one day, but this had come out of the blue for her. Betty swallowed and placed her hands together on her lap.

'Will you be selling the house?'

'Of course,' said Victoria, not giving Iris a chance to speak. 'I suggest you start looking for another position. I already have a maid and cook and require no one else.'

'Oh, I see.' She turned to Iris for confirmation.

'I am so sorry, Betty. I had hoped to stay longer, but I have a feeling Victoria might be right.'

'Of course I'm right, Mother.'

Betty nodded. 'I understand. I'll begin looking straight away. Will that be all?'

'Yes, Betty. Thank you.'

She rose to her feet, nodded to Iris, and left the room in a daze.

Victoria left after having something to eat, promising she would be back again in a couple of days to check up on Iris. Betty felt uncomfortable, as if Iris's recent fall was partly her fault.

* * *

'Come up and talk to me, Betty, when you can.'

She was invited to sit in one of the chairs in the window as Iris took the other.

'I'm sorry you had to find out in that way. I was hoping to talk to you about it before Victoria broached the subject. Never mind, what's done is done.

'It came as a bit of a shock.'

'I want to assure you that it is no reflection on you and, whatever Victoria says, Hannah's presence has nothing to do with it. I rather enjoy having her here.'

‘I did wonder. I’ve tried very hard not to let it affect my work.’

‘And you have done an admirable job. My dear, Victoria has been on at me to live with her for some time. Unfortunately, I do believe that she is right this time. I don’t expect Victoria can care for me as well as you have done, and I know from Christmas her cook is not a patch on you, but she’s right about this house being too big for me. To put it bluntly, I am paying you to keep it clean and tidy, but I haven’t been into some of the rooms for ages.’

Betty nodded. ‘You’ve given me a lovely home these past months, Iris. Hannah and I have been so lucky.’

‘I’m glad you think so, but I’ll be sad to see you go. I hope I’ve been of some use to you, setting you on a path to think about the future. It’s why I wanted you to learn to use the typewriter, and brought the bookkeeping course to your attention. You’re a good girl and you could do so much more with yourself. Seize the opportunity, Betty. Don’t just follow in the footsteps of others. Be ready to create your own path.’

‘Do you really think I can?’ ‘I know you can.’

* * *

A week later, Betty received her first letter from Duncan. She needed something to cheer her up while she was looking to plan the next part of her life. She still hadn’t mentioned Duncan to Jean, and although she wasn’t sure why, she told herself it was best to wait to see if their friendship progressed first. Who knew how long her friendships with either Duncan or Jean would last?

14th January 1917

Dear Betty,

I was so pleased to get your letter. The post to and from the Front is very good we're told, but if we move about a lot then there are some delays, so don't worry if I don't reply quickly.

I, too, really enjoyed the time we spend together on Boxing Day. At the end it felt like I'd known you a while.

It is true what you say about your family. There seems to be lots of support. Father and Susan are all I have. It is the first time the three of us have ever been parted. I am so glad you decided to contact Susan. Parting with Father and Susan was so difficult. Father put a brave face on it and Susan tried unsuccessfully not to cry. My only other family in The Potteries are my mother's two sisters who live in Milton and Kidsgrove. Not exactly neighbours, but at least they can be visited.

The boat arrived in [redacted] *on 31st December after a rough sea crossing, so there was not much celebration of the New Year. Most of us had never been on the sea before. The horses suffered the most. We lost two of them due to broken legs. It was sad, but I expect it is something I will have to get used to.*

By coincidence I met my battery sergeant on the train to [redacted]*, Sergeant Williams, he's seen lots of active service having been in France from the start. He was returning from leave, and we travelled together to join our brigade at* [redacted]*. He is from South Wales and has been in the army since he was eighteen. I don't know how old he is now, but he certainly has got a lot of experience. One of the things he told me was we are attached to a battalion of the*

Guards Division who were made up of men from the five top regiments in the British Army. He said we do everything by the book and, to quote him, 'the book might be wrong in places, but it is better for all of us to be wrong at the same time and in the same way'. Not so sure what I think about that.

When I got to Brigade Headquarters, at [redacted]*, I was told I would spend a few days getting used to active service at headquarters before being moved to* [redacted]*. So, I have only just met my comrades. Like the sergeant, some of them have been in the army since before the war but also there are a few like me who are replacements. I've been told we will likely be moving this evening, but no orders have come down yet.*

The weather is wet and cold and the past two nights there has been a frost. They say it might snow.

I agree letters are very important. Each day's delivery is a high spot even for the old hands. So, you know I will be looking forward to your next letter.

Best wishes
Duncan Kennedy
PS — our letters are censored so you might find bits missing. So, don't worry!

She smiled as she finished reading, pleased to receive such a chatty letter. She hadn't heard back from his sister yet, but if Susan was anything like as chatty, she would become another welcome friend. She put the letter safely in a drawer to reply to later, and carried on with her work, humming as she went.

* * *

Iris talked a lot of sense, and it was true, Betty shouldn't let things happen to her as she had in the past. She should be able to say *I did it*, rather than *it happened to me*, she decided, so she invested a penny in buying a copy of *The Sentinel*. Jobs of all sorts were advertised within its pages, although it was mainly domestic jobs and potbank work. The hospital was advertising for maids and the workhouse wanted a couple of probationer nurses. She wrinkled her nose at those. Lots of women were going into munitions work but Betty wasn't keen. Nothing she could see excited her and she couldn't bring herself to get a job in the workhouse.

And then she saw the perfect job. The Potteries Tramway Company, or PTC, required clippies to replace men serving their country, the advertisement said. '*Do your Bit*'. Men were called conductors and women were lady conductors, or clippies for short, because they clipped the ticket to show the stop the passenger was leaving the tram. Of course, she had seen clippies working on the trams but hadn't given them much thought beyond paying her fare. Wouldn't it be wonderful to have a uniform to show the world how grown up she was?

Betty sang to herself all the way back to Iris's. A job paying a man's money, where she could meet all sorts.

Her perfect job.

She spoke to Jean about it and her excitement must have rubbed off. It didn't take long to persuade Jean to apply too. It turned out she didn't want to make pottery petals all her life.

* * *

Both girls received letters inviting them to attend for interview. Betty had some organisation to do before she could take the job if one was offered. She asked Mother to accompany her on a walk to the many shops in Hanley.

'I need to talk to yer,' Betty whispered.

She wrapped Hannah up warmly and placed her in the big old pram that had seen better days. As they strolled along the street, Betty wondered how best to put her request. She had already told Mother she would need to look for a job and somewhere to live when Iris moved to her daughter's.

'Out with it, Betty. What's troubling yer?'

'I've got an interview for a job as a lady conductor with the PTC. It would mean working shifts, but the pay is good. It's the same pay as a man — twenty-seven bob a week.' Betty's words tumbled out once she got started. 'If I get the job, could Hannah come to live with yer full-time? Shift work would really upset her routine. I shall only be working six days a week but my day off won't always be Sunday. I could give yer board money for Hannah and rent a room somewhere. It'll give me experience and time to find a new job. Iris is hoping to move in with her daughter by Easter, so it'd be a big help to everyone. Please, Mother, say you'll do it. I promise I'll get a —'

'Hang on, Betty, duck. Me head's whirling.'

She let her mother take in what she had said.

'So, you are going to be a clippie?'

'Yes.'

'You'll get paid the same as a man, yer say?'

'Yes! But I couldn't do it without yer.'

Mother stared at her. Betty couldn't tell from her face how her mother felt. Mother continued to push the pram.

'Well? What d'yer think?' she said, when she could stand it no longer.

'Let's see how yer get on then.'

'Oh, Mother I'd be ever so grateful. What about Father?'

'I'll talk to yer father, duck. Dunner werrit about him. He'll do as I say.'

Betty returned to Belgrave Road and told Iris her good news. Iris was almost as excited as she was.

It would be difficult spending so much time away from Hannah but it was for the good of them both that she was doing it. Even so, it didn't stop her from having a little weep later when she was alone in her bedroom.

Part Three

27

February 1917

Betty arrived at the Potteries Tramway Company offices in Stoke and tapped on the enquiry window as requested by a little card pinned to the wall next to a large model of a tram. Iris had told her to sell her good qualities while she had the opportunity.

A man who looked to be in his middle thirties let her in. He might have been younger but his receding hairline, and tinge of grey, suggested not. He led the way to an office and offered her a chair before sitting in the chair behind the desk.

'I'm Mr Adams, manager of the Goldenhill Depot.' He leaned back in his chair. 'So you've come for a job as a clippie, have yer duck?'

'I'm conscientious, Mr Adams. And do a good job, whether I'm cleaning privies or giving people tram tickets.'

He laughed. 'Pleased to hear it. Have yer got any experience of working with cash?'

'Well, I look after me own money — and am careful.' She spoke without taking a breath. 'I work for a lady as housekeeper and look after the household accounts. I am also studying a bookkeeping course at the WEA, which started last September. In service you meet all sorts of people, both masters and servants, and some can be right nowty, but I manage all right and that's just as important isn't, Mr Adams?'

Her words left him bewildered. 'I suppose so, Miss . . . er . . . Dean . . . You'd be working same hours as the men, early mornings, late evenings, forty-eight hours over six days.'

'I'm used to early starts and late finishes. How much will I get paid?'

'Four shillings and sixpence a day, and you'll work six days a week, and two bob a week war bonus.'

A gasp flew from Betty's lips before she had chance to control it.

'We're only taking on clippies for the duration of the war, until our blokes come home. Can't have our heroes coming back to unemployment, can we?'

That was a disappointment. She could understand men would need jobs to come home to, but what about the clippies who need to keep their jobs? Still, she would have experience to draw on. She had to make the most of it while she could. No harm in making herself indispensable.

'Got any references?'

She nodded. Iris would give her one and so would Mrs Stone. She was glad she had left Stowford on good terms.

'Bring yer birth certificate. You are British, aren't yer?'

Anybody would think as she was about to become a spy or summat. She thought of Jean answering his questions, and almost snorted.

'Yes, I am, Mr Adams.'

'Right then. I'll get things moving. I've got a couple more ladies ter see in the next few days, so you'll get a letter in the post.'

'Ta very much.'

She opened the door to leave and cast a glance back

over her shoulder, and grinned.

'Terrah, Mr Adams.'

* * *

A letter from the PTC arrived on Saturday offering Betty the job on the terms discussed and telling her to start on Monday, 12th February, at eight o'clock prompt at the Goldenhill depot.

Iris was thrilled. 'You see what you can do when you put your mind to it, Betty? Remember that and you won't go far wrong. I'm so proud of you.'

'Thank you, Iris. I couldn't have done it without you. I have not told them about Hannah now she is going to live with her grandma for the duration. It seemed pointless as she won't be living with me.' The tears were back and she blinked furiously.

'I don't think it will matter to them, dear,' said Iris.

'I'll look for a room straight away, so you can make your plans to sell the house and move in with Victoria.'

'You've been like a breath of fresh air to me. I shall miss you so much.'

Betty gave Iris a hug. 'I've learned a lot from you, and I won't forget.'

The arrangements had all been agreed. As Mother had predicted, Father gave no trouble in agreeing to take Hannah. Either that, or Mother had brow-beaten him into it. Whichever it was, it was good news.

She didn't know how long the job would last, nor what would happen next, but everything she did from now on would give her more and varied experience for the time when she could make a real home for Hannah.

* * *

Cheap lodgings were more likely to be advertised in corner shops than in the newspaper. Betty found what she was looking for — a room with a Mrs Milly Clowes, in Jasper Street, just a few streets away from both her family and Jean. In days gone by, she would have included Martha too, but she hadn't seen her to speak to since the day Betty had said she was expecting.

From the outside, the house appeared well kept, judging by the clean, polished windows and the immaculate stone step to the front door. She knocked, taking care not to put her foot on the step, and could've sworn the lace curtains at the window moved.

Mrs Clowes looked to be in her forties and wore a pinafore.

'What can I do for you?' she said.

'I'm here about the room you advertised in the corner shop.'

'Oh, I was expecting to rent to somebody older.'

'I'm reliable and no bother, Mrs Clowes. I have a job and can easily pay me way. I won't give yer no trouble.'

'Mmm.' Mrs Clowes tapped a foot as if it might help her come to a decision. 'Best come in then,' she said at last. 'What's your name?'

'Betty Dean'

'Joan's daughter? The one with the baby?'

'Yes, that's me.'

'There's no children allowed here.'

'The room's for meself. Mother's looking after Hannah while I work.'

'I don't allow children in the house at any time.

Too noisy.'

'No, Mrs Clowes.'

'I heard about your misfortune with the father.'

Betty smiled and bowed her head. She stepped inside. There was a flight of stairs in the tiny hallway and Mrs Clowes waved her up to a room on the left. She reached into a large pocket in her pinafore and took out a key.

The room was even smaller than she was used to, with a bed, a small wardrobe, a table and two chairs, and a washbasin. Mrs Clowes folded her arms under her small chest.

'I expect you to keep it clean and tidy. I'll take a month's rent in advance. And I want no gentlemen callers in rooms as well.'

Betty nodded. The rent in advance could be a problem but she would get it somehow.

'It sounds fine, Mrs Clowes. Could I take it?'

'It's a minimum of six months.'

It sounded a long time for the war to continue, but at least she would have somewhere to be based while looking for her next job.

The deal was struck, and everything was in place.

* * *

'I hope it does not take too long to settle into your new lodgings,' said Iris. 'I feel quite guilty.'

Betty grinned. 'It will feel strange to be on me own, but I shall be fine, I'm sure.'

'On a related matter, but something rather personal: You've never mentioned having a young man in your life. Is there someone?'

'I did meet a boy at the Christmas dance, and we

met a couple of times afterwards. But you know how it is, he was a soldier and duty called.'

'So it is with most young men unfortunately these days.'

'He gave me his address to write to him.'

'And did you?'

'Yes, I wrote to him on New Year's Eve and he's written back. He's from Hartshill, but he's away in France.'

With a twinkle in her eye, Iris said, 'Do you realise when you mentioned him, you had a smile on your face?'

Betty was surprised Iris had picked up on something that she, Betty, was unaware of.

'And while we're talking about the future, I must tell you before I forget — I want you to take the typewriter with you. It's old and I have no use for it. It'll remind you that you're in charge of your life.'

'Oh, but I couldn't.'

'I want you to. You have the makings of a fine young woman, Betty. I have a feeling you are going to be a busy lady.'

Betty hugged her. Putting it the way Iris had put it, she couldn't wait to make the world her own.

There were tears when she said goodbye.

'Look after yourself and little Hannah. I shall miss you so much. You have made the house come alive again.' Iris pressed an envelope into her hands.

Betty gave Iris another hug, as much to say thank you, as to control her tears, which were welling up inside her. 'You have been so kind to me. I'll never forget you.'

Michael helped her with the move. He took her case and the typewriter, and put them in his barrow.

Betty pushed Hannah's pram.

The only heart-rending point came when Betty said goodbye to Hannah, this time knowing it was for keeps. She could visit Hannah whenever she wanted, but Hannah's home for the foreseeable future would be Wellington Road.

It was all getting too much for her, saying goodbye to two people in her life that meant so much to her. At least Hannah was too young to understand.

Michael and Betty arrived at Jasper Street and were greeted by Mrs Clowes without the need to knock. She had probably been waiting for them behind those lace curtains. Mrs Clowes lost no time asking who this young man was, which pleased Michael no end. Once Betty explained he was her brother, Mrs Clowes relaxed and supervised the move. It only took a few minutes.

'Hold on! What is that contraption?' asked Mrs Clowes.

'It's a typewriter. I am learning to touch type so I will have a better chance of getting a job after the war ends. It ma —'

'Well, no clacketing after ten at night and before eight in the morning.'

Michael sniggered over her shoulder and Betty nearly laughed, but best not get off on the wrong foot. 'Yes, Mrs Clowes.' It sounded just like being in service again.

Betty sat on one of the chairs and then tested the bed. Everything was clean. She opened the letter Iris had given her. It contained her final week's wages and a reference should she ever need one. Also, there were two ten-shilling notes and a letter clipped to them: '*To get you started on your new journey, Iris.*'

She burst into tears.

To help her feel better, she wrote to Duncan with news of her new job and address, and her excitement that she would be paid a man's wage — even if she would be required to finish at the end of the war. She had arranged to visit his family on Sunday. She asked him if he needed knitted socks or gloves because it seemed to be a major pastime for a lot of women. Another thing for her to learn.

* * *

Betty was a little nervous as she set off to see Duncan's family. She would've expected to accompany him to a first visit, but the war had prevented that. Now, here she was about to introduce herself to strangers, in their own home, to talk about their son who wasn't there.

Hartshill was a village just up the hill from the town of Stoke. The house was in a terrace of well-maintained homes built higher than the road, meaning they had a view over urban Hanley and the smoking chimneys of the potbanks.

She stopped at number fifty-six and checked again the note she had received from Duncan. She opened the gate as the door was flung open and a young girl with a red face beamed at her.

'You're Betty, aren't you?'

She grinned. 'And you're Susan!'

'I'm so glad to meet you. Duncan never stopped talking about you before he left. Come in, do.'

The walls in the hall were half-clad with wood, and, with no windows, it was dark as Susan guided her to the parlour where a man with grey hair sat waiting.

He rose as soon as she entered and moved forward to clasp her hand.

'Father, this is Betty come to see us as Duncan said she might.'

'I'm pleased to meet you both,' she said.

'I'm glad you have, my dear.' Mr Kennedy's voice was gruff, with a strong Irish accent. He bade them both to sit. A tray of cakes was sitting on the table together with three cups, saucers, and side plates.

Betty smiled. 'You shouldn't have gone to all this trouble, Susan.'

'It was no trouble at all. Duncan doesn't have guests very often so we make the most of it. I'll make the tea. Excuse me.'

'She's a good girl,' said Mr Kennedy as he watched her hurry out. 'Grown up before her time after losing her mother. Thinks the world of Duncan.'

'It must have been terrible for all of you.'

'It was, my dear. Susan will make some man a fine wife someday. In the meantime, I have her all to myself.'

It didn't take Betty long to discover the love circulating in the close-knit family. How lucky Duncan was. For their sakes, as well as her own, she prayed he would be one of the lucky ones to come back.

She told them about her life in service and her interview for her new job. Susan's eyes were alight with pleasure as Betty talked about her family and meeting Duncan for the first time.

Betty noticed some knitting on the table and remarked she had promised to knit Duncan some socks.

'I dunno why — I've never knitted any before. I just wanted to do something for him.'

‘I can show you. I’m knitting him some too.’ They spent the next half-hour chatting about knitting while Mr Kennedy dozed in the corner.

All too soon it was time to say goodbye. She gave them a written note of her address and promised to stay in touch. Mr Kennedy shook her hand and gave her a light kiss on her cheek. Susan accompanied her to the door where they hugged each other before Betty stepped into the street and waved her goodbye with the happiest of smiles.

* * *

Betty and Jean arranged to meet at the tram stop for their first day as clippies. They headed for the front seats so they could watch everything. Neither had travelled regularly on trams so every journey was a novelty. They pointed to the shops they passed as they headed towards Burslem, then Tunstall and on to Goldenhill at the end of the line.

When the clippie came to ask for their fares, Betty piped up. ‘We’re clippies now, starting today. Dunner think we have ter pay, do we?’

‘Betty!’

‘Mr Adams said as much, didn’t he, Jean?’

‘Hello ducks. And yer’d be quite right an’ all. Yer dunner have ter pay no more. Me name’s Doris. Glad ter see yer. Yer’ll have a good time. Mark me words.’

‘Well, I’m Betty and this here’s Jean,’ Betty laughed.

‘I’ll see yer around then, duckies.’

Doris moved on and the two girls grinned at each other.

They chatted away as passengers ascended and descended from the tramcar along its journey. By the time it arrived at Goldenhill depot, there was only one other person left, a smartly dressed young woman, whose clothes certainly hadn't come from a cheap stall in the market. The type of person that would put Jean on edge.

'Good morning,' the woman said.

'Morning, duck,' said Betty, deliberately. The woman didn't look like anyone's 'duck'. Why had she got off the tram at the depot and not the shops?

'Er . . . good morning, Miss.' Jean sounded nervous.

'Are you here to be a conductor?' The woman asked.

Betty nodded.

'I am too. I'm pleased to meet you. I'm Connie Copeland.'

Betty nearly choked. *This . . . this smartly dressed woman . . . a clippie . . . well, I never.* She was dumbstruck, leaving Jean introduce herself. Finally, her mouth started to work again. 'I'm Betty Dean. You really going to be a clippie?' She grabbed the woman's hand to shake it. 'You look a bit posh for it.'

'It's all so new, isn't it? I'm a bit nervous.'

'It was Betty what persuaded me to come,' said Jean. 'She said it'd be a good laugh.'

'Better than being beholden to some toff and never having no time for yerself, Jean duck —'

Betty clapped a hand over her mouth. Wave upon wave of flushes covered her face. She'd only been in the depot minutes and already she'd put her foot in it. The first day in a new job was not the time to go upsetting people.

Thankfully, Mr Adams chose that moment to arrive. He took them upstairs to a small room on the first floor and bade them sit while he went through a long speech about the Potteries Tramway Company.

All the drivers were men, and they were in overall charge of the tram although when the tramcar was moving, the clippie would oversee the saloon.

'I'm sure we are all looking forward to working on the trams, aren't we, girls?' In her excitement, Betty couldn't help but chip in. 'If yer need any drivers, I wouldn't mind giving it a go, an' all' No harm in telling him, was there?

'Like I said, Miss er . . .'

She wouldn't let go of the smile that was now fixed to her face. 'Betty Dean.'

'As I said, all our drivers are men. The company believes driving trams is not a job for ladies. Turning the tram and changing the trolley pole in the trolley head is far too heavy work for ladies to consider.'

Betty looked at the others. Even Connie had a blank look on her face. No doubt it would mean something eventually.

There was more information about the job, the shifts, rests, and pay packets. They had tests on numbers and handing out change. Jean was the slowest, probably due to nerves as she fumbled through her bag for the right coins. Finally, Mr Adams asked how they would handle a drunken passenger. Betty thought carefully. She had an idea what he was looking for and decided to go with that rather than say what she would do given the chance.

'I would summon the driver, Mr Adams. You said the driver would always be a man? And that he would always be in charge?'

There, it proved she was listening.

'And you would be quite right, Miss Dean.'

Betty beamed. She had told him what he wanted to

hear. It was clear Mr Adams was a man who thought it his duty to take care of ladies.

Next, they were taken into the yard and given a tour round a tramcar. It didn't last long as the PTC only ran single-deck tramcars. They were shown the driver's compartment and reminded they would not have cause to enter it.

The last thing they did was report to Miss Emily Norton, a lady clerk in the office, who measured them for their uniforms. Then they would be true clippies. Once they were in uniform, the differences in class would be less noticeable, but still there. Connie was sure to have seen the holes at the cuffs of her sleeves and would never have worn a coat with holes in it.

The three of them caught the same tram back home, Connie to Burslem while Betty and Jean continued to Hanley. Connie smiled and waved when she got off as the tramcar pulled away.

'What d'yer think of her, Jean?'

'Seems all right.'

'She's a toff. And always will be.'

'Yes, but she's nice. Doesn't seem bossy'

'Wonder why she wants to be a clippie? She could likely have any job she wants.'

'She's probably got her reasons, Betty.'

'Mmm.'

'She might need the money. Lots of people are suffering money problems at the minute, what with the war an' all.'

'As long as she doesn't come the lady bountiful.'

'Oh no, I don't think she will. Wouldn't it be lovely if we could become friends, the three of us?'

'Us? Friends with a toff?' Betty snorted.

Her mind went straight back to Stowford House

and the Delhavens. That's what being a toff meant. Throwing their weight around and ignoring people who weren't like them. She supposed she should give Connie a chance to prove she wasn't like that. And if she was, Betty would prove *she* wasn't there to be ignored.

* * *

A letter was waiting for her when she got home. Mrs Clowes had left it on the sideboard in the hall. It was Duncan's handwriting. She ran lightly up the stairs to her room. Still in her uniform, she ripped open the envelope.

A rush of excitement ran through her, happy to receive a letter that hopefully did not contain bad news. She began to read.

24th February 1917

Dear Betty,

I hope you are in good health.

We have just returned to the rear after our second period on the line. I can't tell you where, they would only cross it out. There is not a lot going on here. Both sides regularly take pot-shots at each other. We have dugouts in each gun position under the ground where we sleep and take turns on guard duty, so we never really get a good night's sleep. When we are back in the rear, sleep is the main thing we do.

I will take you up on your offer of socks. Keeping our feet warm and dry is very important. We have a foot inspection every week. You can get trench foot, whatever that is. Sergeant said I would know when I got it.

The routine of life is simple here. We get three meals a day when in the rear but at the front it's more hit and miss. We also have a tot of rum, which I usually give to someone else as I don't drink.

Your new job was quite a surprise. I never expected you to say you were working on a tram, but on reflection I think you will enjoy it. Not sure about Jean though. Arthur said she was like a school mistress. It's nice to know employers are honouring their commitment to hold jobs over for us soldiers at the end of the war.

I understand your problem with Hannah. You need to work to live, but you can't work with children. Women have children and their husbands look after them with no allowance made for the results of war. It was the same when my mother died. Father was only thirty years old. But Grandma took us both in and looked after Dad, so he could work. It's what I said in my last letter — you need a family around you.

Thank you for asking about Arthur. The last time I saw him was in Woolwich. I shipped out before him. He's in a different brigade. I'll write to him to see if he's well. He didn't say much but, like a lot of us, when you get to talk to him, he fears what might happen. Most of us try not to think about it. They have a saying out here: 'If the bullet has your name on it then there is nothing you can do.' Unfortunately, Arthur is a worrier.

I hope you liked Susan. She is a good knitter, by the way, so will probably give you some help if you want it. She is sending socks as well.

I'll post this letter now and then get some sleep if Fritz allows us!

Take care of yourself and be careful on the trams.

Best Wishes
Duncan

She clasped her hands to her chest. He was thoughtful and kind, particularly to Arthur, and even nicer than she'd originally thought. She was glad he wanted to keep in touch.

28

March 1917

Betty had been surprised how quickly they had all settled to their new lives — because that was what it was for each of them. Even Jean looked to be enjoying the work. They got on well with the drivers, most of whom were older men. Inside the tram as it trundled through the six towns, Betty felt she was in her own little world. Most of the passengers were obliging and responded well to a smiling face. The ticket machine slung over one shoulder and her heavy money bag over the other caused bruises by the end of her shifts. She folded her handkerchief under the strap, which held it in place until, gradually, her skin became accustomed to it. At night, she soaked her feet in a bowl to help them relax. Who would've thought walking up and down a tram all day would be so painful?

As regards Connie, who was so different to them, Betty had her doubts at the start — a toff playing at work. She had it in mind Connie would try to supervise the rest of them and there was no way Betty would put up with that. As it was, Connie had been quiet and hadn't pushed herself forward. She had even talked about soaking her feet too! Surprisingly, Connie talked a lot about her friend Ginnie who was a working-class girl, like her and Jean. It seemed to Betty Connie deliberately chose friends who were worse off than herself. Had something happened in her past that made her choose to ignore her own class?

Betty was dying to ask but couldn't find the right time or words. After all, she wouldn't want people prying into her own affairs, would she?

It was when they sat around waiting for their money to be balanced with the tickets handed out they got talking about themselves. When it was Betty's turn, she shrugged. A job was a stop-gap between school and wedlock, and all she needed was a husband with some money in his pocket.

* * *

Betty had not made a mistake in becoming a clippie. She loved every minute of it. How much better than being in service. In her next letter to Duncan, she asked if he enjoyed her light-hearted banter, given the trauma he was going through. He had assured her he looked forward to receiving news that helped him to forget, however briefly, the world around him. She told him of the test she had been put through after her first week when a horrible woman gave her a dressing down on the tram in full hearing of one of the inspectors, Inspector Caldwell. He was very particular. Strangely, there seemed to be some clashing of wills between him and Connie. Perhaps no one had told her what to do before.

This woman might have spoiled everything, but it turned out she was part of the test! Her friends, Jean, who he had met, and Connie, who was a toff, were put through the same test. They laughed about it later, but at the time the result mattered too much. She was, she said, more than happy to have controlled her temper throughout and had a feeling that might have been the whole purpose of the charade. She was smiling as she described it, replaying it in her mind. The rest of the job was going well too, although there was more paperwork to complete, and balancing of tickets against the money she had collected.

She told him how much she had enjoyed meeting his family, and how she had enjoyed chatting and knitting with Susan, with his father reading a book and smoking a pipe in a chair opposite. She got the feeling he enjoyed listening to their prattling although he did his best to pretend he was nodding off. His father seemed a lovely man and she had arranged more sock-knitting lessons with Susan, so Duncan was not to worry about his feet getting cold for he was sure to be inundated with them and should never run out.

Lastly, she chatted about Hannah. He always mentioned her in his letters.

29

April 1917

Another letter arrived in early April. Duncan was certainly keeping his promise. She opened it eagerly and began to read.

8th April 1917

My dear Betty,

Thank you for your letter. It arrived a few days ago. We have been on the move since my last letter, so yours took a little bit of time to catch up with me. We have been pursuing the Germans who have retreated to something called the Hindenburg line. It is named after their top general. The retreat started in the middle of March. We got word we would all be moving and we knew something was up. Some thought the Huns were giving up, others that it was a trap. Well, now we know. All the Germans have done is moved back to strong defences and have shortened their line. We have now dug in and are back to the usual routine.

The battalion we support is made up of men from all over Britain and Ireland. They are a tough bunch. Some of the best soldiers we have, according to them. We get to mix when we are off the line and a lot of them have seen plenty of action. They know what they are doing.

It sounds as if you are really enjoying your new job. At least you are getting plenty of fresh air on those trams, and I hope they provided you with warm clothes!

Things are warming up in every sense around here. Spring seems to have arrived, although the ground is still quite muddy. It means military activity will start to increase.

We had our first casualty a couple of days ago.

Most of the infantry units were trained together and now fight together. In the artillery, it is different. I thought we would fight as a unit, but I am the only one from my artillery class in this brigade. It was a strange sensation relying on men I hardly knew. However, it has been nearly two months now and I feel I am part of the battery and my own gun team have accepted me. I think they trust I can aim the gun properly, which means they are not wasting their time. Our gunnery officer is efficient and decisive, and the sergeant keeps us all on the straight and narrow.

It is two o'clock in the morning and I am writing this letter by the light of the moon. Do you think that sounds romantic? I think you might laugh at that! We are on strict blackout so the Germans can't see our position. We might even get orders to move to a new location. There is no advance warning, and we must be ready to move quickly.

Every so often flare rockets are sent up to illuminate the area. This is a constant activity as both sides try to catch reconnaissance patrols, sappers and engineers, and snipers out in the open.

Rumours are going round we are going to get a 48-hour pass, which will be most welcome. Most of the lads will go to the nearest town and get drunk or visit places ladies shouldn't know about. I won't be doing any of this, so you needn't worry about me!

Please take care of yourself.

Love
Duncan

Betty lowered the letter to her knee. It sounded so bleak out there, wondering when it was all going to end. She thought about the men who had no one writing to them and the loneliness they must feel when there was nothing but men, guns, and mud.

* * *

In her next letter, Betty was able to tell Duncan how pleasing it was to be treated like a grown woman at last. In service, she felt she was treated like a girl, and being with Iris was like being with part of the family. Each morning, she walked into the depot with her back straight and her head high. It was the best feeling in the world.

Most of all, she had loved to read his letters, particularly the one where he mentioned he was writing to her by the light of the moon. How wonderful it sounded and how romantic!

She enjoyed the freedom the new job had given her. She had time to herself every day and a full day off every week.

She was on her way to Wellington Road to see Hannah when she saw Martha. They had not crossed paths since that awful day when she had told her former friend she was expecting. Should she continue walking and avoid eye contact, or cross the road and duck out of the need to speak? Martha had plainly seen her. Her face was flushed pink and Betty would have loved to say hello, but she still felt the sting of Martha's last words to her. In the end, Betty crossed over to the other side of the street, leaving Martha to continue her journey alone. It was cowardly and she cossed herself for her lack of confidence

Afterwards, she wondered what Martha would have done if she had stayed on her side of the road.

* * *

When another letter from Duncan arrived towards the end of the month, Betty was delighted. She hadn't expected one so soon. Even Mrs Clowes had remarked when she picked it up from the hall.

'My word, Betty. You seem popular in some quarters. The young man is obviously quite taken with you.'

She grinned. Mrs Clowes was fishing for information, but Betty refused to tell her, enjoying her power to annoy the older woman. When she first moved in, they had spoken only in greetings. Now, they passed the time of day together and Mrs Clowes would try to whittle out updates on the state of Betty's love life. As the custodian of the post, Mrs Clowes would always know when someone had been in touch with her lodger, giving her the upper hand.

'I'm a bit rushed at the minute. Terrah, Mrs Clowes.'

With that, Betty ran quickly up the stairs to avoid further questioning. Mrs Clowes was a one, there was no doubt about it.

She unbuttoned her coat and slung it over the chair, and sat on the bed to read Duncan's letter.

21st April 1917

Dear Betty,

Some of us have been given seven days away from the front to learn some new artillery tactics. I thought I would write to you, now I have a bit more free time. We have had some casualties and some replacements, so I am not the new man any more. I am an old hand to these men, Betty; everyone out here soon becomes an old hand.

Susan wrote to me saying she really enjoys your visits.

I am glad you are still enjoying your job. I suppose, like any job, it starts to become routine. At least there is one thing you could say about this job — it's never routine.

You cannot believe how much I look forward to your letters. Although we have only known each other for a few months, you are in my thoughts constantly. I have never felt this way about someone before. There you go — I've said it. I am starting to fall for you, Betty Dean. I know they say absence makes the heart grow fonder, but I really think we could make a go of it. What do you think?

One thing I ask is whatever your reply, we continue to write to each other. I understand what I have said may be something you were not prepared for. You may not want to get involved with me so soon after Hannah's father. But if anything were to happen to me, I would've hated the thought I had not told you my feelings.

I will close for now. It's back to the classroom!

All my love
Duncan

Hearing how much he looked forward to her letters and was constantly in his thoughts had Betty's heart pounding and the most exciting — he was falling for her!

She sat back and read it over and over. *All my love*, he wrote. She savoured the words. But was it too soon to think about becoming more involved? She knew him — and yet she didn't. Was it love or loneliness he was feeling? How could she explain to him in a letter that Alastair was Hannah's father, that he was still alive, and that he was violent? It would be easier to say nothing. If they started walking out when he came home, she would have to tell him. Would he be disappointed she had lied to him all this time, however long it might be?

It was a quandary she never thought she would be in. The problem was: what should she do about it?

30

May 1917

Everything was going well at work and at home. Hannah had settled in with Betty's mother, which was quite a relief. Betty ached with sadness at being parted from her daughter. She had thought she would get over it, but every time she left Hannah, she did so with a tear in her eye. She reminded herself she was doing it for best, as the alternative — the workhouse — was too horrible to contemplate.

Betty had a couple of letters from Duncan and one from Jeffrey. They were both fine, thank goodness. She wrote back swiftly, although she didn't have a great deal to say, just a few words of encouragement to show she was thinking of them. One event did surprise her, but it was nothing to do with either of them.

It was the day of Jean's twenty-first birthday and she had asked Betty to call by. Betty had promised to make Jean up to show off her best features, curl her hair, which was usually tied in an unbecoming bun, and add a red lipstick to bring out the generosity of her mouth.

'Jean, duck, there's only one reason I can think of for a girl to get herself all done up and that's because she wants a certain man ter notice her.'

'Can't a girl decide such things for herself? Doesn't have ter be a man, even though *yer* might think so.' She wriggled uncomfortably.

'Since when have you bin such an expert?'

Jean looked away.

'Come on, have yer got a bloke or not?'

Jean's mouth opened and closed.

'You bloomin' well have, haven't yer?'

Jean was about to speak but Betty held up her hand. 'No lies — if you haven't got someone then yer've got yer eye on one. Yer can't fool me.'

'I'm not.' Jean hesitated. 'There *is* someone —'

'I knew it!'

'Let me finish . . . there is someone. But he doesn't know.'

Betty frowned. 'Haven't yer talked to him?'

'Course not. Supposing he doesn't like me?'

'Well, the way you're going, yer'll never find out, will yer?'

'It would make life . . . difficult.'

'Do I know him?'

When the colour rushed back into Jean's face, Betty clapped her hands. 'I do, don't I?'

Jean nodded miserably. 'You can't say nothing.'

Betty sat back, arms folded, with a cheerful grin. 'So, who is it?'

'Mr Adams.'

Betty clicked her fingers. 'Stephen Adams? I knew it. Isn't he a bit old? He walks with a stick. How'll yer be able to dance with him?'

'For one thing, he's not old. He's only thirty and he walks with a stick because of serving his country in 1915.'

It was Betty's turn to blush.

'Dancing's not everything, Betty regardless of what *you* might think.'

'I didn't mean to have a go. He's all right.'

'You can't say nothing. He's not allowed ter be . . . friendly with his staff. Promise me yer'll keep yer mouth shut?'

Betty nodded. So, Jean was smitten with Mr Adams! When she thought about it, she believed he could be the perfect man for her pal. In all the dealings she'd had with him at work, Betty had found him considerate and a gentleman. She smiled inwardly. Jean had been so anxious to keep her feelings for Stephen quiet, she hadn't bothered to ask Betty about her prospects. Best keep it that way, for now.

As she walked home, she thought about Duncan. She still hadn't written back to him since he mentioned he was falling for her. What should she say? Of course she liked him . . . a lot . . . but should she encourage him? Would it not be best to wait until he returned and then think about their relationship? In some ways, she felt she was getting to know him better than she would by meeting him in person. Perhaps she should slow things down a little — continue to write, but not be too communicative on her feelings. After Alastair, she felt she really couldn't trust herself until she knew him better.

* * *

Betty took out her writing paper to reply to Duncan. They had been writing to each other for less than six months and had only seen each other three times. How could she be sure it wasn't the loneliness of his current life talking? She had thought she knew Alastair, and look how that turned out. She couldn't go through it again. It was best to tell him she was happy to take things slowly and see how it went. She believed everybody needed to be able to talk to someone in times like these and she was so glad to count him as a friend. She tried to be as positive as she could, not wanting to let him down but needing to be as truthful as she could.

She changed the subject and told him poor Connie had been assaulted on the tram since her last letter, and had been greatly shaken up by it. She wondered what he would think of her news. Would he be shocked and tell her to find a job less dangerous or would he believe women should have the right to jobs and not to feel threatened? If it was the former, it would be pot calling the kettle black, given the job he was doing.

She told him receiving letters was a good way of getting to know people.

He was beginning to sound like a nice bloke but she was not quite ready to give that kind of commitment to any man.

* * *

A new driver, Joe Cumberbatch, was transferred from the Longton Depot to Goldenhill to cover driver shortages.

Doris, a mother figure to the rest because she had been there the longest, knew him from when she worked at Longton. She said he was a well-known trouble-maker and a big union man. Whether, in her eyes, they were one and the same Betty couldn't say. He had an eye for the ladies. Perhaps Doris was jealous she was too old to attract his attention.

He jumped down from the tram and strolled towards them. He looked handsome, younger than the rest of the drivers, perhaps in his early twenties.

He was tall and slender, and, when he removed his cap, Betty's eyes were immediately drawn to his black hair and dark sideburns. If it wasn't for the sideburns, he might have looked even younger.

'This is Joe Cumberbatch come from Longton to help us out.' He had travelled on Jean's tram and she quickly introduced each of them in turn.

'Nice to meet yer, Joe. Are yer planning ter be here long?' Betty raised her eyebrows.

'Might be. I'm covering for those blokes you lost last week. Always like to help where I can.'

More banter followed.

Betty watched and listened. His blue eyes swept over each of them in turn. He was so attractive. He was bound to be married or courting. *Don't be greedy, Betty*, she thought, as Duncan filled her mind with guilt.

'. . . and you believe that do yer?' Joe was saying and he was talking to Connie.

'I do believe it, Mr Cumberbatch and might I remind you that you have only just arrived here. I believe I know them both better than you. And you should get your tram out if you want to keep your job.'

'You're posh for a clippie! That was some speech. I'll consider myself told off, ma'am. Fancy joining the union?'

At that point, Connie turned on her heel and left.

'Come on Joe, we'd best get on our way,' said Betty.

'Posh for a clippie, isn't she?'

'What d'yer mean? You saying as us clippies aren't up ter much?'

'Course not. She looks the sort of person who would shop in Burton & Dunn's rather than the market.'

Hands on hips, Betty tried to chastise him, playfully. 'She started same day as us in February, so we don't know her well. But from what we've seen of her, she's nice.'

Joe nodded and clocked on before springing into his cab at the front of the tram. Betty walked round to her platform and stepped aboard. Slowly, the tram pulled out of the depot and headed for their first stop.

* * *

On the return journey, Betty and Joe had a ten-minute break in Stoke so they stood outside chatting.

'Thought as I might stretch my legs,' Joe said, running on the spot for a few seconds. 'So, what's a smart girl like you doing working on the trams?'

'Oh, you know. I was in service mostly. But, as the war went on, I decided I wanted summat more interesting. I wanted to meet people, get experience of doing more. Who knows what'll happen when it's all over? I want to live for the moment.'

Betty felt as if she was answering questions to get a job, but she wanted to make a good impression on him. She might be writing to Duncan, but there was no reason why she shouldn't get to know Joe too.

'What about you? Where d'yer live?'

'Longton. Just off Railway Street. D'yer know it?'

'I don't know Longton. Only where the tramcar goes. I come from the other side of The Potteries. I'm boarding out now up Hanley. How long have you been at Longton Depot?'

'Two years just over. I was working in Birmingham and when the PTC advertised for drivers after blokes enlisted, I decided to give it a go. Nothing to lose.'

'Doris said you're a trouble-maker and one for the ladies. Is it true?'

'No, I support people who have problems and help them where I can. Sometimes you need to annoy others if you're seeking justice, Betty. As for the ladies, they need my help too and it stands to reason I have to get to know them — but not in the way Doris thinks. I've always been a union man. Seen too many good men lose their jobs because of the bosses. Without the working man all businesses would be nothing, yet they treat us like dirt.'

'They're all right at the PTC. Treat us very well.'

'That's because they need you. Without you they couldn't run the trams. You wait until this war is over and all the men come back. Then you'll see what the bosses are like.'

'I never thought of it like that, Joe.' Betty was quiet for a moment. 'So, what more can yer tell me about yerself? Have yer got any family?'

'Mum and Dad live in Birmingham. That's where I come from.'

'I thought you didn't come from these parts, cos of your accent,' she smiled. 'So yer've not bin in the war?'

'No.' He started to walk away. 'Better get going,' he said over his shoulder, not waiting for an answer.

31

June 1917

Joe and Betty were sitting in the rest room waiting for their shift to begin.

'Do yer really believe unions can make a difference, Joe?

'Of course I do. For the first time in their lives, lots of women are getting paid the same wages as men. They've seen the differences in pay and in the way they're treated. Stands to reason they're beginning to wonder why men get so much more and why women aren't allowed to do men's work. Women are proving to the world, and to themselves, they can do whatever they set their minds to. It's a golden opportunity, Betty.'

'But there's lots of jobs women can't really do. Heavy work and the like.' She could see their discussion excited him. His eyes had a brightness about them that made her want to understand more.

'Take us, for example. The PTC. What work did men do before the war?'

'All sorts I suppose. Conducting, driving, keeping the trams going, the office work —'

'Right. And what are women doing now?'

'Conducting and office work.'

He nodded. 'And?'

'Well, that's it . . . isn't it?'

'Why aren't they driving?'

'I asked Mr Adams if I could do some driving when I started. But he said it was too heavy for women, what with changing the pulleys an' all.'

'So why are there lady drivers in other parts of the country then? In Glasgow, for example. Don't you see, Betty? You women have your chance to prove you can do it.'

He was right. And if women did the same jobs as men, then it followed they should get the same wages.

'Is that what you're fighting for, Joe? For women?'

He nodded. 'But it's not all. If the bosses take on women to do men's work, but for less money, the bosses might well lower men's wages when they come back from the war. If women work for lower wages, why pay men more?'

'You're not thinking of helping women get their rights, you're protecting men's rights to higher wages.'

'Course not. Don't you see? The unions must protect all workers. It's not men against women, but workers against the bosses.'

32

August 1917

Wakes week, Monday

Wakes week in August, also known as Potters' week, was always looked forward to. It was a time when the potbanks shut down for annual maintenance and other such vital work. The Monday was also a public holiday, and both Betty and Joe were not working.

To the employees, it was a time of enjoyment and jollity. Lucky people who could afford such luxury as a few days away could catch a train to Blackpool or Llandudno to sample the sea air. Betty had no such luck, but a day out at Trentham Gardens would be a real treat, walking around the formal gardens and the huge lake, set against the backdrop of the enormously posh house.

It was the Friday before Wakes Monday and Betty hoped to persuade Joe to accompany her. It would be an ideal way of getting to know him and it wasn't every day a girl had the opportunity to have a good-looking man on her arm. Despite the exterior Joe often wore, she thought there was more to him than he allowed people to see. She had thought they were becoming friends and then, every so often, he seemed to shut her out as if the consequences of letting her get too close would be . . . problematic in some way.

She was chatting to Jean and Doris in the yard when Joe arrived, whistling. Already the sun had begun to warm up and he had his coat slung over one shoulder.

Doris folded her arms and tutted. 'Be a good idea if yer come to work dressed of a morning. Mr Adams won't like it.'

'I'm not officially at work until I clock on, Doris.'

'You're in uniform so yer should look the part. Dunner want people thinking we're dropping our standards now, especially them what do for the union.'

Joe tutted. 'You're a spoil sport, Doris.' Nevertheless, he slipped into his coat and added his cap. 'Meet with your approval now?'

Doris grinned while Betty stared at him. He did look good especially in his uniform. She couldn't let the chance go.

'Fancy coming out to the Wakes carnival tomorrow, Joe?'

Joe's eyebrows lifted. Jean nudged her and gave her a warning look, but she didn't care.

'Go on Joe, we could have such fun.'

He shook his shoulders. He must've seen her disappointment because he grinned. 'Course I'll come. Can't turn down a young lady now, can I?'

Betty nearly clapped her hands but stopped herself sharpish and tried to look demure.

'Come on then, Doris. Best be on our way.' Doris and Joe wandered off to their tram, with her muttering and Joe whistling, neither taking much notice of the other.

* * *

They arranged to meet at the corner shop on Jasper Street at eleven o'clock. Even Betty thought twice about asking Joe to call at the boarding house when they barely knew one another.

She took care in dressing. Since she had become a clippie, she had run up two new dresses in a red that set off her dark-brown curls. She wasn't fat. In her opinion, she was rounded and had lost some weight recently. It surprised her because she hadn't lost weight working in service. Possibly, now she was living by herself and responsible for her meals, she ate less of them. Whatever it was, she was more than pleased with the result after applying a new red lipstick enhancing the colour of the dress.

Rather than wear her coat, she slipped it over her arm, ready to be worn if she should need its warmth. She stepped out of her room and made her way downstairs just as Mrs Clowes entered the hall.

Betty gave her a warm smile. 'Morning, Mrs Clowes. Looks like a good day for the carnival.'

'That where you're off to?' Mrs Clowes sniffed. 'Dunner have no time to be gadding about meself.'

'It's only a few hours. Wouldn't do no harm if you was to have a bit of fun?'

'Too much to do, Miss Dean. But I'm sure you'll enjoy yerself any road. Yer look pretty as a picture.'

The compliment was unexpected. 'Thanks for saying, Mrs Clowes. Terrah then!'

She opened the front door and almost skipped along the road. Even so, she was relieved to see Joe waiting for her.

'Hello, Joe,' she said, shyly. He was all hers for a few hours and she would need to make the most of it.

'Good to see you Betty.' He smiled and she thought he too looked a little nervous.

'I've been so looking forward ter this. I love carnivals, don't you?'

He nodded vigorously. 'I do that.'

'Come on then.' She grabbed his hand and pulled him along.

Soon the iron gates of Hanley Park were in front of them, and beyond they could see the various rides, stalls and games that had been set up to tantalise visitors. A roundabout, dobby horses — oh, she loved the dobby horses — shooting ranges where men could show off their prowess . . . Those women lucky enough to have a man with them walked them proudly around the park.

Betty ran towards the dobby horses. 'Come on, Joe. This one first.' Her hair had come loose and was flying round her face. She forced it behind her ears with one hand and waved to her companion with the other.

'I don't know. Never been on one,' Joe shouted back but following her, nevertheless.

'Then you must give it a go. Come on!'

He protested but let himself be pulled along until he had no choice but to climb aboard one of the grand horses with exotic manes and decked with fancy bridles.

'Are you sure it's safe?'

'Dunner be a ditherer. Yer can't not try it. Jump on!'

She climbed aboard the nearest horse and Joe took one by her side. He grabbed hold of the vertical pole and held on as if his life depended on it. For a tiny moment her heart thumped. Should she be so forceful if he really didn't want to ride?

Too late. The horses moved, slowly at first, round and round, up and down as if they were taking part in an actual race. She couldn't take her eyes off him. He was laughing as she hadn't seen him laugh before.

She returned his laugh and knew he'd been joking about being scared.

'You liar! You were having me on,' she shouted above the music and the noise of the crowds around them. She couldn't be angry with him. The day was far too good to be wasted.

Laughs and jokes abounded. She had never enjoyed herself so much. She was lost in the fun of it all. And it was all down to Joe. It was close on five o'clock when he took her home. He didn't have to, but he did. When they arrived at the corner shop, Betty turned to him.

'Thanks for a lovely day. I've had such a good time.'

She stood still, watching him as the smile slowly left her face. His eyes seemed to burn with excitement. She moved her head closer to his, hoping he would lean to meet her. Their lips were only inches apart when he seemed to startle himself out of what must have been a reverie. He jumped backwards, his cheeks slightly flushed.

'What are you —'

Betty stopped at once. She had thought it was meant to . . . had she read it wrongly? Wasn't he going to kiss her?

She had to get away. She wasn't about to throw herself at him.

'I'm sorry, Betty,' he blurted out. 'I hope I haven't upset you. I don't know what I was thinking.'

Betty shook her head, her face drained. 'No, I . . . forget it, Joe.'

She turned and ran up Jasper Street and arrived at the front door, panting. She looked behind her. He hadn't followed.

Whatever had possessed her? She wasn't that awful to look at, was she?

After the day they had shared, a kiss seemed so natural. How could she look him in the face when she next saw him?

33

August 1917

Later in Wakes week

Betty had no idea what she would say to Joe. She kept her head down and hoped he wasn't going to be her driver for a few days.

At the end of the second day, she called into a couple of shops on her way home. Mrs Clowes was waiting for her when Betty opened the door.

'I've got a message for you, Miss Dean. A young chap called earlier today. Wanted a word, apparently. Said his name was Joe and you'd know what it was about.'

Betty could feel a burning sensation, first in her neck and gradually making its way up her face.

'Thanks, for telling me, Mrs Clowes.'

'You'll not be encouraging him to call on a regular basis, will you? Remember my rules.'

'I remember. It'll be summat to do with work. He's one of the drivers.'

Mrs Clowes nodded. 'I see. That's all right then. Just wanted to check.'

'Yes, Mrs Clowes.'

Betty did her best to smile and ran lightly up the stairs to her room.

Joe wanted to talk. It pleased her he had tried to speak to her. She wished he'd left a note. She would have to wait until tomorrow to find out what he wanted to say.

* * *

When she saw him the next morning, he was sitting on a barrel reading a letter. She was in two minds whether to speak, but he must have heard her because he looked up, his face pale.

'Hello Betty. I need to talk to you.'

He jumped to his feet and grabbed her hand, then pulled her towards the corner where the tools were stored.

'I wish you'd make up yer mind, Joe Cumberbatch. One minute yer pulling away from me and the next yer dragging me up a corner.' Betty pulled her hand away.

'You've got it all wrong. I need to explain.'

'You've got two minutes to tell me why I shouldn't just go and leave yer?'

He stuffed the letter into his pocket. 'I'm sorry I upset you the other day. I never meant to.'

'You didn't upset me.' She couldn't let him know how she had felt as she left him.

'It wasn't I didn't want to kiss you Betty . . .'

'Don't say anything yer don't mean. It's not your fault if you don't have feelings for me.'

'I do have feelings — but not the sort you're looking for. Meet me outside the Empire Picture House at eight tonight and I'll explain.'

* * *

She was ten minutes early and was able to watch people dressed in their finery walking up the street towards the centre of the town. Her belly was full of knots. Whatever Joe wanted to say sounded serious.

She turned in the opposite direction, like a soldier on sentry duty, towards Stoke and watched people, mainly women, but some arm-in-arm with men in uniform. They were the lucky ones. Women dressed in furs covering long skirts, and others in everyday wear, heading for the picture palaces or a good old knees-up.

'Hello, Betty.'

She jumped as Joe's voice came close to her ear. 'Oh! I must've bin miles away.'

'Penny for them?'

She shook her head. 'No, they're not worth a farthing, never mind a penny.'

'Can we walk for a little while?' he said quietly. 'I have something important I need to tell you.'

He held out his arm for her to link it and they set off, both staring ahead as they walked up Piccadilly towards Market Square. More people were loitering here, in the centre of the town. It had been good fun to go to the carnival with Joe — until she had attempted to kiss him. Whatever possessed her? She liked him, but there was Duncan to consider.

'I don't believe we can chat out here, Joe. Would you like ter come ter mine if you want a proper talk?'

'I thought your landlady'd chuck you out if you brought men back?'

'I'm only talking about one man, Joe.' She tried to look affronted.

'Sorry. You caught me by surprise.'

Betty relaxed and returned her arm to his. 'Mrs Clowes is out tonight. I'll sneak you in. We can go out again soon as we've finished talking.'

They were almost at Betty's house and, as she had said, there was no sign of Mrs Clowes. Betty put her finger to her mouth, and tiptoed towards the door. Joe came up close behind her. Silently, she turned the key in the lock and opened it. They crept upstairs and, once inside her room, she let go of the breath she'd been holding.

By the look on his face, he wasn't impressed. Still, she wasn't planning to ask him to move in with her. 'It's all right, Joe. We must've looked like a couple of sleuths off the films.'

He grinned. 'It's small, isn't it? Do you like it here?'

'Don't need much when it's just me and I'm at work all day.'

'I suppose not.'

She slipped out of her coat. 'Come on Joe, take yer coat off, make yourself comfortable.' She waved him to the chair. 'What did you want to tell me?'

Whatever he had to say seemed important. Maybe he thought her feelings for him went much deeper than they did, and he wasn't ready.

'I want us to be friends.'

'We are, Joe.'

He stared into her eyes, his own eyes bright. He tried to speak but the words wouldn't come.

'— I don't know if I can tell you. I thought I could, but now, I'm not sure.'

'Why Joe? Why can't yer?'

He shook his head. 'You don't know the half of it.'

'But I'm willing to try if you are. I won't say nothing to the others.'

He stood up quickly. 'It won't work. I can tell you now.'

'How can yer be so sure?'

'I am a homosexual. I do not like women. I like men.'

Betty put her hand to her mouth, mainly because he had said the word, 'sexual'. She tried to speak. She hadn't heard of such a thing before. A man that liked to be with men rather than women. How did that work? It explained why she had never seen him, even in the beginning, with a woman, or a man, for that matter, despite what Doris had said.

There was a long pause.

'I don't understand.'

Joe looked serious. 'Listen, Betty, what I am about to tell you is against the law so if you tell anyone else then I could go to prison or be sent to a special hospital. You have got to promise me, on your life, you will never tell a soul.'

Betty's heart stopped. 'I promise I will never tell anybody. You can trust me, Joe.'

He paused for a few seconds. The room was quiet. The sun had begun to set, and an eerie glow lit up the room.

'Do you understand what homosexual means, Betty.'

'No . . . not really . . . maybe . . . but whatever it is, it sounds wrong.'

There followed the most embarrassing five minutes of their lives while Joe explained to Betty what being homosexual meant. At the end, Betty felt her face was the same colour as the setting sun. She fought to regain her composure.

'I promise, Joe, I will never tell anyone what you have told me. I don't think I would dare even if I wanted to.'

'You're a great girl, but you're just like a sister to me.'

A sister!

'You were the sister I always wanted but I misjudged the situation. We got on so well from the start. I thought you were interested in my union and political views. The thing is, Betty, you have good potential for my sort of work. You are intelligent and you can talk to people. You could be a force to be reckoned with. The union movement needs people like you.'

She never expected such words from him. 'I do want to make summat of meself but it's difficult for women to be taken seriously. Let alone a working-class girl who left school at thirteen.'

He took hold of her hands and stared earnestly into her eyes. 'You need to believe in yourself, Betty. 'We are still mates, aren't we?'

She nodded.

He left soon after. She followed him down the stairs and he stood back while she opened the front door.

'Goodbye, Joe.'

He kissed her forehead, gently. 'See you tomorrow, Betts.'

'I'll think about everything you said.'

She walked back upstairs slowly. She made a cup of tea and sat in the chair Joe had recently vacated, her hands taking warmth from the cup.

She had prepared herself for his refusal because he wasn't in love with her. She had prepared herself he might be overcome with lust, and she might have to fight him off. What she wasn't prepared for was the possibility he didn't fancy women at all.

* * *

The day after he told her, she was reluctant to go into work not knowing what her reaction would be. The simple truth was she didn't know men could have feelings . . . about other men. Joe wasn't going to be her driver for the next few days and that made it easier. Everybody went about their business. It was just a normal day.

The more she thought about Joe's revelation, the more it fitted into place. Since she had first met him, she had thought part of him was too shy to walk out with her. She had tried to put him at ease, but he never made any approach. He seemed caught up in his work. He was always talking about it and the war, and how it would change things for the working class.

Now she knew what was behind his behaviour she was shocked and uncomfortable, but he was still her friend Joe. It must have taken a lot to open up to her. She should count it an honour he had spoken of it at all.

34

August 1917

She had not heard from Duncan for so long, she thought he had taken umbrage at her last letter for hinting at slowing down their relationship. So when a letter finally did arrive, she snatched in off the tray on the cupboard and shot up to her room. She felt the envelope, wondering how much he had to say.

11th August 1917

Dear Betty,

Hope you are all right and everything is fine back in The Potteries? They keep us busy out here. We constantly move the guns around to prevent the Germans from getting a fix on our positions. At the beginning of July, the whole division was moved to a new location. Almost immediately we started to stockpile shells, so we knew there was something in the offing.

Our division took part on the opening day with an attack on [redacted]*. We had quite a bit of success at the beginning, but in the afternoon the heavens opened and the whole battlefield became a quagmire. We tried out a new system of firing, which seemed to work well.*

I've spent the last week at an aid station and field hospital recovering from an injury in the shoulder from a piece of shrapnel. I didn't bother to write to you or my family as it was a routine injury, and I couldn't hold a pen. Once the shrapnel was taken out and the bone had a chance to heal, I was back on the line. I was told again that infection was more dangerous than the wound, and to keep it clean. Fat chance out here! It gives me no problems now, but the sergeant said to watch out in the winter.

There was another reason I have not written before now. I was disappointed by your reply to my last letter. Your letter seemed so reserved, I concluded you are not interested in our friendship going further.

I will of course continue to write these letters as you've become a good friend to me. But I think your last letter has made it clear you do not wish for us to become any more than friends.

This war does not lend itself to slow and measured relationships like we have been used to in the past. The maxim is: 'If I don't say what I think today, I may never get an opportunity.'

Well, that's all for now.

Your friend,
Duncan

Betty read his letter with tears in her eyes. He had been injured! And the last he had heard from her was she wanted to slow their relationship down. Her heart thumped as she read the words, almost taking her breath away. No wonder he hadn't written. The next bit was worrying, too. He had indeed taken her letter to mean she was no longer interested in him, in that way. The frostiness of his letter pricked at her heart. She was so stupid. Once she had committed the words to paper, she couldn't undo them again.

She felt sick as she thought about him reading her letter and then, finally, responding to her in such an off-hand way. In his eyes, he had given her what she had asked for. But was it really what she wanted and, if it wasn't, how could she put things to rights between them?

* * *

Betty knew her reply to Duncan's letter would be of huge importance and she took a few days to think before writing back. She was desperately in need of advice and wished she had told Jean about her letters from Duncan, or better still, that she could talk to Martha or even Iris. But she had to work this out for herself.

How could she make things clear to Duncan when she wasn't clear about her true feelings? How would she feel if he disappeared out of her life? She held her head with both hands, as if to keep hold of her thoughts.

This was no good. She thought about the Duncan she had left on the platform at Stoke station and wasn't ready to let go of him — not yet.

She wrote the letter carefully, running back over each word to check it was what she was meaning to say. She mentioned his injury and the guns, and pleaded with him to take care in the trenches. She told him how difficult it was to talk about feelings in a letter and it was so easy to say something that could be misinterpreted. She was happy if their friendship grew closer, but at a pace she could cope with. She felt she needed to be strong in reminding him she had Hannah to think about, although she wasn't using her as an excuse.

She closed the letter by telling him how much she looked forward to receiving his next letter.

* * *

Betty continued to be paired up with Joe, causing much amusement with Jean and Connie. In fact, it suited her this way because she could pretend she was chasing Joe. Since starting work at the PTC she had kept her private life hidden from everyone to avoid questions about it. Now, she could have them believe he was her sweetheart. She mentioned it to him, casually, and he had no objections, probably because she could act as his shield, should the need arise.

They spent a lot of time in each other's company but avoided the company of others. She quizzed him about the union, what their role was, and what it could do for women like her. It made her wonder what would happen to her when the war ended. Having had this taste of freedom, how could she possibly go back to the girl she was? It would be like setting a caged bird free for a while and then expecting it to return quietly.

* * *

It was nearly a month before she heard back from Duncan. During that time she thought about him a lot. There was no doubt in her mind she liked him, but the extent of that liking was difficult when they could only meet through letters. She must hope they could continue to write until they were able to get to know each other in person.

She grew increasingly anxious as the days passed by, wondering whether he would forgive her truthfulness regarding her feelings. She visited the Kennedys in the hope they had received word — they hadn't. She tried to tell herself this must be good news but it was difficult to believe.

Then, at last, the waiting was over. She picked up the envelope from Mrs Clowes with glee, much to that lady's amusement.

'You'll have a happier look on yer face once you've read your letter, I'll bet.'

Betty laughed. Sometimes, it was good to have a nosy neighbour.

31st August 1917

Dear Betty,

I seem to have put my foot in it. I did not mean to sound cool on our relationship or to upset you in anyway. I can make no excuses; I can now understand how difficult it is to carry out a friendship via letters. You are right in the points you make; I cannot see your face or hear your voice. I can only interpret what you're trying to say. But I still feel the same about you. That has not changed.

You need to understand although we are busy physically out here, our minds have plenty of chances to mull over problems, and you can talk yourself into thinking something is a lot worse than it is.

I am a person who tends to take things at face value. I am not good at reading hidden meanings in what people say. I suppose I have a similar problem when it comes to written communication. Betty, I would ask if you have something to say then just say it. I will not get offended at the directness. In fact, it will make things much easier.

Like I said above, I still feel the same about you and I want you to understand when I say I miss you, I am also including Hannah in my thoughts.

I fully agree with you that we should take things slowly. I think I was impatient to make sure you knew how I felt. Betty, there's little chance out here to meet women, but back home, and especially now you're working on the trams, I worry you might find somebody else, and I wanted to let you know how I felt. I didn't realise you were worried we were taking things too quickly.

From now on, we will be one good friend writing to another. None of us know what is going to happen and while that is hanging over our heads any decisions we make will be tainted by this war. I also think when we meet again, which cannot come too soon for me, we should talk about our feelings as openly as we can. Let's face it, we will know enough about each other, even though we've only met for such a short period of time.

Please be assured I want us to continue to write and I want us to be frank with each other, if we've got problems or things we want to say. The frankness helps me to cope with what I am going through.

I will close now, and I too will look forward to your next letter.

With love,
Duncan

Betty looked up from the letter with a sense of relief. She had been convinced she had upset or angered him so much by wanting to slow things down that he had decided to stop writing altogether. She had got herself into a relationship too quickly in the past, and was trying to be fair to him and to herself.

In thinking he might stop writing altogether, she had begun to understand how much she would miss his letters.

But all that was in the past. He was writing and she was happy. She must be careful in future on what she wrote about and how. If only the war would end, and he would come back, and they could begin to get to know each other properly. She was sure she would know quickly if he was the right man for her.

35

November 1917

In the depths of the winter months, it was easy to become despondent and this war certainly made everybody feel as if it would never end. If it was like that in The Potteries, how much worse must it be for all the men away from home, fighting. During the past few months, Duncan's letters had become more informative on his life over there and her heart went out to him. She knew he didn't tell his family as much as he told her. She had seen them a few times now, and knew this to be the case.

Betty had taken to reading *The Sentinel* more and more, hoping to pick up snippets of longed-for good news. In the autumn of 1917, there had been major battles around Ypres and especially at a place called Passchendaele. There had been lots of British casualties and the fight had been made worse by the torrential rain turning the roads and battlefields into quagmires. Duncan had said in one of his letters they were unable to move the artillery in support of an attack for several days because the mud was so bad.

At the beginning of December there had been a major battle at Cambrai, where tanks were used in large numbers. The newspapers hailed it as a great success.

Duncan's letters at this time lacked his usual cheerfulness and Betty realised his morale was suffering.

How could it not after so long?

The pain inside her grew with each letter, particularly when she read their sergeant had lost his leg, and Duncan had been made acting sergeant of the gun crew. Good news, but in terrible circumstances.

He asked about Hannah, and whether she was walking, which Betty loved. When he said he wasn't too sure when exactly babies began walking, Betty's heart went out to him.

Everyone was waiting for the war to end.

36

June 1918

Betty was on her way back from work and jumped off the tram at Shelton Church. A newspaper seller's placard read:

FRENCH STRIKE BACK —
Checking the thrust for Paris

She bought a copy of the special edition of *The Sentinel* and ran in the direction of Jasper Street. She hadn't received a letter from Duncan since 21st March, when his unit was been refitted and reorganised. It was only a few days later when heavy fighting broke out on the Western Front.

By the time she arrived she was out of breath and had to stop momentarily for fear she might collapse.

Although the newspapers often didn't tell the full story, it was impossible for them to hide the success the Germans were having on the Western front. During the spring, fresh troops released from the war with Russia and slow American involvement had left the German Army in a strong position. The Allies had been driven back towards Paris and the British had suffered setbacks all along their Front, especially in the north near a place called Arras. She had no idea where Duncan was thanks to all letters being censored.

In the last week of May a massive German surprise attack burst through the Allied lines around the Rivers Aisne and Marne. They advanced as close to Paris as they had done in 1914, with reports of many British prisoners and artillery pieces captured.

A shiver passed through her body. Betty, unable to bear not knowing whether Duncan was safe, called on Susan for news. There was none and neither had the family received the dreaded telegram from the war office. They both concluded no news was good news.

It had been a hard day at work and Betty was considering soaking her feet to ease their throbbing. There came a knock at her door. It was Mrs Clowes.

'Betty, there is a young lady downstairs in the hall asking for you.'

'Coming!' she shouted back. She hoped it wasn't Lily with some bad news about Hannah. She followed Mrs Clowes.

Susan stood in the hallway. Betty's legs buckled and she grabbed hold of the banister. Luckily, Mrs Clowes turned to steady her when she heard Betty's intake of breath.

'It's all right, it's good news,' Susan called. 'We've had word from Duncan.'

'I'll leave you two girls to talk.' Mrs Clowes clutched her chest, looking relieved and returned to her room.

'Come up, Susan.'

Once in Betty's room, Susan caught hold of her. 'I'm sorry if I frightened you but Father said you would want to know immediately.' She handed over the letter.

Betty skimmed through its contents. Duncan had written letters to them both, but because of the German Offensive, her letter must have gone astray or been lost. He had been in heavy fighting. But, following a lull in his area, he was no longer at the front. Betty's heart sang.

There was some other personal stuff he had written to Susan and his father, but it was enough for Betty to read Duncan's words on the page again.

Susan stayed a bit longer talking about how worried they had been.

It was getting late, so Betty took Susan home as she would have to change trams in Hanley or Stoke and it didn't feel right to send the girl out alone. Betty had a brief word with Mr Kennedy, who was quite chatty, before she left to catch the tram back home.

* * *

Betty wrote to Duncan that night, to say how thankful she was he was safe. She didn't say she and Susan had shared a few tears. All along, she had tried to tell herself 'no news was good news,' but it was easier said than done.

A load had lifted off Betty's shoulders. It was around this time Connie's friend, Ginnie, received a telegram to tell her that her Sam was 'missing in action'. It was so close to what Betty had been experiencing that she sobbed into her pillow that night.

Betty had lived her own life through the letters she received over the past six months and hadn't dwelt on her feelings. She couldn't have borne not knowing. She told Duncan her heart had almost stopped when Susan popped by. She ended her letter: 'Thinking of you, always.' It came from her heart.

As she readied herself for bed, Betty sank to her knees and gave thanks Duncan was safe and prayed that Ginnie would soon receive good news about Sam.

* * *

Betty hadn't heard from Jeffrey for ages. She had managed to put him to one side for a while. It was as if she could only keep control of her life if she had a series of boxes she kept closed most of the time. Her brother had a box she tended to open in the early mornings. Visions of him sitting in mud-filled trenches, while she was lying comfortably in her bed, haunted her.

She opened Hannah's box when she was in bed at night when sleep was especially hard to call. No amount of counting sheep or saying the Lord's Prayer over and over in her mind, could help.

Joe's box was shut and was never likely to open again, although she would say she now considered him to be her best friend, next to Jean and Connie. She still thought about Martha and hoped that, some day, they might become friends again.

Duncan's box, which had been closed for what seemed like a considerable time, was now open after having sight of the letter to his family. How wonderful it had been to see his handwriting on the page after so long. She still hoped his letter to her would arrive and was keeping her fingers crossed. If anything, waiting to receive his letter had shown her thoughts about him had changed, and she would feel devastated if he did not play a part in her life.

Dearest Duncan. She said his name over and over. There was no doubt in her mind. She loved him.

18th June 1918

Dear Duncan,
I hope this letter finds you well.

Such happenings around here presently! Everything was going smoothly, and we were all getting on with our jobs when suddenly there is talk of a strike, would you believe. Joe, who is the union man, called all us clippies together and told us the men were going to get a five-shilling war bonus this year, but the women were not. Although we have equal pay with the men, the war bonus is not classed as part of our pay. This means the bosses can get away without paying it!

You can imagine the uproar that went on when we were told. Joe wanted us all to join the union — for our protection, he said. It was also to protect wages for all the men coming back to their jobs. Joe says if the bosses can do that to the clippies, what's to stop them doing it to the men too, by making women cheaper to employ. Any road, we all agreed Connie should speak for us women. She went off to see the boss, Mr Adams, and came back saying as it was true. It seems as we are going to have a strike on our hands, and women don't get no strike pay.

I'm so worried, Duncan. I must be careful what I say because I've never told no one about Hannah and if there is to be a strike, I don't know how I will manage to pay my rent and give money to Mother for Hannah's upkeep. Each day we go into work, I dread being told we'll be out on our ears. I might have to look for some charring to do to tide me over. If it happens, Pray God it does not last long.

Please take care of yourself and write back when you can.

Love
Betty

37

July 1918

Betty and Joe were talking about the upcoming union meeting, which was to take place at the end of the month. Joe had spoken to Connie and the other clippies trying to encourage as many women as possible to attend the meeting. The disagreement over the war bonus was still going on.

Betty then mentioned the article about Czar Nicholas being executed and his family being taken to a 'safe place'.

'It still doesn't seem right to execute a king.'

'We have. Charles the first.'

'That was ages ago.'

'In Russia, the ruling classes had absolute power over life and death of their serfs. They owned them and they could be executed on the spot without trial because the local landowner had caught them stealing a rabbit. The Czar was the head of that ruling class.'

'How can someone own another person? It's not right. At least it doesn't happen here.'

'It does. You can pay someone just enough not to starve but not enough to put something by for a rainy day. Isn't that a form of serfdom?'

'Yes . . . I think.'

'We might have votes but we are all economic serfs. We don't get hanged for killing a rabbit or answering back; but we do get the sack and are forced into the workhouse.'

Betty nodded. 'I know people like that.'

'The workhouse is a fate worse than death.'

She thought over what he'd said. Was it so different in this country, or was every country just as bad as each other? 'Do you think there will ever be a revolution in England, Joe?'

'Look at all the men who have been killed over the past four years, yet the government is still arguing over payment of pensions to widows. One MP even suggested a widow's pension shouldn't be sufficient for a person to live on or else the women would just stay at home and live off the state. I think after what these women put themselves through, they deserve to live with dignity. Lots of women out there are not too sure how to claim what they're due. The government needs every man and woman they can get to help with the war effort. But what happens when the war is over?'

'At the PTC the men will get their jobs back and the women will be thrown out.'

'And what about those men who don't make it back? What'll happen to their jobs?'

Betty shrugged. 'I dunno.'

'That's the point the unions and the Labour Party are concerned about. There'll be lots of young men who won't be able to return to their jobs. Do you think they'll allow women such as you to stay on permanently? Mr Adams told you women were too delicate to drive a tram in The Potteries. They aren't too delicate in Glasgow. If they allow you to stay on, do you think they'll want to pay you the same wage is a man?'

Something clicked inside Betty's head. 'So, if we don't win this and get the bonus for women, then it will prove they'll work on the trams for a lower wage than the equivalent wage of a man.'

'That's it, Betty. You're getting the hang of this now. It's called divide and rule. And the British are past masters at it.'

'So what can we do about it?'

'Be active in politics. I have a friend, Jessie, who is passionately concerned with women being represented by unions, not just unions for women. You should speak to her one day.'

'What are you going to do?'

'Me? I'm going to work for the labour movement and primarily the Labour Party. Lots of men are going to get the vote and we don't want them throwing it away by voting Tory or Liberal. Those parties are only interested in the status quo.'

'I think Lloyd George is a good leader, he's from a working-class background.'

'But his party doesn't want to see too much change. That's why it is so important the Labour Party gets as many MPs as possible.'

'But won't it be different now there is universal suffrage for men.'

'It will only be different if the men know there is a difference. We need to get our message over to the working man and woman. I say woman, because until there is universal suffrage for women, their only voice will be through their husband. Only women over the age of thirty and who own property or are married to a property owner have the vote. So how many women do you know who will be voting in the next election?'

'None'

'Like I said to Connie a few weeks ago, it wasn't the suffragettes who got women the vote. It was the

Kaiser. Parliament wanted to keep women quiet and committed to the war effort. Mrs Pankhurst and her followers were happy to receive the vote as it meant only their class would get the vote. A nice cosy arrangement.

'This war has left us with fewer men, and more women looking for work. Women have proved they are as capable as men. Why should employers pay more to employ men when they can employ women more cheaply. This is the biggest challenge we will face whenever this war ends.'

38

August 1918

Sure enough, the London Clippies, conductors and associated workers called everyone out and, as news spread, other transport workers joined them until the whole of London came to a standstill. Other towns and cities joined them.

'They are out! Can you believe it? The buggers in London are on strike.' Joe waved his newspaper in the air and slapped his thigh. 'I'll be damned.'

'You probably will, Joe Cumberbatch,' said Connie.

Joe was fired up, handing out leaflets to all and sundry asking for support. Betty had to admit her excitement grew at the support the strike was mustering. She sometimes accompanied Joe on his campaign and she talked to the women who, despite their money problems, would strike if asked.

26th August 1918

Dear Duncan,

I hope you are well.

The news from the front is looking much more encouraging. The Allies seem to be making major advances. I know you will be part of this fighting and I pray for your safety each night. I try not to think we are getting close to the end of the war in case it tempts fate.

The bosses were trying to stop women clippies from getting the five shilling a week War Bonus, and it came to a head last week. The clippies and women transport workers in London came out on strike! The men supported their action, and London was at a standstill. Joe, the union man, said it was only a matter of time before others joined them. He was including us! All I could think of was how I would make ends meet. Some clippies have been crying in the privies, wondering where their next loaf of bread will come from. I've warned Mother it might happen. She said if the workers come out on strike, I will have no choice in the matter. She wasn't very happy, but at least the rest of the family's working. It could be a hell of a lot worse.

I helped him out, when I could, handing out information. It was good, and talking to the clippies helped me to see what others were going through. Joe said he wished there were more women like me in the union.

The newspapers started to cover the strike, but events in your part of the world overtook it. The spectacular successes of the past few days made me feel guilty that we were striking over money, when men were losing their lives. Joe said we were fighting to protect the jobs of those men when they return.

Connie says we will have to fight for this bonus every year, but with the news from the Front, we may, pray God, have no need for a War Bonus.

Love
Betty
PS We won! All employees will now get the full War Bonus this year. I feel I can breathe again.

39

September 1918

Newspapers were full of Allied victories. They were pushing the Germans back and Duncan's letters reflected the optimism the men must have felt. But men were still dying

Today was Betty's twentieth birthday. She had arranged to meet Jean and Connie at the tearooms in Parliament Row, their first get-together for ages. She felt over the moon having received letters from Duncan and Jeffrey, wishing her well on her birthday. Her friends still thought she was walking out with Joe. It suited her to let them think so. However, it didn't stop her from questioning her friends closely about their relationships.

Once settled in their seats, Betty opened the conversation. 'You two need to get a move on. I told you when we started work that we need to keep an eye on the men if we don't want to end this war as spinsters.'

'You're not still going on about that?'

'Look at you, Connie. You're older than us, and there's still no sign of any blokes running after you. And yer pretty enough. You should be able to catch yourself a man.' Betty turned to face Jean. 'And you, Jean, you're just as bad. You want to snap up Mr Adams before yer lose him. Both of you should take lessons from me.'

'We don't need a man,' retorted Connie. 'We are

quite happy the way we are.'

'Of course you want a man. You don't want to work all your lives, do you? Once you've got a man, he'll be the breadwinner.'

'That's if he dunner spend all his money in the pub and belt you when he gets home. There are women where I come from not much older than you, Connie, who have seven kids, and a husband they would love to see the back end of. It's not all fun.'

Once again, Martha came to mind. She felt guilty she had left it so long before trying to re-kindle their friendship, but Martha had caused their breakup and it was up to her to put it right. Nevertheless, she hoped Martha was all right.

'I'm too young to think about children,' said Connie, stretching her legs and yawning. 'I want to enjoy myself first.'

'This war cannot go on forever, so dunner werrit yourself, Betty. You've plenty of time to find yer man,' Jean was quick to point out.

'But if you leave it too long there won't be no men left. Or at least the men left will all be cripples.' Betty put her hand over her mouth, quickly glancing around to check if her comment had been heard by anyone.

Jean flushed. 'How can you say that? Mr Adams has done his bit, and he will make someone a nice husband. The fact he has to use a stick makes him no less of a man.'

Betty thought of saying she was sorry, but she wanted to make them understand. 'But it's true, can't you see that? Look at the men at the depot. Joe's the only decent bloke among them who is close to my age.' She bit her lip — she shouldn't have drawn attention to him. Damn!

'Why isn't your Joe in the army, Betty?' asked Jean.

'I haven't a clue. Never asked him,' she said, evading the question. 'If he was in the army, he wouldn't be here with me now.'

'But he's content to let others do the fighting for him, is he?' Jean's face was bright red.

She had dug a hole for herself and didn't want to pick a fight with Jean, who was sensitive about Stephen Adams and his war wounds. Unusually, Connie said nothing. Betty would've expected an outburst from her, rather than Jean, with her being a former suffragette.

They finished their drinks, and cakes that appeared to have shrunk since they had first become patrons of the teashop.

'Let's walk down towards Burton & Dunn's,' said Jean, keen to change the subject. 'Have a gander at what they've got in their window. I can't afford to buy nothing; it's far too expensive, but it's nice ter look.'

Betty hung back to look in the milliner's window. The others carried on walking. Her secrets were weighing heavy. She would have to be more careful.

Later, she made her way to Wellington Road where Hannah had a birthday present waiting for her. She didn't have to pretend to be shocked — she genuinely was. The thought had not occurred to her — and she loved it. It was a tablecloth, edged with embroidery, not as fine as that on the borrowed christening gown, but precious all the same.

* * *

Betty was running out of time. Now the war was moving in the right direction, she needed plans in place.

If her job was to end at the conclusion of the war, as the clippies had been told, then she may well not have long to work. Getting a well-paid job was going to be the most important thing and that didn't come by working in service. She needed to use the skills she possessed.

Becoming a tram girl had given her a view into a life that could hold so much for her, as a woman. Iris had made her see that. It would be silly to throw away the knowledge and experience she had gained just to get a husband. She'd had a taste of what a woman could do and she rather liked what she had seen. She wanted a good husband and a good job. She wanted to be her own person.

Romance might be on the horizon when Duncan eventually came back, and she hoped it would, but he would need to accept her for what she was now rather than what she was when they first met. She had changed — and he would need to understand that.

40

October 1918

Jean and Stephen Adams were developing a friendship. Betty could see it in Jean's face every time she looked at him. Betty had thought he was too old for her, but now she could see that not only did he smile more now than in the early days, but that he'd be good for Jean, too; they would get on well together. Most of the time, Jean acted beyond her years and seemed content with her lot.

Connie was good at keeping her feelings hidden. So far, she hadn't spoken about any close men friends, and she was not the sort of person Betty felt she could ask. If the truth be told, she was still a bit in awe of Connie. She had heard her and Joe talking about unions, politics, and the suffragettes, all sorts of things, and didn't think she knew enough to join in, but would listen to pick up what she could.

Connie had said suffragettes didn't want to speak for women; women should feel confident to speak for themselves. It was a funny old world. Women who didn't want men to speak for them, but they were happy for toffs to speak on their behalf. Trouble was working-class women like her didn't speak out generally. It was something she would have to learn. She had an idea.

That night as she and Connie had finished their shifts and boarded the tram for home, she had a favour to ask.

'Connie, Jean said you wanted to keep yer dealings with the suffragettes quiet for fear of making trouble?' When Connie rolled her eyes, Betty jumped in. 'Oh, she was only warning me ter say nowt cos it might cause a bust up.'

'What do you want to know, Betty?'

'I'd like ter find out a bit for meself.'

Connie looked surprised. 'You're interested in the work of the WSPU?'

'I hope you don't mind me saying, but are all suffragettes toffs, like you?' *Oops!* There she went again, not thinking what she said before she said it.

'Oh, no. One of the leaders of the Women's Social and Political Union was Annie Kenney. She started work in a cotton mill at the age of ten and by thirteen was working twelve-hour shifts. She came from a large working-class family just like you — eleven siblings although one died in infancy, I believe. I'm sure the library will have plenty of articles about her if you want to find out more.'

'Don't the suffragettes have a newspaper or journal or summat?'

Connie smiled. 'Yes. I can lend you some of mine if you like?'

'I'd like that very much.'

'I'll bring them in tomorrow.'

The conversation went on to other things but soon ended when Connie alighted in Burslem. Betty continued to Hanley with a broad grin on her face.

* * *

Connie was as good as her word. When Betty went up to the rest room to start her shift the next day, she found a pile of old copies of *The Suffragette* and *Britannia* newspapers waiting for her, along with a pamphlet about Annie Kenney. She skimmed through a couple of pages and placed them in her shopping bag before starting her shift.

She would begin reading tonight.

41

November 1918

To cheering crowds, the Prime Minister announced an armistice had been signed, in France, on 11th November 1918, at five o'clock in the morning. A ceasefire on all fronts would be in place from eleven o'clock. Later, in the House of Commons, the Prime Minister warned the men wouldn't all be coming home immediately. It would take time to organise the demobilisation of so many. But, at least there would be no more killing. Crowds sang '*For he's a jolly good fellow*' and '*Rule Britannia.*' And then the booming of maroons.

What excitement! Such celebrations!

'I would love to have been in London to watch it all happening,' said Betty, wistfully.

It was her day off and she was at home with her family. Mother had heard from Jeffrey last week. But there was no word from Duncan.

Father and Michael had gone to work as normal but were sent home as the winding men had not turned up. Mary-Ellen and Lily also could not work because there was no clay ready for working. Tommy wouldn't go to school if nobody else was working. It wouldn't be right.

'Come on kids, let's go out and join in the fun,' Betty cried to everyone. 'We should all go.'

She dressed Hannah in a warm coat and hat, put

on her own coat and chivvied the rest of them to do likewise. She and Hannah headed for the door. She shouted over her shoulder: 'Come on, you lot!'

In the end even Father put on his coat and went with them.

Crowds had gathered and most people had knocked off work to join in. It should have been obvious to her that with all the crowds there was the likelihood of meeting someone. It turned out to be Martha, who looked as if she was returning from work. When Martha's eyes caught hers, Betty looked away, expecting to be ignored.

'How are yer, Martha?'

It was Mother that spoke.

Martha flushed. 'I'm fine, Mrs Dean. Hello Betty.'

'Hello,' Betty mumbled.

Martha seemed rooted to the spot. Betty was sure she'd seen the pram, but Martha never looked Hannah's way. If she had — just one tiny glance — the ice between them might have melted.

'Best get a move on. Come on, Betty.'

Betty pushed the pram forward and away from Martha.

Mother tutted when they were almost out of earshot: 'I was determined that girl wasn't going to ignore us. I've a good mind ter give her a piece of me mind.'

'Why?'

'Didn't yer know as one of the twins, Peter, I think, has got a girl into trouble.'

'Has he? Well I never!'

'There was no way I was going to let that little madam ignore us with her high and mighty ways.'

A parade for the 'Feed the Guns' campaign had been scheduled for the 11th, requesting investment in war bonds processed from the Town Hall to Market Square at noon, where the guns were stationed, with the mayor due to open the campaign. However, the appeal was soon forgotten, and turned into a celebration of the Armistice and the end of hostilities. Children waved union jacks; even little Hannah waved one. At three, she couldn't walk too far, and she was fast asleep in the pram before they arrived back home.

Tommy wanted to see one of the trams Betty worked on, so the whole family walked across to the main tram stop. As luck had it, a tram was waiting, and another turned the corner and pulled up behind the first. Both Tommy and Hannah called out with excitement and the whole family turned to watch.

Betty heard a voice shout from behind her.

'Hello, Betty.'

She turned to see a beaming Jean. 'It's great ter hear the news, isn't it?'

'I'm surprised they haven't cancelled all the trams, but I suppose people have got to get back to their homes.'

'We must be the only ones working. We're going to have a bit of a do at the end of our shift, but for now it's strictly teetotal and business as usual.' She glanced down at Hannah. 'Who's this you've got with yer? What a gorgeous little face.'

Betty was mortified to be caught out amid all the celebrations. Glancing quickly at her mother and then back to Jean, she spoke quietly so the rest of the family couldn't hear. 'This is me little sister, Hannah. Say hello to Jean, Hannah. She works with me.'

Hannah stared and stuck her thumb in her mouth.

Jean grinned.

Hannah hid her face.

'I didn't know you had a sister that young, Betty.'

Thankfully, Mother joined in to help Betty out. 'Hannah's me youngest. It's nice ter meet yer after all this time.'

'Pleased to meet you too, Mrs Dean.'

Hannah looked up at Jean — and gave her an angelic smile.

'What a lovely little girl.'

'You may as well meet the rest of the family while you're here. This is me husband, Charlie; the lad is Tommy and that's our Lily with him. Over there, laughing and giggling's our Michael and Mary-Ellen. As Betty will have told yer, Jeffrey, our eldest, is away in the army.'

The driver appeared from his cab and shouted to Jean. 'Come on, stop gassing to Betty. We haven't got all day.'

'I'd best go. It's been lovely to see you all, but I must get on. We're due out now. See you again sometime, Mrs Dean.'

Betty and Mother gave each other a relieved look as the tram took Jean on her way.

Betty wiped her brow. 'That was close.'

* * *

That evening, Betty wrote to Duncan about the excitement and celebrations. It would take time for him to come home, but now she knew it was over, she would wait for him. She wasn't the most patient of people. She needed to hear from him and had to admit her surprise at the strength of her feelings for him.

* * *

It was nearly two weeks later when his letter arrived. She ripped open the envelope.

16th November 1918
[redacted]

Dear Betty,

I am safe and well and about [redacted] *If you look on a map you can see how far we've come. If the censor erases this then I will show you myself when I get home. It sounds so good to say that.*

We have not heard anything about when we will come home. Although the Germans have signed an armistice, it will take a peace treaty to end the war officially. At least we're not fighting any more.

We are still facing the Germans, in case hostilities do break out. We've had a couple of shelling incidents since the 11th, but they have only been a few rounds and not too accurate. It's just a few stubborn officers who cannot accept their defeat.

Today, we went to our forward observation post to watch the Germans leaving their lines. They had to leave all their arms behind, so no rifles. But they still marched away in good order. I don't know how long they kept that up, but they certainly weren't going to let us see them in disarray.

We have been told to maintain our readiness and so our days are much the same, but without the firing.

Hope you are all well. I have written a letter to Susan and Father. They should get theirs at the same time.

I think you and Susan can stop knitting socks now!

We will have so much to talk about when I get home. And tell little Hannah I am looking forward to meeting her.

That's all for now. Keep well.

All my love
Duncan

She held his letter to her chest and muttered words of thanks he would be coming back to her. A load had gone from her mind, much she hadn't even been aware of until now. During the two years she had known him, she had come across no faults. Of course, he probably did have some — after all, no one could be that perfect.

Every day, her first thoughts were . . . could it be today?

* * *

Since the Armistice, Betty and Joe had taken to meeting once a week for a drink in Hanley after work. They always had something to talk about, and afterwards Joe would walk her home and catch the tram back to his digs.

They sat down at a table in the corner.

'Betty, I have decided to leave the PTC in the New Year. Nothing is finalised yet but I am going to work for the Labour Party and their prospective candidates in Birmingham.'

'You'll have a lot of work on.'

'Yes,' Joe said with a smile, 'this is for the next election. It's going to be the important one. All the men that *are* coming back from the war, will be back and we'll see whether Lloyd George can make good on his promise, 'A fit country for heroes'.'

'I shall miss having you about Joe. I shall have nobody ter talk politics with.'

42

December 1918

Betty was on a split shift and was sitting in the rest room with her feet up on a chair eating her snapping of oatcakes and cheese. She was hungrier than she realised.

Emily Norton came from the office, all mithered, and not at all like her. She always came over as so capable.

'Are you all right, cos yer don't look it?'

'I'm handing round these letters, and I must make sure they all get delivered before everyone clocks off, else there'll be hell to pay.'

'Letters for all of us?'

'For the clippies. Here, I've got one for you, Betty, duck. You can have yours now and it'll be another off my list.'

Betty got to her feet. 'Is that what I think it is?'

'It is, duck. I've got one an' all. I'm not a clippie, but a man can do my job just as well as I can.'

'But you're so organised. Mr Adams'll be lost without yer.'

Emily shrugged.

Betty tore open the envelope to reveal the typed letter inside. The clippies would end their employment on different dates, which was necessary if the company was to keep the trams going. She looked up from the letter and stared at the wall opposite with its stained 'Rules and Regulations' poster. She got to her feet and slipped into her jacket, hardly aware of what she was doing. Then she put on her money bag and ticket machine, which hung like weights around her neck. Funny their heaviness should come to her now. She had worn it for almost two years and hadn't noticed after the first week.

She stuffed the letter into her pocket and descended the stairs. Two of the drivers, Fred and Bert, were talking beside a tram. They stopped as she walked into the yard. The maintenance men did the same. Did they all know the letters had gone out?

She put on her hat but remained by the door, wanting to be in full control of herself before approaching anyone, to pretend she wasn't upset and she had many irons in the fire. Connie walked around the corner and into the yard.

'Hello Connie. How's things?'

'Not so bad, thanks, Betty. What about you?'

'A bit fed up. I never felt as I'd feel this way when I finished here.'

'I don't suppose it'll happen quite yet. Have you any idea what you're going to do next?'

'To be honest, I was hoping I wouldn't be working at all. I thought I might meet a decent bloke and be married by the time the war was over, not thinking about looking for the next job.' Betty said the words as if she was joking. And then more soberly, 'I'm not that bad-looking, am I?'

Connie grinned and patted her shoulder. 'You're not bad at all, Betty. But what about Joe? Everyone knows he thinks the world of you.'

She shrugged. 'I don't think as he wants to tie himself down.' That, at least, was true.

'Anyway, don't you want to have a career or find

your way in the world before you settle down?'

'Nope. People like me don't get careers, Connie. They get jobs.' Betty sniffed as the contents of the letter seemed to swim in front of her eyes. 'Whatever pays well that dunner require too much brain, and then they get wed.' She was feeling sorry for herself.

'Betty! Please don't say that. You're worth so much more. Are you saying you would find a man, any man, and marry him, so you don't have to find a job?'

'That's it in a nutshell.' Betty thought about snatching the words back. She was on the brink of telling Connie everything about Hannah. And what about Duncan? She felt foolish and depressed.

'You're selling yourself short, Betty.'

'It's all right for you to talk. You can do as you like. College. University even. Or a posh job in an office. That don't happen to us. No point in wanting what you conner have, is there? Any road, we'd best get our thinking caps on cos we've had our letters telling us we're finishing.'

Connie's mouth fell open and she set off at a run towards the office. Betty watched her go, realising the news had come as a shock to her posh friend, too.

* * *

Connie, Jean, and Betty had agreed to get together for a Christmas party at Jean's house, which would be the last time they would all meet as clippies. Her landlady said they could use the front room. Betty was the first to arrive and Connie shortly afterwards. She had brought mince pies and a few other treats, including a bottle of sherry.

Betty had a lot on her mind and wasn't in a party

mood. She was losing her job and had no idea what she could do. Tonight, she would try to forget about everything and enjoy herself.

'It's lovely to see you both outside of work. I'm sure we have lots to talk about,' Connie smiled expectantly. 'Any thoughts on what you are going to do next?'

'Not really, how about you, Connie?' said Jean, shrugging.

'We know what you'll do,' Betty grinned and winked.

'I don't know what you mean.'

'Come off it, Jean. We've both seen how you look at Stephen and how he looks at you. You'll be Mrs Adams inside six months, I'll bet.'

Connie smiled. 'He's a good man, you could do a lot worse, Jean.'

'He's so old, he's hardly going to sweep yer off your feet.'

Jean folded her arms. 'I'll have you know, he's a very nice man.'

Betty laughed and pointed her finger. 'So, there is something between you two.'

Jean's face flushed a violent red and she refused to say any more.

'I left school at fourteen,' said Betty keeping her fingers crossed on her lap. She was not going to tell everybody she was only twelve when she was sent out to work, 'and me mum took me straight into service. One less mouth to feed and a few bob coming in. That was what I was to her.'

'Oh, that's terrible.'

'No, Connie, that's life.'

'I think the sherry's going to our heads, we all need a cup of tea.' Jean stood up and disappeared into the kitchen, leaving Betty to speak to Connie.

'You were a suffragette and stood up to the bosses. Until I met you, I had one plan:. To find a man and get married. I'm going to do something with my life. I just don't know what yet. But it will be something for me. If I need a man to get it, so be it.'

'Betty, I don't know what to say, it's such a sudden change.'

'I've been thinking about it for a while. I just haven't spoken about it. Less questions that way.'

'Do be careful, Betty.'

Jean returned with three cups of tea. 'So, what are your plans, Connie?'

Connie talked about doing an office job, but Jean felt she could do better. The two girls were shocked when Connie confessed to having financial problems and needing a job, otherwise her family might need to sell their home.

When Jean asked Betty, she said she needed a job that paid the rent and if that meant leaving The Potteries, so be it. When they asked about Joe, she quickly changed the subject, but swore that the man she married would not be poor.

Jean stared at her, horrified. 'Be careful, Betty, whatever you do. I think a loveless marriage for money might be the worst thing.'

'No Jean, being poor, that's the worst thing.'

* * *

Betty was not starting to work until midday, so after a lie-in, she walked downstairs to find a letter from Duncan waiting for her.

Mrs Clowes was returning from a shopping trip, moaning she couldn't get sugar and flour and had to go to three shops before she could find some. 'Any word of your young man coming home?'

Betty waved her letter. 'I'm hoping this might tell me,' she grinned.

9th December 1918
Maubeuge, France

Dear Betty,

Just a quick note to let you know everything is fine here. The local people are so friendly, and I suppose grateful after being under German occupation for over four years. They have told us some horrible stories.

My big news is the division is going to be transferred to the area around Cologne in Germany, as part of the occupation force. We've been told the artillery will stay with the battalion. Then we'll be redeployed to France, prior to demobbing. I don't know what sort of reception awaits us. We'll wait and see.

Looking at the government's demobilisation plan, I think I shall be in one of the last groups to come home, so don't build your hopes up too much. I will keep you posted.

We're being transported by lorry. They expect the journey to take five days so we should be in place by 15th/16th December. We'll spend the nights in tents. It is cold or 'es ist kalt' in German, here. I hoped I might pick up a few words, but we are under strict orders not to fraternise, so we'll see.

It's time to go now. I hope you and Hannah have a nice Christmas. I am not sure when you'll get this letter so it might well have already passed.

Love Duncan

Betty had read about the occupation force. The Germans had been told they must vacate all the land west of the Rhine. She hoped he would be safe. His letter had taken two weeks to arrive, which she supposed is not too bad. She had expected the news about Duncan's lowly position in the demob order; it was only right and proper essential workers, volunteers, and married men returned first. But the waiting was unbearable.

* * *

Betty had a good Christmas Day with her family. Hannah was a lot more attentive now and she seemed to recognise everyone was happy. There was only one seat empty when they had their meal. Jeffrey was due to be home the first week in January. As a miner, he would be among the first to be demobbed.

Mary-Ellen and Michael both had lives of their own now. Mary-Ellen had her eye on a young man, although he didn't know it yet. If the war had continued, Michael would have been eligible for conscription in March next year. He said he was upset he could not do his bit, but Betty suspected he secretly was relieved, as were the rest of the family. Both he and Mary-Ellen were working and lived with Aunty Ella, while Lily was training as a lithographer at a local pottery. Much to Tommy's disgust he was going to have to stay at school until he was fourteen, according to the new Education Act. But Betty thought he might get a job this Easter and ignore the new rules.

Everyone had gathered at Wellington Road and they had much to celebrate. They would sing Christmas carols and tell stories after tea, but it was while

Betty helped her mother to prepare a little food for the festivities to come, that a knock came on the front door.

'I'll go,' Betty called out.

She wiped her hands on her apron and headed to the door. Though the glass, she could see the figure of a man.

She opened the door and immediately the man pulled her into his arms and gave her such a hug, she could barely breathe.

'Hello, duck,' he said in her ear. It was Jeffrey, returned a month earlier than expected.

'It's our Jeffrey,' she screamed as soon as he let her go.

Mother came running and he caught her up in his arms.

What jollities they had in store that Christmas! Everybody was home, everybody was earning, and everyone had a roof over their head. In The Potteries that was a perfect Christmas.

* * *

When Betty got back to her room on Boxing Day evening, she needed answers to questions that had been plaguing her.

While she was waiting for Duncan's letters to arrive, she had been convinced she was in love with him and couldn't wait for him to come home. Now that time had arrived, she was worried she had built him up into something he wasn't. She couldn't bear the thought he might turn into another Alastair — that when she got to know him, she would be disappointed. Was that why she hadn't mentioned him to anyone yet?

Her thoughts returned to Iris Shenton. She would pop over to see her in the next couple of days. She needed Iris's words of wisdom.

She was as good as her word and, two days later, she stood on the steps of Victoria's house where she was welcomed with open arms. In no time at all, she was settled in a chair in the front room sipping tea with Iris. Victoria soon made an excuse to leave the two together.

'How are you, my dear?'

'All the better now the war's over,' said Betty. The room was like Victoria, prim and proper, not a thing out of place. Almost too tidy for comfort.

Betty could feel Iris's eyes scrutinising her. 'Is all well with you and your family?'

'Yes, Jeffrey's just come back.'

'Oh, I am pleased for you all. It must be such a relief.' Iris paused for a moment. 'And what about your young man? Dare I ask if he too is back?'

Betty shook her head. Iris gave a start. 'No . . . no Iris, I don't mean that. He's coming back soon, but he's part of the trouble.'

'Whatever do you mean, child?'

'Now my job with the PTC is over, I need to find work.'

Iris nodded encouragingly.

'That's the trouble, Iris. I'm so confused. I can't imagine Duncan not being around, but equally I don't know if I'm ready for our relationship to take over my life. I've been talking to someone at work and feel there are things I need to do before I settle down with any man.'

'I see. You feel the need to spread your wings while you have the chance?'

Again, Betty nodded. 'I want to be someone, and use the skills I've been building; and I want ter give Hannah a good home.'

'Very admirable, Betty, but you need to have thoughts for yourself in all your planning, too. If you're unhappy, then Hannah will feel it. Duncan might be coming home, but why do you have to make decisions now if you are not ready?'

'He told me he was falling for me in one letter. I think he will want to talk about it when I see him.'

'If he is the man for you, he will wait, will he not?'

'He's done everything I've asked so far.'

'Then you have your answer.'

Betty pondered as she returned to Jasper Street. Iris was right. She needed to be in control. Only that way could she do what was best for herself and her daughter.

43

January 1919

Jean was the first clippie to receive her official letter terminating her employment from 10th February — only two weeks away. Betty and Connie were told later Mr Adams couldn't approach Jean while she was a worker under his command. As soon as he was able, Stephen asked Jean to marry him — and she said yes! Betty had witnessed their growing affections and, in her mind, it was only a question when, rather than if, the two would be wed.

How strange it would be to call him Stephen!

Betty caught Jean alone.

'You're a jammy beggar. Fancy being the first of us to get married and keeping your feelings from us all this time.'

'It was hard; I really wanted to tell you and Connie — but I couldn't. You would've done, too, if you had to, wouldn't yer?'

Betty thought of all the secrets she was keeping from Jean and let the subject drop. 'Well, am pleased for yer, Jean. You deserve ter be happy.'

'We're getting married at Hanley Register Office. We didn't want all the fuss of a church wedding. But I have a favour to ask yer. Will yer be a witness for me?' Jean was grinning and held out her arms to Betty.

'Yer want *me*?'

'You and Connie, cos we're all mates, aren't we?'

Betty's agreement was lost as she hugged Jean so hard the two of them could barely breathe. So, Jean, the shyest of the three was to be the first to get wed. Who would be the next? She had noticed Connie's eyes on Robert Caldwell, but they always seem to be arguing. Betty had no idea why.

With Joe having returned to Longton Depot, Betty's circle of friends had been considerably reduced. Who would be the next to go? She didn't know if she would miss the place. It was turning into something different. It wouldn't be the same without her tram girl friends. Once they had all finished on the trams, she would consider telling them everything and hope they could remain friends.

She would miss her talks with Joe too. She had learned so much from him about workers and their rights, and the role unions played in looking after them. The strike had kindled her thirst for knowledge and taught her the power the workers had if they stood firm.

44

February 1919

Betty's tram pulled into the stop in the centre of Hanley where she waited with Bert, the driver, for the Longton tram to arrive, before continuing on their way. She had a few minutes to herself when she heard a familiar voice.

'Hello, Betts.'

'Oh! Joe, you made me ju—' He was dressed in plain clothes, and obviously not working. Before she could ask what he was up to, he interrupted her

'I've got some good news. I've got a new job in Birmingham as a local union organiser. I start at the beginning of March. I'm only giving in my notice a week before, so don't tell anyone.'

She beamed. 'That *is* good news. You'll enjoy working for a union full time. It'll help your political plans.'

'My friends in Birmingham have been encouraging me to do something like this. Working on the trams and being the union man has given me an insight I wouldn't have had.'

'Are you waiting for the Longton tram?'

'Yes, it's my day off and I've been shopping. Need to look me best for the new job.'

Betty sighed. 'I wish I could get a job somewhere like Birmingham. It would be good to make a life starting with a new job, and I reckon I'll have more opportunities than in the Potteries.'

'Not found anything yet?'

She shook her head.

'There are a lot more people down there, so it'll probably be no easier. Still, if I see anything, I'll let you know.'

She sighed. 'A girl can only dream.' And there was always Hannah to think about.

* * *

A few days later, Joe drove the Longton tram into Goldenhill Depot. The trolley head needed adjusting before the tram could return to Meir. While the work was being done, he had some news for Betty.

'I've organised a meeting for Sunday in Birmingham for you, Betty. I think you might be interested in it.'

'So quick! I'm not sure, Joe.'

'Have you heard of the Association of Women Trade Unionists?'

'No.'

'You have a meeting with their local secretary, Jessie O'Neill. She's on their national committee and is a strong believer in men and women working together, rather than separately. She thinks it works better that way. In one way or another, we all want the same things in this world, don't we?'

'Did yer say, *she*?'

He nodded, with a smile. 'I thought that might pique your interest.'

'Well . . . yes, it does.'

'I wrote to her telling her about you and your experience and how much help you've been to me'

Betty's eyes widened. 'You did?'

'It so happens she's looking for some office support and she suggested you might be just the person.'

Now Betty's eyes really were wide open. 'I don't believe it. Why would she say that?'

'Because she's practical. Because she needs help. Because you're a working-class woman who wants to better herself. It doesn't matter, Betts. It's the chance you've been looking for. You need to grasp it with both hands.'

'It'd mean moving to Birmingham?'

'Yes, but think what you would be gaining: something you would never get if you stayed here. At least think about it.'

She bit her lip. The time had come to tell him about Hannah. 'Yes, I will, but there's summat I need to tell yer.'

'Oh yes, what's that?'

A shout went up from the other side of the tram where a clippie was waiting. 'Joe, get a shift on, our tram's ready to go now and we can still make the start time,' said a conductor Betty didn't recognise.

'I'll have to go, Betty. I'll send you a note about the arrangements. You can tell me on the train on Sunday.'

Before Betty could say any more, he jumped into his cab and left.

* * *

It must've been Stephen who organised for Jean, Betty, and Connie to be on duty on Jean's last day at the PTC. They gathered during the last hour to say their goodbyes properly and to allow Jean to say goodbye to as many of her friends as possible, many of whom she might not meet again.

Betty did her best to act normally, even though she was excited by the prospect of a good job in Birmingham. She wanted to tell the others, but she decided to keep it quiet until she knew she had got the job and Mother would continue to look after Hannah, to enable her to create a better home for her daughter.

From the side-lines, Betty watched Jean's reaction as people came and went. How her face lit up and her eyes watered with each goodbye. Betty was glad she wasn't going to have to go through all this. She was going to slip off without making a song and dance about it. But that's where the differences between them showed so well. Jean, the quiet, reserved one, revelled in the fuss and attention she was receiving, whereas Betty, usually so out-going, didn't want her feelings on show to anyone.

* * *

Betty arranged to meet Joe at Stoke station and to take the train to Birmingham New Street station. Although Birmingham was miles away, the journey was not as long as she had thought as it took them from the grey towns of Stoke, through fresh, green countryside with the odd village strung along its route. Joe was immersed in a newspaper, but periodically looked up and smiled at her.

She had to tell him about Hannah. It was thanks to him she was meeting Jessie today. She wanted to be truthful with Jessie — it had worked with Iris. What a pity he'd had to rush away just as she had prepared herself to tell him.

He looked up from his newspaper. 'Is something

wrong? You look edgy.'

Betty swallowed. 'Remember I had summat to tell yer when I last saw you?'

He nodded. 'I do. If that's why you're anxious, it must be important.'

'It . . . it is.' She stopped talking, swallowed and began again. 'I should've told you, Joe. I have a daughter.'

Joe stared. His mouth opened and closed like a fish. 'A . . . a daughter? You've never said. Where is she? I mean, who —'

'Mother looks after her so I can go to work. She's no trouble at all.'

'But why have you never mentioned her?'

'It's complicated.'

'I recommended you to Jessie in good faith, Betty. I think I'm due an explanation. Are you married?'

'No, I'm not married' She trotted out the agreed story. It would have to do for the time being.'

'Oh. I'm sorry to hear that.'

'I didn't tell anybody at the PTC because it was nobody's business and I didn't know how long the war was going to last. I might've been out of work a month later. D'yer see, Joe?'

He leaned back in his seat and closed his eyes. 'I don't think Jessie'll hold it against you. She's a decent sort. But you'll have to tell her — and better now than she finds out later.'

'I thought you should know first.'

'Thanks for trusting me.'

Betty let out a jagged breath.

Soon after their conversation, the train pulled into the station. It was huge. Fifteen platforms and crisscrossing metal structures held the roof in place.

Bridges over the railway lines enabled passengers to get to their required platform once they could find it.

Even though it was the middle of the day, it was dark in the station after the light of the sun shining through the carriage windows. The train edged along the platform and came to a halt. They descended and followed the signs to the exit. Everyone was in a hurry and seemed to know where they were headed. Joe looked more relaxed than Betty had thought after being on the receiving end of such news, but she had forgotten he was originally from these parts and was going home.

* * *

They had arranged to meet Jessie O'Neill in the Queen's Hotel on New Street. They made their way towards a woman sitting alone at a table close to the window. She smiled when she saw Joe, who rushed to shake her hand.

'Good to see you again, Jessie. Can I introduce you to Betty Dean, the friend I was telling you about?'

Jessie turned to face her, the warm smile still there. 'I am so pleased to meet you, Betty. Joe has told me a lot about you.'

'I hope it hasn't put you off,' she laughed nervously.

'He's been highly complimentary, Betty. You've no need to worry.'

She had expected Jessie to be older, but she couldn't have been much over twenty-five. Her clothes were plain but well-kept, reminding her a bit of Connie. Her blonde hair of neatly pinned curls was set off by a charming suit showing off her slender body.

'Now, Betty, come and sit beside me and let me get

to know you.' She patted the chair beside her. 'Joe is going to give us an hour to chat in private. Thanks, Joe.'

He nodded and winked at Betty before strolling off towards the entrance.

Jessie opened the conversation. 'You can start by telling me a little about yourself.'

Betty had practised what she would say, and she was happy to have remembered everything. Jessie listened attentively as she spoke of her experience of working in service and of getting out and meeting people on the trams.

'I've also taught myself to type, and I've done a bookkeeping course, too. I am trying to learn shorthand at the WEA and from a book. It's difficult, but I'm getting the hang of it. I wanted to get on. To prove to myself I'm bright — just like my teacher, Mr Wells, said I was.'

'That's a splendid thing to do, Betty and I'm sure he would be proud of you.'

'I've never heard of a lady organiser before. How did you start?' Betty surprised herself with the question, but Jessie was so easy to talk to, she couldn't stop herself.

Jessie breathed in deeply. 'Where to start? Father is a manufacturer of armaments. He's a Lord, and I'm left-wing and a grave disappointment to him. I want to see the working men and women of this country better their lot.'

'Blimey! So do yer not speak to yer family?'

'Oh yes. We tend to avoid those areas of conversation that would put ourselves at war with each other. It was important to me to get to know what issues caused the most concern for working people and how they could be prevented.'

'That's what I want, but I don't expect people will take any notice of someone what's been in service and talks like me.'

'Stuff and nonsense!'

Betty's eyes opened wide. 'What d'yer mean?'

'Sorry to be blunt, but maybe I can help you there, Betty. You need to believe in yourself before you can get others to believe in you. I found that out for myself.'

She sighed. 'I think I believe in me . . . most of the time.'

'And when something or somebody causes you to question that belief, you need to be ready for it. Do your homework before you take on a challenge, and be ready to answer.'

Everything Jessie said made sense. How wonderful it would be to work with this woman. Jessie hadn't said a word about a job, but being here, listening to her, felt uplifting.

'Betty, I have a job available doing clerical work in my office, assisting me. The job has grown and I need an extra pair of hands. I wondered if you —'

'Oh, yes.' Betty blurted out the words and then realised she hadn't given the poor woman time to finish her sentence. 'Sorry!'

Jessie laughed. 'I like enthusiasm, Betty. I do believe you'll fit in perfectly. Would you have any concerns about moving to Birmingham?'

'I maybe shouldn't have jumped in so quickly, Jessie.' Betty bit her lip. 'I do have something to tell you that might make you wish you hadn't offered the job to me.'

Jessie frowned. 'Go on.'

'Well, you see . . .' She wondered how to approach

the delicate matter. She looked down at her hands and wished herself somewhere else. Then, taking a deep breath, she burst out, 'I have a daughter.'

Jessie's eyes opened wide. 'You? Have a daughter? You don't look old enough.'

Betty nodded miserably. 'She's lovely. She lives with my mother in The Potteries so I can work. She's no trouble at all.'

'Right. So why do you think this information might make me change my mind?'

'I'm . . . not married. I haven't told nobody. Most people think she's my sister.'

'And her father?'

Betty kept to the story she had told Joe. 'He was killed in 1915. He never knew about Hannah.'

'I see.'

'I'll understand if you change your mind. I should've told you sooner, but I got a little carried away.'

'Well, Betty. Thank you for your honesty.' Jessie paused and seemed to make up her mind. 'You are just the sort of person I'm looking for. You will be able to relate to many of the women we are trying to recruit into the unions — for their own benefits. You understand some of the problems they face from your own experience. They will relate to you.'

'Does that mean —'

'The job's yours . . . if you still want it?'

She grinned happily. 'I most certainly do.'

Betty explained her situation and that she would be leaving the PTC on 14th March. 'It is a Friday, so I could start on the following Monday. I would need to find somewhere to rent. I don't know the area so I've no idea how long that might take. Joe suggested somewhere like the Young Women's Christian

Association or the Girls' Friendly Society. They both have cheap lodgings and might be able to help until I can get somewhere more permanent.'

Jessie thought for a moment. 'I've a better idea. You can stay at my flat. It is about five minutes' walk from here.'

'Your flat?' Betty couldn't believe her ears. But could she afford it?

Jessie looked earnestly into her eyes. 'You would be doing me a favour. I have one person currently sharing and it would be good to have another. We could have fun. And I promise I won't lead you astray,' she added as she saw the excitement disappear from Betty's face.

'Oh, but I couldn't afford —'

'No rent to pay. My father pays for it. I'm sure he wouldn't object if I share it with two well-brought-up young women. If you subsequently decide to find somewhere more permanent once you've settled in at work, then that's up to you.'

Betty shook her head in disbelief. This couldn't be happening. She looked Jessie in the face. 'D'yer mean it?'

'Of course, I do. When you get to know me, Betty, you will discover I never say anything I don't mean.'

'Then I accept with thanks, Jessie.'

* * *

'So, everything went according to plan.' Joe's face beamed as they returned to the station.

'I can't believe what just happened, Joe. Not to people like me. Thank you for setting it up. I would never have the confidence to do it for myself.'

He took hold of both shoulders and turned her to face him. 'Betts, you did it — nobody else. Remember that.'

His eyes were earnest and there was no doubt he meant what he said.

'I told Jessie about Hannah and you were right, Joe. She seemed to take it all in her stride. In fact, she thought it was a good thing that I would know what troubles a lot of women are going through.

He looked surprised, but nodded. 'You can trust me. We have both got parts of our life we don't want people to know about. Your secret is safe with me.'

Plans had to be made. First and foremost, she must speak to Mother about Hannah. Would she be happy to continue the arrangement while Betty established herself in Birmingham? The offer of a room in Jessie's flat made the move to Birmingham a lot easier, as she would have time to look for somewhere suitable to live.

But fancy that! If she could make it work, she, Betty Dean, was going places!

* * *

Betty hardly slept that night and the following day her mind was not fully on the job. She hoped everyone got the ticket they were expecting and the cash would balance. Surprisingly, when she cashed up, she was sixpence over.

She had a quick bite to eat and then rushed round to Wellington Road to tell Mother of her news and to ask about Hannah. As usual at that time of the day, Mother was on her own. Betty jumped straight in.

'I've got the chance of a job in Birmingham. Well, I

should say I've got it, if I want it.'

'You'd move to Birmingham? How could yer look after yerself down there on yer own? Worrabout yer rent. Where's it going ter come from?'

'It's a good job. Not in service, nor in a factory, but in an office. I think it'd do me good. I'll earn good money and, even more important, I've been offered somewhere to stay. Five minutes' walk from the office and not a penny of rent to pay.'

'It's not somewhere . . . you know . . . somewhere nice girls dunner —'

'Course not. I'd never go to a place like that.'

'And worrabout our Hannah?'

'I thought if you could carry on looking after her, just like yer doing now, I could do this job and get some experience. Perhaps be able to move back to Stoke with some money in my pocket. Like you said, Stowford House gave me a good background, which meant I could work for Mrs Shenton with no problem. This will do the same. I'll come home whenever I can. The train's quick and not too expensive, so it'll be just like before.'

Mother nodded. 'Hannah's no trouble. Course she can stay with us. I half expected she would any road. You've still got ter earn yer keep when you've left the trams, haven't —'

The rest of her words were smothered in a hug as Betty clung to her.

45

18th February 1919

Everything was falling into place, Mother agreed to keep Hannah so as not to disrupt her young life. Betty had a job and somewhere to stay. All that was left was to tell Jean and Connie her good news. Obviously, she couldn't say anything until Joe handed in his notice next Monday. It was what she'd agreed with him.

She hummed as she went about her duties on an almost-full tram. The sun had nearly gone and there was a reddish hue between the clouds.

As she reached the last of her passengers, she swung round to face him. The humming died on her lips.

It was Alastair Macdonald.

Blood drained from her face.

'Fancy seeing you here. What brings you to Stoke?'

'Looking for you.'

'When did yer get back?'

'I'm on three days leave and I wanted to see you as soon as I could. I've come back for you, lass, just as I promised.'

She was confused. She had told him she wasn't interested before he left, but the middle of a tramcar was hardly the place to remind him.

'We can't talk here,' she whispered. 'We'll arrange summat, before you go. Sit still, we're nearly at Goldenhill.'

Betty forced herself to return to her job. It was

nearly four years since she had seen him, since she had made it plain to him it was over between them.

When the tram stopped at its turnaround in Goldenhill, Betty jumped off and hurried round to the cab to speak to her driver.

Fred, the driver, grinned when he saw her. 'Alrate, Betty duck?'

'Listen, there's this bloke I need to have a word with. You turn the trolley head, but keep an eye on us.'

Fred's eyebrows knitted.

'It's a long story. Just keep yer eyes on us, please'

'You'll be alrate, will yer?'

'Yes, Fred, I'll see yer in a few minutes, I promise.'

'Okey-dokey!'

The tram pulled away.

Alastair began talking immediately. 'I've been to see the head gamekeeper at Macclesfield Hall. He says there will be no problem for me returning to my old job. In fact, the Duke is impressed by my war record and wants me to return to Pitlochry in the autumn. So, like I said earlier, I've come back for you as I promised I would. I was sorry you couldn't write to me but I forgive you.'

She stopped. 'What are you talking about?'

'When we go back to Scotland, the Duke will give me a cottage on the estate. Betty, it is magnificent up there. Lots of fresh air and space for the children to run around and none of this horrible smoke and soot you live with every day. I'm surprised you returned here after living in Stowford, but Pitlochry is so much nicer than Cheshire.'

Betty groaned. He had taken in nothing of their previous conversation. It would take more than five short minutes to go over it again and she didn't have time for that. Fred would be calling her shortly as they we due out immediately. There were already people waiting on the tram.

'I'll be finishing my shift at six. Can I meet you somewhere?'

'Yes. Not too far away. I could come to your place?'

Betty shook her head vigorously. 'No. How about up Hanley? Look for the big store, Burton & Dunn. You can easily get to Stoke station after.'

'Ok, if that's what you want?'

Betty looked across to Fred who beckoned her to join him. She was holding up the tram.

'Wait at this tram stop. The next tram will take you back to Hanley. I'm on a different route. I'll see you later.'

He nodded and made a move towards her, which she managed to avoid.

* * *

Betty had two hours to decide what to say to Alastair. What was he playing at? Hadn't she made her position clear? It suddenly dawned on her she had never received any letters from Stowford House after she left. If he had tried to contact her, she would never know. Perhaps he'd had her in his mind all this time. He certainly sounded as if he planned a lot. Her heart missed a beat.

She didn't change out of her uniform. She didn't want him to know she lived close by. She just wanted to get this whole thing over with.

He was waiting, as agreed, outside Burton & Dunn's.

'Aye, aye. Betty!'

She glowered back, angry. 'What the bloody hell do you want, Alastair?'

He looked at her quickly and shrugged. 'I thought I'd get a welcome hug and a kiss at the very least. And don't swear, the Duke doesn't like it'

He reached out for her, but she stepped out of his reach.

He frowned. 'You're beginning to worry me. You should be pleased to see me. I've come for you as I promised I would, even after the nasty things you said.'

He looked stone-faced. Betty swallowed nervously. 'I told yer there was nothing between us.'

'You were upset at me going to war without telling you, I know. But you must've thought a lot of me after what we did. I understand how you must have felt, so I forgive you.'

He forgives me!

Betty thought quickly. If he knew about Hannah she would never get rid of him. She needed him out of the way — now.

She stopped walking. 'After what happened with John Makepeace and the way yer manhandled me . . .'

'I did nothing wrong. He needed a good hiding. He was after my girl. They say you left Stowford in a rush.'

'No I didn't, I gave a week's notice and left on good terms. I even got an excellent reference from Mrs Stone.'

'That's how I knew you were working down here on the trams. I told Ruth you were my girl, and she took pity on me. I can be quite charming when I want to be.' A grin spread across his face.

Betty could, quite happily, have kicked Ruth if she

had been there. 'We had problems at home, and I left Stowford quickly to help my family, nothing more.' She swallowed. 'Be that as it may, Alastair, I made it clear to you I didn't want anything more to do with yer. You are a violent man and can't control your temper. How long will it be before I deserve a good hiding?' She stabbed her chest.

'You'll only get one if you deserve it. Be a good wife and mother and we shall have no problems. Bring the kids up as God-fearing children and we'll be a happy family. We can start to plan our future. I am going to be demobbed in May and I shall return to Scotland in September. We can get married here and then have a blessing at the Free Kirk in Tummel . . .'

She couldn't believe what she was hearing. 'Alastair! Will you please listen? There will be no marriage, no children, no cottages, no Scotland! I would not marry you if yer were the last man on earth. I want you to leave now and don't try to contact me again.'

Alastair stepped forward and grabbed her by the shoulders. His eyes bright and glaring. Was it fanciful that she could see madness in them? She ducked, convinced he was going to hit her. Instead, he calmed down and let her go.

'See, I can control my temper. I'll give you time to think about what I've said. It's a good offer. After what we did, no man will want you. You're damaged goods.'

It was the last straw. He might have controlled his temper but Betty certainly had no intention of doing the same. One advantage of not changing was she had her heavy winter boots on and a precisely aimed kick on the shins sent Alastair crumpling to the floor. She ran back to the safety of the shops and people.

She had nothing left to say to him.

* * *

Betty rushed home, constantly looking over her shoulder. She had a quick wash and changed out of her uniform. She was still shaking when Joe turned up at seven o'clock to finalise arrangements for the move to Birmingham.

Her heart missed a beat, just the man she needed to see. He was even getting on well with Mrs Clowes, who opened the door to him.

'Good evening, Mr Cumberbatch,' Mrs Clowes gave him a broad smile.

'And good evening to you, Mrs Clowes,' he returned, taking off his hat. 'You are looking well if I may say so.'

'Of course, you may. Come in out of the cold, won't you?'

If it had been at any other time, Betty would have laughed at their formalities. Joe knew how to woo the ladies, even though he would probably never make use of his knowledge.

By the time this exchange had been completed, Betty was halfway down the stairs, pulling on her warmest coat.

'Thank you, Mrs Clowes, but we're not stopping.'

Joe looked at her blankly. 'What?'

'We're leaving Joe. I'll tell yer on the way.'

'Where to?'

'You'll see.'

Betty led the way down the street, looking around to make sure there was no sign of Alastair.

'What's happened, Betty? You're worrying me.'

If there was any chance Alastair might come back and force his way to seeing Hannah, then Betty needed to have plans in place. It would be stupid not to.

'You've definitely made a hit with Mrs Clowes, Joe.'

'Don't change the subject. Aren't you going to tell me what's the matter?'

'Alastair Macdonald's turned up.'

'And who's he?' He caught hold of her shoulder. 'You'd better start at the beginning Betts.'

She shook his hand away. 'You'll know soon enough. First, we are going to see Mother and Father and then I can tell you all. No point in repeating meself, is there?'

* * *

Betty, with Joe following, strode up to Wellington Road, and stopped suddenly outside her parent's house. She turned to him.

'I haven't been entirely honest with you. There are things you should know, especially now Alastair's turned up. I need you to promise to say nothing to anyone about what happens inside. Remember you asking me to say nothing about your secret — well, it is the same for this too.'

Joe's face paled. 'Betts, you haven't murdered him, have you?'

She couldn't laugh. She didn't know if he was joking.

She opened the door quietly glancing around to see who was in. Hannah was, most likely, in bed and the rest were in the kitchen judging by the mix of the voices.

She stood in the open doorway unable to speak. Everyone stopped talking and stared. Mother rose, unable to take her eyes off Betty, with Joe standing behind her.

'Come on you lot. Let's be having yer upstairs now,' she said, herding everyone except Father and Jeffrey out of the room.

They could all see the anxiety in Betty's eyes and went off without so much as a whimper.

'Yer look awful,' said her father. 'What's going on? And who's this?'

'Hello Mrs Dean, Mr Dean, and you must be Jeffrey.' He held out his hand. 'I'm Joe. I work with Betty at the PTC.'

'Nice ter meet yer, Joe,' said Jeffrey. 'Why's our Betty in this state?'

'I'm not too sure myself. She told me to come with her and here I am.'

'Everybody sit down. I've got summat to tell yer all. And dunner say a word until I've finished.'

Betty looked at each one in turn until they each nodded. 'I met Hannah's father today. His name is Alastair Macdonald. He's in the army, but he lives in Stowford. He got on my tram.'

'Hang on our Betty, yer said Hannah's father —' interrupted Jeffrey.

Joe's mouth fell open. 'But you said —'

'Shut up will yer. You both need to wait until I've finished.'

Betty quickly recounted it for the benefit of Joe and Jeffrey. Redness spread across Betty's face. She swallowed several times, but pressed on while she had the courage.

She glared at each of them and laid her trembling hands face down on the table. 'When I came home, I told Mother and Father the whole story. I couldn't tell you, Jeffrey, because you were going back to war and I didn't want to worry yer. Any road, we agreed we would say Hannah's father was killed during the war, better that than being talked about by all and sundry.'

Jeffrey shook his head. 'So yer lied to me?'

'And me,' said Joe.

Betty nodded. 'And now, I'm telling yer the full story, if you'll let me? I came home and had Hannah and everything was fine — until today. The last time I saw him, I made it clear I didn't want to see him again. Somehow, he's got the idea it was all a mistake and he is ignoring what he doesn't want to hear.'

'Does he know he's Hannah's father?' asked Mother.

'No. And he must never know that. He's only concerned about marrying me and taking me to Scotland to be his wife and look after our children. Touching really, if he wasn't such a bully and good with his fists.'

'Are yer saying he's hit yer?' Jeffrey's eyes were black. His clenched fists rested on the table.

She turned to Jeffrey. 'That's why I didn't tell yer. I didn't want you going off to find him and getting into a fight. I met him again about an hour ago and told him there was no chance of us getting together again, that he was a bully and I wanted nothing to do with him.'

'What did he say ter that?' Mother enquired. She had been quick to grasp the situation.

'I thought he was going to hit me, but he then turned all nice saying he could control his temper. I took the opportunity to kick him in the shins with my winter boots on. I ran as hard as I could back to Burton & Dunn's and then home to Jasper Street. He didn't follow me. I am sure of it. But I'm frightened.' Betty could hold her emotions no longer. She had to cry, both out of desperation and anger.

'Where is he now? I'll show that jock what a coal shovel feels like,' growled Jeffrey.

'Alastair's gone back to his unit, but he'll be back before long. He says he's going to marry me whether I like it or not. He says I should be grateful. Oh, Mother it's such a bloody mess.'

In true Potteries style, Mother said they should have a cup of tea and think about what to do. The five of them sat round the table in silence.

'What's he got ter do with all this?' said Father, pointing at Joe.

'Joe's a friend.'

'Lord above, I thought you said you had a room in a flat with a woman. Yer never said she's a man!' said Mother.

'No! Jessie's the person who has offered me a room in her flat and she is a woman. But I have known Joe since I've been on the trams. He's got a job in Birmingham as well.'

'Yes, I'll keep an eye on Betty, Mr Dean, and she will have me there to help her if needed,' added Joe. 'And before you ask, I'm not living in this flat.'

Betty felt the mood change and was keen to build on it. 'The other person is a doctor, and highly respectable.'

'So, it is a man,' interrupted Jeffrey.

'Stop! This is what I didn't want to happen. You're confused. I'm going to work for the Association of Women Trade Unionists, whose representative in the Midlands is Lady Jessica O'Neill. Her father is Lord Eccleston, the armaments manufacturer, and he owns the flat. I will be sharing the flat with both Jessica and Doctor Rowena Paget, who works at

Birmingham Children's Hospital. It's all respectable and above board. Joe is going to work for the Labour Party and will have his own place.' Betty paused for effect. 'Does everyone understand?'

She took their silence to mean yes.

'Does this Alastair know where yer live?' asked Jeffrey.

'I don't think so.'

Mother put her hand up for silence. 'Only the five of us know the full story — that's still true is it?' She glanced at each of them in turn.

'Yes, Mother.'

'The rest of the family and the neighbours have all been told you were going ter marry the father but he was killed in the war. So if he comes snooping around here, he'll not get any joy.'

'Yes, Mother.'

'And, if you're not here and no one knows where yer've gone at the PTC and the PTC have only ever had Jasper Street as your address, he won't be able to find you. If he does make his way ter our door, we will deal with the situation at that time. If you go to Birmingham now, before he comes back, and dunner tell anybody where you're going, he won't know where to find yer,' said Mother.

'Your mother's right, Betty,' said Joe. 'We haven't said anything at the PTC yet and let's keep it that way. You mustn't tell Connie or Jean anything. Nothing at all.'

She had wanted to surprise Connie and Jean with news of her job, but now it looked like she could tell them nothing. Just disappear.

'I'll talk to Mrs Clowes about the rent and you can do a moonlight flit. It won't be the first time it's happened to Mrs Clowes.'

'I dunno whether I could do that.'

'You dunner have much choice,' said Mother. 'Let this Alastair have time ter come ter his senses. Me and yer Father'll make sure the kids say nowt if anybody comes sniffing around.'

'I'm so sorry, Joe,' murmured Betty. 'You got more than you bargained for.'

Before she left, she tiptoed upstairs to Hannah's room and quietly let herself in. Hannah was asleep, her soft breath barely noticeable. She lay on her back with her finger in her mouth looking so peaceful, so beautiful. She leaned forward and planted a kiss on her daughter's forehead. Hannah moved slightly but settled again. Betty closed her eyes and tried to imprint the picture in her mind. Who knew when she would see her little girl again?

An overwhelming sense of fear and protection welled up. She would do everything she could to keep Hannah away from Alastair.

As they said their goodbyes, Father took Joe's hand and shook it. 'You'd best look after me girl, young man. If I hear you've touched her in any way, yer'll have me to reckon with.'

Betty cried again when she arrived at Mrs Clowes's that evening. Sitting alone in her room brought home to her the enormity of what she was planning — to disappear completely without telling a soul. This is what it would be like all the time. No girl friends to share her thoughts with. Missing out on celebrations, of not being together through thick and thin. Could she really bring herself to do it?

She hated Alastair for forcing this life on her.

46

Late February 1919

Before she left, Betty wrote to Connie. Given both she and Joe would be in Birmingham before anyone knew they had gone, she came up with a story that might explain why she had not told them of her plans. She would pretend it was all part of her plan to wed, and she would show Joe off in the best possible light so Connie wouldn't think the worst of him for his part in it. She had to explain he was taking care of her and she shouldn't be worried. She said she and Joe would live together as brother and sister — because it was cheaper that way. She also asked Connie to tell Jean she was sorry for missing her wedding.

She wanted to say so much more about what she was doing and why she felt so safe with Joe, but it wasn't her place to divulge his personal secrets. She read the letter through several times and concluded she had said enough. One day, when they were well settled in their new lives, she would write again, and she hoped it would be soon. Until then, it would have to do. She quickly stuffed the letter into an envelope, addressed it and sealed it.

She dashed off a quick letter to Iris explaining she had a new job and told her to write care of Mother's address. She would be in touch soon. Iris might read her letter and feel surprised, but would be the first person to tell her to make the most of the opportunity, for herself and for Hannah.

The letters were done; she was committed. She would post them on Saturday morning in Stoke.

* * *

It was for the best. There was every chance Alastair would come back, still disbelieving her. She couldn't take the risk. He had changed so much since she had walked out with him. He had always been a little fiery; perhaps it was the red hair! But she was surprised how much effort it took him to hold himself in check when his temper was raised. At one point she had thought he was going to slap her. Calling her a whore in the street — she could never forgive him for that.

She would be heartbroken to miss Jean's wedding. Perhaps, when everything was eventually sorted out and she knew where she was with her life, she might make it up to Jean in some way. At least Jean and Connie would still have each other. A streak of envy cut through her mind, its intensity surprising her.

She would be leaving before her notice period at work was up, but it couldn't be helped.

Betty paced up and down her tiny room. She needed air, otherwise she would choke. She snatched her coat from the back of the chair, wrenched the door open and hurried outside. Once on the street, she took in huge gasps of air. She slid into her coat and fastened it before the heat that had got her this far disappeared and left her icy cold.

How much she would miss them all? What hurt most of all, was leaving little Hannah. Again.

She was such a bad mother.

* * *

Betty rose early and packed away her remaining chattels, without stopping for breakfast. She wasn't hungry. It was normal for her to be up and out this early so it wouldn't be unusual. Mother would be speaking to Mrs Clowes over the weekend about the rent money.

She folded her PTC uniform neatly on a chair and added a note asking Mrs Clowes to hold on to them until she could get someone from the company to collect them.

She sat on the bed, staring round the small room. She wouldn't miss it, but she would miss what it stood for: independence. The silence hurt her ears. No one moved in the house and even the road outside sounded quiet. She grabbed her bags and let her eyes sweep along the drawers and into the open wardrobe to make sure she was leaving nothing behind. She twisted the door handle slowly and stood on the landing, listening. Satisfied she could hear no one, she tiptoed down the stairs with her large bag in front of her, expecting the stairs to creak, but she was lucky.

Once outside, her whole body relaxed.

She pushed her key back through the letterbox, and then she was running down the street to where she had arranged to meet Joe. Sure enough, he was there looking smart as ever, smoking a cigarette. He smiled when he saw her, and took a last drag and threw the remaining butt away.

'Did you have any trouble Betts?'

'Nah. Mrs Clowes gets up later. If she did hear me, she would think I was off to work. Didn't have much to pack any road.'

'I've got us train tickets to Birmingham. You don't

mind walking to the station do you? Don't think as we should use the trams, for obvious reasons.'

'I'm quite happy, Joe. I'm just glad it's all over. I couldn't have kept quiet for much longer.'

He took a bag from her. 'Sure you want to go ahead with it?'

She nodded. 'Yes, I'm sure.'

He patted her arm. 'Good, I'm glad.'

Part Four

47

March 1919

Joe had booked a room in a small hotel just off New Street for Saturday night. They climbed three flights of stairs and walked along a never-ending corridor to arrive at their room. Joe unlocked the door and stood aside for Betty to enter.

The first thing she noticed was the double bed.

'There's only one bed, Joe.'

'It'll be because I was originally coming on my own. I'll go down to see the man at the desk. There must have been some mistake.' He backed out of the room with a bright-red face.

He returned with a face even brighter than before.

'I'm so sorry, Betts. It's all my fault. I asked my mate to get a cheap room somewhere for the night so as we can sort ourselves out. I said as I was bringing my sister. My mate decided we wouldn't mind . . . sleeping in the same room . . . just for the one night.'

'I don't mind that, Joe. But the same bed —'

'I'm sorry. There's only this one left. I'll sleep on the floor.'

This wasn't a good start and Joe looked mortified. Betty put her head in her hands and closed her eyes. A picture formed in her mind of the two of them, in the bedroom, at a total loss with the one, and only bed between them. And she laughed. And laughed.

The anxiety on Joe's face was soon replaced by a

rueful grin and then he too laughed.

Betty threw herself backwards on to the bed.

'Oh, Joe. What have we done?' She managed to squeeze out the words in between the chuckles of laughter. 'Who cares? Nobody knows us here. That's why we came isn't it?'

'Suppose so. I didn't want it to start like this, you thinking as I'm taking advantage.'

'Dear Joe, I'm not thinking anything of the sort. If I was, then I wouldn't be here with you now, would I?'

Whether it was consciously done or not, they stayed out of their room for the rest of the day. After a quick tea at a cafe close by, they wandered round the shops that were so tall, with many floors, they made Burton & Dunn's look small by comparison. There was so much temptation if she had the money to spend: clothes, trinkets, household goods, books. She reckoned she could buy anything she wanted from that one street.

Joe didn't bother looking through shop windows. He appeared content to follow wherever she led.

Eventually, they returned to their room. Unsure what to do, Betty took off her coat and slowly sank into one of two upright chairs. She folded her arms on her knees as if waiting for Joe to give some sort of order. She couldn't return to the girlish laughter of earlier in the day. This had become grown-up stuff.

'I think . . . I think I might go to bed now,' she stammered.

Joe's body jumped physically. She was sure he was lost in his own world, wondering how to approach the subject.

'I'll take a stroll, Betts. Give you time to . . . get . . . in bed and I'll sleep on the floor, like I said.'

'Don't leave me on me own, Joe.'

'I'll lock the door while I'm gone. Will ten minutes be enough?'

She nodded quickly.

Once the door was locked, she tried to relax. She rummaged through her bag to take out her night clothes and, in five minutes, she jumped into bed and pulled the blankets up to her neck to await Joe's return. She studied the two chairs — even if he put two together, he couldn't sleep on them, and the floor was much too hard. Could she possibly allow him to sleep on the bed, or would she be inviting trouble? It would be selfish of her not to offer.

The turning of a key in the lock sounded louder than she'd expected; Joe walked into the room.

'Are you all right?' he said.

'Course I am.'

'Well, forgive me, Betts, but I can only see your eyes and they don't tell me anything.'

'Well . . . I've been thinking . . . you won't be comfortable on the floor. You can sleep on the bed. If you like?'

His eyes widened. 'Share your bed?'

'You can lie on the top. Put yer coat round yer. You'll be comfortable and warmer then.'

'You sure?'

'It's only for one night.'

He nodded back with a look of relief, and she was glad she had made the offer.

She turned her back towards him to give him the privacy to undress. Then she felt the bed sink as he lay down beside her.

Joe's breathing steadied. She could just make it out over the sound of traffic. It sounded nice, comforting in this strange place.

* * *

On Sunday morning, the two friends strolled through the city towards Jessie's flat, with Joe carrying the larger of Betty's bags. She had tried to picture in her mind what her new home would look like, but failed. Jessie had told her it was a large, stone building in a quiet street within walking distance of the offices. From the outside, it looked much grander than Betty was prepared for and she felt nervous, especially when Joe opened the large wooden door from the street only to be met by a military-looking man in a smart uniform.

'Miss Dean is moving in to Flat 12 with Miss O'Neill, Ted.'

'Good morning, Miss Dean, Mr Cumberbatch. We've been expecting you. Do you need help with your bag?'

'No, Ted, I've got it,' said Joe and motioned to Betty to follow him.

They climbed the stairs to the second floor and walked steadily to number twelve.

'Who's he?'

'It's Ted. You'll get to know him. He is the building's caretaker, doorman, handyman. He lives with his wife in a flat in the basement. His wife cleans for people, including Jessie. You'll like them. If you need anything, Ted's the one to ask.'

Joe knocked and, almost immediately, Jessie opened the door.

'Come in, come in.' She stood back to allow them in.

The door opened into a large sitting room, with a ceiling that could easily be fourteen feet high. A marble fireplace provided a central point in the room;

three large, small-paned windows looking over the centre of Birmingham allowed light to fill the room. Velvet curtains, with large pelmets, framed them. Two matching settees and four comfortable chairs with fancy legs looked a pleasure to relax into. Betty swallowed. It was all too grand and she wasn't required to pay a penny. She must be dreaming!

Jessie led her past the door to the kitchen one side and bedrooms along the other. Betty's room was the door at the end.

'It's smaller than the others, but cosy.'

It was like a palace. There was a large wardrobe, a bed, and a dressing table, all to match; a small desk in the window alcove, and two upholstered wing chairs with fancy legs.

She put her hands to her cheeks. 'Th-thanks, Jessie. It looks wonderful. I don't know what to say.'

Jessie laughed. 'It's no bother. It will be a pleasure to have your company.'

'Looks like you've drawn the lucky straw here, Betts,' Joe pursed his lips, and nodded. 'Thanks for all your help, Jessie.'

'Not at all. As I said, I'm sure we'll have a fabulous time.'

'I'll leave you to settle in, Betts. I've got a few things of my own to sort out. I'll be in touch.'

Jessie saw him out, while Betty could do nothing but gaze at her surroundings.

She was standing by the window, looking out when Jessie reappeared. 'Now then, Betty. You'll want to unpack. I'll get us a cup of tea.'

Left on her own, she wandered around the room, touching things, and marvelling that she would be living in this place.

They spent the afternoon getting to know each other. She reminded Betty a little of Connie. A young woman, making her own way in the world, brimming with confidence.

* * *

As Jessie had said, the AWTU office was just a short walk from Great Western Arcade. It made a pleasant change and didn't cost a penny. Betty watched as people hurried by, office workers most likely, as most factory workers would probably have started to work a couple of hours ago. She didn't pay much attention to the shops she passed along the way. She would have plenty of time for that in the coming weeks and months.

Jessie stopped at a wood-panelled door and took out a small bunch of keys. Once inside, they entered a passageway to a flight of stairs. The union office was on the second floor. It consisted of two rooms, a small kitchen, and a privy. There was enough room to work in without being over generous. The door from the stairs opened into a reasonably sized room, which Jessie referred to as the reception room, and it was where Betty would be working. There was a desk, on which sat a typewriter, more modern than the old one she was used to, but much the same in its operation. To the right of the typewriter sat a large black telephone, which caused Betty's heart to miss a beat. She had never spoken on the telephone before. She wouldn't know where to begin in answering any calls. A coat stand stood in the opposite corner right next to a second door, which led to a bigger room that was Jessie's office, and meeting room for clients and employers,

Betty was told.

'Take off your coat; we can get started.'

Betty did as she was bid and, together, they walked into Jessie's office so they could talk more about the job she was to undertake. She was to become the first person from the Association that members, officers and employers would meet. She would need to be courteous and always welcoming. Often, the people who contacted the union had major concerns about their employment, and needed to be treated carefully and empathetically.

Betty nodded, taking it all in. She had heard from Joe about some of the matters Jessie raised, but it was fascinating to hear it from Jessie's point of view. Jessie asked her if she had done any Pitman's shorthand when she learned to use the typewriter.

'Yes, I am halfway through a WEA course on Pitman's. It is so complicated. It's English written in another language.'

'That's a good way of putting it. When I have some correspondence to do, you can use your shorthand.'

'I don't think I could do that.'

'Another thing, Betty: You do not say you can't do something until you have tried to do it.'

Betty felt her face redden. Jessie must have seen it.

'I don't mean to be bossy, but it's true. You don't know what you are capable of until you try. It is why some people get on in life and others don't. Now, shall we start with a cup of tea? I have some letters for you to type.'

Betty returned to her office, and headed for the kitchen and the kettle. The gas ring sat on a metal tray in the corner of her room, almost as an afterthought. At least she would see it boiling, but what a strange place to put it!

She settled down at the desk and started to type. She was now Betty Dean, office worker, and she couldn't have been prouder.

At dinnertime, Betty took a cup of tea to Jessie. Her boss smiled her thanks and suggested she join her.

'It's been a good morning. How do you feel, Betty?'

'I think I'm going to enjoy it. Thank you for giving me the opportunity.'

Jessie sighed. 'The war's over and the men are coming home, and we should all be truly thankful. I worry for the women, like yourself, who have experienced the independence paid work brings. I don't believe they will feel happy returning to the kitchen to be housewives looking after their husbands and children. I feel for the widows and spinsters who will have neither men nor jobs.'

'I need to continue working. Mother always said getting a man was the only route I had to happiness. She found her happiness with six kids and a husband who needed nearly as much looking after as her youngest child. I don't need a man to rely on; I want a man to share my life with.'

* * *

She had been working at the offices with Jessie for two days and it was time she wrote to Duncan to tell him her new address, and about what had happened over the past month. She wouldn't mention anything about Alastair. How could she possibly explain all of that in a letter?

She hadn't heard anything from him since the letter he sent just before Christmas, and she was concerned about the newspaper reports saying the German people were extremely short of food and the Allies were still blockading German ports to prevent imports. Did Duncan have any idea when he would be returning?

Her biggest concern was the post. Since the war had finished a lot of the army was now on the move. Post took longer to arrive than it did when the fighting was going on. To be fair, Duncan had mentioned this might be the case when he told her about his move to Cologne. Nevertheless, she was longing to hear from him.

48

April 1919

It took Betty some time to settle in Birmingham. The people were different. The way they spoke sounded more like Joe. Sometimes she felt as if she was in some far-off country trying to make sense of the world around her. It made her aware of her own way of speaking, so she endeavoured to speak properly at all times.

The housing was just the same as The Potteries, though. The terraces, the back-to-backs with outside privies, and the posher ones with only one neighbour. She could almost believe she was back in Stoke-on-Trent until she heard them speak. Is that what they thought of her? She must remember to speak nicely on the telephone, so people could understand her, Jessie had said.

Jessie had organised some shorthand tuition for her. At first Betty didn't know which was worse — the shorthand or the accent of the person teaching her. She would need to get used to both if she wanted to continue working with Jessie.

She was missing her friends, particularly in the middle of April when Jean was to marry Stephen Adams. How disappointed she was to be missing such a celebration. She could've travelled to Stoke from Birmingham to be a bridesmaid, worn a pretty dress, and celebrated with her friends. She and Connie would have had a great time ribbing Jean, but most of all, they would all have joined in her happiness. If Alastair hadn't turned up, everything would be so different.

* * *

Betty and Jessie were in the reception office going through the items left in the diary that would need to be carried over to the following week.

'By the way, Betty, I have a meeting on Tuesday in the offices of Jackson, Bond and Company about a request for information from some of their women who want to join the union. It's a good opportunity for us, so I plan to take you along, too, to take notes. I may also call on you to speak to them if you feel comfortable. You have a good deal of personal experience to offer the meeting.'

Betty flushed with pride at the news. 'It will be my first time talking in public.'

'I will talk you through my plans before we go. You won't be in the dark. And it will be a chance for you to use your shorthand. It would be an enormous help to me if you could take notes, and leave me to concentrate on the message I want to get across.'

At that moment a knock came on the door and a messenger boy walked in. Betty and Jessie looked at one another and then at the boy waving a telegram.

'Telegram for Miss Betty Dean?'

Betty went hot and cold. She didn't want to take it, afraid of the news it might contain.

'That's . . . me,' she said in a quiet voice. She took the envelope gingerly, as if it might burn her fingers, and laid it on the desk.

'Is there any message, Miss?'

The boy looked at her sympathetically. How many telegrams had he delivered over the years? He was about the same age as Betty, but his eyes looked so much older.

'Would you like me to open it for you?' asked Jessie, softly.

'No, I'll do it.'

She tore open the envelope and closed her eyes as she removed the telegram, from its envelope, her hands trembling.

25/04/19 at 11:56 am
To Miss Betty Dean, AWTU Offices,
17 Pinfold St. Birmingham
Meet me 26/4 noon, main door,
New Street station.
Duncan.

Betty could barely see. She read the telegram again.

'It's from Duncan. He's back,' she cried, cupping her blazing cheeks with her hands. 'He wants to see me tomorrow!'

Jessie put her arms round Betty's still-quivering body. Betty was sure she saw tears there, too.

'That's wonderful news. I'm so happy for you.'

The messenger boy grinned. 'It's a change to bring good news. Any reply, Miss?'

Betty turned the message over, but there was no address. She glanced at the messenger boy, eyes still brimming. 'No thank you. There's no message.'

'Right, Miss.' The boy nodded and headed out of the room.

'He says to meet him at the station. That's all.' She handed it to Jessie. 'He'll be in Birmingham tomorrow.'

'Then we must go shopping at lunch-time to buy you a new dress so you can show him what he's been missing.'

As the contents of the letter sank in, the smile left Betty's face. 'Suppose we've changed and it just doesn't work?'

'Then so be it. You'll never know unless you meet him, will you? What have we been talking about with our members? Be bold, decide what you want, and go for it. How can you convince others if you can't convince yourself?'

* * *

She was on her way to meet Duncan in the pale-blue dress she had bought yesterday. It met with Jessie's full approval. She had called it a day dress and Betty had no idea what the difference was between day dresses and ordinary dresses, but had been delighted with the outcome. The dress was gathered at the waist and brushed her legs mid-calf. A large pale-blue collar set off the top of the dress, showing her neck to best advantage. Jessie had pinned Betty's hair up in a becoming bun, with curls framing her face. She looked confident and smart, like a woman who felt comfortable with the world. Just now, the dress was hidden under her coat, and she couldn't wait to dazzle him when she took it off.

Her heart was beating so hard inside the dress it nearly took her breath away. She might look good, but what would Duncan think? She had been the one to slow down their growing relationship because she had worried everything was happening too quickly.

War tended to do that to people because they felt they had no time to wait. Since the men had started to return, she'd heard many women say they felt they were living with strangers, or children didn't recognise their fathers.

She came into view of the station, a towering building of six floors, with tall arches at ground level. The time on the station clock was five minutes to noon. She had taken her time, not wanting to arrive breathless. Her eyes panned round searching for him. At first, she couldn't see him because he had his back to her. When he turned, she saw him before he saw her. He looked slimmer and taller than she remembered. His cheekbones stood out. He was still dressed in his army uniform, but he looked very much the man she remembered from the dance — so handsome it took her breath away.

He saw her and it was as if a light had come into his eyes. He hurried towards her.

'Betty! Oh, Betty.' He dropped his bag, and his arms went around her. 'I was beginning to wonder if this day would ever come.'

He hugged her tightly and let her go.

'I was so glad to get your telegram.'

'Sorry, but it was the only way I could contact you in time. I didn't upset you, did I?'

She shook her head. 'Course not. I can't tell yer how happy I was to read it.'

'It's been so long. I'm happy just to stand here looking at you.'

'I've booked a table at a hotel so we can have something to eat,' she said.

She walked beside him wondering if she would be able to eat anything at all. The hotel was near to the station so, in no time at all, the two were seated and a waitress had taken her coat.

'You are looking even more beautiful than I remember, Betty.'

'Thank you.' She was lost for words. She had thought they would have so much to talk about and now, here she was, speechless.

'I'm so pleased to see yer. How does it feel to be back?'

'Words can't describe it. What about you? Are you enjoying working in the big city?'

'Yes, I am. Jessie, who I work for, has been good to me. I'm learning a lot from her.'

They were silent for a moment. The waiter arrived and they ordered their meals. Betty stared around her in the relative darkness of the hotel. Tables were beginning to fill.

'How long did it take you to get here?'

'I got my demob papers on 18th March. I think the date will be fixed forever in my mind. I was in Cologne, and we moved to a transit camp near to Calais. We'd heard lots of soldiers died in the transit camps because of the influenza, but by the time we got there it was almost over, thankfully.'

'How awful — to survive the war and then to die from 'flu.'

'We were all waiting to get our passage home. I had to report to a Demob Centre at Crystal Palace in London and was there for a week. As soon as I got my travel papers, I sent you the telegram. I couldn't wait to see you. I hope you don't mind me saying that?'

'Of course not. I still can't believe you're here.' She reached out and touched his hand. It sent a shockwave up her arm.

'. . . and, like I said, I have a month's leave before I must go back to work.'

She had lost her concentration. With an effort she heaved herself back and said the first thing that came into her head. 'Do they let you keep your uniform?' What must he think of her?

He looked at her blankly. 'No, I need to return all my kit within the month. I have various documents, one of which is a voucher to get signed to say I've returned my great coat.' He laughed. 'I'll have a meeting with my boss on the railway in the next couple of days to organise my return, and then everything'll be back to normal. Or that's the plan.'

'I suppose you'll have given them time to get rid of the woman who is doing your job.'

Duncan's eyebrows knitted together. 'That's all agreed. Although I can't imagine working inside after all this time.'

Betty closed her eyes. Ever since the war had ended there had been disagreements about women losing their jobs and being discouraged from working outside the home. It was a large part of the work she and Jessie had been dealing with ever since she came to Birmingham.

'I'm sure Susan and your father will be overjoyed to see yer. Is that where you're going next?'

'That's right, we've been given passes for the train. I'm on the two o'clock to Stoke.'

'We don't have long then.'

'It's enough just to see you, for now. It's a long way, but I'm hoping we can keep in touch, Betty. It'll mean more letters again, and the odd visit?'

Betty smiled at him. 'I'd like that.'

They talked some more. At times, their conversation was a still a little strained, as if neither was quite sure what to talk about. All too soon, it was time for him to catch his train.

She walked back to the station with him. He looked hesitant as he stood in the doorway. 'We are still good friends aren't we, Betty? This first meeting face to face, was bound to be a bit awkward, but we can get over it. I would like to see you next weekend if you have no objection?'

She beamed at him. 'I would love to see you.'

She was sure he was going to kiss her. She waited. He leaned forward and kissed her on the cheek.

'Goodbye, Betty . . . for now.'

She watched until she lost sight of him and then slowly retraced her steps to Great Western House. She had been afraid she had built him up in her mind, but he was every bit the gentleman and had treated her as a friend, as she had asked.

By the time she was back at Jessie's, she had decided it was not enough. She wanted more from him. She had not done well with her choice of men friends, rushing into relationships, if you could call it that, and she had wanted to take her time with Duncan. She felt she had done that. Now, she hoped to make their long-distance friendship into something more.

49

May 1919

Duncan was on Betty's mind throughout the week. She had received a brief note from him confirming he would be on the eleven o'clock train, on Sunday. As she headed towards New Street station, she became filled alternately with joy and trepidation. He must have things he felt needed to be said, too.

He walked towards her. He was wearing a grey suit rather than his uniform and he looked even better for it. She caught a breath in the back of her throat and she rushed into his arms. He pulled her towards him to plant a friendly kiss on her cheek.

'It's good to see you again, Betty. The weekend couldn't come too soon.'

'I'm glad you said that. I feel the same.'

He gave her a quick glance but didn't say anything.

'I thought we could go to the flat if that's all right? Jessie is dying to meet you, just to say hello,' she finished quickly.

'Does it mean I've passed the test?'

'What do yer mean?'

'I don't believe you would have invited me if you were about to end everything.'

'End everything? No, Duncan. That was the last thing on my mind.'

He stopped her, his eyes watching her keenly. 'Have you changed your mind? About wanting to take things slowly?'

She swallowed. 'I . . . I have, if you still want me?' She held her breath.

'What? When you've been on my mind every single minute?' He ran a hand through his hair. 'I'm lost for words. I thought I'd have to woo you all over again — never thought you'd change your mind so quickly. I want to kiss you!'

She caught his lop-sided grin before negotiating the crowds near the entrance to the Great Western Arcade and the entrance to Great Western House.

'I'd like that. But we shall have to wait a bit longer, because we're here.'

She opened the door with her key and walked towards the man in uniform. 'Morning again, Ted. This is my friend, Duncan, recently returned from Flanders.'

'Pleased to meet you, sir. Did you have a good journey?'

'Yes, I did . . . Ted.'

As they climbed the stairs she heard an intake of breath, and Duncan whistled.

'Wow, Betty. This is a bit unexpected.'

'I know; I still can't believe I live here. It's good to know Ted's looking after the place,' she said over her shoulder.

She opened the door to number twelve and walked into the sitting room where Jessie and Rowena were relaxing. They jumped to their feet immediately.

'This is Duncan Kennedy, from Stoke. He is the soldier I've been writing to.'

'Hello, Duncan, how lovely to meet you' said Jessie, every inch the lady, shaking his hand.

He nodded to both women. 'Pleased to meet you

both. It's good to meet Betty's friends.'

Rowena came forward and shook his hand, too. 'Pleased to meet you, Mr Kennedy.'

'Call me Duncan, please'

'As I explained, Jessie's my boss and Rowena lives in the other room.'

'We are going out now so you will have the place to yourselves. I'm sure you will have much to talk about. Come on, Rowena.'

The two women left. The room was quiet. How strange it seemed to have him here, in this empty room. All those times she had thought about him and what she might say . . . and here she was, with all the time in the world . . . and she was speechless.

'Nice views from the windows,' said Duncan.

It was as if he knew how she felt. She gave herself a talking to. She was a grown woman, not a shy schoolgirl.

'Would you like to sit down?'

'Before I do, do you think I might kiss you?'

She couldn't see his face — he was still facing the window. Her face burned. He turned to look at her. Her heart missed a beat. She nodded.

Before she could get a word out, she was in his arms, their lips searching each other.

'You don't know how long I've been waiting for this,' he murmured, his lips against her hair.

Tingling sensations spread throughout her body. She pressed closer to him. He seemed to hesitate for a moment, and she didn't pull away. His kiss became more urgent.

Gradually, they parted.

He grinned. 'You can't tell me you still want to take things steady after that kiss.' His face became serious as he waited for an answer.

She stared at him. Was this the time for her to tell him everything? She moved towards the settee and sat, motioning him to do likewise.

'Why did you get cold feet?'

There had been times when she had appreciated his directness. She wasn't sure if this would be one of them.

'Duncan, there are things I need to tell you that I couldn't put in a letter.'

His eyebrows raised, but he nodded and said to carry on.

'I told you about my family and that I had to go into service when I left school because there was not enough room at home. When I found out I was expecting Hannah, I went back to The Potteries. I worked for a lady, Iris, who employed me even though I was pregnant. I had Hannah when I was working for her. I was still there when we met. Iris's health wasn't too good and she decided to move in with her daughter's family so I had to get another job. That's where the PTC came in. When that job finished, Joe, one of the tram drivers, knew Jessie and he helped me to get this job. He works for the Labour Party now and hopes to become a politician one day.'

'Is this . . . Joe still around?'

He sounded a little jealous to Betty. 'Yes, he moved down here at the same time. Well, he got a job first and then I got mine. He thought I would appreciate having someone I knew down here when I started.' Duncan scowled, so she quickly added: 'He's a good friend, nothing more, I promise.'

'Is he why you wanted us to be *just* friends?'

'No, Duncan. Cross my heart.'

He said nothing more, so she carried on talking. 'Because I knew Joe, Jessie has let me live here rent-free.'

'Rent-free? Who can afford to do that?'

'She can. She's a toff like my friend, Connie, but more so. Her father is a lord and money doesn't worry her.'

He whistled. 'You do drop on lucky!'

'I have more to tell you. I need you to promise not to tell a soul, not even Susan or your father.'

His face stilled. 'Sounds serious.'

'I wasn't entirely truthful with you about Hannah's father. He was never dead — that was a story the family made up to explain why Hannah's father wasn't around.' She couldn't look at him.

'Betty, are you trying to tell me you're married?'

'No, nothing like that.'

'So . . .'

'He was violent, and I finished with him. It was after that, I discovered I was pregnant.' Betty told Duncan about her relationship with Alastair and how the violence had showed itself.

'You must have been very young, and very frightened,' he said.

'I was. Anyway, once I left Stowford, I never gave him another thought. You know how it was, no one who knew a man serving at the front could make any long-term plans. They lived each day as it came. Then we met, and I realised that I would have to resolve the situation with Alastair at some stage'

'He's the reason you wanted to take things slowly with me?'

'No, it was like I said in my letters.'

'I see.'

'There's more.' Betty told Duncan in detail the events leading up to her departure from The Potteries and her new life in Birmingham, and how supportive Jessie had been.

'There, you know everything now.'

Duncan groaned. 'What an unholy mess! Have you heard anything from him since you came here?'

She shook her head.

'What does Jessie know?'

'She knows about Hannah, that's all.'

He pulled her to her feet and kissed her, his hands gently cupping her head. 'If only I'd known,' he murmured.

'You *do* see why I couldn't tell yer?'

He nodded. 'But you're safe now.'

'I know. I hope it doesn't affect the way you feel about me.'

He smiled but didn't answer. It was a lot to take in, she supposed.

The rest of the day passed far less eventful than the morning.

When it was time for him to leave, they put on hats and coats, and she walked with him to the station. She put a hand on his arm. He looked at her. She tried to read his face, but it was closed to her

'Will I see you again soon?' she asked.

'I'll be in touch Betty.'

He gave a brief wave before disappearing into the jaws of the station.

She took a slow walk back to the flat. After all she had told him, it was up to him to decide on his next step and whether he would see her again.

* * *

'So, Betty dear, how did it go? You look a little agitated if I may say so.'

Rowena had just left, and it was the first time Betty and Jessie could get together to talk about her meeting with Duncan.

Betty slumped into a chair. 'I thought everything would be so much easier once he was back and we could talk about everything.'

'Tell me — if you want to, that is; I don't wish to make your life more difficult.'

She wrinkled her nose as she thought how to begin. 'When we were writing to each other, he said he had . . . feelings for me and wanted us to be more than friends. I had only met him three times before we started to write, and I said I thought we should slow things down a little, but I was happy to write.'

Jessie pursed her lips and nodded. 'It sounds the right thing to do if you're not sure.'

'I liked him, but after Hannah's father, Alastair, I didn't think I could trust myself to choose the right person.' She paused and tried to think of the right thing to say next. 'Before we go any further you need to be in full possession of the facts.' Betty went on to recount the story of her relationship with Alastair and Duncan.

'Oh, you poor girl. I never realised.'

'I apologise for not telling you at the interview, but I had got so used to telling the agreed story that I think it had become second nature to me.'

'Don't worry yourself about that, you told me the most important part, the most necessary part. Alastair's violence, while it is abhorrent, is a detail which would not have affected my decision to employ you.'

'I told Duncan the story and he went so quiet. When it was time for him to leave, I walked with him to New Street, and he hardly said a word. I asked about another meeting, but he just said he'd be in touch. Oh, Jessie, I think I might've lost him.'

'He seems decent, and you've been incredibly brave. The good news is that, if he visits again, it means he has accepted what you have told him.'

'And if he doesn't?'

'Then, my dear, you need to think about whether or not he's worth fighting for.'

* * *

It was nearly two weeks later before Betty received a letter from Duncan and she was nearly out of her mind with worry. Jessie had picked up the post as usual and she handed Betty the letter. Her heart thumped so hard it hurt.

'I don't know whether I can bear to open it.' Betty's hands were shaking so much she had difficulty opening the envelope. In the old days, she would have taken it somewhere, to open on her own. Now she knew the value of having someone with her who could support her if it had all gone wrong.

'Take it easy, Betty. Deep breaths. I don't want you passing out on me.' Doing as Jessie suggested, she calmed herself as much as circumstances would allow, before slitting the envelope open and taking out Duncan's letter.

14th May 1919

My Dear Betty,

A good sign, she thought.

My Dear Betty,
I'm sorry it has taken so long to write to you. You gave me a lot to think about, and thank you for telling me. It took courage and it must have been painful for you to open up like you did. I think I can appreciate now why you decided to slow down our relationship.
Having said that, I think there are things we need to talk about and suggest, if it's all right with you, I come down to Birmingham on 18th May and talk in more detail. I will be on the eleven o'clock train unless I hear otherwise from you.
Susan and Father send their best

Love
Duncan

Betty blinked as she gazed up at Jessie, her eyes bright. 'He wants to see me on Sunday. He says he'll come down on the eleven o'clock again.'

'That's good news. I'm so pleased for you.'

'He says we need to talk.'

'For what it's worth, Betty, I believe he wouldn't come all this way just to tell you it's over.'

'I wish I could believe it. Considering how much Mother drummed it into me that getting a husband had to be my aim in life, it's the part I've had the most trouble with.'

'Oh, a man is important, Betty, don't get me wrong. But it must be the right man and if Duncan, or any other man you meet, isn't the right one, you're better on your own.'

'Is that the advice you gave yourself, Jessie?'

She nodded. 'I was walking out with a man who went to war. He didn't come back.' A faraway look crossed her face. 'He was so good to me. We were going to get engaged during his next leave. Then I had the dreaded telegram and he never came back.' She seemed to shake herself back into the present. 'Anyway, I have never found anyone good enough to replace him.' She opened her arms wide. 'So here I am, waiting, and I'll wait for as long as it takes to find someone as good as he was.'

'Oh, Jessie.'

'Don't worry — when the right man comes along, you'll know it, just as I did.'

* * *

Betty spent the rest of the week thinking about her feelings and what Jessie had said to her. When Duncan kissed her, her body seemed to come alive. She hadn't experienced anything like it. He was constantly in her thoughts. Was he truly the man for her?

On Sunday Betty took special care to dress for Duncan. She flew around her room panicking about everything going wrong. Despite the help of Jessie and Rowena, anxieties had been building up in her mind, and threatened to overtake her reason.

Everyone must have been relieved when there came a knock on the door. Betty was in the kitchen and froze. Rowena, tutting, went to let him in. Duncan was wearing the same suit, but with a different tie, Betty noticed. He couldn't see her, so she was able to take in everything about him. He could, most definitely, be her young man, there was no doubt about it.

Hearing the three voices chatting quite freely, she

tried desperately to pull herself together. She had a feeling today was going to be one of the biggest days of her life. She straightened her back. She, Betty Dean, was going to meet it head on.

She patted her hair and walked into the sitting room. Duncan turned to look at her with a smile on his face, which was a good start.

'It's lovely to see you.' She moved forward and stretched up to kiss his cheek. 'I thought we could have a talk first and perhaps go out for a walk later?'

'Suits me.'

'We might see you later, Duncan,' said Jessie, with a quick wink at Betty. 'If we don't, have a good journey back.'

She took hold of Rowena's arm and pulled her towards the coat stand to don their jackets before disappearing through the door.

'Nice girls, aren't they?'

Betty nodded. 'Yes, and I can't thank them enough.'

She stood in front of him determined, this time, she was going to stay in control of both herself and the conversation.

'I am glad you came, Duncan. I was afraid you would think twice about it after everything I told you.'

He wore a wry smile. 'I was a bit overwhelmed, I don't mind saying. Life doesn't seem dull when you're around, Betty.'

She smiled back. 'But you came back.'

His face became serious. 'Over these last weeks, I've done a lot of thinking. I can see why you were reticent about getting involved with me when you had so much to think about, and I also understand you couldn't say much about it in a letter. For my part, I think I let my disappointment get the better of me and I was frustrated I couldn't explain it better.'

He put his arms around her and hugged her, and she relaxed against him. Some of her anxiety had melted.

'Will you ever go back to Stoke?'

'I love my job. I don't know if I could get anything similar in Stoke, but I would like to think I will go back — when the time's right.'

'What does that mean?'

'When I know Alastair isn't going to appear again, I suppose.' She could've said *when there was something to go back for. Or someone.*

He pulled away from her. 'I've heard of men who have come back fit and healthy, but sick in their minds. Even men from the Somme are still reliving the war every day and that's nearly three years ago. Betty, when I told you, in my letter, I thought I was falling for you, I meant it. No, I didn't *think*, I *knew*. I was angry with myself for telling you so soon, but had to tell you. I might not have had another chance.'

Betty shuddered.

'It's what soldiers think.'

'Have you forgiven me?'

'We all have pasts, some more eventful than others. But the past is the past and we can't let it influence our futures.'

They kissed, slowly this time, enjoying the closeness she would never take for granted.

Duncan lifted his head. 'There is just one thing.'

Frowning, with her head on one side, she waited for him to speak.

'If you are happy about it, do you think it might be time for me to meet Hannah?'

Betty didn't have to think. Her arms went round

him, and she hugged him so tightly he had to protest about not being able to breathe.

* * *

Betty organised the trip back home so Duncan could meet Hannah. She told the whole story to her parents: how she had met him before he went to war and had been writing to him, as a friend, ever since. She even told them he knew about Alastair and the problems she'd had with him.

'And he still wants ter walk out with yer?' Father gave a pretend laugh — at least, Betty hoped he was pretending. 'He sounds alrate — mad, but alrate.'

'Father!'

'Listen ter me,' said Mother. 'If this bloke knows what our Betty says he knows, and he still wants ter see her and her little girl, then he's definitely alrate by me.'

* * *

She arrived at Wellington Road on Saturday afternoon but didn't tell three-year-old Hannah about their guest until Sunday morning.

'Hannah, darling, I have a friend who is coming for dinner today. Would you like to meet him?'

'A man?'

'Yes. His name is Duncan.'

'Will he play with me?'

'He might — if you ask him nicely.'

'You can play as well.' Hannah put her finger in her mouth, which enabled her to think.

'Thank you, Hannah, I would love to.'

It had been up to each member of the family to decide whether they would like to be there, although, if it had been left to Betty, she would rather it had been Mother, Father, and Hannah. Still, the bridge had to be crossed sooner or later.

She didn't have time to warn Duncan in advance, and so it was that he turned up, as smart as ever, to a house full of the Dean family. He managed to control his face as he walked in and was introduced to everyone. He was given a seat in pride of place beside the fire grate, even though it wasn't lit. Betty sat next to him to prevent him becoming overwhelmed. Hannah tried to sit next to Betty and, when she was introduced, couldn't bring herself to say a word.

Sunday dinner was informal. There was no room big enough to fit all of them and so the older members of the family sat round the table leaving Mary-Ellen, Michael, Lily and Tommy to sit in the kitchen. Father quizzed Duncan on his war experiences and his job on the railway. He appeared disappointed that Duncan worked in the office and wasn't a driver.

When dinner was over, Betty suggested she and Duncan took Hannah for a walk. Tommy wanted to go, too, but was persuaded not to by his mother. Betty got Hannah ready to go out in the pram, fearing she might not be able to walk far after eating her dinner.

It was a lovely day and it felt good walking beside Duncan.

'How do yer feel?' she asked with a grin. 'You know, walking with me and Hannah? Are yer embarrassed?'

'No, do you think I should be?'

'No. I was only thinking it must be so different ter what you were doing only weeks ago.'

'I see what you mean, but I couldn't be happier.'

She stopped pushing the pram. 'Do you mean that?'

'Every word,' he smiled.

'Every word,' echoed Hannah.

They burst out laughing.

It was over all too soon and Betty had to catch the four o'clock train to Birmingham. Duncan took her home to drop Hannah off, and then to the station.

'So, Duncan, you know all about me and me family. Rather a lot to take in all at once I should imagine.'

'It's a happy family, from what I can see.'

'I suppose we are, although we have our ups and downs, like every family.'

'Betty, I can't carry on with my life until I know where I stand with you. Do you think we might possibly have a future together?'

She beamed. 'I was hoping you'd ask me, Duncan, because if you hadn't, I had vowed I would have to ask you!'

It was a wonderful summer, quite the best Betty had ever had. She and Duncan saw each other whenever they could. Usually, Duncan would travel to Birmingham because of his free tickets from the railway. When Betty went north, they would have the opportunity to take Hannah out with them. Sometimes, they would call in to see Susan and Duncan's father, Sean. Hannah was getting used to meeting people and had lost some of her shyness. It would be wonderful to be a proper family, but difficult when they were living so far apart.

50

September 1919

Betty had been working in Birmingham for over six months. It hadn't taken as long as she had anticipated to acclimatise to the huge city and working routine. Jessie and she worked well together, and Betty had begun researching the attitudes of employers towards women and their effects on rates of pay. Jessie was convinced of the need to encourage all women to join their unions and to fight for their rights as workers.

They usually had dinner in one of the little cafes in the centre of the city. Often, they would meet Joe and some of his friends and colleagues. They would exchange ideas and information, and Betty revelled in being part of it.

It was at one such dinner Joe announced he would be working in London for the next few months, maybe up to a year.

Betty's eyes lit up. 'I've always wanted to go ter London. It sounds exciting, Joe.'

'It's an interesting place, although it isn't all glamour,' said Jessie. 'You think there are poor places in Birmingham, but the same applies in London.'

'I'll keep in touch with both of you. I expect you to have changed the world by the time I get back,' said Joe, eyes twinkling.

'No, I think it's you that wants to change the world, Joe Cumberbatch. Remember Doris from the PTC?

She was right about you being a troublemaker! But I shall miss you so much.'

She reached up and planted a kiss on his cheek, and laughed as his face burned red.

51

November 1919

At the beginning of November, Betty was in Birmingham Central Library carrying out her usual task of scanning national newspapers for articles of interest to the AWTU. She was halfway through her pile of papers when an article headline caught her eye.

WAR HERO COMMITTED TO
MENTAL ASYLUM

At Perth Sheriff Court, the Procurator Fiscal heard evidence from the police about an incident that took place on the Blair Tummel Estate of Lord Caithness. Alastair Macdonald, the gamekeeper, was accused of assaulting two hill walkers and threatening them with a loaded gun. He then disappeared into the trees but was later arrested.

Macdonald had received the Military Medal for bravery in carrying out many risky sniping operations on the Western Front to kill or severely wound German Officers.

He stated he had not done anything wrong. 'I challenged the Germans [the hill-walkers] and when they were clearly not officers. I let them go with a warning,' he said.

After examination by several leading doctors, it was agreed Macdonald was still living under the illusion he was fighting the war. It was a type of shellshock.

Macdonald is potentially a danger to himself and others, and has been committed to a secure mental hospital for further assessment, before standing trial for his offences.

As she read, she felt cold inside. She couldn't believe what she was seeing. It felt like a dream. She copied the article into her notebook, her hand shaking. She completed the rest of her task and returned to the office.

* * *

Betty ran up the stairs to the office and flung her coat on the stand. She must have been breathing heavily because Jessie's voice rang out from her office.

'Is that you, Betty?'

'Yes, I've had such a shock. You'll never guess.' She hurried into Jessie's office.

'Whatever's happened? You look awful.'

'I was at the library going through the papers as usual and I found this.' She handed her notebook to Jessie, whose eyes scanned over the words.

'You've been a lucky girl,' she said at last.

Betty sank into the chair facing Jessie's desk. 'When I read the article, I panicked. I never thought he could be that bad, Jessie. I really didn't.'

'You've had a lucky escape.'

Betty shook her head. 'We were determined if he came looking for me, he wouldn't find Hannah.'

* * *

Betty was desperate to share this latest news with Duncan. On Sunday, his house was the first stop.

Susan opened the door at her knock. Her face must have betrayed something of her feelings because, once inside, Susan took her coat and immediately called for Duncan. He appeared smiling at Betty and held out his arms to her. She threw herself into them.

'Hey, what's all this?' He held briefly and then pushed her gently away.

'I have to talk to you.'

Duncan frowned. 'What's happened? Come with me.'

He led her into the sitting room and deposited her gently into a chair.

'I'll make some tea,' said Susan, glancing from one to the other. She hurried out, closing the door quietly behind her.

He held Betty's ice-cold hands. 'Now, tell me?'

She nodded. He let go of her hands. She felt into her bag and pulled out her notebook and passed it to him without a word.

'What's this?' He took the notebook.

'It's about Alastair. Go on, read it.'

He read it quickly and placed it on the table.

'You were right to feel frightened Betty. Thank the Lord you got out of his way before he did anything to you.'

Betty shivered and he put his arm gently around her shoulders. She felt anxious and cold inside as her mind returned to the night Alastair threatened her.

'You'll feel safer now.'

'The article does not say how long he was committed for, but Jessie spoke to our solicitors, and they confirmed he would have to improve considerably before being considered fit to stand trial. He would then have to serve his prison sentence. So it looks like a long time.'

'I've heard of men like this who are still hospitalised several years later. I don't think you will see Alastair for a long time.'

His voice was gentle. She turned to him and reached forward to meet his lips.

'I feel numb. It'll feel strange, visiting The Potteries and not looking to see if he's around.'

'You're safe with me, Betty.'

He kissed her again, just as Susan chose that moment to bring in the tea.

'No problems then?'

'No problems, Susan. There was, but not any more.'

After leaving Duncan, she carried on to Wellington Road and gave her news to her parents. It was a relief to all concerned, although Mother said it must be terrible for Alastair's mother.

She gave Hannah a big hug.

* * *

'You must be thankful your problems have been resolved,' said Jessie. 'I suppose there's nothing to stop you returning to Stoke permanently, if you decide to.'

'I don't suppose there is. And having Duncan in Stoke makes it more likely I will — but not to work in a dead-end job. You have taught me so much, Jessie. I am not going to throw it away just to go backwards. When I started, you told me I had a lot to offer women at work, and I would understand their problems and needs. I intend to stay in Birmingham until the right job comes along.'

Rowena said: 'I am pleased about that. I think you have the potential to make something of your life. I really do. But there's nothing to stop you re-acquainting yourself with your friends, is there?'

'There's a few things I haven't told them. I need to build myself up to do that.' Betty lowered her head. 'There is one friend I told about Hannah — and she wasn't very nice about it.'

Jessie shook her head. 'Then you're better off without that friend.'

'I can't just leave what I'm doing here. I've worked so hard.'

'You'll know when the time is right, Betty,' Jessie smiled. 'Until then, we shall be glad for you to stay.'

52

December 1919

'Look who's here, Hannah. It's Mummy.'

The little girl squealed in delight and ran into Betty's open arms.

'Have yer come straight here, or have yer seen Duncan?'

'No Mother, I came straight here. Duncan will be at work.' She dropped a kiss on Mother's forehead. 'Where's Lily? I could give her a hand?'

'Sent her out ter get some last-minute stuff. She was letting things get on top of her. Thought it best ter send her out. Her's taken Tommy an' all.'

'Mummy play.'

Hannah had taken hold of Betty's skirt and was pulling her towards the cushion she had been sitting on.

'Mummy sit . . . now.'

The little voice had grown more urgent. Betty chuckled. Hannah certainly was attention-seeking. Working in Birmingham, Betty had missed so much of Hannah's life: her first steps, first words, the beginnings of her personality. To make up for it, she tried to spend longer with her on each visit. Little kids tended to become shy around adults they didn't see regularly and she didn't want that to happen to her daughter. She flopped on to the cushion beside which Hannah was kneeling, and read three stories, and then played marbles until her daughter's red curls stopped bouncing and she curled up to sleep beside her mother. Feeling her little body, curled up so trustingly beside her, sent an overwhelming feeling of protection through Betty.

* * *

At Christmas this year there was plenty of food on the table and good company. They played games and made merry, and sang Christmas carols because everyone knew the words, thanks to regular attendance at Sunday school.

Betty sat playing with Hannah but thinking of her tram friends. What were they up to today: Jean, the quiet one, and Connie, the toff.

She had been away for nine months, without a word to either of them, and it had broken her heart. Jessie was right. For better or worse she should see them and beg for forgiveness for her disappearance. Surely, when they knew of her reasons, they could become friends again.

Each time she had returned to The Potteries to see her family, they were in her mind. How were they? Did they miss her as much as she missed them?

Now that Alastair was out of the way, she could begin to make plans to see them again.

53

January 1920

Her mind was made up. The start of a new year and a new decade was also a day for making resolutions, for putting decisions into practice, and a day for renewing those friendships she had missed so much. She wouldn't write to them — that would be cowardly. She would call on them, starting with Connie because hers was the only address Betty had, now that Jean was married. She would march up to the front door, bold as brass, and announce herself. She'd had enough of hiding herself away. She wanted them to meet this mature, responsible Betty, the new Betty who worked in an office, who wore decent clothes that were not second-hand with frayed cuffs.

She lay in bed, staring at the ceiling, and, despite her thick head after celebrating the New Year with Jessie and Rowena, a grin began to develop in the corners of her mouth. She knew what to do.

She scrambled out of bed, and dressed in her best work suit and restrained her curls into an efficient bun at the nape of her neck. She looked every bit the confident woman of the new decade. A quick glance in the mirror and she was ready to leave. She left a note for Jessie and Rowena telling them her plans.

She caught a train to Stoke in the darkness of the early morning, and a tram to Burslem. By the time she arrived at Sneyd Street, and Connie's home, the morning was well advanced. Her walk had kept her warm. There were few people about. She hoped she wouldn't arrive too early. She knew Connie lived somewhere rather grand but, even so, she wasn't prepared for what she saw. Flabbergasted would be an understatement. Betty's jaw dropped. A brass nameplate with the words '*Holmorton Lodge*' was attached to the wall of the largest house she had ever seen in The Potteries. She stared, unable to take her eyes off it. How could someone who lived in such a house have taken a job as a clippie? Had she got the wrong address?

A cold chill ran down her back as she recalled being that girl who had stood with her mother looking up the long drive to Stowford House. Now, she was a grown woman of twenty-one years, with a decent job, and a posh house still put the fear of God into her.

The house had three stories and was quite square-looking. There were big bay windows, crowned by parapets on two sides of the house and arched windows on the other two. Every window was framed in a smooth cream cement. The house was set in a well-maintained garden. It looked like a castle.

She came to her senses and hoped no one would be looking through the windows at the strange woman standing with her mouth open. She took a deep breath, marched up to the front door and knocked.

Betty stood back from the step and waited. No using the servants entrance this time.

Moments later the door was opened by a girl of similar age to Betty, dressed quite prettily, not in a uniform of any description, so Betty didn't know if she was part of the family or not. To her knowledge, Connie had never mentioned having a sister.

'Can I help, Miss?'

The girl didn't talk like Connie neither, so Betty was none the wiser.

'I've come to see Connie. I'm a friend of hers,' she said boldly.

'Who shall I say is calling, Miss?'

'Betty Dean.'

There was a slight lifting of the girl's eyebrows as if she recognised the name.

'Best come in and I'll get Connie for you.'

Betty stepped into the hall and waited for the girl — who she now realised must be the maid, Alice — to close the door. Connie had spoken of her many times. The wood-panelled hall looked warm and smelled of polish and in one corner there was a floor-to-ceiling Christmas tree.

At that moment, Connie came through a doorway on her right. She was reading, what looked to Betty, like a letter.

Alice smiled. 'Someone to see you, Connie.'

Connie stared at Betty and froze. Her eyes widened as if she couldn't believe what she was seeing. 'Betty Dean? Is it really you? You look . . . incredible!'

Betty flushed with pleasure. 'Hello, Connie. I hope as you don't mind me coming without telling you. Only, I was just passing,' she lied.

'Well I never. Of course, I don't mind. I should have minded much more if you hadn't called, after all this time!'

Then, Jean appeared, her eyes nearly popping out of her head.

Betty held out her arms. 'Fancy catching you here an' all!' Tears sprang into her eyes. 'I'm so sorry, Jean. If there had been any way to get ter your wedding, wild horses wouldn't have stopped me.'

'I'd just called by to drop in some books for Alice and Connie, and we got talking about things.'

The three of them hugged each other to within an inch of their lives.

Connie let go first. 'Alice dear, Betty was one of the clippies from the PTC.'

'Am pleased to meet yer Betty. Would you like some tea?'

'We shall be in the drawing room, Alice.'

Alice nodded and disappeared, leaving the three of them together. Connie herded Betty and Jean through a door to the drawing room and closed the door.

* * *

Connie rounded on Betty.

'Betty Dean! What the hell did you think you were doing — disappearing off like you did, leaving us with no idea where you were, or why you left? Throwing your life away with Joe! We were worried sick about you.'

Connie's green eyes blazed. Her sharp words took Betty by surprise. She had so much to tell them, some of which she had taken for granted — such as Joe and all his help.

'Why did you go? Why has it taken you so long to get in touch? What on earth have you been doing all this time?'

The old Betty would have hung her head. Could she expect anything else when even she could see her behaviour looked bad. The new Betty stood, chin up.

'I'm sorry, Connie. I never meant ter hurt any of yer. I had me reasons for what I did.'

'Why didn't you send a letter? Anything — to say you were all right?'

Jean nodded, also looking for answers.

'As I said, Connie, I had me reasons,' Betty said, quietly. 'Have you two never had no secrets?' She lifted an eyebrow. There had been times in the past when she was sure Connie had a past she kept secret, and so had Jean and her Stephen. She used that knowledge now. She wasn't going to let either of them get the better of her before she had said what she had come to say.

They stared at each other. It was Connie who turned away first, much to Betty's satisfaction.

'We've been so worried,' said Jean.

'It was a case of needs must. I wouldn't have done it if I hadn't had to. You should both know that.'

Alice came back with a silver tray holding dainty cups, a teapot, and a plate of homemade biscuits. She glanced at Connie and Betty before laying the tray down on a small table.

'Would you like me to pour the tea, Connie?'

Connie was silent.

'I'll do it. Thank you, Alice' intervened Jean after glancing at the faces of the other two.

Alice smiled and beat a hasty retreat.

Connie's anger seemed all but spent. Betty began to speak. 'I am sorry, Connie. I didn't realise just how worried you were about me.

Connie stared at her. 'I'm sorry I was so cross with you. It was the anxiety talking, but I shouldn't have gone on at you like that. Please forgive me, dearest Betty. You'll be wishing you had never returned.'

'I appreciate your concern. I thought about you both all the time and I promise that if there had been any other way, I wouldn't have done what I did.'

Connie smiled a sort of watery smile, Betty thought. She really does care. All three girls came together in an embrace. The worst part of the visit was over.

⋆ ⋆ ⋆

'So, Betty,' said Connie, 'we want to know everything that has happened since you left.'

'It all a bit strange now. You remember the party we had that last Christmas — when we were telling each other our plans because we'd had our leaving letters? It had all been so good at the PTC. You, me, and Jean, together, with money in our pockets. The end of the war ended all that.'

'But you didn't have to go away? You could have found work in The Potteries, couldn't you?' said Jean

'But things were changing. It was obvious you were in love with Stephen Adams and, if yer don't mind me saying, you, Connie, were feeling more than you let on for Inspector Caldwell.'

Connie smiled. 'Very perceptive of you, Betty. I didn't even know myself.'

'I like ter watch people. Anyway, I was going on about the end of the war spoiling things before you arrived and Jean told me as I should stop thinking about me and think instead about the blokes coming back. Then you came in and we started ribbing Jean about Mr Adams, remember?'

Connie laughed and nodded. 'And you said he was too old! It was a lovely wedding, Betty. Just a registry office ceremony, and a dance. That's when me and Robert —'

'You and Robert? So, I *was* right about you pair?'

Connie nodded with a huge grin. 'Yes. You are a good judge of character it seems. But he hasn't asked me to marry him yet. Anyway, you asked me about my time as a suffragette. Do you remember?'

Betty grinned. 'You left some of the Suffragette journals for me to read. It started me thinking about union work. While I was in service, I learned to type and took a course in bookkeeping. I always said I wanted summat better. When Joe got a job with the Labour Party in Birmingham, he asked if I want a fresh start because he knew of this job going with a woman called Jessie O'Neill, a friend of his, an area organiser for the AWTU. She's very good. I was tickled pink when she offered me the job.'

'What about Joe? What's he doing?'

'He's working for the Labour Party. It's early days, but he's ambitious. He knows Jessie. He turns up occasionally as a friend, nothing more, I swear.'

'It sounds as if everything was fine for you, so why leave without telling us? That's what we couldn't understand. We tried everywhere: we went to your boarding house and spoke to your landlady. She wasn't much help.'

'I'm sorry. She was only doing what I asked.'

Jean shook her head as if she didn't understand.

The time had come. 'I was so excited about the job and looking forward to telling you both. But something happened.' Betty forced herself to carry on. 'I have a lot to tell you, but first, I have to say Joe is one of the best of men and I won't have a word said against him. When I've told you everything, you'll understand. I promise. The first thing you need to know about me is . . .' she took a deep breath. 'I have a daughter —'

Their gasps were audible. Betty could almost laugh but held back. 'And before you ask, she isn't Joe's.'

'The little girl I saw you with . . . you said she was your sister.'

'Don't interrupt, Jean. Let me tell you everything. Then it'll start to make sense to yer.'

Connie and Jean looked at one another but did as they were told.

'My daughter, Hannah, was born when I was seventeen.'

This time there was a gasp from Jean. A warning look from Betty stopped her from speaking and Betty was able to carry on with her story.

'And yes, I had her before I started to work with you both. I was in service and, with the war and everything, I had . . . relations with a man, Alastair, before he went off to basic training. I thought I was in love with him but I saw a side of him I didn't like. He had a temper and could be violent. I realised I couldn't love him if I couldn't trust him, so I ended it. After he went away, I found out I was expecting.

'I couldn't continue to work at Stowford and I gave notice to leave. Mother and Father were none too pleased, but in the end decided nothing could be done about it, so we made the best of it. Mother looks after Hannah for me, so I can go out to work.'

'You poor thing,' said Jean, with eyes full of sympathy.

'I was going to surprise you both about the new job, but Joe didn't want to hand his notice in straight away and asked me to say nothing. The week before Joe and I were going to hand in our notices, Alastair arrived wanting to pick up where he left-off.'

Betty met Connie's eyes boldly. 'The war had

changed him. He really frightened me. I was concerned for my safety and for Hannah. I had told him it was over, but he didn't believe me. He threatened to come looking for me as soon as he was demobbed. Joe and I talked it over with my parents and agreed it would be best if I left The Potteries straightaway, but if it was going to work, I had to keep it a secret. So, I told nobody where I was going.'

'But you knew you could trust us,' said Jean.

'I couldn't tell you because I would've had to tell you about Hannah, too.'

Connie's green eyes pierced Betty's brown. 'Why didn't you?'

Betty hung her head. It was painful to carry on, but she was determined. 'I was too embarrassed. I thought you wouldn't want anything to do with me. Honestly, if I hadn't had Joe, I don't know what I'd have done. Me and Joe never slept together, we didn't even live together. When I wrote you that letter, Connie, I couldn't think of anything else to say. I just wanted you to know I wasn't on my own.'

Connie flopped back in her chair as if exhausted. 'I don't know what to say. All this going on and you never said a word. I think this calls for more tea. I'll go and get some.'

'I think it calls for something stronger!' said Jean.

* * *

'What are you doing in Birmingham?' asked Connie.

'I work for Miss Jessie O'Neill, she is the Midlands' representative for the AWTU. She is Lady Jessica O'Neill, but you wouldn't think so. She is left-wing and a supporter of women's rights at work. I get paid the same wage as a man would get.'

'Oh, that Lady Jessica. She is very emancipated. I heard about her from one of the WSPU women a few years ago. Her father made millions from the war as an armaments manufacturer. I'm surprised he allows his daughter to carry on like that.'

'I think Jessie can handle her father, Connie. They have agreed to an informal truce. She doesn't speak of his work, and he does not interfere with hers.'

'What does the job entail?'

'I'm Jessie's assistant. I type, organise meetings, deal with correspondence, take notes of meetings in shorthand and anything Jessie wants. I like the work. I get to go to meetings with the bosses and other union representative and take notes. I do research for Jessie and talk to women in the factories to understand what their problems are. Jessie says I have the common touch and I can get women to talk to me. And, what's more, I earn enough for both Hannah and me, and can save some money as I live rent free —'

'With Joe!' gasped Jean.

'No! With Jessie. I'll tell you more later, but now I want to know what I have missed here apart from you getting wed, Jean?'

Jean spoke first. 'Not much. We're living with Stephen's mother near to Tunstall Park. You must come and see us now you're back, Betty.'

'I am only visiting. I must be back in work tomorrow morning. I haven't been to see my family yet, I came here to talk to Connie and find your address, Jean, so we could meet again.'

'Oh, I see. But you must still come to see us as soon as you can.'

'What about you, Connie? You must have lots to

tell me.'

'Father passed away in October, last year,' said Connie, blinking. 'I still expect him to come through the door. We have money problems, but like you put it, Betty, we're not proper poor but things will have to change.'

'Oh, I'm sorry to hear about your father. Was it sudden?'

'Yes. His heart.'

'Are you working now?'

'I have an interview on 12th January with our solicitor, Mr Railsford, in Burslem. One of his ladies is finishing because she's having a baby.'

Betty raised her eyebrows. So, Connie *did* have money problems. To lighten the mood, she said coyly: 'What about you and Inspector Caldwell?'

'We are getting on well. He was seriously ill last year and had no one to look after him so I helped nurse him, together with Alice.'

'I thought there was something between you two.'

'He hasn't asked me to marry him yet.' A wistful look crossed Connie's face.

'Bet he will.'

'I hope so.'

'What about your friend, the one whose young man was missing?'

'You mean, Ginnie? That's good news. Sam came back in March 1919, just after you left. It was so wonderful. They got married during Wakes Week and she's expecting a baby in June. I'm so happy for them. But they've got their problems. Sam was badly affected by the war. He has terrible nightmares. Ginnie says it's as if he is re-living the war. He must have seen such horrible things out there and it sounds as if he's brought some of them back with him.'

'Sounds a bit like our Jeffrey. He takes himself off outside when it gets too much for him, even when it's dark. He can't stand being shut inside.'

'Robert's illness was made worse because he had been gassed during the war and it had affected his lungs. And then there's your Stephen, Jean, with his bad leg.'

They were silent for a moment, each thinking of their men and what the war had done to them.

'If you're not walking out with Joe, Betty, are you walking out with anyone else?'

'Yes, his name's Duncan.'

'Duncan? Not the Duncan you were dancing with . . . Arthur's friend?'

Betty grinned, delighted Jean had remembered. 'The very same one.'

'How did you two meet again?'

'We exchanged letters regularly during the war and once he was demobbed, we started to see each other again.'

'Were you writing to him all the time you were a clippie?' interrupted Connie.

'And you never said a word?' asked Jean.

'Yes, it started as letters between friends. I didn't want to get involved after my experiences.'

'I'm glad, Betty. He was rather nice. How much have you told him?'

'Everything'

'And he is still walking out with you, he must be a tolerant man. Has he asked you to marry him?' Connie raised her eyebrows, with a grin.

'No, not yet, but you never know.'

All too soon she had to leave. She wanted to pop into

Wellington Road to see Hannah before she returned to Birmingham. She said her goodbyes promising to stay in touch from now on.

* * *

It was a different Betty that trudged over to Wellington Road.

Her thoughts turned to Duncan. Their relationship had grown, but at a distance. She had been more open and spoken about more things to him than she had ever talked about to anybody, even Jeffrey. Recent events had begun to show her she only had to set her mind to something and she could do it.

Later, she sat back in the carriage back to Birmingham and closed her eyes. It had been a busy day, but it had given her so much. She had seen her daughter and her little group of friends. Not being in touch with them for such a long time had reminded her how important they were. She must not lose sight of that.

54

February 1920

Snowy weather prevented Betty from returning to The Potteries for a couple of weeks. She caught up with some mending and finished a scarf she was knitting. She had discovered a liking for knitting after making numerous pairs of socks for Duncan and cardigans for Hannah. Her next mission would be two bonnets for Hannah. On her last visit, Mother said she was growing fast and needed a bigger size. Knitting kept Betty occupied during the evenings. She had even taught Rowena, although that lady was too busy to complete anything.

Betty was delighted to receive a letter from Connie and ripped it open with glee.

4th February 1920

Dear Betty,

I was so happy to see you again after all this time, and I know Jean was too. We agreed never to refer to it again, but I must tell you one more time your friends in The Potteries really missed you and want you to promise never to disappear again, no matter what. We will always be there to help you. Robert was thankful, too. I didn't realise how anxious he was about you. He had been blaming himself for transferring Joe to Goldenhill Depot!

I am pleased to tell you I am doing quite well at Railsford Solicitor's Office. My time on the trams has served me well because I am able to control my tongue a little more than I had in the past, although you might not think so! Mr Railsford does not allow me to make any decisions for myself yet. He says I am to do as I am told. Still, it is early days. I am sure I can make some improvements in the future when Mr Railsford has become more acquainted with my ways!

Anyway, I have some news to share with you. Could you come to Holmorton Lodge on Saturday 14th at seven o'clock? I would love to tell you and Jean both together. You can stay here overnight if it is more convenient.

Love
Connie

Betty smiled. She thought she had an idea what Connie wanted to say and she wouldn't miss it for the world. And she could always snuggle up with Mary-Ellen, Lily, and Hannah for a night.

* * *

When she arrived at Holmorton Lodge, Alice was there to open the door and welcome her inside. This time, she was greeted as a friend and was shown straight into the sitting room where a group of women was gathered. There was Connie, of course, an oldish lady who Connie introduced as her mother, Agatha, Ginnie White, Connie's friend from before she became a tram girl, and Jean, who jumped up immediately to give her a hug. Alice joined them too.

There was joking and frivolity going on and Betty would not have been surprised to find the sherry bottle open. It seemed Betty was the last guest to appear for, shortly afterwards, Connie raised her voice and asked everyone to remain quiet.

'Thanks to all of you for coming out on this cold, damp night, especially to Betty for coming so far, but I had a good reason for dragging you away from your fires tonight.'

She paused and she looked at each of her friends in turn, savouring the moment, Betty thought.

'I wanted you all to be the first to know. Of course, Mother knows already —'

'Come on and tell us, Connie. We're on pins here.' That was Ginnie, and Betty took to her immediately.

'Very well, I am delighted to tell you Robert has asked me to marry him, and I have said yes.'

They all jumped up and hugged each other, happy for Connie to have her own dream come true.

'Of course, I knew it would only be a matter of time, Connie, duck,' grinned a delighted Ginnie. Now that Ginnie was on her feet, it was obvious to Betty she was expecting. She smiled at her and turned to Connie. 'I told yer not to let him go, didn't I?'

Jean had tears in her eyes. 'Stephen will be so glad to know you and Robert have finally admitted your true feelings.'

In witnessing Jean's tears, Connie's eyes filled too.

'And about time too,' Betty couldn't help but add.

Agatha Copeland watched the goings on from her chair with a faraway smile. Betty watched the emotions cross her face. Maybe she was remembering the day her husband had asked her to be his wife.

‘We are to be married on 26th June, and we hope you can all be with us.’

‘Wouldn’t miss it for the world, Connie — all being well,’ said Betty feeling a little embarrassed.’

‘I’ll do me best, but it depends on the little one,’ said Ginnie, hands on her stomach, protectively. Connie picked up Betty’s hands and held them tight. ‘Don’t you dare run out on us again, Betty Dean, or you’ll have me to answer to and next time I won’t be so lenient.’

55

April 1920

Alice, Jean, and Ginnie spent many happy hours with Connie helping her to prepare for the wedding, which was to take place at St John's Church, Burslem. Betty joined them whenever she could. Connie would've liked to have all her friends as bridesmaids but had chosen Jean and Betty to take on those special roles. It should really have been Ginnie and Alice but, Connie explained, Ginnie's confinement was due the week after the wedding. Not wanting to let anyone down, Ginnie had suggested Connie's two tram friends would be best in the circumstances, with Alice agreeing to be on standby to look after Ginnie, should the need arise.

The many hours the group spent together allowed each of them to catch up with news, and for Betty to get to know Ginnie and Alice better. The party of friends grew closer as the weeks went on. Betty learned Ginnie had been in the workhouse in her younger days and now worked at Royal Edward's pottery in Burslem, where she planned to stay for as long as she could. She lived with her husband, Sam, her sister Mabel, and Mabel's daughter, Florrie. Ginnie and Sam had been looking for a house to rent near to Burslem Park, where Sam was a gardener. So far, they hadn't been able to find one they could afford but they continued to look.

Jean had hoped she would get pregnant quickly and she confided in Betty she was growing increasingly more disappointed as her monthlies continued to flow. Betty reminded her she had only been married a year, so it was to be expected. She tried a joke, saying, in her experience, babies tended to come more quickly if the woman wasn't married, but it didn't really help. To take her mind off her worries, Jean had returned to her old job as a flowerer at Newtown Pottery, where she worked before becoming a clippie. She and Stephen could put the money by for that wonderful day when they would become parents.

After one of those meetings, Connie opened up to Betty about some concerns she had with Robert. He had been estranged from his family for many years, something Betty hadn't known about. It was to do with the war. He'd had a disagreement with his father. Connie didn't say what it was about, but it meant Robert hadn't spoken to his family since the beginning of the war. Connie had an idea to call on them in the hope she could persuade them to come to the wedding.

'Do you think it wise, Connie? You would be interfering with family matters that don't concern you.'

'Yes, but I'd be doing it for Robert and it does concern me. He deserves to have his family at his wedding. I couldn't bear it if he was there, celebrating all alone.'

'Have you spoken to Robert about it?'

Connie nodded. 'He said it was best left. They knew where he lived and if they couldn't be bothered to get in touch, then he couldn't see any reason for inviting them.'

'Poor Robert. What a terrible thing.'

'That's why I need to go, Betty. To try to bring them

together.'

Betty sighed. 'It's a big step to take.'

'I know, but I feel I have to try.'

56

May 1920

A couple of weeks later Betty received upsetting news from Connie.

5th May 1920

Dearest Betty,

I should've heeded your warning. I am in trouble with Robert when all I wanted to do was to make him happy. Now, I can see I was interfering into matters I knew nothing about. Let me explain.

I went to see Robert's father to tell him of our impending marriage, and to ask if he and the rest of the family would like to attend. And he refused without even discussing the matter. He was waiting for Robert to make the first move.

Of course, I told Robert what I had done and he said I had wilfully ignored his wishes. Honestly, Betty, it was like standing in front of his desk getting told off over something I had done as a clippie. He was so angry. I can't believe they are grown men — they were both as stubborn as each other, Betty!

I have pleaded with Robert to forgive and forget but I am beginning to think I have crossed a line. I do hope he comes round soon. I would hate to have a second marriage called off before it has begun.

I hope you are faring better than I, dear, and shall

let you know whether you need to cancel your train ticket for the wedding.

Very best wishes,
Connie

Betty shook her head after reaching the end of the letter. Connie may have been an intelligent young woman but she was hopeless at listening to advice. Betty wished she was back in Burslem with her so they could talk face-to-face. And Robert was just as bad. The pair of them needed their heads knocking together, and she would tell them so when she next saw them — if the wedding was going ahead!

It was funny: she had spent a long time being wary of Connie and her posh life, when really, she was just as likely to make a mistake which might ruin her life, as anyone else!

* * *

'Good afternoon, AWTU office.'

'Could I speak to Betty Dean, please?'

Recognising Connie's voice, Betty was afraid it could only mean one thing. 'Are you all right?' she asked.

'It's all sorted; that's what I'm ringing to tell you. Robert's come to his senses.'

'Thank goodness for that. I thought you'd both messed it up.'

'I still wish his parents would come to the wedding, but I don't think there is anything else I can do.'

'Connie, *leave well alone*. I know you when you get an idea in your head. It will gnaw away at you. You must learn when to stop.'

'Yes, I understand. You're right, of course.'

'So, I can book my railway ticket after all!'

The friends chatted for a few more minutes.

When Betty put the phone down, she did so with a sense of relief that the matter was sorted. Connie and Robert were both capable of being stubborn enough to cancel the wedding on a matter of principle.

57

June 1920

It was the beginning of June, the month of Connie's wedding and everything was going well. The dresses were finished and Betty felt like a princess when she put hers on for the final time. She had never had such a dress, and couldn't wait for Duncan to see it.

Hannah was going to be a bridesmaid for the first time in her young life, so she was there for a fitting, too. It brought tears to Betty's eyes, seeing her daughter dressed in a lemon silk and lace dress, with a bonnet of the same material, which set off her red curls.

'Am I a princess, Mummy?' asked Hannah.

'The very best in the world,' she said, hugging her tightly.

'We will get you a little posy of flowers to carry too, Hannah,' Connie said, laughing as mother and daughter did a little dance round the room. 'You're just like your mother.'

* * *

Betty took Hannah back home early, not wanting to keep her from her bed. Surprisingly, everybody was out, and she had to use her key to get in. She had just put Hannah to bed and had arrived downstairs when there came a knock on the door. She opened it to find Duncan standing there, carrying a bunch of flowers, in the middle of which were six red roses.

Betty gasped with delight and pulled him inside. 'Duncan, they're truly beautiful. Thank you so much. But what've I done to deserve them?'

She took them to the kitchen to put in a bowl of water until she could put them in a vase.

Duncan had gone quiet. She stopped talking and turned to look at him. 'Is summat the matter, Duncan? Your father isn't poorly, is he?'

He shook his head. 'I couldn't wait any longer,' he said, his face looking deadly serious.

Betty's heart thumped. 'What do yer mean?'

'Haven't you guessed, after all this time?'

She couldn't say out loud what she thought, hoped. She would feel such a fool if she'd got it wrong.

He stepped towards her. 'For a woman of the world, you can be dense at times, Betty Dean.' He took hold of her left hand. He lifted his eyes, burning with intensity, to meet hers. Her breath caught.

'Would you, Betty Dean, do me the honour of marrying me?'

'Marry yer,' she whispered, although there was no one to hear.

'What did you think I was going to say?'

'I . . . I dunno.' But she did know. As soon as she saw the look in his eyes. She just couldn't put it into words.

'Well? Are you going to give me an answer?'

'Yes! Oh, yes! I mean I would love to marry you.'

She threw her arms round his neck. His lips found hers and suddenly the world was spinning around her. All that time since their first misunderstanding, when he had told her he was falling for her, but had agreed to wait a while, upon her request, she had regretted it. She had dithered because she couldn't admit her feelings to herself. They had grown close since he'd returned, especially over the business with Alastair. Now, at last, he was hers.

'Mother will be so pleased when I tell her.'

'She already knows. I had a word with your father, to ask him for his permission. How do you think I managed to get the house to ourselves tonight?'

It was the best day of her life. She'd had a proposal of marriage from the man she loved. She couldn't believe there might possibly be two weddings for her to attend this year — and that one of them would be hers.

They sat, arms around each other, waiting for the family to return so they could give them the happy news. When they arrived, there was no need to ask any questions. It was clear from their faces the news could only be good. Hannah was carried downstairs to join in the celebration.

'Am that pleased for yer, our Betty,' said Mother, hugging her. 'I think yer've got a good 'un there, so mind yer hold on to him,' she whispered.

Father and Jeffrey both shook hands with Duncan and would, no doubt, have some words of wisdom to pass on to him at some stage.

'Are you going to be my daddy?' Hannah stood in front of Duncan who had turned a shade of pink.

'I . . . er, I —'

'Would you like him to be your daddy, Hannah?' said Betty softly.

Hannah stared at him, her head on one side and a finger in her mouth. 'I think so. Will yer read me stories?'

'I would be very happy to.'

Hannah trotted off, happy with the answer. Duncan was getting ready to leave when she reappeared with a book in hand. She had taken him at his word and he would not be allowed to leave until he had satisfied her request.

* * *

Betty and Duncan paid his family a visit to celebrate news of their engagement. Susan couldn't have been happier, and Mr Kennedy said he was pleased his son had finally met someone who could challenge him.

'We don't argue, Father,' said Duncan, eventually. There was a twinkle in his father's eye.

'There isn't a marriage today that doesn't have ups and downs, my lad, and you'd do well to remember it. These women have a way of getting what they want without a bloke even noticing. Is that right, Betty?'

She laughed. 'I couldn't possibly give away such secrets.'

Mr Kennedy joined in with the laughter. 'The brass-neck of the woman!'

Betty joined Susan in the kitchen to prepare supper.

'I know you've worked hard to get your job, after the setbacks of your earlier life,' Susan said.

Betty nodded.

'I think Duncan might be hoping you will give up work when you get wed.'

'Give up? Why should he think that?'

'You've heard him going on from time to time about families, and little Hannah? He was telling us you would probably be giving up work soon, so she could live with you, rather than stay with your mother, and you wouldn't have all the travelling to do.'

'No, Susan, you've got it wrong. Hannah will come to live with us, yes, once I get a job in Stoke. But Mother would pick her up from school and the like, so I can carry on working. It's a long way off yet.'

Susan shook her head. 'I thought he might have it wrong but I'm afraid he thinks that's what will happen. Look, don't tell him I've said anything, but you really need to talk to him about it before you make any plans.'

* * *

They took their suppers to the table and they sat talking. Betty wondered how to raise the subject of work, when Mr Kennedy did the job for her.

'Now, young Betty, how's that job of yours going?'

'I love it, Mr Kennedy. I feel I am doing summat worthwhile. My boss, Jessie, has taught me well and I shall always be grateful to her. She is giving me more responsible work, and I sometimes go out to meet the workers to take notes. We were talking with members of the Birmingham Labour Group, who are keen to set the groundwork for universal suffrage of women on the same basis as men, whenever a favourable government is elected. Of course, we hope it is going to be a Labour government. I am working on ways of getting the message to factories with female workforces. We don't need unions for men and others for women — we need single unions for all workers. It's all very exciting.'

This was it, she had to get Duncan talking now. 'Jessie has put a lot of trust in me and the job pays well, doesn't it Duncan?' she added.

He nodded.

'It'll be a help then, when you set up house,' said his father.

'It won't really, Father.' Duncan smiled at Betty, and leant back in his chair, languorously. 'I'm sure you'll want to give up working once we've got our own house, won't you? You certainly won't be able to work in Birmingham.'

Betty frowned. 'I am used to working and looking after myself. Besides, I can't leave my job until I get something else as good as this one.'

'But we'll have Hannah with us, and when we have children of our own you'll —'

'I'll what?'

'You'll give up working then? How can you look after our kids and keep a job?'

'Lots of women do, Duncan.'

'But not my wife, Betty. You'll have people feeling sorry for us that I've had to send you out to work.'

'Come on, Father, let's leave them to it,' said Susan

Betty barely noticed them leave. 'I thought you didn't mind my job. You seemed pleased about it when I told you.'

'That was before we talked of getting married. I naturally assumed you would finish as —'

Betty jumped to her feet. 'You know how much I enjoyed my jobs. I've learnt to be a good cook, shorthand typist, bookkeeper, and research work for women's rights. I'm confident when I talk to people, whoever they are. I don't want to give it all up just because I have a husband, Duncan, and I don't think it's right of you to ask it of me, when we haven't even set a date.'

'And I don't think it right you should put a job

before our family.'

'We share our family. We share the responsibility for it.'

'You mean you want me to share the housework and the cooking, so you can go to work?' If the argument hadn't been deadly serious, she would have laughed at the shock on his face.

They were both on their feet, glaring at each other

'You need to think hard about our future, Duncan. We appear to have different views on how we each want to live, and they are poles apart.'

'Perhaps you'll feel differently about it when you've slept on it, Betty.'

She clenched her fists. How dare he assume, having slept on it, she would be the one to change her mind. 'I think I'd better go now.'

He didn't move. He didn't say anything.

Betty shook her head in frustration. 'I would be grateful if you could walk me to the tram stop, Duncan, and I will make my own way home — unless you would prefer for me to ask your father?'

* * *

The friends gathered at Connie's house the night before the wedding. There was much hilarity. Everyone joined in, even Connie's mother, Agatha, who was particularly happy because her brother, James, had come down from Manchester and was staying in one of the guest rooms. The two of them were quite happy joining in with the conversations, but then took themselves off to the drawing room or the library to talk of the private matters they were rarely able to discuss, being so far apart. Betty and Jean were to stay two nights and their men would join them at the church.

Alice and Connie had laid out a table of snacks and drinks in the dining room for them to keep them going during the evening.

'I am so glad you are here, my dearest friends. There was a time when I thought this day would never come. It will be such a wonderful day and we shall have great fun. We are each about to settle down with the men we love, and will be so much better for it.'

Betty couldn't help blurting out: 'I don't think I will. Me and Duncan have had a row.'

Everyone groaned.

'What have yer gone and done now?' asked Jean.

She sounded exasperated, as if Betty was always doing something wrong. Well, this one was not her fault. She told them how close she had been getting to Duncan, and had high hopes of him being the one she had been waiting for — then he went and spoiled it by coming over all controlling, talking of her giving up work to have children and turning her back into a skivvy.

'You were always going on about getting a bloke, and that a job was only a stop-gap between leaving school and getting wed. Now yer've got one and you're still not satisfied.'

'I had my reasons, Jean, as I've said. I dunner think I'll be engaged for long.'

'I could speak to him tomorrow for you, Betty. He can't disagree with me on my wedding day.'

'No, don't, Connie; leave it. He'll come round eventually.'

'I think as everybody goes through problems when they get wed,' chipped in Ginnie. 'Me and my Sam have known each other since we was about eleven, but we spent a lot of time apart, for various reasons, just like Betty and Duncan. It took some doing for us to get ter know one another again when he come back. He was really poorly at times, thinking back to the war, having nightmares, and screaming for help, and being cuddled like a baby when yer try to keep them warm. As regards your Duncan, Betty, yer hardly knew him when he went ter war and yer love blossomed through yer letters. Now yer've both got ter get ter know the real people behind the letters yer fell in love with.'

'I thought we'd done that.' Betty stared at Ginnie. She sounded wiser for her years than the lot of them. 'You'll soon have to get to know a new little person, Ginnie. You'll make a wonderful mother. Sam's got a lot to be thankful for.'

'I hope so,' she said, caressing her belly, which looked ready to burst no matter how much she tried to hide it.

'It won't be long now, Ginnie,' said Connie.

'Next week, all being well.'

'You're so lucky,' said Jean, 'and you too, Betty. You'll soon be surrounded by children. Me and Stephen are still waiting.'

'But you've only been married just over a year, Jean. I'm sure it'll happen for you.'

She shrugged and took a sip of sherry. 'I'm glad I've gone back ter work. It gives me summat ter do.'

Everyone had become silent, each thinking of their own problems, when in walked Agatha and James.

Agatha glanced at all the faces. 'James, did you ever see such glum faces? I thought you girls were celebrating a wedding!'

'We are, Mother. You chose the wrong time to come

and join us. Please, take a seat, both of you.'

'We have finalised our plans, you will be happy to know,' said Agatha, with a smile. 'I shall be moving in with Uncle James sometime after the wedding, as I mentioned to you Connie. I know we have talked about putting the house up for sale, but I have decided when I move, I will give you Holmorton Lodge as a wedding present. With both of you earning, you should be able to manage comfortably. It will be for you to decide what to do with it in the future.'

Betty's eyes were on Connie as she received the news, unable to believe her ears. Connie looked just as shocked, pale and then flushed in turn, as she took in what her mother was saying.

'Oh, Mother! Are you sure you want to do that?'

'For my only daughter, I would do anything.'

'And I will have my precious sister all to myself, instead of visiting only for weddings and funerals,' said James. 'You will have nothing to pay to run the house — I have agreed to settle a regular income to cover the running and maintenance costs of the house for as long as you own it.'

Agatha smiled sadly. 'I hadn't the heart to sell your father's pride and joy, Connie.'

Connie hugged her, looking just about as happy as any bride could be.

'I can't wait to tell Robert. He will be so happy for me, I'm sure.'

Agatha turned to Alice. 'Alice dear, you are very welcome to come with me as my companion. Of course, you will need time to think about it.'

Tears welled up as Alice looked at the old lady.

'But, I promised Alice years ago she could stay with me,' burst out Connie.

'Connie — let her think about it.'

Alice wiped away her tears. 'It's very good of you, Mrs Copeland and I appreciate it. But, if you don't mind, I would like to stay in The Potteries, with Connie.' She flushed bright red. 'There is this boy . . .'

'Alice! You're a dark horse. You never said.'

'I can still look after things here to pay my way . . . and look for a job too.'

'That's wonderful, and we can convert the top floor into a flat for you. No more answering the door . . . I think Robert and I can manage that task quite well!'

'And there's me thinking I might have to teach Connie how to cook,' Betty chuckled.

Her eyes swept around each of them. 'So much happening for all of us. I'm so glad. We can show the world we are The Potteries Girls and we're in charge of our lives.'

58

26th June 1920

Five happy chattering girls for breakfast. Connie, Jean, Ginnie, Alice and Betty: their voices could be heard echoing throughout the house. Hannah had to stay, too, and thought it a good game to run through the house searching for each of them in turn.

Betty felt content with her friends and tried her best to join in with the banter, but Duncan preyed on her mind. If only she could have seen him before the wedding.

Uncle James was due to walk Connie down the aisle, with Betty and Jean as bridesmaids, following. Stephen was best man, with Duncan and Sam as ushers, and Alice charged with looking after Ginnie.

A large car had been ordered to take the bride and her retinue to St John's Church in Burslem. When they turned off Moorland Road and on to Swan Square, the crowds of Saturday shoppers watched the bridal party make its up Queen Street. So many happy smiling faces greeted them as the car drove slowly, passing the Wedgwood Institute where Alice's art courses took place.

The car pulled up outside the church at exactly twelve o'clock. Uncle James opened the door and helped, first Betty and Hannah and then Jean, out. He put out a gentlemanly hand to Connie as she too stepped from the car. Betty heard the oos and arrs from the crowds that had stopped to watch.

Betty and Jean pulled Connie's long, lace dress into a train behind her. Her veil was draped around her and held in place by a tiara, which Agatha had worn on her wedding day. She had given it to Connie that morning, having her daughter in tears as they both thought of Connie's father missing her, finally, getting married. And how beautiful she looked.

Then began the slow walk into the darkness of the church after the brightness of the summer day, first Connie and Uncle James, then Hannah with a posy, followed by Betty and Jean. Music started as she moved through the doors and, as one, the congregation rose to their feet. Betty spotted Duncan looking smart as an usher, and her heart leapt, but she told herself to concentrate on the task in hand. As they turned to walk down the aisle, Betty heard a gasp from Connie. Glancing over the bride's shoulder, she saw two men in uniform standing next to Robert. As Connie walked towards them, the three men turned. Robert's face was a picture as the other two raised their arm in salute. Betty felt a sudden rush of emotion and happiness for Connie as she realised: they must be Robert's brothers — Connie's trip to see the family had not been for nothing after all.

Connie turned to give the posy of flowers to Betty. Their hands clasped each other momentarily. Duncan put out his hand to Hannah and she moved to sit next to him. Betty smiled. They looked so good together. She mouthed a quick thank you to him, and turned back to concentrate on the service.

There was silence as the ceremony began, prayers were said and hymns sung, and then the magical words pronounced them man and wife.

When Connie turned to look at their friends and relatives, her face was a picture of happiness.

The party moved towards the vestry to sign the marriage register. Betty and Jean, who were required to sign the register, followed.

Suddenly there was a huge cry. Turning quickly, Betty saw Ginnie was on the floor.

'Me waters have broke!'

* * *

Betty closed her eyes.

A torrent of words and murmurings echoed round the church.

'Oh, no. I can't believe it. At least this time I managed to get married before it was interrupted,' wailed Connie from the vestry. 'Please tell me she's all right.'

'I'll see what's happening,' Betty called over her shoulder and rushed over to Ginnie. Sam was pale-faced, kneeling beside her and holding her hand.

'Dunner werrit, Ginnie duck. We'll get yer sorted.'

Sam looked up blankly as if waiting to be told what to do. Others stood around gawping, but no one stepped forward to help poor Ginnie. The baby was on its way whether the time was right, or not.

'Anything I can do?' It was Uncle James. His calm, practical manner soothed Betty so she could think straight.

'Can we get hold of the midwife or a doctor, or somebody what knows what to do?'

'The midwife's in Newcastle Street. I can go for her,' said Sam, 'if you can take care of my Ginnie?'

'Yes, do.'

Sam rushed off.

Ginnie's face was bright red and creased with pain.

'We need ter get her home, quickly,' murmured Betty. Out loud, she asked for Alice. The girl pushed through the crowd around them. 'Alice, I need to go home with Ginnie and stay with her until help arrives. Can you tell Connie? And can you sign the register for me?' Alice nodded. 'And tell her I'm sorry I won't be there.'

Alice placed a hand on Betty's shoulder and patted it, gently. 'Just make sure as Ginnie's all right. That'll be foremost in her mind.'

Betty felt Duncan's hand rest on her shoulder. 'Don't worry, I'll take care of Hannah.' She hugged him swiftly and turned back to Ginnie.

They got Ginnie to her feet and helped her out of the church. The driver of the car was sitting on the church wall, smoking a cigarette. He jumped up when he saw the party moving towards him.

'Quick, get us to North Street,' ordered Uncle James.

'Her's not going ter have it in me car, is she?'

'Not if yer get a move on,' shouted Betty, in a voice that refused to take no for an answer.

The car, taking Ginnie, Uncle James, and Betty, sped off towards the home Ginnie shared with her sister, Mabel, and Mabel's six-year-old daughter, Florrie.

'Lord above!' Mabel squeaked as she opened the door to see a sorry-looking Ginnie. 'Is it coming? I told her as she shouldn't go, but would she listen? Let's get you up to the bedroom —'

'I don't think I can get up there,' said Ginnie, sagging into her sister's arms.

'You walk with her, Mabel, and push from behind

and make sure as she dunner fall. I'll be here ter make sure she gets up there,' panted Betty.

'Mr . . . can yer keep yer eye on little Florrie for me?'

It wasn't a question. Mabel didn't think twice about ordering people about when it was necessary, even important people such as Uncle James. Betty didn't have a name for him, apart from Uncle James. She grinned at him. 'Thank you, Uncle James.'

Uncle James must've decided he'd done his bit, and sat beside the table.

'Boil some water will yer? And plenty of it.'

Betty could picture him smiling as he caught Mabel's order from half-way up the stairs.

* * *

Thankfully, the midwife arrived soon after. Betty and Mabel were able to hand over responsibility for the delivery, but both stayed to support her should the need arise. Ginnie was exhausted after each contraction.

Betty found herself thinking of her mother, who had gone through the pain of childbirth so many times, and had gone through her own birthing of Hannah. She felt the pain as if she herself was giving birth. As she held Ginnie's hand, talking to her about something and nothing, she let her thoughts rest with Hannah. She could almost feel herself pushing Ginnie's baby out with her, willing her on.

If everything had gone according to plan, Connie should have been there; but babies don't stick to plans. The labour seemed to take ages.

'Betty?' Ginnie's voice was almost a whisper.

'Where's Sam? I dunner want him to be on his own.'

'Connie's Uncle James is with him. Would you like me ter check on him?'

Ginnie nodded and her body tensed with a scream and then sank back into the pillows. 'Tell him I'm alrate and not ter worry.'

'Course I will.' Betty let go of her hand and slipped out of the room. Trust Ginnie to be thinking of Sam rather than herself.

Betty made her way carefully down the steep stairs. Sam jumped to his feet as she opened the door.

'What's happening?'

'She's still in labour, Sam. But she's doing well. She asked me to tell you not to worry. Midwife thinks it'll happen soon.'

Sam passed his cap from one hand to the other, as if it was a comforter. 'We're sorry yer missed the rest of Connie's wedding. She'll be on edge, waiting for news. Pity it had ter happen today, of all days.'

'Am sure Connie doesn't mind. She'll be thinking about Ginnie, make no mistake.'

Another scream came from upstairs. Sam's face contorted as if it was him who had cried out.

'I'd best get back, Sam. We'll tell yer soon as there's news.' Betty crossed her fingers behind her back as another scream rent the air. Sam groaned. She gave him a quick hug and ran back upstairs.

She opened the door to the bedroom. The midwife bent down to see if there was any sign.

'Baby's coming,' Mabel announced as Betty opened the door and quickly shut it again. 'Baby's coming! Push, Ginnie, duck. Push.'

Once again, Betty picked up Ginnie's hand, although she didn't think Ginnie even noticed. The tension built up in Ginnie's body as she pushed with all her might.

Suddenly, the baby was out and picked up by the midwife. A tense moment followed as she gently wiped the baby's face and nose, waiting for the cry of protest from the new arrival. Little arms fought back, an angry cry went up, and there were grins all round.

'You've got yourself a son, Ginnie,' said the midwife.

Once the baby was given to her, the new mum would forget the pain. It would be just her and the baby, and Sam as soon as he was allowed into the room. The midwife passed the bundle, now wrapped in a soft blanket, to Ginnie, who gazed at her son.

Betty's eyes filled with tears. That's what she must've looked like — so young, lying there, cradling Hannah. She smiled at Ginnie and then the midwife. 'Is it all right for Sam to come in? He won't rest until he's seen for himself they are both safe.'

The midwife stepped to the door and shouted for Sam, who arrived before she had the need to repeat his short name.

Ginnie looked at him from her bed. 'We've got a son,' she whispered.

Sam's face had a look of pure joy. He opened his mouth, but it wasn't working. The midwife pushed him gently towards the bed as Betty let go of Ginnie's hand and moved out of his way.

'My boy.' There were tears in Sam's eyes as he bent forward to kiss them both.

'We're a proper family now, Sam.'

He bent and kissed her gently on the forehead and then turned first to the midwife, then Mabel and finally Betty. 'Thank you for bringing my lad into the world.'

The whole birth had taken three hours from when Ginnie's waters had broken. To Betty, it had seemed so much longer.

* * *

'Our Connie does have some exciting wedding days,' muttered Uncle James on the drive to the North Stafford Hotel, where the wedding breakfast was taking place.

Connie had insisted they get a cook to prepare all the food because she wanted Alice to attend the wedding as a valued guest. Alice had protested but Connie would have none of it. Alice had told both Betty and Jean, and they could see she was proud to be included as such. She still insisted on making the wedding cake, and supervising the table on the day, so everything was perfect for the bride and groom to return to.

It had been agreed Betty would join Agatha, Jean, and Alice at the hotel in Stoke in readiness to greet the guests if she possibly could. Photographs would be taken at the hotel rather than the church to give Connie and Robert time to pay a quick visit to Ginnie before joining the festivities.

The newlyweds stayed with Ginnie, Sam, and Young Sam for about forty minutes before leaving, reluctantly, to re-join their guests.

* * *

Everyone cheered when Connie and her new husband entered the hotel. Robert called for quiet and everyone stopped talking.

'I am sure you will all wish to know that Ginnie and Sam were, today at three o'clock, safely delivered of a son,' Robert paused as a cheer went up, ' . . . a son who will be called Sam. He will most likely be called Young Sam so when, at some time in the future, he gets into trouble, it will not be his father who gets the blame.'

Laughter filled the room.

'I want to thank you all for coming to today's . . . eventful wedding. My beautiful wife . . .' he turned to Connie, whose eyes were sparkling with love, 'and I hope those of you who have travelled from both near, and far, think it all worthwhile,' he said, smiling at his brothers.

Stephen Adams rose. Betty had never seen him looking so nervous. Perhaps a wedding party was far more daunting than speaking to a couple of dozen clippies.

'Robert and I became friends in unusual circumstances. I still remember many of the conversations we had while in the field hospital.' He went on to tell a couple of funny stories about the war and their work on the trams. 'But there is one thing I will say to all of you: this is a brave man. Thanks to him, and his comrades, there are many men alive today who otherwise would not be.'

Robert nodded to him and the two men who stood beside him during the wedding ceremony raised their glasses to him.

Stephen called for a toast and Betty swore there were tears in his eyes.

The speeches over, Robert turned toward Betty.

'Betty and Jean, can we have a word with you both?

I would like to introduce you to my brothers, Stanley, and Andrew.'

'Thought they must be. I can see the resemblance,' said Betty.

The older-looking man smiled. 'I'm Colour Sergeant Stanley Caldwell, Warwickshire Regiment, ladies, and Robert's older brother.'

'Sergeant Andrew Caldwell, 4th Btn of the Essex Regiment, serving in the Middle East. I'm the youngest Caldwell but probably the best looking.'

'Oh!' Betty covered her cheeks with her hands. 'We're so glad to meet you both, aren't we, Jean?'

'Oh, yes.'

They stayed talking to Robert's brothers for a short time, hearing about their careers in the army and especially Andrew's adventures in the Middle East.

Betty was excited when she returned to Duncan and Hannah. 'I'm glad his brothers turned up for Robert. He's such a nice man. I don't know whether his father will ever forgive him, but at least his brothers were there for him today.'

Duncan nodded. 'Families are important, Betty. We'd be lost without them.'

* * *

It was late evening. The wedding celebrations were going well, given a baby had decided to come into the world earlier than expected during the ceremonies. Betty's day would have been perfect if it hadn't been for her disagreement with Duncan over her future. So far, he had changed the subject when she tried to talk about it. She wanted to tell him the world had moved on, that women had greater expectations at work than ever before.

Betty glanced across the room. He was talking to Robert, and both seemed oblivious of the rest of the room. What were they finding to talk about? As far as she knew they only had their war years in common. She smiled. Let them carry on. She could do with a bit more time to herself.

She admitted to herself she was tempted to give in to Duncan's demands about giving up work to concentrate on a family, but then Jessie O'Neill and Iris Shenton popped into her mind — the two women who had had such an effect on her life. How could she tell them she had given up on the ambitions they had helped to cultivate? Now the wedding was over, she would talk to him, make him see why her job was important to her.

She slipped outside into the street, still light with a summer breeze, and rubbed her arms although she didn't feel cold. Throughout her life her plans had varied, as most people's did. In the early days she had been swayed by her mother to look at a job as a stop-gap until a man came along. Joe's big secret had put an end to any romantic relationship with him before it had even begun, and she shuddered as Alastair came to mind. Now, there was Duncan who had the power to give her everything she wanted, if only he could let go of some of his old-fashioned ideas on what women should do with their lives.

She had no doubt she loved Duncan. That's why she hadn't sent him away before now. But it would be a mistake to go into a marriage with the hope of changing someone from the person they were — and he needed to recognise that as much as she did.

She sighed. When she had set out on growing up,

she had thought life would be so easy. How naive she had been!

'Betty!'

Duncan's voice called to her. 'Where are you going?'

She shrugged. 'Nowhere. I wanted a breath of fresh air, a little time to myself. Time to think. Where's Hannah?'

'Jean's got her. I think she wanted someone to look after,' he said.

'Poor Jean. She's desperate for a baby.'

'I thought it might be the case.'

Betty smiled. 'Anyway, you and Robert seemed to be engrossed in conversation just before I stepped out. Anything interesting?'

'He was warning me.'

Betty stopped walking. 'About what?'

'That I might risk losing you if I don't stop being so bloody stubborn. Sorry to swear, but that's what he said.'

'Robert said that?' Betty chuckled. She couldn't imagine it of him.

'He basically said if we have chosen strong women because we love them, we can hardly complain when they have a mind of their own.'

Betty put a hand to her mouth to try to stop the laughter that threatened, but it didn't work. Instead, it burst from her lips and set Duncan laughing too. 'Connie must've said something to him.'

Duncan grabbed her shoulders and turned her to look at him, all traces of laughter gone. 'Darling Betty, our relationship hasn't had the best of starts, with letters passing back and forth, and living a distance apart — but I truly do love you. You came into my heart at a time when the world was going crazy, and when people made plans without knowing whether they would ever come to fruition. I honestly thought you would love to stop working and concentrate on raising a family. I was shocked when you told me, quite firmly, it wasn't the be-all-and-end-all for you.'

'I've been thinking too, Duncan —'

She had been about to tell him she would think about how her life might need to change when a family came along. Until then, Hannah was settled, and she would rather keep her job and save the money to give their future family the best opportunities. She didn't get the chance.

'Betty . . . I see it now. I would like us to build a life together. A life we can both enjoy. You can work for as long as you wish, my dearest. I'll not stand in your way. I love you too much to do that.'

Her arms went round him, not caring what the neighbours might see or think.

'And I have Robert to thank! I never thought I would see the day when Inspector Caldwell would come to my aid!' she laughed.

'Truly, Betty. Robert asked me if I was prepared to lose you for the sake of my principles. I knew what I had to do.'

'I think we've both learned something, Duncan. I think marriage is a partnership. We talk about things and sort out problems — together, always.'

Slowly, they walked back towards hotel.

Just before they reached the entrance, Betty turned to Duncan. 'I love you, Duncan Kennedy, and I want to kiss you.'

'I love you, Betty Dean. Will you marry me? No conditions needed.'

Her lips found his. 'I will.'

Reluctantly, they drew apart. 'I suppose we must go inside,' said Betty. 'They'll be wondering where we are.'

Duncan grinned. 'I don't think so.'

'Why not?'

'I told Robert I was going to ask you to marry me — again. And hope this time nothing will stand in our way.'

Her eyes watered as she opened the door and walked into the hotel. Connie was the first to see them. 'They're back everyone!'

All eyes turned towards Betty. She took up Duncan's hand and smiled at him. 'I said yes!'

There was a great uproar as Connie squealed and rushed to hug her. Hannah went to stand beside Duncan. She stared up into his eyes. 'Does this mean you will be my daddy?'

With a wry smile, Robert said. 'You'll need to be on your toes, Duncan. I rather think these two'll run rings round you otherwise!'

Betty smiled at her family and friends, full of love. She was Betty Dean, soon to be Betty Kennedy, and she had everything she wanted.

A letter from Lynn

Thank you so much for choosing to read *The Potteries Girls on the Home Front,* the third book in my Potteries Girls series, set in the Staffordshire Potteries. I enjoy immersing myself in the place of my birth as it was during the second decade of the twentieth century. Each of the books in the series picks up a key theme facing young women of the time and the difficulties they had to overcome.

Much of the research I did for the previous two books has been well used in this book too. I would, again, like to add my thanks to the help I received from Crich Tramway Museum. In addition, I have spent happy hours researching the lives of servants from a range of sources, to the point of procrastination. For the work of the trade unions — in particular The Ceramic and Allied Trades Union or CATU — I found the publication *A History of the Potters' Union* by Burchill and Ross particularly helpful. Any mistakes of interpreting the information are entirely my own.

As always, there are people who authors come to rely on and whose contributions help to create even better stories. I must give my heartfelt thanks to Keshini Naidoo and Hera Books for having enough faith in me to continue the stories of the Potteries Girls: Ginnie, Connie and now Betty. Her patience and advice has been gratefully received. The final book in the series will be published in the summer of 2023.

My books continue to benefit from the comments of faithful beta-readers and dear friends, Jacquie

Rogers, Lesley Colclough, and Amy Louise Blaney, and I thank all of them for their ongoing support and very helpful suggestions.

It has been enjoyable to create people, organisations and employers, and locations to populate this book. The people only exist in my imagination but the locations have all been inspired by my own recollections of my childhood in Stoke-on-Trent, and have a mix of fictional and real places within the six towns that made up the County Borough.

I also send a note of appreciation to my wonderful husband, Michael, who has become my go-to assistant for help, guidance, and support during the writing of this book. He knows all of the characters and has been a pillar of strength throughout my writing.

Finally, I want to take the opportunity to thank readers of the first two books for their amazing comments, and hope they get as much enjoyment from *The Potteries Girls on the Home Front* as well as catching up with old friends. For new readers I very much hope you enjoyed meeting new friends and discovering how the Great War changed one girl's life forever.

Other titles published by Ulverscroft:

WARTIME WITH THE TRAM GIRLS

Lynn Johnson

July 1914. Britain is in turmoil as WW1 begins to change the world. While the young men disappear off to foreign battlefields, the women left at home throw themselves into jobs meant for the boys.

Hiding her privileged background and her suffragette past, Constance Copeland signs up to be a Clippie — collecting money and giving out tickets — on the trams in Staffordshire, despite her parents' disapproval.

Constance, known as Connie, soon makes fast friends with lively fellow Clippies, Betty and Jean, as well as growing closer to the charming, gentle Inspector Robert Caldwell.

But Connie is haunted by another secret; and if it comes out, it could destroy her new life.

After war ends and the men take back their roles, will Connie find that she can return to her previous existence?